# Praise for F[?]

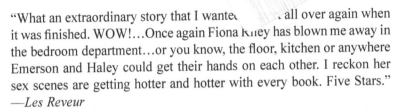

## Media Dar[.]

"What an extraordinary story that I wante[.]　[.] all over again when it was finished. WOW!…Once again Fiona Riley has blown me away in the bedroom department…or you know, the floor, kitchen or anywhere Emerson and Haley could get their hands on each other. I reckon her sex scenes are getting hotter and hotter with every book. Five Stars."
—*Les Reveur*

"{A] sweet romance with the addition of a critique of the media role in their portrayal of celebrities. Both main characters are multi-layered with their personalities well defined. Their chemistry is absolutely off the charts…an entertaining, poignant and romantic story with a side of social critique to celebrity culture and the media. Five stars."
—*Lez Review Books*

"I really dig the way Fiona Riley writes contemporary romances because they're sexy and flirty with a whole lot of feelings, and *Media Darling* is no exception."—*The Lesbian Review*

"A great mix of characters, some great laughs, and a good romance. A great well written read that was emotional and fun."—*Kat Adams, Bookseller (QBD Books, Australia)*

*Media Darling* "was well-executed and the sex was well-written. I liked both of the characters and the plot held my interest."—*Katie Pierce, Librarian, Hennepin County Library (Minnesota)*

## Room Service

"The sexual tension between Olivia and Savannah is combustible and I was hoping with every flirtious moment they would jump each other… [A] sexy summer read."—*Les Rêveur*

"*Room Service* is a slow-burn romance written from the point of view of both main characters. Ms. Riley excels at building their chemistry that slowly grows to sizzling hot."—*Lez Review Books*

"Riley is a natural when it comes to delivering the heat between characters and undeniable chemistry."—*Book-A-Mania*

"*Room Service* by Fiona Riley is a steamy workplace romance that is all kinds of fabulous...Fiona Riley is so good at writing characters who are extremely likeable, even as they have issues to work through. I was happy to see that the leading ladies in *Room Service* are no exception! They're both fun, sweet, funny, and smart, which is a brilliant combo. They also have chemistry that sizzles almost from the get-go, making it especially fun to watch them grow in ways that are good for them as individuals and as a couple."—*The Lesbian Review*

### Strike a Match

"Riley balances romance, wit, and story complexity in this contemporary charmer...Readers of all stripes will enjoy this lyrically phrased, deftly plotted work about opposites attracting."—*Publishers Weekly*

"[A] quick-burning romance, with plenty of sex scenes hot enough to set off the alarms."—*RT Book Reviews*

"*Strike a Match* is probably one of the hottest and sexiest books I've read this year...Fiona Riley is one to watch and I will continue to get extremely excited every time I get one of her books to read." —*Les Rêveur*

"While I recommend all of the books in the Perfect Match series, I especially recommend *Strike a Match*, and definitely in audio if you're at all inclined towards listening to books. Fans of the other two installments will be happy to see their leads again, but you don't have to have read them to pick this one up. It's sweet, hot, and funny, making it a great way to spend a day when you just want to hide away from the world and immerse yourself in a lovely story."—*Smart Bitches, Trashy Books*

"*Strike a Match* is Fiona Riley's best book yet. Whether you're a fan of the other books in the series or you've never read anything by her before, I recommend checking this one out. It's the perfect remedy to a bad day and a great way to relax on a weekend!"—*The Lesbian Review*

"I love this series and Sasha is by far my favourite character yet. I absolutely loved the gritty firefighter details. The romance between Abby and Sasha is perfectly paced and full of wonderful grand gestures, magical dates, and tender, intimate moments."—*Wicked Reads*

"Fiona Riley does a nice job of creating thorny internal and external conflicts for each heroine...I was rooting for Abby and Sasha, not only to be together, but also that both of them would grow and change enough to find a true HEA. The supporting cast of family members, friends, and colleagues is charming and well-portrayed. I'm looking forward to more from Fiona Riley."—*TBQ's Book Palace*

### Unlikely Match

"The leads have great chemistry and the author's writing style is very engaging."—*Melina Bickard, Librarian, Waterloo Library (UK)*

"Two strong women that make their way towards each other with a tiny little nudge from some friends, what's not to like?"—*The Reading Penguin's Reviews*

"*Unlikely Match* is super easy to read with its great pacing, character work, and dialogue that's fun and engaging…Whether you've read *Miss Match* or not, *Unlikely Match* is worth picking up. It was the perfect romance to balance out a tough week at work and I'm looking forward to seeing what Fiona Riley has in store for us next." —*The Lesbian Review*

### Miss Match

"In this sweet, sensual debut, Riley brings together likable characters, setting them against a colorful supporting cast and exploring their relationship through charming interactions and red-hot erotic scenes… Rich in characterization and emotional appeal, this one is sure to please."—*Publishers Weekly*

"*Miss Match* by Fiona Riley is an adorable romance with a lot of amazing chemistry, steamy sex scenes, and fun dialogue. I can't believe it's the author's first book, even though she assured me on Twitter that it is."—*The Lesbian Review*

"This was a beautiful love story, chock full of love and emotion, and I felt I had a big grin on my face the whole time I was reading it. I adored both main characters as they were strong, independent women with good hearts and were just waiting for the right person to come along and make them whole. I felt I smiled for days after reading this wonderful book."—*Inked Rainbow Reads*

## By the Author

Miss Match

Unlikely Match

Strike a Match

Room Service

Media Darling

Not Since You

# NOT SINCE YOU

*by*
Fiona Riley

2019

THIS TRADE PAPERBACK ORIGINAL IS PUBLISHED BY
BOLD STROKES BOOKS, INC.
P.O. BOX 249
VALLEY FALLS, NY 12185

FIRST EDITION: NOVEMBER 2019

---

**CREDITS**
EDITOR: RUTH STERNGLANTZ
PRODUCTION DESIGN: STACIA SEAMAN
COVER DESIGN BY TAMMY SEIDICK

# Acknowledgments

This whole story idea came about when two wonderful people decided to get married on an island in the Caribbean, and they thought the best way to get there would be by traveling at sea on a giant cruise ship. With all their friends and family. And unlimited booze and food. As one does. Now, I know what some of you might be thinking, and the answer is yes, I had all the fruity cocktails. I ate at all the restaurants, and everything you read about cruising life is totally true—it's the best people-watching, juicy gossip about the crew is as abundant as the prevalence of hand sanitizer stations at every doorway, and if you can, you should try it, even if just once. Because there is nothing quite like a city at sea. So, thank you Josh and Gailyn for including me on your special day (week), and happy (belated) first wedding anniversary. Lots of love to you both, xo.

To Brendan Noonan and his helpful family and friends: thank you for giving me the inside scoop on all things cruise related. Thank you for answering all of my annoyingly specific questions without expressing any irritation (to me, at least ;) ). Your insight, technical knowledge, and vast cruising experience were invaluable. You made doing research really, really fun. Plus, you're a super cool guy to cruise to the Caribbean with. I owe you a frozen cocktail, or six. Thanks again.

To Ruth Sternglantz, you are the best at everything, but especially helping me map out my timelines and keeping me on target when I start to flail. I am so grateful for you. You need a raise. Let's talk to someone about that.

To Kris Bryant, thank you for taking my ranting phone calls and helping me work through my storyline issues. Your enthusiasm for all things romance related is unmatched by anyone I have ever met and it's infectious, in the best way possible. Thank you for the early, before work phone calls and late-night texts, I'd be lost without you.

And to the readers, I'd be nowhere without you. I hope you enjoy this second chance romance as much as I enjoyed writing it. Thanks again for your reviews, comments, tweets, and likes. They mean so much to me. Thank you. You're the greatest.

For Jenn.

An adventure at sea with you inspired this novel.
Truthfully, all my adventures with you inspire novels,
but that's because every minute of this crazy life is an adventure.
And I wouldn't change one second of it.
Thanks for always taking a new adventure with me.

To my Love, to my ladybug, and to my dream girl:
thank you for this wonderful life.

# Chapter One

*Cruise Day One: Departing for Vacation*

"I sincerely doubt that overly enthusiastic sign," Charlotte Southwick muttered as she stepped toward the obnoxiously large, brightly colored banner that read *Paradise Awaits, Ladies*. Charlotte wasn't sure paradise was even a thing, let alone a thing that awaited her once she passed under this insultingly cheerful welcome archway made of balloons and the promise of endless possibilities.

A Barbie lookalike with a broad smile nodded at her and held up a bottle of what looked like hand sanitizer. "Welcome aboard, Mrs."—she leaned forward, straining to read the tag on the lanyard around Charlotte's neck—"Mrs. Vallencourt."

"Southwick." Charlotte tried not to growl her reply. "It's Southwick, and not Mrs. anything, contrary to what the fancy laminated pass says since my ex-fiancée is a lying cheater who only thinks of herself. Can I get this changed? Or better yet, just pitch it into the ocean with the rest of my hopes and dreams."

The smile dimmed on the woman's face. "Um, sure?"

"Great." Charlotte yanked the lanyard off her neck and shoved it into her purse with every intention to bury it at sea like the diamond in *Titanic* as soon as they were far enough from shore for it to feel remotely cathartic. She nodded toward the bottle of gel the woman held in the air. "I interrupted you—that looks important. You were saying?"

The woman blinked. "Uh, right. Yes." She shook her head and her plastic grin returned. "Welcome aboard, Miss Southwick. We're glad to have you with us. Please allow me the opportunity to acquaint you with our sanitizing routine in order to help keep everyone on board healthy and safe."

Charlotte extended her hand toward the woman, mirroring her posture, with the intention of retreating to her room as quickly as possible. It was then that she noticed the name tag resting on her unrealistically perky chest. Angela. She looked like an Angela, Charlotte thought.

Angela squeezed a generous dollop of the clear gel onto her palm and continued her spiel while Charlotte rubbed it in. "We're here to make sure your every desire is met and fulfilled. We can do that best with clean hands and cheerful smiles. We are at your service, every step of the way."

She paused long enough for Charlotte to interject again. "Great. That's all very clinical and sanitary." And a little creepy, she thought. "But I get it, thanks."

Unfazed, Angela continued. "Right. Well, I can see here that you are a VIP guest, so you'll be following Enrique over to your stateroom. He'll make sure you have everything you need."

"Fantastic." Charlotte was glad to leave the perky plastic woman behind and see what awaited her in this stateroom.

"Right this way, ma'am." Enrique gave her a nod and reached to take her carry-on bags.

"*Charlotte* is fine, thank you." She handed him her belongings but pulled her laptop bag closer to her body. She had no intention of letting this out of her sight—she had to finish the Davenport Hospital project before they got to Aruba if she had any intention of enjoying her vacation.

"As you wish." He gave her a genial smile and raised his arm to gesture toward the back of the monstrous cruise ship. Charlotte didn't miss the way his shirt strained in an apparent attempt to contain his rippling muscles. Enrique, like Angela, was perfectly fit. Like, perfect. She was feeling a little insecure all of a sudden.

He led her along the lower deck by the dockside toward the back of the boat. Charlotte tried not to stare at the many lesbian couples looking happy and holding hands, waiting for their turns to board the ship. She was grateful when he took her toward a set of double doors that led into the center of the ship and away from the crowds of people eager to start vacation.

"Have you cruised with us before?" he asked.

"No. I've never cruised anywhere, actually." Charlotte tried to contain the bitterness in her voice. It had been Veronica's idea to book this cruise. She'd raved about these types of cruises throughout their courtship, and she'd been eager to get Charlotte into the cruise ship lifestyle. Charlotte had only agreed under the condition that they did something she'd like as well: nothing. She wanted nothing more than to spend two uninterrupted weeks at a fancy resort on a beach, someplace warm. The compromise was fifty-fifty—Charlotte would get her island time, but they would cruise to that destination. And then really spend their honeymoon soaking up each other's company. But Veronica liked to *cruise*…and that included into other people's beds, it seemed. So here she was, on their honeymoon, alone and unmarried. During Lesbian Week. Because, of course.

"Wait." Enrique stopped short and she almost walked into his overly muscular back.

Charlotte looked around to see if there was something she'd missed to cause him to freeze on the spot. Just a few dozen more lovey-dovey couples. Nothing to see here.

"You've never cruised before?" He looked surprised.

"Nope. I'm a cruise virgin." Charlotte shrugged.

"Well, that changes things." Enrique puffed out his chest and gave her a sly smile. "Your room won't be ready for another hour or so. Let's drop off this bag and I'll give you the secret behind-the-scenes tour."

Charlotte hesitated. She'd told herself she could stomach boarding alone if she could hide in her room and wallow in self-pity for a day or two or six until the ship reached Aruba, at which point she would disembark and start the part of the vacation she was most looking forward to and skip the last few days of cruise life, since that was Veronica's preference, not hers. And since that was what she'd talked herself into agreeing to, Enrique's proposal seemed like a daunting social experiment she wasn't sure she had the energy for.

When she didn't reply, his expression softened and he leaned in a little closer. "Look, I overheard what you said to Angela back there at the ramp. And I can tell from your baggage tags and the paperwork you handed her that you're VIP and staying in the presidential honeymoon suite, alone. On your first cruise."

"You don't miss a thing, do you?" Charlotte asked, unsure of whether she should be annoyed or ashamed that he'd so easily pegged her.

"It's my job to pick up on little details. Well, that, and to deliver cocktails on the main deck to the lounge chairs, in addition to dancing my booty off at the onsite night club six nights a week as a go-go dancer." He shimmied in front of her and she had to laugh. "Let me ease you into this week, okay? I promise there will be only as much talking as you can handle. I swear."

Charlotte laughed and touched his forearm affectionately. "I heard you say drinks in there somewhere. I assume there can be drinks on this secret tour?"

"Duh. That's the first stop." He extended his elbow toward her. "Let's go cause some mischief."

She slid her arm into his and let the last bit of apprehension leave her body. "I'm all yours."

❖

Lexi Bronson tapped her fingers on the bar as she reviewed the checklist before her. The list seemed endless, and she had about ninety things to get done before the ship left the port, but none of that mattered because this was her favorite week of the cruise season. Truthfully, it was her favorite week of the year.

"I know that smile." Her roommate and closest friend Zara Thompson tossed a lime at her, the decorative beads at the ends of her long braids dancing and singing with the movement.

She caught it easily and gave her a sly grin. "I don't know what you're talking about."

"Oh yes, you do." Zara pointed the knife in her hand at Lexi briefly before resuming her lime prep duties, her golden bronze skin looking healthy and flawless as always. With those braids and that small gold ring in her left nostril, she looked every bit the part of a Caribbean queen. Zara often joked about her Caribbean-by-way-of-Connecticut heritage. She looked like a local while on this cruise route, because even though her entire immediate family resided in New England, her grandparents were islanders. That was one of the reasons she'd taken this gig, to reconnect with her roots. "That's your lady-killer smile. That's the smile of a woman who is going to flirt her single-and-ready-to-mingle ass off while she shakes all the drinks for all the beautiful gay ladies all week long. That's a predatory smile. You're a predator."

Lexi feigned offense. "You wound me."

Zara raised the knife again and made a playful stabbing motion at her "Ha. Not yet. But I think about it every time I trip over your dirty laundry in our tiny, minuscule little bunk. All these years and you still don't know how to use a hamper." She shook her head and reached for a new handful of limes.

Lexi laughed. Zara was totally right—she wasn't the cleanest roommate. Or even the most organized, but she was the most fun. And the easiest to get along with. Lexi didn't like drama and Zara didn't cause any. And for the past five years, they had been a match made in tight-quarters cruise-ship bunking heaven. "You'd be lost without me."

Zara rolled her eyes. "I'd have significantly more floor space without you or your soiled laundry. But, yeah, I suppose you're right."

Lexi gave her a gentle punch to the arm and dodged the lime wedge Zara rocketed toward her head. "Hey. Don't forget I'm the boss around here."

"Too bad I work in the spa and the fitness area and not the bar, but who's counting?" Zara gave her a head nod and a curtsy. "How could I forget, your Royal Intoxicologist? Where are my manners?"

"That's right, and don't you forget it." Lexi picked up the errant lime and tossed it into the sink. She'd been promoted to head bartender on the main deck two seasons ago but had recently also been given the role of VIP liaison on her time away from the bars. This was a big deal for her. In the near decade she'd been with the Majestic Princess cruise company, she'd made huge leaps in responsibility and pay grade, but this opened up new possibilities for her. And new cruise routes. And the option of corporate advancement, not that she had any interest in that, but still. Lexi oversaw a whole fleet of people now, and that wasn't something she took lightly.

"All right, that's all I have time for today, Boss Lady." Zara dumped the prepared fruit into the containers that lined the bar and rinsed off her hands. "I'm due downstairs for the Safety Protocol presentation and rah-rah dance routine until I can go hide in the spa and play *Candy Crush*."

"Have fun." Lexi gave her a high five and wished her luck, grateful that her roomie had agreed to spend the last of her free time before departure helping out at the bar. "See you later, around dinnertime? The usual spot, with the boys?"

She was referring to the far back corner of the El Capitan, the only Mexican restaurant on the ship. Crew weren't allowed to eat or socialize in the guest areas, but she and Zara had started this tradition, one that was secret save for their friend Manuel in the kitchen, about four years ago when a nasty stomach bug had infiltrated the guest area and left most of the restaurants empty. Lexi made sure to keep Manuel and the servers of El Capitan well liquored at the crew bar, on her dime, to ensure they got their secret little back table, out of sight of the guests.

"It wouldn't be the start of lesbian-cruise-week-palooza without our traditional pescatarian enchiladas and tequila, now would it?" Zara gave her a toothy grin.

"That's my girl."

"Oh, before I forget"—Zara reached into her back pocket—"Ahmed pulled some more real estate listings for you. A couple of different choices on this cruise route this time. I'd be happy to pop off the ship with you and check them out if you want."

"Thanks." Lexi accepted the paper and made a mental note to look at it later. She'd been casually looking at restaurant and bar properties for sale on this cruise route for the last six months. She didn't have any immediate plans, but she liked to watch the market and see what was out there. Owning a beachfront bar was a pipe dream for her, but it had nagged her more than usual lately. Maybe someday.

"See ya, Lex," Zara called out as she slipped under the bar top and headed toward the main deck.

Lexi waved good-bye to her friend and hummed as she went down the rest of the prep list. She was so grateful to have Zara's friendship. Everything felt more manageable with her there. But more than that, Zara had long become family. And since Lexi had no bio family, it made Zara that much more important to her. She was glad to have Zara by her side, always. She'd do anything for her, and she knew the same was true for Zara.

She looked out at the ocean; the skies were clear blue, and the water looked calm. She took in a deep breath, smelling the salt in the air. The excitement of the week was palpable even while the ship was docked. She hummed the tune her father used to sing her to sleep with, a ritual she did at the start of every new cruise week. The tradition had originated after her father's death nearly a decade ago, when she'd joined the cruise life. She'd joined to run away from her past and fulfill a dream he'd had his whole life: to live by the sea, free to undertake any adventure. And oh, how she'd done that ten times over by now. She looked up at the sky once more before she returned to her bar prep duties and found the biggest, fluffiest cloud. That was her dad's cloud, she just knew it. "It's gonna be a good week, Dad. I can feel it."

## CHAPTER TWO

Charlotte marveled at the beauty of the ship. Enrique made good on his promise, and she got the tour with a cocktail in hand, but it was mostly neglected since she was completely blown away by the architecture and detail of the ship. She was sure half the tour she had her mouth open, gaping in an unattractive manner. But she couldn't help it—this was unlike anything she had ever seen. The ship was like a city on the water, with multiple levels and layers, something for everyone. And she meant *everyone*. If you couldn't find something to do on this ship, that was on you. Because they seemed to have covered every base.

Enrique took her through the main atrium, the center of which was open, and you could see nine stories up. The space was flanked with three sets of glass elevators on each end, so you could people watch the whole center of the ship as you went floor to floor. There was a glass dome at the top of this massive space that provided a protected view of the weather, while offering natural lighting to complement the ambient glow of chandeliers and recessed lights on every floor. On the floor they were on, Charlotte noticed a Starbucks positioned across from a small dance floor, where jazz musicians played soft welcoming music for the vacationers. The ten or so small, intimate tables were filled with eager tourists reviewing the cruise packets handed out by the cheerful excursions coordinator they passed, as Enrique pointed out the duty-free shop and internet café located on the same floor.

They walked up the grand *Titanic*-esque staircase to the next level, and he took her through the art gallery located at midship before he showed her the lounge, equipped with two dueling pianos and a fancy martini bar with bartenders dressed in formal white dress shirts to match the area's aesthetic.

"On this floor, at the forward of the ship—that means the front," he said, "there is a salon, a spa and fitness area, a library, and a few sports bars." He pointed to one of the dozens of maps located by each corridor and elevator. "The majority of the guest rooms are here and here"—he showed her on the map—"and the crew and staff are down here."

"Underwater?" she asked.

"Some, but not all. Officers are above water, as well as higher-level staff positions like entertainers or musicians. Crew are at water level or just below, but that's mostly the kitchen and cleaning staff, maintenance, et cetera." He shrugged. "We are so infrequently in our rooms, rooming on a low deck doesn't really bother most people since there is a view just about everywhere you go."

"Are there a lot of staff and crew?" she asked as they moved to the next section of the ship.

"Oh, for sure," he replied. "It's a two-to-one ratio of Majestic Princess employees to cruisers. We have our own cafeteria and bars, gym, and social spaces down there—we're like a hidden underwater city in the city."

"That's wild." Charlotte couldn't even fathom the enormity of responsibility managing all of those moving pieces, and people.

"It's cruise ship living. You get used to it." He showed her the humidor and cigar bar located next to the rear entrance of the casino and highlighted the restaurants located on each floor, a total of twenty in all, each with a different theme or dining style. Some were plated, some were buffet, a delightful variety to accommodate whatever mood you were in: sushi, Mexican, Thai, Brazilian, French. You named it, they had it.

As they headed toward the rear of the ship, or the aft as he called it, he showed her the reservation desk where she could secure dinner reservations at the most popular places.

"You can do it that way if you want to look at each menu," he said, "or you can have your VIP attendant do the footwork for you. That's their job, too."

"VIP attendant?" Charlotte asked as she poked her head into the main showroom, an amphitheater where Enrique said they had nightly performances and shows, like comedians and magicians. It was cute in there, intimate but with plenty of stadium seating so everyone had an unobstructed view.

"Oh yeah. You're fancy, girl," he teased as he walked her toward the next entertainment area. "This is the on-ship nightclub that I mentioned before. There's a nice lounge area in there, too. And multiple bar stations to make it easy to get a cocktail without waiting too long. There will be a few events in there during the week that will be posted on the digital screens around the ship and on your daily itinerary. The biggest draw is usually the White Party toward the end of the cruise. The dance floor is big enough that you have room to get your groove on, but there are plenty of casual seating spaces so you can people watch, if that's more your speed."

As they meandered back through the ship, Enrique took her to her floor.

"Okay, this is where I leave you." Enrique gave her a bright smile and carried her suitcases from the doorway of her suite into the room, depositing them by the desk.

"Well, damn." Charlotte looked around the room for the first time and pinched herself to make sure she wasn't dreaming; the room was magnificent. The king-sized bed to her left looked plush and welcoming, but the real showstopper was just beyond the bed, where the floor-to-ceiling double glass sliding doors opened out to a private balcony. Sheer white curtains framed the view of the water and billowed gently in the breeze as the ship slowly pulled away from the shore.

"Yeah." Enrique's voice sounded far away as she walked closer to the balcony. "Most people have that reaction."

Charlotte nodded, her reply stuck in her throat when she noticed the double set of *everything* laid out on the chaise at the end of the bed: two robes, two champagne flutes in front of a bottle on ice, two boxes of gourmet chocolates delicately arranged on a plate within a heart made of fresh strawberry slices…the perfect gift for honeymooners in love. There were even delicately monogramed *hers & hers* napkins under each glass. No expense had been spared. And why should it? This vacation had cost her a fortune. These details were a blatant reminder of that. That and the fact that she was here alone.

"I can have those removed." Enrique surprised her, his voice close to her shoulder.

She shook her head, willing the tears to stay at bay. She looked out at the balcony to quiet the storm of emotions brewing inside her. After a moment, she faked a smile and looked back at him. "It's fine. Really."

His deep brown eyes flashed the pity she was so desperate to avoid, and her face must have shown that because he stepped back and coughed. "Well, uh-oh." He reached over to the desk and picked up the folder, changing the subject. "You're in good hands this week. It says your VIP attendant for the week is Lexi. She's great. And she's the best bartender on the ship as well, so she'll make sure you're good to go."

"Lexi?" Charlotte thought she'd misheard him. That was a name she hadn't heard in a very long time. And yet, even after all that time, just hearing the name did something to her. "I knew a Lexi once. A lifetime ago." It had been another life entirely.

"Oh yeah? That's cool. Well, this Lexi's a character. She's been on this ship forever. She'll be able to tell you all the quiet hideaways on board to get away from the other cruisers if you get overwhelmed," he said, a seemingly subtle nod toward the last topic she'd rather not revisit. "Anyway, she'll be here shortly and explain to you all the stuff in this folder and fill you in on all the ship's happenings. I'm due up top for a salsa class in a bit—feel free to stop by and say hi. I'll be here all week if you need anything."

"Thanks." She meant that. She was glad to have run into him.

"Oh, before I forget"—he slipped the messenger bag she had relinquished to him during the tour off his shoulder and handed it to her—"you said this was important. I kept it safe."

"You did." She took it from him and held it to her chest. "Thanks again."

"Anytime." He gave her a small wave. "I'll see you on the top deck. Don't be a stranger."

"I won't be." She watched him leave the suite and she sat on the chaise with a heavy sigh. Alone at last. In so many more ways than one.

She put aside her messenger bag and reached for the envelope resting against the ice bucket between the offending doubled glassware. She ran her fingers along the raised gold font on the front before she pulled out the card that waited inside. *Thank you for choosing the Majestic Princess as your first stop on making your forever memories with your special someone. You are someone special to us and we are happy to serve you. Cheers.*

"Cheers indeed." She hated the bitterness in her voice. Deciding not to dwell on anything for too long, since she felt so fragile already, she plucked the bottle out of the icy water and examined it. It was a smooth brut, not one of the obnoxious, overpriced versions Veronica preferred, but not an inexpensive one either. Since Veronica had been a big champagne drinker, Charlotte had grown quite knowledgeable about the bubbly in the years they'd been together. *Years.* All those wasted years. The thought morphed her sadness into something darker, something angrier. "This was a bad idea."

She submerged the bottle with probably more force than was necessary and stood. She momentarily considered unpacking the suitcase into the drawers next to the desk but decided against it when she noticed that the curtains nearby had picked up their movement. She'd rather lose herself in the view from the private deck than face what awaited her in that luggage.

A look out at the water told her the ship was well on its way to the adventure that awaited. She let that sink in a bit. As hard as it was to imagine in this moment, this was an *adventure* and she ought to remember that. Her grandfather had been the one who had encouraged her to take this trip, even as her world fell apart around her. He'd been adamant about it, and who was she to argue with his ninety-one years of life experience? She thought back to their conversation as she settled into the lounge chair on her veranda.

"Lottie," he'd said, a nickname he'd used for her since she was very little and one that was exclusively his, "every moment in life you are given the chance to make a decision and take a chance. This is one of those moments. You can't get your money back anyway, so go. Have fun. Hit the reset button and come back to your Paw Paw with stories of tropical islands and beautiful women."

Her mother Cookie, on the other hand, had been less supportive. As per her usual. "Charlotte, don't you think it'd be better to forget the trip and try to work things out with Veronica?"

She'd bristled at that comment. "Work things out? Mom, she was cheating on me. For months. Maybe more than that. There's nothing to work out."

Cookie had shrugged and examined her manicure in that infuriating way she did when she was being dismissive of Charlotte's feelings. Which was basically always. "That sounds like you're giving up. I didn't raise a quitter."

Charlotte had bit back the part where she was going to mention that her mother hadn't *raised* her really at all, the nannies and her grandparents did. But that didn't seem like it was going to get her anywhere, so instead she challenged back, "You didn't raise a doormat, either. So, no thanks. Veronica can live happily ever after with whatever woman she can con into thinking she's capable of being monogamous. Because I'm not that woman."

Her mother's look of disapproval at her directness fell short of its likely intended effect due in large part to the fact that her grandfather was giving her the thumbs-up behind her mother's perfectly coifed blond head. She'd always preferred her grandfather to, well, anyone in her family, but especially her mother.

The sound of laughter from a nearby deck brought her back to the moment. Her eyes settled on the crashing waves cast off by the boat's motion. The angry whitecaps blurred into one another with each successive deep blue swell, and Charlotte felt like the sea was mirroring her emotions in that moment. She thought of her failed relationship with Veronica, and her hurt morphed back to anger again. And that anger brought her back to her continued failed relationship with her mother—a crack in their family that seemed to deepen with time, not lessen.

She stood from the chair, feeling restless. She began to unpack her clothes as she mentally unpacked her relationship with her mother. It hadn't always been that way. They'd been close until halfway through high school—well, as close as you could get to someone like her mother. But that all changed the summer of her junior year. Everything changed that summer. That was the summer of Lexi.

Enrique's comment had stirred something in her, the memory of a ghost from her past that Charlotte had long since tried to bury. Whatever had become of Lexi? She'd done everything she could to forget about her first love. She'd tried without success to fill the void in her heart that never seemed to heal after Lexi was gone. Charlotte had chalked that up to first-love scars and expected it to stay that way forever. She supposed it still would.

Lexi had been paired with her to help with some math tutoring for her SATs, but their relationship quickly morphed into something more, and Charlotte spent the end of high school sneaking away to find alone time with Lexi. It was the first time she gave her heart to someone else. And she found herself falling head over heels for the girl whose life and family couldn't be more different from her own. But when Charlotte went off to college, she made a decision that changed things forever. She chose the path she'd planned since she was a little girl, the path mapped out for her by her mother long before Lexi was in the picture. Because suddenly it was time to grow up, but she'd grown around someone else, and that wasn't in the plans. Charlotte had had to choose, and a part of her always felt like she'd chosen wrong. A big part of her. But that was in the past and there was no going back.

"Okay." She closed the last drawer and looked at herself in the mirror. Her reflection looked tired. That just wouldn't do. "You can do this, Charlotte. You can start over and find the part of you that you lost over the last few years. You can do this. You have to." She nodded to herself and forced a smile. Now her reflection looked tired *and* pained.

She shook her head and closed her eyes. "Warm sand, hot sun, cool breezes, blue skies, clear ocean water, bottomless frozen cocktails... No worries, no one to report to, nothing stopping you from having the vacation of your life, alone." She opened her eyes and widened her stance, putting her hands on her hips and assuming the Superhero Pose. "You can vacation alone. You are cruising to paradise on a luxury ship with hundreds of queer women in a safe space, then spending a week in the nicest, most posh resort Aruba can offer. It's going to be fucking fantastic, and you're going to love every minute of it."

Charlotte swore she saw the light come back into her reflection's eyes. This was happening. She was doing this. "I'm gonna make this vacation my bitch."

## CHAPTER THREE

L exi checked and double-checked her uniform. Since she was playing double duty as bartender extraordinaire and VIP attendant, she had to make sure the often sticky and dirty parts of the bar life didn't spill onto her VIP life. Literally.

Satisfied that she looked presentable, she jogged down I-95, the main corridor the crew used, toward the package room, but that was no small task. The I-95 was jammed with luggage still being sorted for the guest rooms, and there were dozens of crew members darting back and forth to and from the small stairways that led to the main floors. It was strict cruise ship policy that the crew goings-on were out of the public eye and behind closed, often hidden, doors.

"Slow down, Bronson," Captain Lynn Correia called out as Lexi had to leap to the left to avoid a falling suitcase.

"Captain, my Captain." Lexi gave her a broad smile. "What's good?"

Captain Correia gave her a look. "Not you if you end up in the infirmary with a broken ankle."

Lexi halted her progress to shimmy side to side before diving into a full-blown moonwalk. "I've got moves for days, Captain. Don't worry about my skills—they're impressive."

"If you say so," Correia replied. Correia was one of only a handful of female captains in the luxury cruise ship business. She'd been a decorated sailor in a past life and maintained the order and routine of her military career in the way she ran the cruise ship. But she had a pretty decent sense of humor and self-deprecation if you got to know her. She'd been Lexi's captain for going on five years now, and Lexi had been spending more and more time with her and the other officers now that she was working the VIP angle. Lexi had grown to consider the captain a friend and she knew the feeling was mutual.

Correia adjusted the cap on her long, perfectly braided silver-blond mane, of which, not a hair was out of place. Her uniform was blindingly white, and somehow all her medallions managed to glisten under the gross I-95 lighting. They really needed to spruce up the crew quarters—it was like a dungeon down here.

"Did you hear me, Bronson?"

"What?" Nope, she definitely did not. "No, I was just thinking that we could use some better lighting in here. Either that or your uniform shirt is looking a little dull."

Correia's eyes widened and she looked down. Lexi tried to hold back her laugh but failed, miserably.

"Bronson." Correia's mouth held the hint of a smile when she made eye contact with Lexi again.

"You mustn't take anything I say too seriously, Cap." Lexi gave her an exaggerated eye roll. "It's the first day of a new cruise and the last week of work before my vacation in Key West. I'm positively buzzing with excitement."

Correia laughed and shook her head. "How could I forget? It's your favorite cruise week."

Lexi looked left and right before adding quietly, "Yours, too, if I recall." Correia had been the driving force behind hosting a queer women's cruise week, something that had previously been balked at by the corporate offices. It was one of the reasons Lexi felt she and Correia got along so well. They shared a common interest. "Plan on meeting the lady of your dreams this week, Captain?"

Correia's eyes narrowed but her expression remained playful. "You know the rules, Bronson. No fraternizing with the guests. That's grounds for an immediate dismissal."

Though they were only joking, Lexi knew that rule was a non-negotiable one. Cruise ship employment contracts were for six months at a time, and aside from the basic safety and no-fighting rules, the cardinal rule here was not to get tangled in the sheets with a guest. Ever. Or else you'd find yourself at the next port with all your bags and walking papers in hand. The corporate suits didn't mess around about that. They wouldn't even fly your sorry ass home. They'd just drop you off. Lexi had seen many a colleague fall victim to lust. It wasn't worth it, not ever.

Correia stepped closer as the commotion around them grew, the hustle and bustle of moving luggage to guest rooms and crew members running to assignments in full swing. She lowered her voice and said, "I want you to think about our discussion last week. Let's make plans to chat before we get back to the mainland."

Ah, the talk again. Okay. Lexi knew this was the time to be serious. "Yes, Captain. Will do."

As if on cue, Correia's right-hand woman, Staff Captain Sally Dashel, appeared at the Captain's shoulder with a tablet and a no-nonsense disposition. She was a serious woman who always seemed to have a worried, pinched expression—that wasn't new, but the blinking red text Lexi could see on the tablet was. "Captain, you're needed on the top deck."

Correia regarded her with a small smile. Nothing ever seemed to faze Correia. "Thank you, Sally." She looked back up at Lexi and gave her a wave. "See you 'round, Bronson."

"Bye, Cap." Lexi watched Correia stride down the causeway with that relaxed confidence she exuded so well. Sally took two steps for each of the towering ship captain's and looked like an eager Chihuahua at her heel.

"She's got it bad for Cap, huh?" her friend Ahmed Rahim said as he leaned out the doorway of the administrative and package office to her right.

Lexi nodded. It was a common assumption amongst her closest friends that Sally was in love with the captain. But as far as she knew, it was only gossip. Juicy as it was. "Seems that way. I feel bad for her."

"Why? Because Correia won't act on it? Or because you think she's out of her league?" Ahmed stepped back into the office and sat behind his tiny desk as she followed him into the quieter space.

"Both. More that I think it's likely unrequited. I mean, they've been working together for years. Every time the assignment roster rolls through, they're on it. You'd think something would have happened by now." Lexi slid the pocket door almost all the way closed to block out some of the crew noise. "Crew dating other crew, even officers, isn't unusual. It happens all the time. This is a hard lifestyle in which to maintain a relationship unless you're both on the same ship. You know?"

"Maybe they are having a relationship, though, and we just have no idea. Now that would be something." Ahmed's hazel eyes shone with mischief. "Can you imagine if they had some secret, naughty sexual dalliance behind closed doors? Sally might oversee the ship's staff and be a rule-following disciplinarian, but I could see her easily relinquishing that role for Correia. Tightly wound Sally bottoming for easy, breezy Correia feels like it fits. I bet that Correia is a demanding top."

Lexi scrunched her nose at his statement. "Correia's beautiful. And dashing. And incredibly smart and shrewd, but I'd rather not think about her sexual proclivities."

"Buzzkill." Ahmed huffed, seemingly annoyed at the nonstarter of a gossip session. He pushed his stylish black-rimmed glasses up higher on his nose. "I assume you're here about your new VIP assignments for the week."

"You know me so well." Lexi plopped into the chair facing his desk. Don Julio, his little drinking bird toy thing, was slowly sipping away on his desk. It was mesmerizing.

"I know you're about to go on vacation and there's a ship full of beautiful ladies up there that you'd like to get back to." Ahmed clucked. "It's not like you're here to visit with your good friend Ahmed, who's locked below the ship like a caged animal in this tiny office, managing schedules and boring administrative tasks, all hours of the day—"

Lexi held up her hand. "Point taken. I will visit you more this week—I promise."

"You say that now." Ahmed's tone was light as he continued to tease her.

Lexi stood and saluted him. "I solemnly swear to visit you in the bowels of the boat—"

"And bring me juicy gossip from topside," he interjected.

"And bring you juicy gossip from the part of the ship that sees the sun." Lexi crossed her heart.

"Fine." Ahmed unfolded his arms and leaned back in his chair. "I accept your terms."

"Phew." Lexi dropped back into the chair before glancing at her watch. "I gotta fly, guy. How about those assignments?"

"And just like that, we're back to the bitch work." Ahmed shook his head and laughed. He reached to his right and pulled out a file folder. "Hmm, this is unusual."

"What's that?" Lexi leaned forward and poked Don Julio's bobbing head to make it drink the water on the desk faster.

"Stop that." Ahmed swatted her hand away. "You're going to spill the water."

"Am not." Lexi poked Don Julio again, this time with more force. The beak bobbed into the water with more gusto.

"Alexandria," Ahmed warned.

"Ahmed Mohammed Ayaan Rahim," she replied.

He chuckled. "One time, you get ahold of my pay stub one time."

"I'm a sucker for details, what can I say." Lexi knew Ahmed appreciated that she'd taken the time to learn about him. Although he'd been working for the cruise company for a couple of years now, this was their first shared contract. They'd become fast friends in the past six months, and he'd blended easily with her, Zara, and their friend Enrique. They were inseparable in their off time. And she felt like she'd known him forever. They'd spent many nights talking about his very strict, religious Muslim family, and how he had ended up on a cruise ship. His story wasn't that different from everyone else's: they all were searching for something. Most people joined the cruise life in hopes of seeing the world and experiencing different cultures that their previous life wouldn't have afforded them the chance to experience. But they were all a little lost, too. The cruise ship *lifers*, anyway. Though, Ahmed didn't strike her as a lifer. He was different, special. All that aside, she also knew that this job was very important to him. He took pride in it. Even though it was isolating in a way. She knew that all too well.

"Have you decided about recontracting after this?" She made a mental note to see him more this week, unsure of whether he would be assigned to her ship again. She knew they would remain friends, even after their assignments together, but still, she wasn't in any rush to lose him.

Ahmed let out a sigh. "I reapplied. I'd like to stay, but…"

Lexi nodded in understanding. Ahmed had a serious crush on Enrique. But he'd never had a boyfriend before, and he was afraid to act on those feelings—for a multitude of reasons, he'd assured her, but she knew one of them was along the lines of something he'd said about Sally earlier. Ahmed thought Enrique was out of his league. Lexi wasn't so sure.

"You know, if you just ask him for a drink, you'd know where things stand between you two." Lexi gave him an encouraging nod. "I know a really kick-ass lady bartender who makes a mean mojito. Which I have on good authority is our Latin hunk's favorite cocktail."

Ahmed frowned and sank deeper into his seat. "He's too muscly and handsome to be interested in a bookworm like me. There's a reason he's up there looking all tanned and gorgeous serving drinks and dancing in those teeny tiny spandex booty shorts at the club, and I'm down here hidden in paperwork and shift assignments." Ahmed waved his arms around, pointing at the very neat and organized—but immense—stacks of paper around him. "I'm cruise ship basement office material, and he's Mr. Congeniality with perfect abs and—"

"Crap." Lexi had started to zone out and gave Don Julio a too hard nudge, and the little cup of water under his beak spilled onto the desk.

"Lexi," Ahmed whined and grabbed a handful of tissues to minimize the damage.

"My bad." Lexi winced and leaned back. "All I'm saying is tell him you're into him. Before it's too late and we're all off the ship."

"We'll see." Ahmed's frown looked permanent and Lexi's heart hurt for him. "Well, like I was saying before you violated my bird and made a damn mess," he scolded, "your assignment this week is unusual."

"Unusual how?"

He handed her the folder she'd long forgotten about. "You only have one VIP room for the week. Not sure how that happened, but that's what it says here."

"Huh. Weird." Lexi took the folder and thumbed through its contents. Her heart sank. "Newlyweds. Lady newlyweds at that." She looked up and saw that Ahmed was regarding her curiously. "What?"

"I dunno. You sound kinda sad about that." He shrugged. "Who doesn't like newlyweds?"

"I'm not. It's not. I…it's fine." The truth was that Lexi hated newlyweds. Like, a lot. She hated how lovey-dovey they were with each other, and she especially hated working as their VIP liaison because she never knew when she could safely stop by their rooms without walking into some crazy sexcapades. Because all newlyweds seemed to be sex crazed, which she understood since they were usually starting their honeymoon and all, but she'd had more than her fair share of threesome inquiries to be wary. And lesbian week was one of the busiest for those types of offers. "It's fine."

"You said that already." Ahmed stood and walked to the front of his desk, shooing her away as he lifted Don Julio and wiped beneath it. "I just think maybe you shouldn't be giving romantic advice when you've never been in a long-term relationship and you hate monogamous people."

"Rude." She scoffed. "I *have* been in a long-term relationship."

He waved the wet tissue at her, dripping water everywhere. "That was in high school."

She dodged the droplets and shrugged. "Still counts. And I don't hate monogamous people."

"Just people in love." Ahmed raised an eyebrow at her, and she felt judged. Like, really judged. Which was doubly rude.

"I don't hate people in love." Lexi's high-pitched reply was convincing no one, least of all herself.

"Right." Ahmed patted her on the shoulder. She didn't miss the wet handprint that accompanied it.

"I'm sure"—she stood and made her way to the door, pausing to glance at the names of the guests—"the Vallencourts are lovely people and they won't ask me to join them in a threesome or be a royal pain in my ass the whole week. There. I said it. I put that positive thought out into the atmosphere and if it crashes and burns, it's not my fault."

Ahmed's mouth was agape. "Who said anything about a threesome?"

"Never mind." Lexi threw up her hands. "Dinner at the usual spot?"

"With Zara—"

"And Enrique," she added.

He sighed and nodded. "I wouldn't miss it. Oh, did Zara give you that real estate hit list?"

"She did," Lexi replied. "You know I have a Realtor I work with."

"Yeah, yeah. Omario, I know. I've been blind CC'd on all the emails between you two." Ahmed waved her off. "But he only focuses on Aruba and Curaçao, and he's busy. I've got eyes all over the islands here. It gives me something to do when I'm bored. I get to dream big for you, with the clear understanding that I will always drink for free at whatever location and bar you open up. Right?"

"Right." Lexi didn't mind agreeing to that. He would have drunk for free anyway, in her fictional future bar and restaurant, regardless of whether he helped her or not. But it was nice to have someone in her corner cheering her on. It was fun to dream with someone.

"Okay, I'm out." She turned to go but halted when he called to her.

"Don't forget to pick up the two dozen long-stem red roses before you get to the room. They were specially requested by one of the Mrs. Vallencourts."

"Of course, they were." She rolled her eyes and opened the pocket door to his office the rest of the way. She was immediately greeted with a buzz of excitement and noise from the corridor. "I'll get those right away, don't worry."

"Be nice," Ahmed called from the door as she speed-walked down the hall.

"I will," she called back. And she would. Because she had to. It was her job to make sure that every cruise guest was happy and well attended to. This was a vacation for them after all, and they *were* headed to paradise. She only had one set of VIPs to worry about, and by this time next week she'd be on vacation herself, not responsible for making or keeping anyone else but herself happy. Which was something she was very much looking forward to.

## CHAPTER FOUR

No sooner had Charlotte vowed to have a good time on the ship than she heard a knock at the door. She wondered if this might be the Lexi Enrique mentioned before. His Lexi, not her Lexi. Not that she had a Lexi to begin with, but now that he'd said the name, her mind wondered all the same.

"I'll be right there," she called as she scanned the room to make sure all her unmentionables were tucked away.

She made her way to the door and pulled it open with a smile, one that quickly died.

"Charlotte?" Behind a mass of red roses, Lexi Bronson's expression matched what Charlotte was currently feeling: shock, surprise, disbelief. Definitely disbelief.

Charlotte felt faint. No, not faint. Sick. Like she was having an out-of-body experience at the very tippity-top of a too high roller coaster and she was going to pass out on the ride and be pitched off the coaster into oblivion. That kind of sick.

The room began to spin, and she grabbed for something, anything, to keep her from falling.

"Whoa, Charlotte, hang on." She became aware of Lexi's hand gripping her shoulder, steadying her in place. But only vaguely. Because this was a dream, right? Her ex-love was not delivering flowers to her non-honeymoon honeymoon suite. On a ship. In the middle of the ocean. Because that stuff didn't happen. Nope. Not a chance.

"I need to sit. Or lie down. Maybe both." She would've been amazed at her ability to form words if this was really happening. If she wasn't still in complete and utter shock at the concerned blue eyes that met her gaze. Familiar eyes. Eyes from her past.

"Yeah, sitting is good. Sit." Lexi looked around, panicked. "Is there someone else? Hello?" she called to no one. "Is there someone here I can—"

"Ha." There was that all too familiar bitter laugh Charlotte seemed to have perfected lately. "No. Just me."

Lexi helped her to the edge of the nearby bed, juggling the oversized and rather obnoxious bouquet of roses. Which looked heavy. Very heavy. Or maybe Charlotte was still just feeling weak from the near fainting. "Oh, um, okay."

Charlotte took in a few steadying breaths, her body shaking a bit from the surprise of it all. She leaned forward on her elbows and rested her head in her hands. "This is some kind of sick joke, right?"

"For which one of us?" Lexi's voice sounded like a mix of sarcasm and nervousness.

She looked up at her. "I was talking about for me. But I could see why you would feel that way, too."

"Harrumph." Lexi hummed and Charlotte felt bad. They hadn't broken up on the best terms and she knew that was entirely on her. But that was a long time ago. She was different now, and she wondered if Lexi was, too.

Lexi placed the glass vase on the nearby table and leaned against the wall. She looked good. Great, even. Her long dirty-blond hair was swept back into a ponytail; her sun-tanned skin glowed beneath her uniform shirt. She looked tall and lean and...*tattooed*. From what Charlotte could see, Lexi's left wrist to elbow was covered in brightly colored ink. That was unexpected. Well, besides all of this being unexpected.

Lexi cleared her throat and Charlotte realized she might be staring. "So, you're one of the Mrs. Vallencourts, huh?"

"No." Charlotte leaned back on the bed, resting her weight on her hands. The new position afforded her some room to breathe, and she took it, inhaling deeply, trying to gain some composure. As if that was a possibility with the ghost of her past standing no more than four feet away, looking incredible and like no time had passed at all. "Not married. Not a Vallencourt. Still a Southwick."

Lexi raised an eyebrow and looked more delicious. "Are you in the wrong room then?"

"Nope. Not in the wrong room. Just not married."

Lexi looked adorably confused. "I'm not following."

Charlotte nodded. "It's kind of a long story."

"I bet." Lexi moved from the wall she was holding up and

gathered some paperwork from the floor. That hadn't been there before. Charlotte figured maybe Lexi had brought it with her and dropped it to help her during her near fainting episode.

"Thank you for making sure I didn't pass out." Charlotte felt her cheeks flush.

"Sure." Lexi gave her a small smile. "The medical staff on the ship is pretty great, but there's no reason to start your vacation with a concussion."

"That would put a definite damper on things." Charlotte was starting to feel normal again, whatever that meant.

"So, this is a little awkward but"—Lexi pointed toward the flowers—"those are from someone named Veronica. Do you know a Veronica? Or is this a mistake?"

Charlotte scowled. Of course, Veronica sent her flowers. She was so manipulative in that way. "Probably not a mistake. But I'm not interested in them, just the same."

Lexi looked at her a little dumbfounded. "You don't want them?"

"Not even a little, no." Charlotte was sure of that.

"Would you like me to remove them?" Lexi tucked an errant hair behind her ear and Charlotte was reminded of the nervous habit Lexi had as a teenager. Was Lexi nervous?

Charlotte shrugged. "Yes. No? I don't know. They look heavy."

Lexi exhaled with a laugh. "They are super heavy."

A buzzing noise came from beside her and she followed Lexi's gaze to her cellphone's screen. She had forgotten she'd tossed it on the bed while she was unpacking. She'd meant to shut it off, to avoid something just like this.

"That's some picture." Lexi leaned in to get a closer look as Charlotte reached for it.

Veronica was calling. Charlotte had set the last photo she'd ever taken of Veronica as the photo ID: Veronica in bed with another woman, in the throes of passion, oblivious to Charlotte standing there in their bedroom doorway with her phone out to surprise her with an impromptu lunch date. She'd been glad she had the camera set to photo as she walked in, and not video. The picture was painful enough. She couldn't imagine having video footage of the moment her whole world collapsed.

She looked at it a moment before holding it up briefly for Lexi to see. She pointed at the screen, to the dark-haired, mostly naked woman on top. "That is Veronica. My ex-fiancée."

Lexi peered at the screen, a deep blush on her cheeks as she indicated the woman below Charlotte's cheating ex. "And *that* is not you."

Charlotte laughed. The other woman was mostly covered by their white silk sheets, but it was clear that the blonde in the photo was not her. "Exactly."

"Oh." A look of recognition settled on Lexi's face. "Hence you not being married."

"Right." She silenced the phone and turned it off, eager to have the image out of sight. "How long until I lose my cell signal? I'd rather not have to see her calling this whole trip."

Lexi had resumed leaning against the nearby wall. "Well, that all depends on your cell phone carrier, but usually a few miles offshore most people lose their reception."

"Good." Charlotte tossed the phone across the bed.

"Or you could just put it on airplane mode and be done with the whole thing," Lexi supplied. "Your suite comes with a Wi-Fi package if you have to get any emails or need the internet for anything. But that would at least ensure you don't get any more surprise naked photo attacks."

"Duly noted," Charlotte replied.

Lexi looked at her for a moment, not speaking, and Charlotte saw a multitude of emotions cross her face. The quiet felt uneasy, nothing like the quiet they had shared in the past. Being with Lexi had always been so easy. It had felt so right. Charlotte could be near her, not talking for hours on end, and never feel uncomfortable. But this silence now, this felt uncomfortable. Maybe because they were strangers to each other now. Or maybe because they hadn't been strangers, once.

"So, I skipped a few steps and should probably backtrack a bit." Lexi broke the silence and Charlotte was grateful. Lexi walked back to the closed suite door and knocked on it, before walking back in with a broad smile. "Hi, my name's Lexi and I'll be your VIP attendant for the week. Welcome to the Majestic Princess's ten-day-long Lesbian Cruise Week to the Caribbean."

Charlotte burst out laughing. "Oh, sweet Jesus."

Lexi stifled a laugh and continued. "This is your welcome packet." She motioned to the folder and papers she'd gathered from the floor a few minutes ago. "In here you will find the daily itinerary as well as information about the ship, including but not limited to the list of restaurants, a map of the shopping areas, and the casino hours."

She handed it to Charlotte and resumed her rehearsed monologue, making Charlotte laugh harder. "Just as a review, our route is as follows…Day one, vacation! Yay. Today and tomorrow you'll have a day at sea before we visit the islands of Princess Cays and Grand Turk. Another day long party on the waves follows that until we're off to Curaçao and Aruba. And finally, the return voyage home consists of two relaxing and fun-filled days of sea and sun with your favorite cruise ship staff before we get back to the mainland, where life resumes, but you are not required to resume life as usual."

Charlotte was struggling to catch her breath as Lexi pointed to the top page and continued. "You'll receive a daily itinerary as well as a ship newsletter, and on the days we are in port, you'll also receive a detailed copy of a map of the island we're visiting and some key tourist attractions. Please note the re-boarding time will be highlighted in bold print. Don't ignore the bold print, or the boat will leave without you."

Charlotte nodded, tears streaming down her face from laughter. "Pay attention to the bold print, got it."

"You're a fast learner." Lexi smiled wider, her hands moving in excited and theatric motions as she continued. "If there is anything you need, anything at all in the morning or evening, you can have me paged using your room phone, and I'll be by to help in any way I can. Midday you will have another, but less awesome, attendant, as I am stationed elsewhere in the ship. Be that as it may, we're happy to have you as our guest. Welcome aboard and happy vacation." Lexi bowed and Charlotte nearly died.

"Wait a second." Charlotte sucked in a breath to keep from suffocating from laughter. "Do you have to give this spiel to everyone?"

Lexi nodded. "Indeed. I vary it slightly to keep it exciting for myself but, basically, yes."

"Wow." Charlotte wiped away the last laughter tears and exhaled. "I'm really glad you went back and started over. I'd hate to have missed that."

"Yeah, well, now you haven't. You got the whole welcome package." Lexi's smile was genuine now, the fake greeter smile gone. Her casual posture from before now back, she crossed her arms and seemed to hesitate, like she wanted to ask Charlotte something.

"What?" Charlotte felt renewed. She'd needed a good laugh-cry. Lexi had always been able to make her feel better when they were younger, and obviously that much hadn't changed.

"Why did you leave that picture as Veronica's contact photo?"

Charlotte stood from the bed, stretching before she walked to the roses. "To remind myself not to answer. And to remind myself that I made the right decision by calling off the wedding and walking out of that life."

When Lexi didn't immediately say anything, Charlotte turned to look at her. Her face was contemplative, like she was considering what Charlotte had said. Lexi's gaze settled on hers and she had to fight to maintain eye contact. She hated feeling this vulnerable, this exposed.

"I'm sorry, Charlotte. That really sucks." Lexi's voice was soft when she spoke. That was all that Charlotte could take.

She broke eye contact and ran her thumb along one of the ruby petals in front of her, the softness in conflict with how sharp and raw she was feeling inside. "Well, you in particular would be more than justified in saying that I deserved something like this—"

"I wouldn't." Out of her periphery, she could see Lexi shake her head. "I wouldn't say that."

Charlotte was grateful. "But you could. And you probably wouldn't be wrong."

Lexi's hand hovered by her forearm but withdrew. "That was a long time ago, Charlotte. A different life. I don't harbor any bad feelings about you, not anymore."

Charlotte could feel the emotions inside starting to bubble up again. Her eyes felt wet. The confident woman in the mirror from before was retreating back inside. "But you did, though."

Lexi gave her a sad nod. "I did once. But I don't now."

"I wouldn't blame you if you did, though. Just to be clear," Charlotte said. "But I'm glad all the same."

Lexi's smile didn't reach her eyes when she replied, "It's all good. You're on vacation, I'm about to go on vacation, and we just so happen to be in the same place at the same time in a very different time in both of our lives than the one that brought us together in the first place. I'd say that's some sort of luck."

"Some sort of luck." She'd heard that phrase before—it was something Lexi's dad used to say. She felt a pang of sadness in her heart, this time for Lexi and not for herself. "How long has it been now, Lex?"

"Almost a decade." Lexi's expression was somber.

"Lexi, I—"

Lexi held up her hand and shook her head. "It's fine. It's in the past." She motioned between them. "All of it."

Charlotte wiped the fresh tears from her eyes and nodded because what else was she supposed to do?

"Try to enjoy your vacation. It sounds like you need it." Lexi pointed toward the flowers. "Shall I take these with me?"

Charlotte regarded them with a new perspective. It wasn't the flowers' fault that Veronica was evil. *Let the past live in the past, Charlotte.* "No. They're beautiful."

"And heavy," Lexi supplied with an easy smile that made Charlotte feel like maybe everything would be okay.

"And heavy," Charlotte agreed. "Why should I let that woman ruin something beautiful? I'll keep them—they smell nice."

"That they do." Lexi stepped back toward the suite's door and bowed her head as she departed. "Oh, before I go"—she stepped out into the hallway and pointed somewhere next to the door—"there's a slider here with three options: one is for privacy, one is to tell the housekeeping staff you want the room freshened up, and one is for us, the crew, to let you know the room is ready for you to return after cleaning. We'll always knock before we drop anything off or enter to clean, but this is just another way to communicate. Okay?"

"I'll pay attention to the bold print *and* the slider—got it." Charlotte saluted her and had no idea why.

"Good, well, let me know if you need anything." Lexi gave her a small wave.

"It's nice to see you, Lex." Charlotte couldn't stop the words from tumbling out.

"You, too." But Lexi was gone before Charlotte could tell if she was being sincere. She hoped she was.

## Chapter Five

A ll right, how was everyone's first day?" Enrique sat down with a flight of tequila shots, delicately balanced on the tray he lowered with care.

Without speaking a word, Lexi grabbed the closest glass and downed it.

"Oh, that well, huh?" Zara gave her a look. "Or are you just thirsty?"

Lexi grumbled and Ahmed pushed his shot toward her. "Here, you need this more than me."

Lexi accepted it with a grateful smile and quickly downed his glass, too. After her run-in with Charlotte, she needed to talk to someone. Zara would have been her first choice, but she was leading an exercise class, and Lexi couldn't wait—she had to tell someone. Enrique was a great listener, but a bit of a softie, and she wanted to vent, not be told to forgive and forget. And Ahmed, well, Ahmed was the perfect amount of snarky and sassy behind those mild-mannered spectacles. And he was a stone—you could tell him anything and it never got out. She appreciated that about him.

"Whoa, whoa, whoa." Enrique put his hands around the other two shots, shielding them. "What's going on here? What happened to toasting to the first day of a new cruise? And manners? What happened to manners?"

Zara poked Lexi in the ribs, interrupting the delightful slow burn of the tequila coating her throat. "What's up? You never hit tequila that hard. Ever."

Lexi sighed and looked out at the ocean. She wasn't in the mood to be social. Today had been weird. So. Freaking. Weird.

"Lexi's first love is on the ship, single and vulnerable, and looking amazing." Ahmed blurted the words out before covering his mouth with his hand.

Lexi shot him a glare. So much for him being a stone. "Traitor."

"Who's Lexi's first love?" Enrique looked confused.

"Charlotte?" Zara sounded dumbfounded. Lexi kept her eyes trained on the dark clouds over the moonlit sky in the distance.

"One and the same," Ahmed replied and Lexi kicked him under the table. "Ouch."

"*The* Charlotte Southwick, breaker of hearts, ruiner of love and all things love-related for our dear Lexi? That Charlotte?" Zara asked, disbelief in her voice. "We're going to need more tequila."

"Well, since Lexi already got a head start"—Enrique handed Zara one of the remaining shots and clinked his shot glass to hers—"anyone want to fill me in here? I'm feeling a little left out."

"I'd rather not." Lexi huffed and looked up at the ceiling, not believing how today had unfolded. Her run-in with Charlotte had left her feeling all sorts of things: anger, confusion, annoyance, pity, affection. But she was most bothered by that last emotion. She'd felt an affection toward Charlotte—hell, she'd nearly touched her arm in an effort to console her. Console *her*. As if Charlotte needed to be consoled. As if Charlotte hadn't ripped her heart out of her chest all those years ago and stomped on it.

"You're doing that brooding thing." Zara poked her in the ribs again, this time harder.

She swatted her hand away but caved when Zara took her hand between hers.

"We should talk about it." Zara's amber eyes were a mix of affection and concern, and Lexi wanted to curl up in her lap and sob about all the memories seeing Charlotte had evoked in her. So many memories. Not all of them good.

"Well, from what I hear, Charlotte was the love of Lexi's life and one day just up and left her. I'd say she broke her, if you ask me." Ahmed cleared his throat and slid his seat back before Lexi could kick him again.

"No one asked you," Lexi pouted, her desire to maim him fading with each squeeze of Zara's hand.

Enrique shook his head. "Okay, so, you used to date someone—"

"Not anyone, *the one*," Zara replied.

Enrique nodded. "Okay, you used to date *the one*—"

"She wasn't *the one*," Lexi sighed, "otherwise we'd still be together, and this wouldn't be the conversation we were having right now."

"There's the jaded bartender we all know and love." Ahmed gave her a look and she rolled her eyes.

"I'm not jaded." That was convincing.

"You sound jaded." Enrique winced as he sucked on the lime wedge briefly before discarding it. He waved over one of the servers and placed their usual order, this time asking for another round of tequila. "Okay, so from the beginning. Lexi fell in love with a girl named Charlotte."

Zara placed their joined hands on the table and patted the back of Lexi's. She said directly to Enrique, "Lexi and Charlotte were high school sweethearts of sorts. Truly, madly, deeply in love."

"I'm right here," Lexi added.

Enrique looked at her and smiled. "Then feel free to tell me the story yourself, since you aren't happy with Ahmed's and Zara's versions."

"I thought my version was pretty good. Concise, to the point." Ahmed pushed his glasses up the bridge of his nose and shrugged.

Lexi closed her eyes and breathed out slowly, trying to organize her thoughts. She opened her eyes to find three sets staring back at her expectantly. "Fine. Charlotte and I dated toward the end of high school. We came from completely different worlds, though, and her world sent her one way and mine wasn't grand enough to keep her interest. Long story short, she broke up with me and then went off to Spain for college and I never saw her again. Until today, when I delivered her two dozen red roses from her ex-fiancée, effectively making me the messenger of sad news because no one wants to be reminded that their wedding dissolved before it happened because the love of their life was sleeping with some hot blonde that wasn't her." Lexi looked up at the stunned faces of her friends. "What?"

Zara blinked a few times before asking, "You brought your ex-girlfriend roses from her ex-fiancée? Damn."

"That's a lot to unpack." Ahmed took a sip of his water, and she was reminded of his bird, Don Julio.

"Does this Charlotte have pretty dark brown hair, a broad smile, and really sparkly green eyes?" Enrique asked, a look of guilt on his face.

"As a matter of fact, she does." Lexi had been trying to forget those sparkly green eyes all afternoon. "But that's awfully specific, Ricky. Something you should mention?"

Enrique ran his hand through his hair and frowned. "Yeah, I kinda gave her the official and unofficial tours of the ship."

"Unofficial?" Ahmed looked scandalized. And jealous. That was there, too. Poor guy. "What does that mean?"

Enrique laughed and put his arm around Ahmed's shoulders and gave him a friendly shake. "Relax, I just showed her where the quietest spots to read were or, more specifically, where to work, because she said she's working on a project or something."

That piqued Lexi's interest. What kind of project? What did Charlotte do for work? She'd always talked about wanting to do something based in art, but she was on the corporate business path last Lexi knew. What else about Charlotte had changed?

Enrique continued, "I showed her where the best chairs were by the top deck pool—you know, the ones where all the servers have to pass by so those guests get the most attention? Just little insider info like that." He shrugged. "She was sweet and seemed a little sad. I felt for her."

"Aw." Ahmed was giving Enrique moon eyes and Lexi was going to be sick.

"So what now?" Zara asked as the server brought them their food and their tequila refills.

Ahmed grabbed his glass before Lexi could claim it. "Well, Lexi is her VIP attendant for the week. And it's her only VIP assignment. So, there's that."

Lexi groaned and dropped her head back against the top of the chair. "This is going to be the worst week ever."

Zara squeezed her hand and she looked over to find her friend's eyes filled with tears.

"What's up, Zee?" Zara never cried, like, *never*. She was reliably steady and not overly emotional and that's why she and Lexi were such perfect friends and roommates.

"I was going to wait to tell you this later, but since there's bad news already all out on the table, maybe it's best to just rip the Band-Aid off and lay it all out there." Zara sniffled and released Lexi's hand to reach for a napkin.

Enrique frowned and nodded knowingly. Ahmed looked as confused as Lexi felt.

"What?" Lexi pressed again.

Zara sighed. "I didn't renew my contract, Lex. This is my last week on the ship."

Lexi felt like someone had punched her in the stomach. First Charlotte showed up on her ship and now this? Zara was her family, her best friend. She started to rationalize: People took time off. This lifestyle wasn't for everyone—maybe Zara just needed a break. "But you'll be back, right? You're just taking a season off, or two, right?"

Zara's face told her everything she needed to know. She wasn't coming back. This was it.

"Well, fuck." Ahmed's glasses were crooked on his face and he dabbed his eyes with his napkin. "This fucking sucks."

Enrique looked out at the water and said nothing.

"You knew?" Lexi asked him and Zara put her hand on Lexi's forearm.

"I had to tell someone, Lex. It was a big decision," Zara reasoned.

Another gut punch. "And you didn't think to tell me? Your roommate? You're my best friend, Zara. We've been together forever."

"I know, I know." Zara's frown looked endless, but Lexi was too angry and hurt to feel bad for her. "I wasn't sure how to tell you. I thought maybe we could just breeze over it—"

"Breeze over the fact that you're leaving? How am I supposed to breeze over that?" Lexi's head was starting to pound. She wasn't sure if it was the stress of the day or the tequila taking effect, but she had the sudden need to take a walk.

"Lex. This is your favorite cruise week and you're going on vacation to Key West and your dad's big ten-year anniversary is later this year and I just didn't know how to tell you, but I'm not going to stop being your friend. You'll have me forever, just—"

"Not as my roommate," Lexi added bitterly, and then something occurred to her. "When did you decide this?"

Zara looked down and Enrique tugged on the collar of his shirt, looking uncomfortable. "About a month ago."

That was the last straw. She stood up from the table, nearly knocking over her chair in the process. "A month? You've known for a whole month and you're just mentioning it now?" Her anger flared and she glared at Enrique. "And I suppose you've known this whole time as well."

Enrique looked between them, seemingly unsure of what to say. Ahmed sat there speechless, eyes wide as everything unfolded.

"You know what, forget it." Lexi tossed her napkin on the table, her desire for food or company having run its course. "It's been a long day. I think I'm going to crash."

"Lexi." Zara's voice was pleading.

Lexi frowned and shook her head. "Maybe we can talk later. I'm not the best company tonight. I'll see you later, Zee."

And with that she slipped out the side entrance of the restaurant, careful to blend in to the shadows and not evoke any guest questions or attention. And as she made her way down the side stairs toward the crew floor, she thought about how much had changed so quickly. How had her favorite theme week—with her favorite crew and friends, on the last week of her contract before vacation—gone so terribly, horribly wrong?

All things seemed to lead back to Charlotte and the bad luck she brought into Lexi's life when she entered it. It seemed some things hadn't changed at all.

# Chapter Six

*Cruise Day Two: Day at Sea*

"All right, so, tell me your story," the attractive older woman with the dazzling gray eyes and spiky white-blond hair to her right asked, her sunglasses perched on the edge of her nose.

Charlotte blinked, surprised by the woman's forwardness. "Excuse me?"

"Your story." The woman sat up on the lounger next to her and nodded toward the bar. "You've been staring at that pretty blond bartender nonstop for about twenty minutes. Something that normally wouldn't be significant, since she's gorgeous and all, but she's looked up at you just about every time you've looked away, which hasn't been often."

Charlotte felt a little violated. "You're observant."

"Or nosy, as my wife would have said." She extended her hand toward Charlotte. "I'm Barb. And you are?"

"Charlotte," she replied as she shook the waiting hand. Barb's grip was strong, but her hand was soft. It was a nice combination.

"So, Charlotte, tell me why you and the sexy bartender are exchanging looks." Barb's tone wasn't invasive—on the contrary, there was a level of sincere curiosity that amused Charlotte enough to answer her. Plus, Lexi had been looking at her?

"That's a long story," she said as she closed the tablet she'd been reading and tucked it into her bag. She hated to admit she'd been thinking about Lexi when Barb had interrupted her, but she knew it was pointless to pretend. Barb had seen through her. She'd bet Lexi had that morning, too. Their interaction earlier had been brief and awkward. She wasn't sure if that was her or Lexi, or both of them, but Lexi had seemed like she was in a hurry to get away from her, and Charlotte was left feeling sad. Which was not an unfamiliar feeling for her as of late, but this seemed different all the same. It was a different sadness.

Barb smiled and pointed toward the ocean behind them. "We've got all day. We're at sea until tomorrow. I've got time to listen if you care to share."

Charlotte scanned the people around them. The pool area was packed, and nearly every lounge chair was occupied. Which had turned out to yield some really great people watching but had effectively ruined her attempts at working. "It's probably boring and whiny and I'm sure you have other better things to be doing on your vacation than gossiping with me."

"Wrong. I've nothing better to do than gossip. And I was speculating before, but now that I know there's *gossip*, I'm all in." Barb rubbed her palms together with excitement.

Charlotte stretched and turned her head to survey Barb a little more closely. She was wearing a neon blue sports bra under a black tank top, her loose-fitting swim trunks went past her knee, even while sitting, and her sandals were the athletic kind with the rubber nubs that always made Charlotte's feet hurt. Barb adjusted her sunglasses over her eyes and tightened the band that kept them in place, the black silicone of the strap leaving a little indentation in the close-cropped hair by her ears. Barb had a playful, welcoming quality to her. Charlotte appreciated that.

"I know what you're thinking." Barb nodded, motioning between them. "I'm old enough to be your mother—that's probably true. But I assure you, I'm not hitting on you."

"I didn't think that." Charlotte laughed because that thought hadn't crossed her mind at all. That was something Veronica would have teased her about. She would have called her obtuse and said she was too in her own head to realize the rest of the world existed around her. Charlotte had been thinking a lot about those things lately. She wondered if there was some truth to that.

Barb frowned. "You're sad. Is it because of the bartender?"

Charlotte shook her head and smiled. "No, it's because I remembered something about someone who hurt my feelings for a moment."

"Oh." Barb looked worried. "Am I that person?"

"What person?"

"The person that hurt your feelings," Barb replied.

"What? No, I just…" Charlotte sighed. "It's a lo—"

"Long story," Barb said. "You said that."

Charlotte slid her glasses into her hair and squinted up at the bright sun above them. The blue sky was tranquil and calm, save for a few thick white clouds off in the distance. The vastness of the deep blue sea between her and those clouds made them seem a lifetime away, even if Lexi had warned her this morning during their very brief, somewhat strained interaction going over the ship's itinerary for today, that there was a storm on the horizon. Lexi had advised her to soak up the sun while they had it. She'd wondered if that was some euphemism at the time, but she wasn't so sure now.

She looked at Barb's disappointed expression and reminded herself of her grandfather's words, to try to enjoy herself. "Okay, I'll give you the full dish, but you have to promise me one thing."

Barb's face lit up. "Sure, anything."

"You have to promise not to let me blab on forever and ever and keep you from enjoying your wife." Charlotte glanced beyond Barb's shoulder to the adjacent lounge chair, but saw the woman seated there turned toward her other neighbor, the two clearly familiar with each other. "Is she here?"

Barb's expression dimmed, and Charlotte was reminded of Lexi's face last night when she'd brought up her father. "She's not. She passed away last year. I'm taking the trip we'd always planned to take together, but never had the chance to take."

"Oh God, Barb. I'm so sorry." Charlotte reached forward and took Barb's hand.

Barb gave her hand a gentle squeeze. "It's okay. I'm figuring things out. It's hard, but I know she's in a better place now." It was only then that Charlotte noticed the ring tan on Barb's finger, the pale line in stark contrast to Barb's heavily tanned skin. She hated herself for being insensitive.

"Still, though, that's…Ugh, I'm sorry." Charlotte's shoulders sagged.

"Don't be." Barb waved her off. She released Charlotte's hand and clapped her hands together, almost as if to reset the conversation. "Tell me about the hot bartender."

Charlotte laughed. "If we're going to talk about her, then I need to tell you a little about me."

"I'm all ears." Barb's excitement from before was back in full swing.

"Well"—Charlotte took a breath before letting go—"I'm here on my honeymoon. Alone. Because right before our wedding, I caught my fiancée sleeping, or decidedly not sleeping, with another woman, in our bed."

Barb's mouth dropped open in an almost cartoonish fashion. "No way."

"Yes way," Charlotte replied. "On our brand-new sheets, no less. Like, brand new. As in, I didn't even have a chance to experience them yet—that's how new they were."

Barb looked offended. "That's just rude. I mean, there's nothing better than new, clean sheets."

"Right? So impolite," Charlotte said.

"Maybe not the rudest part of that story, but worth noting," Barb supplied with a slight smile.

"Thank you." Charlotte still mourned those sheets.

"Wow." Barb paused. "So this just happened, huh?"

"Not really, no." Charlotte had gotten that question a lot once people who didn't know her heard the story. The truth was it had been months since she and Veronica had split. It'd been just long enough for her to pack her things, move back into her mother's house, and withdraw from most of their mutual friends. Her separation from Veronica had uprooted her existence, and she was still coming to terms with that. "We planned the honeymoon for a few months after the wedding, so she could make partner at her firm, so I've had just enough time to get angry and bitter about the breakup and also cranky about not getting my money back for the cruise. It's a confusing combination of emotions."

"I'll say." Barb whistled and waved to one of the servers passing by. "We need a drink. Is it too early to start?"

"Is there a time on vacation that's too early?" Charlotte asked.

❖

Lexi had incorrectly measured three frozen drinks in a row. Three. That never happened.

"I'll have a piña colada," the pretty brunette with the white-framed sunglasses called out, her smile sweet and inviting.

"Sure thing." Lexi dumped the excess daiquiri into a nearby glass, the third spillover glass, to be exact. It looked as though she was making a flight of frozen drinks. "Coming right up."

The line at the poolside bar had been steady the entire time since she'd started her bar shift. That's how she liked it usually, but today she couldn't focus. She felt like a newbie, misplacing her cocktail mixers and repeatedly forgetting the ratio of alcohol to ice. It was like she was in a fog. A fog that was in no way clearing with Charlotte in view, just a stone's throw away, looking fabulous and better than Lexi remembered from their youth. How was that possible?

She looked down at her hands and paused. What had she been doing just then?

"Let me help." Zara's voice sounded over her shoulder and she froze. They hadn't spoken since dinner last night. Lexi had slept in the medical triage room after she'd spent the better part of the night wandering around the boat, keeping out of sight, just lost in her thoughts.

Zara took the shaker out of her hand and asked her what she'd been making.

"I don't know." Lexi didn't fight her.

"Okay." Zara's expression was gentle as she looked at the drink parts in front of them. "I'd say a piña colada. Who's it for?"

"Brunette with the white sunglasses," Lexi replied. She knew that much.

"The one giving you the up and down right now?" Zara teased.

Lexi glanced over at the cruise guest. Yup, she was totally checking her out. Lexi had completely missed that before, her attention on the pretty brunette from her past. "Seems like it."

"I got this." Zara bumped her out of the way and finished making the drink. Lexi was vaguely aware of her taking a few other orders as she slunk back from the bar, slipping into the nearby walk-in refrigerator to clear her head.

"You need to pull yourself together, Lex." She closed the door and rested her forehead on the cold metal rack in front of her. The walk-in was small, but centrally located to contain all the beverage and fruit supplies that any of the three topside bars might need. The pool bar was the biggest by far, but the two smaller ones, at the forward and midship ends, also got a good amount of foot traffic. Part of Lexi's supervisory job entailed making sure this fridge stayed stocked.

She picked up the nearby clipboard and skimmed the item list, looking up from time to time to check the inventory. They needed more limes—she made a mental note to send one of the newer bartenders down to the kitchen to get some. People were drinking a lot today, which was usual for the first full day of cruising, but she expected that to slow considerably when the ship reached the bad weather pattern. Captain Correia had informed the crew that they'd hit the storm around dinnertime. The entertainment and scheduling staff had been scrambling to offer more indoor activities to entice the guests to stay dry but well lubricated. The ship's casino did exceptionally well on rainy days and nights. That meant that Lexi would be at one of the indoor events later, instead of a topside bar, which was fine by her since she couldn't seem to focus anyway.

Her head had been foggy when she'd woken up but had gotten worse when she'd seen Charlotte this morning. She'd stood outside Charlotte's door for a full minute before she'd convinced herself to knock. She contemplated knocking faintly to give herself an out—Charlotte's suite was so enormous there was a good chance she'd never hear her anyway, and she could just slip the itinerary under the door. The hallway security cameras would catch her knocking, but there was no way anyone could say how loud it was or say that she didn't try if they were watching. In the end she knocked louder than she'd anticipated, her subconscious winning out. Part of her wanted to see Charlotte again, just to make sure this was all real, because it didn't feel real.

Charlotte must have been near the door because she'd opened it right away, catching Lexi off guard. She looked great, refreshed and happy, a contrast to how she'd appeared yesterday. She'd smiled and stepped back, inviting Lexi in. Lexi was glad when Charlotte settled by the chaise—that put plenty of distance between them. The distance made Lexi feel grounded.

She'd started her usual morning monologue, but her mind had been elsewhere. Charlotte looked different from how she'd remembered, but the same as well. Her dark hair fell in perfect waves around her face, settling just past her shoulders, light flecks of golden highlights sprinkled throughout. Her hair was longer now, the angular cut from her youth gone. Lexi liked the length. Her body was fuller now, too, more lushly feminine than her teenage self. The curves suited her, her chest a bit bigger, her hips softer. Charlotte was unquestionably fit, but she'd grown into herself.

She was stunning—that hadn't changed.

And she still had that same smooth, flawless skin and those sparkling eyes, the ones that said more than her voice ever needed to. Lexi had always loved those eyes the most. She always felt like

Charlotte could see all of her with those eyes. She couldn't hide from them. Something that she was very aware of in that moment.

Lexi had hurried through the rest of her greeting, not wanting Charlotte to see too much of her, too much into her. She didn't trust herself around those eyes. Mainly because she didn't trust all the feelings seeing Charlotte again had stirred up.

Lexi had a lot of feelings today, it seemed. None of them made easier by Zara's announcement last night.

"Lex." Lexi heard the fridge door close behind Zara and she knew she was cornered.

She sighed and looked up at her friend, her oldest friend, well, aside from Charlotte, who wasn't her friend exactly, but they had once been friends and suddenly she was here, and she had friendly feelings to her. Kind of. It was complicated.

"You didn't come back to the room last night." Zara leaned against the shelves of daiquiri mix, looking pained.

"I was brooding," Lexi admitted.

Zara nodded. "I'm sorry, Lex."

"About leaving me or not telling me you were leaving me?" Lexi took the easy shot but felt bad right afterward.

"Ouch." Zara winced. "Both."

"Zee, I just—"

"No. Let me talk. Okay?" Zara said.

Lexi waited, running her fingers along the hem of her uniform shirt to have something to do with her hands. This conversation felt heavy and it hadn't even begun yet.

"I needed a change. I needed to see my mom and my sisters for more than a week or two at a time. I needed to wake up with a permanent mailing address that wasn't a PO box. I want to get to know my mailperson and leave a cash tip at the holidays. I want to *have* holidays, on land, with weather that isn't tropical." She raised her hand and shook her head. "I know I'm going to regret saying that last part, but I want to see snow, Lex. I want to go back to school and maybe finish my nursing degree and be boring for a bit. I've been at sea for five years, and I've had a million wonderful adventures with you and the crew, but this was never my endgame."

Lexi had known that all along. Zara had a great home life. She had lots of family and friends on land. It wasn't unusual for her to take large stretches of time away from the ship, and Lexi had noticed it had taken her longer and longer upon reentry to re-acclimate to the cruise life.

Zara hadn't been happy for a long time—Lexi had seen it but ignored it. Mostly because she was in denial. But there was no denying this: Zara was leaving, and Lexi was about to be all alone. Again.

"I know." Lexi released her shirt hem to run her hand through her hair. "I know."

Zara gave her a small smile. "I know you do. But I know this isn't easy either." She crossed her arms and cocked her head to the side. "I didn't want to break your heart, Lex. I didn't want to leave you. I still don't. I wish you'd come back with me. Set some roots and do this part-time. Come to Connecticut with me."

The idea of permanence made Lexi recoil. She'd been at sea all this time on purpose. Nothing good had come from setting down roots. She'd lost her whole life in the weeks after Charlotte had left, and as they quickly approached the anniversary of her father's death, the only family she'd ever had, she was feeling even more vulnerable to that fact than usual. Nothing good came from being in one place for too long.

"I don't know about that," she replied. "You know how I feel about being tethered."

Zara rolled her eyes. "I know how you feel about a lot of things, but I think it's time we reevaluated your stance on what being tethered really means. You're afraid of committing to anything longer than a six-month employment contract. Let's face it, the longest relationship you've ever had with another person is with me. And that's kind of unacceptable."

That hurt. "Wow. You just laid it all out there, huh?"

Zara broke eye contact for a moment before she continued. "I'm not leaving you to hurt you. I'm not leaving you at all. I'm just ready for something new and I was afraid to tell you because I knew how hurt you'd be. But you don't have to be. I love you, I'm still gonna be your bestie, but I'm just going to be a phone call or text away instead of five feet away in the next bed."

Lexi tried to swallow the hurt and see this for what it was: Zara was moving on with her life, but that didn't mean she was leaving Lexi behind, even if it felt that way. "This is going to suck."

Zara laughed and stepped forward, pulling her into a friendly and much needed embrace. "It is. But it'll be fine. I promise."

Lexi settled in her friend's arms and sniffled, the tears that had threatened last night finally streaming down her face. "You're going to be the best nurse ever."

Zara chuckled and leaned back, wiping away her tears. "We'll see, you big sap. I have enough savings to sit back and reexamine what I want. I'm not the same twenty-one-year-old that joined this life to get away from her old one. I'm different now. Cruising changes you—you know that. I have to find myself a bit again."

"On solid ground," Lexi added, not ready to be done pouting yet.

"On solid ground, yes." Zara stepped back but held her hands, swaying them side to side as she continued, "But make no mistake, I'll be visiting your pasty ass at all the best islands between your contracts to vacation with you. That's a given."

Lexi warmed at the thought. "I'd expect nothing less."

"And while we're having a heart-to-heart in this cold motherfucking fridge, I'd like to add that I think you should take that promotion Correia's been suggesting. Do the VIP route full-time and drop the hustle of the bartending shtick. That gig pays more, you get your own private room—which is awesome, since your amazing and irreplaceable roommate is leaving—and you're perfect for the job, Lex. You can schmooze with the best of them. You're funny and sarcastic and wonderful, and you'll get tips on top of that ridiculous salary. Rub elbows with the VIPs for a bit, and you'll have that dream beachside bar and restaurant on any island you want. We both know you're sitting on a small fortune as it is. Now's the time to double down and pad that pipe dream account." Zara gave her a knowing look and Lexi blushed.

No one besides Zara knew that little secret. When Lexi's father died just after she'd turned eighteen, she'd sold the family home to a developer for an absurd amount. Her father's longtime friend Jack had helped her navigate the paperwork and legal stuff. Without Uncle Jack, she wasn't sure she'd have been able to pull it off. But there was nothing in that town for her anymore, and a chance like that wouldn't come around again. So she'd jumped at it. Since Jack was her only family, she never went home. She didn't even have a home, really. Just a PO box. If she ever stayed anywhere that wasn't with Jack, she just rented a place for a while. Since she was almost always working, she never spent any of the money she made, which with tips was a considerable amount compared to her peers. But she had nothing to spend it on. Zara had a point, which annoyed her.

"Well, damn. How long have you been rehearsing that speech?" Lexi asked.

Zara tapped her chin with her finger. "About a month. Did it sound convincing?"

"Totally." Lexi was feeling marginally better about Zara leaving. Marginally.

"Pep Talk of the Year achievement unlocked." Zara did an end zone dance in the tiny fridge before shivering. "I love this whole conspire in private thing, girl, but it's cold as eff."

"Says the woman who wants to have holidays with snow," Lexi teased as she shivered, too.

"Oooh, good one." Zara put her arm around Lexi's shoulders as they struggled to squeeze through the now opened refrigerator door side by side.

"I save my best comebacks for you," Lexi replied, glad to have her buddy back by her side, teasing her.

They stepped back behind the bar and Angela, the other senior bartender on the bar looked relieved. "Where have you been? It's crazy out here. I could use the backup."

"Chillax, Angela. We got you." Zara said as she moved a bunch of dirty cups into the express dishwasher next to the sink. "Well, Lexi's got you, I have a spin class to teach in a bit."

Lexi pouted. "You're leaving already?"

Angela cast Zara a frantic look. "Seriously? You're leaving?"

Lexi looked out at the long line that had formed in their absence and Lexi gave Zara her best puppy dog expression. "Catch us up a bit, first?"

"Fine. But only since I'm abandoning you and I feel like I owe you something." Zara said and this time Lexi didn't feel that same pang of sadness from before.

"Oh, there will be so much making up you have to do this week, trust me."

"That's fair, Boo." Zara gave her a high five and danced around her to the blender, her long braids swinging behind her as she moved.

Lexi took a few orders and fell into the easy routine she was used to. With Zara's help, she and Angela cleared the line in no time. She filled a request by one of the servers for a pair of frozen mango margaritas and dropped an extra cherry in each because she was feeling generous. She was wiping her hands with a bar towel when a familiar laugh nearby caught her attention.

"She's got a great laugh," Zara said.

Lexi didn't have to ask who she was talking about. "How did you know it was her?"

"It's all over your face. And FYI, she's way hotter than you ever mentioned. You probably owe that girl an apology," Zara said, her gaze following Lexi's toward the sound of Charlotte's laughter.

"An apology for what? She dumped me all those years ago, remember?" Lexi replied, but she had no bitterness in her tone this time. Talking about it was getting easier. Which surprised her because she'd assumed that seeing Charlotte again would be like reopening an old wound. Which it kind of was but wasn't, all the same. It was confusing.

"You owe her an apology for underselling how beautiful she was. I can see why you were so heartbroken—she's gorgeous."

That comment did not help, at all. "Gorgeous but also heartless in the way she dumped me without a second thought, like I was yesterday's news."

"Mm-hmm. That's your side of the story, anyway."

Lexi gave her a look. "You don't believe me?"

"Oh no. I believe that's what you *believe* happened," Zara added as she walked backward, headed out of the bar area. "Look, I watched you for like five full minutes before I came back here to rescue you from yourself because you couldn't mix a damn drink to save your life. Largely, I'd bet, because you couldn't stop staring at her." Zara ducked under the counter and popped up on the guest side of the bar before continuing, "All I'm saying is you've talked a good game all these years, but now that I see the looks you two keep sneaking each other, I think maybe you left some bits out. Because she's not looking at you like you were yesterday's news. She's looking at you like you're the one that got away."

Lexi dropped the plastic cocktail glass she'd been holding, and it bounced at her feet before colliding with a shin—Angela's, who shot her a dirty look. "She's been looking at me?"

Zara looked back over her shoulder as she walked away. "Seems like there's some unfinished business there. Just sayin'."

Lexi hazarded a glance back at Charlotte in that moment and smiled when Charlotte raised a cocktail in cheers in her direction. It was a mango margarita with an extra cherry. Cherries used to be Charlotte's favorite, but Lexi had made that drink not knowing it was for her. That was an unexpected coincidence or, as her dad would have said, some sort of luck.

Lexi held Charlotte's gaze and waved in response, her heart

rate increasing a bit when Charlotte slid her glasses into her hair and winked in her direction. Attractive women winked at Lexi all the time, especially during this cruise week, and yet, she felt an all too familiar pull toward Charlotte just the same. Maybe Zara was on to something. Maybe there *was* unfinished business there.

# CHAPTER SEVEN

Charlotte wasn't sure what had happened, or how it had happened so fast, but before she knew it, the blue skies above them had turned black and a torrential downpour had begun. She'd lost track of time, chatting with Barb and sipping those endless, sinfully sweet frozen drinks, and had no idea what time it was. Even though she'd switched to water some time ago, she still felt that carefree lull that accompanied day-drinking in the sun. Except now, there was no sun, and everything was wet. Like, so wet.

She'd been so lost in her own thoughts that she hadn't noticed the mass exodus from the pool deck until it was too late. A crack of thunder sent the few remaining people scrambling for cover, Charlotte included. She grabbed her beach bag to zip it shut in an attempt to save her tablet from getting waterlogged before she dashed from her lounge chair toward the only visible place with coverage: the bar.

As she approached the bar, she scanned the scene. Most people had fled indoors, but a handful of cruisers were clustered toward the far end of the bar, chatting and laughing with the hand-sanitizer woman Charlotte recognized from the start of the cruise...Angela, was it? Lexi had been working the bar for the entire time she and Barb had been lounging poolside, but when Barb left a few minutes before the sky opened, Charlotte hadn't noticed Lexi there any longer. Not that she had been looking, or staring, under the cover of her dark glasses. Because that would have been creepy.

A flash of lightning in her periphery motivated her to hustle, and she sprinted to the emptier, quiet end of the bar as the rain picked up. She leaned her back against the bar, making herself as flat as possible, the overhang above protecting her, but just. Not that it mattered anyway—she was soaked. She shivered from the cold wetness of her clothes, but she wasn't uncomfortable. The air was warm still—they were almost in the Caribbean, after all. The rain was falling in sheets in front of her, so thick she almost couldn't see through it. Lightning filled the sky, and she could see the stream of light in the distance, the current racing down from the black clouds above to the water's surface. Thunder clapped again and she jumped.

"Wow." She'd never been at sea during a lightning storm.

"It's beautiful, isn't it?" Lexi's voice sounded over her shoulder. Charlotte kept her eyes on the storm unfolding in the distance as a new one began to brew under the surface of her skin at the sound of Lexi's voice.

"It's incredible. And terrifying, also that." The downpour was lessening, and though flashes of light still danced in the distance, the thunder sounded farther away now. They were moving away from the storm.

"You run into an occasional storm here or there, but they're mostly infrequent. I love them, though. There's something so amazing about them, right? The sheer power and magnitude of a storm at sea makes you feel so small and insignificant." Lexi's voice was soft.

"Like you could just get swept away." Charlotte turned to find Lexi watching her.

"We are just a series of tiny moments in a much larger picture." Lexi placed down the glass she was holding, and Charlotte wondered how long she had been standing there before she'd said anything.

"That was pretty fucking deep, Lex," Charlotte deadpanned.

"I have my moments." Lexi flexed and tipped her imaginary hat. "I'm not just a pretty face, you know."

"Oh, I remember." Charlotte slapped her hand to her mouth, but the words were already out into the world. She might had been thinking that, but there was no reason to verbalize it. Idiot.

Lexi arched an eyebrow at her and placed her hands on the bar, leaning forward a bit. "Charlotte Southwick, are you flirting with me?"

"What? N-no." Charlotte shook her head, her hand reflexively going to her chest. She pressed the tissue to slow her racing heart, a habit she'd had all her life when she was embarrassed or nervous. Lexi's eyes followed the movement and she wondered if she'd remember that. No, that was forever ago, and Lexi was only teasing her. She wasn't serious. They hadn't seen each other in a little over a decade. She was joking. Right?

"You answered that pretty fast." Lexi placed her hand on her hip and looked *delicious.*

How much had she had to drink today? "But if I were, would that be a problem?" Too much. Clearly, she had had too much to drink.

Lexi's eyes widened. She seemed to have surprised her with that response. "No, not necessarily," Lexi replied.

"*Not necessarily* like you wouldn't mind it, or *not necessarily* like you're dating that incredibly attractive bartender that was here before?" Charlotte was already committed—she might as well follow through.

"Zara?" Lexi laughed and reached forward, pushing the plastic cover off a tray holding cocktail fruit. She picked up an orange slice and nibbled on it before tossing the rind somewhere beneath the bar. "First of all, she's not a bartender. She just helps me out from time to time. And secondly, she's not my girlfriend. She's my very straight, very bossy, know-it-all roommate."

"Who you love." Charlotte added, "At least platonically."

Lexi was reaching for another piece of fruit and paused, her hand hovering in midair. "What makes you say that?"

Charlotte had seen their exchange at the bar before they both disappeared. Lexi had looked hurt, a face Charlotte was all too familiar with. The memory of that face had haunted her for years after they broke up. That was the last expression she had seen on Lexi's face— one of hurt. And betrayal. She'd seen it between Lexi and Zara today. The Lexi she had known had a terrible poker face and used to wear her heart on her sleeve. That was one of the things Charlotte had loved most about her. It seemed some of the old Lexi she knew was still around. "You seemed upset when she stopped by initially, but you were laughing and had your arms linked when you reemerged from wherever you went. So I figure whatever it was must be better."

"Because there was laughing?" Lexi's expression was unreadable.

"And arm linking, don't forget that part," Charlotte replied.

"Okay, and affection. So?" Lexi resumed her fruit mission and another orange rind disappeared from Charlotte's view.

"So," Charlotte speculated, "the Lexi I used to know didn't forgive any indiscretions very easily, unless she had a soft spot for someone. Which is my guess in this case, thus the smiles and affection. She matters to you, so you forgave whatever made you upset."

"You saw all this from your lounge chair, huh?" Lexi stared at her for a minute and Charlotte felt naked under her gaze. "That's awfully observant. And boldly speculative."

"And wrong?" Charlotte had no idea where this boldness was coming from but she kind of liked it.

"Not wrong, no." Lexi crossed her arms, exposing more of the colorful tattoos on her left arm that the sleeve of her uniform shirt had concealed. Charlotte had a lot of questions about those. "But pretty fucking presumptuous."

That was fair. Charlotte shrugged. "I have a wild imagination."

"Now *that* I remember." Lexi reached for the fruit dish again and Charlotte felt a blush settle on her cheeks.

"So you're not dating your roommate, and you love her platonically, and you don't mind if I was maybe flirting with you—not that I was but just for clarification purposes—so that means you're single, right?" Charlotte was possessed by an evil spirit, one that was making her say all kinds of un-Charlotte like things. Or tequila. Maybe she was possessed by the tequila from all the day-drinking.

"I'm unattached, yes. Though that reasoning was a little circular and I'm not convinced that you weren't flirting with me, but I'll humor you"—Lexi held up a maraschino cherry with a long stem—"if you'll humor me, of course. Assuming you can still do it, that is."

Charlotte looked at the fruit and felt as though her face was on fire. "Ask."

"Tie the stem in a knot for me." Lexi extended the fruit toward Charlotte and she took it between her fingers.

"That wasn't a question," Charlotte said. The look in Lexi's eyes told her she was aware of that.

"You're pretty confident I'm the same teenager you used to know. I'm not. Maybe I don't do as I'm told the way I used to." Lexi's expression was challenging, though not intimidatingly so.

"I like this Lexi." The heat from Charlotte's face had begun to travel elsewhere. "Okay, let's make a deal."

"Oh?" Lexi leaned forward, resting her elbows on the counter between them. "And why would I make a deal with you?"

"Because we're going to be on this ship together for a fixed number of days and you see me every morning, and sometimes during the day it appears, and I think we should come to an agreement." The cherry felt sticky between her fingers, but she wanted confirmation on her conditions before she relented.

"All right. I'm in." Lexi gave her a broad grin. "What are we agreeing to?"

"I won't make any more suppositions about your life or who you might be now based on the memory of who you were when I was young and dumb and made a lot of terrible mistakes, one of which was how I treated you"—Charlotte rushed that last part out—"as long as you pay me the same courtesy. Because I'm not that girl anymore, like you say you aren't, so I'd like to get to know this version of Lexi, if you're up to it."

Lexi's eyes narrowed. She didn't speak for a long time and Charlotte was convinced she'd insulted her. Fuck.

"Okay."

Okay? "Okay," she parroted.

Lexi nodded toward the cherry still perched in Charlotte's fingers. "Let's hope some of the old Charlotte is still around."

"She is. The good parts of her, I promise." Charlotte popped the cherry in her mouth and went to work. It had been a long time since she'd been tasked with this challenge. After a few attempts, she produced the perfectly tied cherry stem and placed it into Lexi's open palm.

"Well, damn." Lexi looked impressed, and Charlotte preened.

Knowing she had Lexi's attention, she broached the topic Lexi seemed to want to avoid yesterday in her suite. She'd been thinking about it a lot, and she wanted to try to make things right. To try to get some closure. "I meant what I said yesterday. I'm sorry for how things ended between us. And I want to get to know you, if you're open to that." Lexi nodded but said nothing. So Charlotte continued, "Look, that was a confusing time in my life. And although that doesn't excuse me from—"

"Dumping me." Lexi gave her a small smile, but she could tell she was being serious.

"Dumping you, yes." Charlotte sighed. "It was never about you. It was about me and my own fears getting in the way of my dreams. I had spent my whole life planning for my future and mapping out my path, but I found you and suddenly my path was so unclear. And before I knew it, it was time to make some serious adult decisions and act on the plan I had always had in place or throw it away and take a risk on something that burned so brightly in me that it scared me. And honestly, I panicked. I let my mother's influence and my insecurity about growing up and losing you guide my decisions. I put my pre-Lexi life plan ahead of my *actual* life with you. And that was wrong. I had hoped I was saving us both some heartbreak by ending things before the distance did that for us. But I didn't go about it in the right way. I should have talked to you about my fears before I acted on them. You were never anything less than wonderful to me and you deserved better."

Charlotte swallowed hard before admitting the next part. "You know, I came back for you, but you were already gone. I missed my chance to tell you I was sorry and that you were important to me, but I'm glad to have that opportunity now. Because even though we've both moved on from our teenage lives, and you clearly haven't spent your life pining over me—"

"I haven't." Lexi's reply was quick, but not cold, even though a part of Charlotte was sad by that admission. Though she completely understood that and echoed those feelings, a little bit of her was sad.

"Right," Charlotte said, "all I'm saying is, the past *is* in the past, but it was a past we shared, and I want to acknowledge my involvement in the way it ended and try to move past it. If that's possible."

After what seemed like an eternity, Lexi gave her a small nod. "Thank you. And I'd like that, too."

"Great." Charlotte exhaled, feeling like a weight was lifted from her shoulders.

There were a few moments of silence between them as the heaviness of the conversation lingered, but Lexi never looked away from her. On the contrary, actually, Lexi seemed to be watching her more closely than before. Charlotte took that as a good sign.

Eager to resume their earlier banter, she tried changing the subject. "Tell me about you. I want to know about this version of Lexi standing in front of me. What else do you like?"

Lexi seemed to consider this as she rolled the cherry stem between her fingertips. "I like that you were watching me today."

"Good. Because I was totally flirting with you before," Charlotte replied feeling uninhibited after her attempt at closure. She wanted to embrace the apparent honest train she was on at the moment. There was no point pretending Lexi hadn't been the only thing on her mind since yesterday.

"I like that, too." Lexi's blue eyes looked endless and bright. So very bright.

In fact, everything was brighter, Charlotte noted. She glanced back—the dark clouds were gone now. The rain had stopped, and the sun was setting on the angry lapping waves, the only sign that there was any storm at all. "Wow."

"The storms don't last." Lexi was standing when Charlotte looked back at her, a towel resting on her shoulder as she organized some cups nearby. "They're something, though, aren't they?"

"They're certainly something." Charlotte wasn't talking about the weather patterns and the look on Lexi's face told her that was loud and clear.

After a pause, Lexi motioned toward her bag on the counter. "What's in the bag? Anything good?"

"Ah, sunblock, ChapStick, a facecloth I stole from the room, and my work tablet." Charlotte tapped her chin in consideration. "And maybe also a hair tie. Or six."

Lexi took an order from someone who'd ambled up next to Charlotte before she returned to their conversation. "Still losing hair ties, huh?"

"Oh yeah. That part of Old Charlotte still exists. I go through a dozen a week, easily." Those things seemed to grow legs.

Lexi appraised her before speaking. "Your hair is longer now—it looks nice. It suits you."

"Thank you." Charlotte took the compliment and matched it. "Tattoos look great on you. And totally fit, too. Like that does and doesn't surprise me."

"I'm sure I still have some things I can surprise you with." Lexi's tone was playful.

*I'd like to see and experience all of them*, Charlotte thought. When did she get so horny? She chose a more subdued reply. "I bet you do."

"So, work computer, huh? Working in paradise?" Lexi nudged the bag as she asked.

"We're not in paradise yet," Charlotte replied, "but if I finish before we get there, then I'll be able to unwind without worry."

"What kind of work do you do?" Lexi managed to look busy arranging the bottles, but Charlotte could tell by her eye contact that she was paying attention to their interaction.

"Graphic design." Charlotte settled onto the stool across from Lexi and played with a napkin on the bar. "I'm just about done with a big project for a hospital back home. It's my last responsibility at the moment."

"Oh?" Lexi handed Charlotte a water. It was unprompted but greatly appreciated all the same. "Do you do freelance work or work for a company?"

"A company for now, but I've been strongly considering the

freelance route. I think I need a change." That was an understatement. She needed a life overhaul. And fewer responsibilities.

"Graphic design, huh?" Lexi leaned her hip against the bar and shook her head. "I always thought you were on the corporate business track."

Charlotte nodded. "I was. But when I got there, I realized I wanted something different. My mother wanted business school, while I wanted something more artistic. I blame you for that."

Lexi smiled. "I secretly always hoped you'd pursue something artsy—you were always a gifted artist."

"You weren't so secret about it," Charlotte recalled. "If I remember correctly, you filled out an art school application for me and submitted it without me knowing."

Lexi laughed. "I wrote a damn good entrance essay. You got in, didn't you?"

"That I did." Charlotte had been shocked when the acceptance letter had arrived. She'd fallen even more in love with Lexi when she'd found out she'd submitted it for her. That was what she'd meant before, when she said something burned so brightly in her that it scared her. Lexi started that fire in her—she helped her see that there was life and love in art, and that the corporate business track wasn't the only option. And it frightened her—Lexi and how much she meant to her frightened teenage Charlotte. And embracing her love of art as a potential career scared her as well.

She'd known Cookie would never have paid for school if she knew Charlotte was going to pursue art. Charlotte always felt a little cowardly about acknowledging how that weighed on her decision. But she was grown now, and she could see the error of her ways. To be fair, though, she had done the best she could at the time, and she knew that, too. She was done beating herself up about the past. Her recent past, included. This was a new start for her, a new chance to be happy. She wanted to embrace it.

"I still can't believe you scraped together all that money for the application fee." It was money Charlotte knew Lexi didn't have at the time.

"It seemed important." Lexi shrugged. "Plus, I learned some valuable skills about using edging tape when painting."

Charlotte remembered being surprised that Lexi took a painting gig that summer, but it was short lived, so she hadn't pressed her much about it. Little had she known Lexi did it to save money for *her*. Lexi was endlessly thoughtful like that.

Lexi took another drink order, this one for a cutesy newly married couple. Charlotte watched Lexi's seamless interaction with them. Lexi made quick, easy conversation like a seasoned pro. She learned their names and asked all the right questions to make them feel special and at ease. Charlotte half wondered if that was what Lexi was doing with her right now, asking the right questions to make her feel momentarily important and seen. How authentic was this exchange?

"Well, good for you, regardless." Lexi resumed the conversation as though nothing had disrupted it to begin with. "I'm glad you followed your heart."

Charlotte wasn't so sure she had, since a piece of her heart seemed to beat stronger with Lexi nearby. "Eventually, I did, I guess. It's a fun job. I like it." She wanted to know more about Lexi, though. "What about you? Have you been doing this long?"

Lexi filled two water orders and sent them down the bar. "A little over nine years."

"Wow." Charlotte marveled at all Lexi must have seen. She couldn't imagine staying in one job for that long. It occurred to her that that was just about the entire time they'd been apart—or rather, since she'd seen Lexi last. So much had transpired in her life since then. Had it in Lexi's life as well? "And you still like it?"

"I do," Lexi replied. "I like people and being outdoors. And who could complain about traveling to paradise week in and week out?"

She made a valid point. "This is the first trip I've had out of the country in a very long time."

"Exactly." Lexi dropped a few cherries into a small cup and slid them to her. "You can spend your whole life in a cubicle or an office working, but why? When all of this exists." She waved toward the now clear sky. "It's beautiful here."

"It is." Charlotte couldn't argue with that. She snacked on the cherries while Lexi worked for a few minutes nearby, checking a clipboard with Angela and restocking the bar.

"So, you think you'll bartend at sea for life?" Charlotte asked when she was nearby again.

Lexi gave her a look. "That sounds like a judgmental question."

Charlotte nearly choked on the cherry in her mouth. "It wasn't intended to be—I'm sorry. I meant, um, do you think you'll do this for a long time?" She shook her head. "You know what? Sorry. I didn't mean to pry."

Lexi's expression softened. "I don't know. I've been considering switching things up recently. There's an opening for a new gig, one that takes me out from behind the bar and puts me more in the VIP realm of things. It offers more opportunities for travel and on bigger ships. It would be a change, but I might be ready for it."

"That sounds exciting," Charlotte said, because it did. She couldn't imagine having the freedom Lexi was describing. She was envious of how carefree she seemed.

Lexi nodded. "I'm not far off from qualifying for a retirement severance bonus, so I'll stick around for that at least."

Charlotte had wondered about how this all worked. "I didn't realize that was a thing."

"It isn't with all cruise lines, but it is with the Majestic Princess. That's why I chose them to begin with." Lexi leaned against the counter now that the bar was quiet again. "You can make a good amount of money cruising, especially if you work at the bar or in the casino where you can get tips. Obviously, the officers make more, but room and board and food are covered, so if you're careful, it can be a pretty lucrative experience."

"You've got it all figured out." Charlotte was in awe. "I can barely get dressed in the morning and you're already planning for your future."

"I have to have a plan. I don't have anyone to catch me if I fall. It's not like I've got any family to help me out. I have to be proactive." Lexi's tone was softer than the implication of her statement. Charlotte had come from money, but Lexi had come from nothing. A risk for Charlotte was one that had a built-in safety net, even now. She felt embarrassed by Lexi's point, even if she didn't feel like it was made in an antagonistic way. It was a fact, all the same. The differences of their pasts were still evident in the present.

"That just makes you all the more incredible, then." And brave, Charlotte thought.

"But to answer your first question, no, that's not my end goal," Lexi said, seemingly uncomfortable with the compliment. "I like working for the Majestic Princess cruise company, but I don't see myself at sea forever."

"Where do you see yourself?" Charlotte asked, drawn in by the blue of Lexi's eyes again. Lexi appeared to make no attempt to look away. She was being candid with her. Charlotte was grateful for that.

"On a beach, looking out at the ocean"—Lexi laughed—"which isn't so different from this, but I'd like to own a bar and restaurant on a tropical island somewhere. Preferably someplace with a good local following but close enough to a cruise port to keep the place bumping and busy. So I can work and play at my leisure without worrying about making ends meet."

"All while in paradise," Charlotte noted.

"Precisely." Lexi stretched. "I don't mind working, but I like the sand and sun, too."

"Sounds like a dream job," Charlotte said because it did. "Maybe I can visit someday if I start freelancing."

Lexi cocked her head to the side, seeming to consider this. "I'd like that."

Charlotte felt like she meant that. And though she'd said that to make conversation, she also hoped for it to be true someday. Now that Lexi was back in her life, she was in no rush to usher her out of it. She wondered if they might continue a friendship after this week was over. It had seemed fated to have run into her, after all.

"What about you?" Lexi asked, jarring her from her thoughts. "Are you happy with your position in life? Do you feel fulfilled?"

"Not in the least." Charlotte hadn't meant to be so blunt. Or so honest. "I mean, I like my work, but did I expect to be living back at home with my mother and grandfather after a failed engagement as I neared thirty? Not exactly, no."

Lexi gave her a playful grin. "How is Biscuit these days?"

Charlotte chuckled at the familiar jab. Lexi and her mother had never gotten along, and Lexi refused to accept that a grown woman would go by Cookie. So she'd taken to calling her other dessert foods as a way of mocking her. Charlotte had always appreciated her creative food choices. "Oh, you know, stale and dry. As biscuits can be."

"Some things never change." Lexi laughed and crossed her arms. "And Paw Paw? How's he? I'm glad to hear he's still around."

Charlotte's heart warmed. He and Lexi had always gotten along exceedingly well. He'd accepted her into the family the moment they'd struck up a friendship, and when they'd started dating, he hadn't blinked an eye. He'd always been so welcoming to Lexi, which made it easy to spend time with them both. Which she'd always valued. She loved her grandfather, and her girlfriend, and she'd loved seeing them interact. That was something she'd missed when she had ended things with Lexi. And her Paw Paw had noticed it as well.

"He's good. Ninety-one years young this year. He's still playing cribbage and kicking everyone's ass." Her grandfather was a trip.

"And that car? Tell me he still has that car." Lexi's eyes shone and Charlotte felt like a teenager again. She loved that look.

"Oh, he still has it. I think it probably only has about five hundred more miles on it since the last time you saw it." Lexi loved her grandfather's prized '57 Chevy. Lexi's dad had been a car enthusiast, and Lexi had bonded with Paw Paw over the vehicle in the beginning days of their pre-dating friendship. The car was special to Charlotte, too, but that was because it was the first place she and Lexi had ever had sex. Not that she told Paw Paw that. But it had been a life changing night for Charlotte and one that she and Lexi had talked about often when they were still together. It wasn't lost on her that Lexi had brought that memory up, in a roundabout sort of way.

"That's a great car." Lexi looked nostalgic and Charlotte was getting all kinds of feelings, albeit dirty ones, but nostalgic all the same.

"It does have a great back seat," she added.

"Mm," Lexi replied, and Charlotte's heartbeat picked up at the sound. "I do remember that."

"Hard to forget?" She was fishing, and she didn't care.

Lexi leaned across the bar, her voice low as she said, "Unforgettable."

"I'm glad we remember it the same way." Charlotte let her gaze drop to Lexi's lips. She wondered if they were as soft as she remembered. She bet they were.

"Me, too," Lexi said and Charlotte held her gaze in a titillating silence until someone broke them apart with a drink order.

Lexi started mixing a cocktail and Charlotte settled into her seat a little more comfortably. She watched Lexi work and let herself freely admire her old friend while having more than friendly thoughts about her the whole time.

❖

"Captain! Have you got a second?" Lexi increased her speed down the I-95, being careful to navigate the hurrying crew members frantically trying to get to their posts before the start of the dinner rush.

Captain Correia paused and Staff Captain Dashel nearly collided with the back of her. "For you, Bronson, sure."

Lexi skidded to a halt and sucked in a gasp in an attempt to catch her breath. "I wanted to talk to you about that VIP position."

Correia looked surprised. "And?"

"I'd like to know more about it. I think it might be time to make a change." Lexi had been toying with the idea since the first time Correia had proposed it, and with the new knowledge that Zara was leaving, and the pep talk in the refrigerator earlier, Lexi decided it would be in her best interests to remain open-minded. So this was her being open-minded. "Assuming the offer still stands."

"That's great to hear." Correia's smile seemed genuine. "HR manages all the details, but I'm sure with some feedback from the captain, the job is as good as yours." She turned to the staff captain. "Sally, can you get the ball rolling for Lexi?"

Sally had her tablet out and was typing before Correia had finished speaking. "Of course, Captain."

"Okay. We're doing this." Lexi exhaled shakily. She didn't make decisions easily, and she reminded herself she wasn't finalizing a plan, so much as she was just getting all the data on said decision. Even though this was something she had considered for a while, it was still something new, and new scared her. Just like seeing Charlotte again had scared her a bit. But if she was being honest with herself, she did need a change of pace. Zara had been right about that, and seeing the familiar and beautiful face from her past had all but sealed the deal in her mind. It was time. "Thanks, Cap."

"Have a good night, Bronson." Correia turned to leave, but then she paused and turned back to add, "Lexi, make sure Ahmed puts you on the schedule to work in the Officers' Lounge toward the end of the week, for old times' sake."

"Will do." Lexi warmed at the request. She was probably already scheduled to work a night or two behind the bar, but she was touched that Correia had said anything. She really liked that woman.

She checked her watch and cursed under her breath—it was late. She jogged the rest of the way to Ahmed's office and knocked, hoping she hadn't missed catching him before he'd left for the night.

"Come in." The sound of Ahmed's voice was muffled behind his closed office door.

Lexi pulled open the slider and spilled into the room, closing the door loudly behind her.

"Jesus. You're like a bull in a china shop." Ahmed looked up from his desk and rubbed his forehead.

His desk was a mess. There were papers everywhere, some with large portions of text highlighted in yellow and pink in seemingly random patterns. This desk was very un-Ahmed-like. Lexi was intrigued.

"You're here late." Lexi leaned over the desk to see what all the paperwork was about, but Ahmed shielded the majority of it from her view.

"That's none of your business, move along." He shooed her away. "I'm up to my eyeballs in work, so I'll be here a little bit longer."

"I can see that." Lexi reached out and petted Don Julio on the head, but Ahmed stopped his bird's bobbing.

"I can't get these papers wet, Lex."

"Don Julio looks thirsty," Lexi argued and tried to reach past Ahmed's obstructive hand.

"Lex, no." Ahmed swiped at her again, and she stepped out of reach, waiting until he moved to nudge the bird once again. "Seriously?"

"I can't help myself," Lexi teased as she sat down across from him. "I'll be good, I promise."

"I don't believe you for a second," Ahmed said as he folded his hands and leaned on the desk. "What's up?"

"I missed you and wanted to visit," Lexi replied.

"Aw, thanks." Ahmed wrapped his arms around his shoulders and gave himself a playful hug before his expression got more serious again. "But why are you really here?"

Lexi laughed. "Two things. One, I left my schedule at the bar earlier but the storm rolled in and it got soaked before I had a chance to double-check it against the online copy."

"Okay, you need a new schedule, done." He turned around and opened the filing cabinet behind his desk and shuffled some folders around. "And the second thing?"

Lexi chewed on the inside of her lip. "I was wondering if you could access the guest schedules for the week."

Ahmed stopped what he was doing and gave her an incredulous look. "I manage the crew side of things, not the guest side of things."

"I know." Lexi stood up and paced the tiny office as she rambled. "But I also know that you know how to do things that I don't know how to do, and you do them in an awesomely amazing fashion, and I figured you could totally do this for me. Just this once."

Recognition filled Ahmed's face and he cheered. "This is about Charlotte, isn't it?"

"No." Lexi stopped pacing. "Yes. Stop judging me."

Ahmed put his hands up in surrender and shook his head. "I'm not judging you."

She started pacing again, her mind restless like it had been since she'd first seen Charlotte on the ship. It had been an interesting few days, days that seemed to freeze and turn back time simultaneously. Seeing Charlotte here had made her feel vulnerable, and hearing about Zara leaving had made that vulnerability deepen, but things had changed today. Maybe it was Charlotte's apology or how incredibly raw and honest she had been—Lexi wasn't sure. But she had felt something change in her and it started with that storm. Or, more likely, it had started with Charlotte. And suddenly she found herself feeling...brave. Curious even. And that cherry stem thing and all those reminders of awesome back seat car sex had made her feel, well, hot.

"Lexi, stop pacing. You're freaking me out." Ahmed pointed to the chair she had abandoned. "Sit."

Lexi sat but tapped her feet, the need to move overwhelming her.

He handed her a sheet of paper. "First things first. Here's your schedule. Don't lose it."

"I won't." They both knew that wasn't true. Lexi might lose it. It was a thing she sort of did sometimes. She could be absentminded.

"Now for part two"—he reached for the phone on his desk and cradled the receiver against his shoulder—"are you asking for anything in particular? Or just everything I can find out?"

Lexi covered her eyes with her hands, embarrassed that she was even doing this. She peeked through her fingers to answer. "All of it."

Ahmed gave her a knowing look and dialed a number. "Hi, Sarah. I'm good, how are you?...Oh yeah? Sure. Let's plan on that...Listen, any chance you can get me some information on a guest? Yes, I'm trying to make sure the VIP attendant's schedule lines up with the guest's...Uh-huh. Sure. The name is Vallencourt—"

"Southwick," Lexi corrected, but Ahmed held up a hand silencing her.

"Right. Yes, good. Sure, email would be great. Thanks, Sarah." Ahmed disconnected and rolled his eyes at her. "You almost blew that."

"She's not a Vallencourt." Lexi wasn't sure why she felt the need to argue that point.

"But the reservation is under Vallencourt. Don't worry." Ahmed loaded his computer and typed in his password. "I'm fully aware that your dream girl is back from the past and unmarried."

Lexi wanted to argue back for the sake of arguing but she couldn't. Charlotte *had* been her dream girl, way back when. But that was why the breakup had been so devastating for her. At least in some part, anyway. But she also realized that she was young and inexperienced and saw things through her teenage eyes at that time. And though time had passed—and she agreed with Charlotte's point earlier that she hadn't pined over her all these years—there was something about seeing Charlotte again that affected her. She was every bit as dreamy as Lexi remembered, and that was simultaneously alarming and exciting.

Ahmed pulled a piece of paper from the printer and handed it to her. "I have to buy Sarah a drink later, so you'll be covering that debt. Thank you very much." He pointed to the sheet and outlined the details. "These are her scheduled on-ship activities, and these are the VIP activities that you already have access to." He pointed to the bottom of the sheet and continued, "These are the activities and excursions she has planned for her stop in Half Moon Cay, Grand Turks, and Curaçao."

"Nothing for Aruba?" That surprised Lexi largely in part because Charlotte had something booked just about every day of vacation, so why not in Aruba?

"Nope, I guess not." Ahmed shrugged. "So care to tell me why you wanted this?"

Lexi had been thinking about that. "Have you ever had something happen in your life that felt so serendipitous that ignoring it would make you wonder what-if for the rest of your life?"

Ahmed leaned back in his chair and nodded. "I felt that way about taking this job. No one in my family has ever traveled before, and I've been to over two dozen countries in less than six months."

"Exactly." Lexi stood from the chair, feeling encouraged. "Something is telling me not to blow her off and not to fight my attraction to her. It's like there's something pulling me toward her." She looked down at the list in her hand. "This might be my only chance to see her again. And it's not something I ever expected to happen. Like ever." She looked up at him and saw the understanding in his face. "I'm not going to ignore fate knocking on my cruise ship door. Even if this isn't anything more than an opportunity to find closure, you know?"

"I'm proud of you." Ahmed stood and joined her at his office door. He opened his arms. "Get in here."

She stepped into his embrace and tickled his sides. "Listen, I know I'm a little superstitious—"

"You mean a lot superstitious," he corrected as he squirmed away.

Lexi didn't argue because he wasn't wrong. She'd been that way since her father had died. Which had come just on the heels of her relationship with Charlotte ending. And while a tiny, insecure part of her told her to run from Charlotte, who seemed to set off the chain of sad and unfortunate events in her life, the mature and more sane part of her was curious to see what had come of her past love. And what her being here meant in the grand scheme of life.

"Yeah, that. But what I was trying to say before you pointed out my flaws is that I think you should—"

Ahmed placed his hand on her shoulder and squeezed. "Ask Enrique out. I know."

"Serendipity, Ahmed. Same time, same place. It's fate, I'm telling you. You're on the same boat for a reason." Lexi patted his hand and turned to leave. "At least, that's what I'm choosing to think about Charlotte."

"You're wiser than you look, maybe"—he grabbed her shoulder and stopped her from departing—"except you left your schedule."

"Crap." Lexi dropped her head and put out her hand. "I'm the worst."

"The absolute worst." He handed the paper to her and shooed her toward the door. "She's got dinner reservations at the front of the ship in about an hour. If you hurry, you could find yourself in that vicinity, looking inconspicuous."

"This seems a little creepy," Lexi said.

"It is." Ahmed nudged her again toward the door. "I have work. Go, be creepy elsewhere. And report back with juicy details."

"Bye, Ahmed." She pecked him on the cheek. "Thanks for listening."

"Always." He gave her a wave before closing his door and disappearing from sight.

Lexi looked at the list in her hand and contemplated her next step. She'd chatted with Charlotte at the bar for a long time today, and it had been like a breath of fresh air. They'd talked about everything and nothing, but the banter was there—there was chemistry. She could feel it in her bones. When Charlotte had mentioned that she and her new friend Barb would be grabbing dinner later on, Lexi felt like she'd dropped the information in hopes of seeing her again. If she was being honest, she wanted that to be the case.

"Okay, just a casual stroll in the area of the ship she might be dining in. You see her, it's meant to be, you don't, it's not. Simple." Lexi exhaled and headed to her room to freshen up, just in case fate was on her side again.

## CHAPTER EIGHT

Charlotte was so full she felt sick. She'd had a great dinner with Barb, but she'd had way too much of everything and felt the need to walk some of it off. Barb had ventured off toward the casino, but Charlotte had no interest in gambling. That was more of a Veronica thing than something she enjoyed. She didn't like the randomness of it, nor did she think of herself as particularly lucky or skilled in any way. She likened it to throwing money into the ocean, which seemed ironic since this honeymoon trip was literally throwing money into the ocean.

She walked along the top deck, following the designated jogging path, and did some people watching as she went. There were couples scattered along the pool lounge chairs, music playing, and servers bringing cocktails here and there. She'd looked over at the main bar but hadn't seen Lexi. Not that she'd been looking for her exactly, but she kind of had.

Their conversation this afternoon was so very different from the awkwardness of this morning. Charlotte had felt more relaxed, which was probably helped by the cocktailing she'd done during the day, but the more they chatted as the sun went down, the more and more at ease she felt with the reappearance of Lexi in her life. How unexpected and yet welcome it was. Maybe she was feeling more nostalgic than usual being as she was here after what was easily one of the worst endings of a relationship in her life. Or maybe it was just Lexi. She wasn't quite sure, but she was sure that she wanted to see her again and often. Which was inevitable since they were on the same ship, right?

On her second loop around the jogging trail, she headed toward the bridge, stepping off the marked path and weaving through the lounge chairs. This late at night, not many people were out here. They seemed to be clustered near the bars and pools, but the front of the ship was mostly empty.

She headed toward the bow of the ship, the deck gleaming white in the light of the moon overhead. She leaned against the railing and looked out at the vastness before her. The ocean was dark, almost black save for the portion below the glow of the moon. That dark blue water was textured with small breaking whitecaps that moved rhythmically along, like a series of never-ending thoughts running one into the next. Charlotte felt like her head had been that way for the last six months, and though she'd found moments of distraction or calm, her entire being had felt uprooted and frantic in a way. But she hadn't noticed that at all today. It was a welcome respite.

"You're a hard lady to find," Lexi said and she smiled at the sound of her voice.

Charlotte turned to find Lexi in casual clothes. It was the first time she'd seen her out of uniform. She looked great. "I didn't know you'd be looking for me."

"Are you disappointed that I was?" Lexi gave her an easy smile as she leaned against the railing next to her.

"Not in the least. I would have made myself easier to find if I knew, though," Charlotte replied, glad the banter from earlier was back. "You look nice."

Lexi glanced down at herself and dramatically tossed her dirty blond hair over her shoulder. "I do own more clothes than cruise-ship issued ones."

"Good to know." Charlotte let herself imagine what other kinds of things Lexi had to wear, or not wear. Worried that she might be staring, she decided to attempt casual dialogue. "How was your day?"

"Busy. But good. Yours?" Lexi didn't seem bothered by the potential staring. If anything, she looked amused by it.

Charlotte looked back out at the ocean to regain some composure. "Good. I spent most of my day sipping margaritas, and in an unexpected twist, I ended my day tying cherry stems with my tongue. So, overall, a good day."

"Sounds like it."

She was aware of Lexi's gaze on her profile. She turned to face her, and her heart stopped. Lexi was closer than she'd realized, and those endless blue eyes were watching her with curiosity and something else. Charlotte had spent the last of her high school days getting lost in those eyes, falling into them as she'd fallen into Lexi's arms like Lexi was the only security she had ever known. And to some extent, that had been true. Lexi was *definitely* the one that got away. She held a piece of Charlotte's heart that had never healed, but it was a self-inflicted wound and Charlotte knew that. She'd been the one to end things, for all the wrong reasons. Reasons she'd regretted immediately. But like she'd mentioned to Lexi at the bar before, she'd gone back to make it right, but Lexi was gone. She thought she'd missed her chance to ever get lost in those eyes again. She wasn't about to let that happen again.

"I don't think I realized how badly I missed you until you walked into my room with those roses." Charlotte took in Lexi's beauty under the moonlight, her sun-kissed skin and freckle-free complexion looking as young and vibrant as she remembered. But she was more mature now, too. She had a confidence and a swagger that was hard to ignore. Charlotte had watched her interact with cruise guests all day and felt jealousy pool in her stomach. Lexi was charming and funny and kind, on top of looking incredibly sexy and natural behind the bar. And Charlotte was drawn to her like a magnet.

Lexi gave her a small smile and exhaled. "I can't tell you how many times I dreamed of hearing you say that, after you left. I used to dream that you would come rushing back in a dramatic fashion, apologizing for breaking my heart, and sometimes I would just kiss you in those dreams, like it was all I could do."

"And the other times? The ones without the kissing?" Now Charlotte could only think of kissing Lexi. She was suddenly very aware of the shimmered gloss on Lexi's lips. How sparkly.

Lexi's lips parted and her perfect white teeth shone blindingly. "The other times I cussed you out."

Charlotte winced. "I deserved it." She did. "But I would have much preferred the kissing."

"Some days I would, too," Lexi replied, her body still close enough to touch.

"And days like today?" Charlotte was painfully aware of how close her hand was to Lexi's abdomen. She'd been bracing herself on the railing when Lexi sidled up next to her, and with just a millimeter of movement, she could graze her stomach. She wanted to. The only physical contact they'd had, had been when she'd almost fainted. But she didn't have the chance to appreciate it then. She'd sure as hell appreciate it now.

"Days like today I wonder about who you are and who you became after you left. I wonder if you remember me, the way I remember you."

Lexi scanned her face and Charlotte closed her eyes, focusing on Lexi's words.

"What do you remember about me?" Charlotte blinked her eyes open to find Lexi looking at her intently.

Lexi laughed. "What don't I remember about you? That might be an easier place to start."

"Okay, I'll help." Charlotte turned to face her, mirroring her position against the railing. "What was my favorite comfort food?"

Lexi replied without hesitation, "Kraft Mac and Cheese. Fake orange cheese and all. You were a savage."

"Still am." Charlotte gave a small cheer. "I don't care what you say, that shit is still amazing."

"You're a mess." Lexi shook her head. "Do you remember mine?"

Charlotte paused. "That's a trick question."

"Oh?" Lexi gave her a pleased expression. Clearly, Charlotte had answered correctly. "Go on."

"You hated soup, like, *hated* it. But you loved your dad's clam chowder. When you were sick, it was the only thing that made you feel better. But when you just wanted to binge on comfort food and rock sweats on the couch, you could eat your weight in that Ellio's microwaveable pizza from the big box stores that your dad used to fill the freezer in the garage with. You were an endless pit for that stuff." Charlotte remembered being shocked how much pizza Lexi would put down without ever gaining an ounce. Lexi had been naturally athletic like her father, Timothy, who was a young dad compared to the other parents of kids in their grade, and he was a total stud. Every girl had a crush on Mr. Bronson, except for Charlotte, who had a crush on Mr. Bronson's daughter.

"I'm pretty sure my dad had stock in that company. There was no other way he would have agreed to keep buying that stuff in the mass quantity that I required to sustain life." Lexi looked away for the first time tonight, her attention directed toward the moonlit water in front of them.

A quiet fell between them. Charlotte knew it had to do with the talk of Lexi's father. "I'm sorry I wasn't there when it happened, Lex."

Lexi nodded but didn't look at her.

She'd just started her semester abroad in Spain during her second semester of college, when she'd heard about the drunk driving accident that had taken Timothy Bronson's life. He'd been helping a stranded motorist with a flat tire on the side of the road when an intoxicated driver lost control of his car and hit them. The stranded motorist lived, a single mother with three kids. But Timothy, the Good Samaritan, did not.

She continued, "I'm sorry for a lot of things, but I'm most sorry about that."

Lexi was quiet for what seemed like forever. When she finally spoke, it was to the water below. "The other day, you asked me if I harbored bad feelings toward you, and I told you I used to, but that I didn't anymore. I meant that. I hated you for leaving, but not for leaving me. I hated you for not being there when he died. I needed my best friend when I lost my whole life that night. One bad decision by a nameless, faceless asshole changed everything, and I couldn't breathe. It would have been so much less isolating if I hadn't been truly alone. But I was. And I hated you for a while for that. Not because it was your fault he died, but because you weren't there when I needed you most."

That had been what Charlotte had feared more than anything, that she'd let Lexi down. Never once when she had made the decision to ends things with Lexi did she believe, even for a second, that they wouldn't get back together. But she was leaving for school and going abroad, and it didn't seem fair to string Lexi along while she was off living her life. Her mother's bullying about their relationship didn't help, and though for years she blamed her mother for the demise of her relationship with Lexi, she knew a part of her had been too cowardly to stand up to her mother.

Lexi and her father never met Cookie Southwick's standards. But no one ever did, least of all Charlotte, who'd turned out to be gay-gay and not just gay for a phase, something that took a long time for her to accept and come to terms with. She knew that embracing herself would mean that she would never be close with her mother again. It took coming home after her father's death to find Lexi, and not being able to make it right with her, to change Charlotte's fear and cowardice to some semblance of resilience. She'd lost Lexi, but she wouldn't lose herself. Nothing was ever the same after that summer. Nothing.

Charlotte didn't know what to say. She felt a million emotions in that moment, but none of them were appropriate to share right now. Lexi was right and deserved to have her feelings heard. Charlotte would respect that. "Thank you for telling me that."

"You said earlier you came back for me. What did you mean by that?" Lexi continued to stare out at the sea and Charlotte wondered what she was thinking.

"I did. When I heard what happened, I took the first flight back, but I was too late." Charlotte could remember that phone call from her Paw Paw like it was yesterday. She'd been traveling on holiday with some school friends and had been off the grid for a few weeks backpacking through Europe. By the time she'd heard the news and got back home, Lexi was nowhere to be found. "Your house was dark and there was a lockbox on the front door. I heard through the local gossip channel that you'd packed up and moved out. I didn't know where to find you, or where you'd gone. You just vanished." Charlotte couldn't remember a time when she had been more devastated, when she had cried harder, in her whole life. She'd lost Lexi that day, in a way so unlike the day she'd broken things off with her. The memory of it gave her that same visceral, helpless feeling even now.

Lexi looked back at her and her eyes were wet with tears. "You know, all those times I fantasized about seeing you again, those happened before I lost him. For a long time after that, I stopped dreaming altogether, which was a relief from the nightmares that followed for months afterward. But it's strange when you don't dream. It's like a piece of yourself is never at rest enough to be free and get lost in your subconscious. A life without dreaming isn't much of a life. And, if I'm being honest, I thought you were a distant memory of my past. A mirage, even. Something I dreamed up when I still had the capacity to dream at all." She wiped her eyes and added, "But then you were there, standing in front of me, nearly fainting—"

"In a very dramatic fashion." Charlotte wiped tears from her own eyes before she rolled them.

"Exactly." Lexi laughed and shook her head. "You came rushing back into my life in an overly dramatic fashion, apologizing for breaking my heart, and I just forgot that I was supposed to hate you. Because I didn't, not really, anyway."

Charlotte felt that familiar twinge in her chest, the one that told her there was still a love of some kind between them. "I'm happy to hear that."

Lexi held her gaze for a moment before appearing to notice something over Charlotte's shoulder. "Hey, check that out."

Charlotte turned to see what Lexi was pointing at and gasped. Four wild dolphins were jumping through the air before diving back below the water. Their smooth wet gray skin shimmered like glitter under the moonlight when the pod reemerged. They frolicked and played, each pair weaving and dancing in the water almost in competition with the other. They were seemingly weightless, so graceful and elegant in the water. Charlotte couldn't believe her eyes. She'd never seen dolphins in their natural habitat. They were breathtaking.

"Those are bottlenose dolphins," Lexi said. "They're common in the waters of the Dutch Caribbean islands. They're super friendly and amazingly intelligent."

"And gorgeous," Charlotte said, aware for the first time that her mouth was agape. She snapped it shut. "I'm such a tourist. You must see these guys all the time."

"Not often under the moonlight," Lexi replied, "they seem more magical this way."

Once the dolphins were out of sight, Charlotte looked up at the moon above them. The sky was clear, and stars twinkled here. There was no city smog or pollution. Charlotte felt like she was in a planetarium, seeing constellations for the first time. "It's wild being out here, in the middle of the ocean. Everything seems so vast and deep and enormous."

"Makes you feel small, huh?" Lexi's voice was soft.

Charlotte looked at her and let herself get lost in Lexi's eyes. "Teeny."

Lexi squeezed her hand and Charlotte looked down, shocked.

"How long have we been holding hands?" she asked.

Lexi ran her thumb along Charlotte's knuckles before letting go. Charlotte's hand fell back to the railing. "Oh, since I told you I couldn't hate you even though I wanted to."

Charlotte had no recollection of reaching for Lexi, but she was glad she did. Of course, this was now twice that she's touched Lexi and not truly appreciated it. Dammit. "Hey, Lex?"

"Hmm?"

"I'm glad you don't hate me."

"Me, too." Lexi's lips parted and Charlotte felt herself lean in.

"And I'm glad you didn't mind me flirting with you earlier." She licked her lips and saw Lexi's eyes drop to her mouth, so she did it again for good measure. "Because I like flirting with you, and I want you to know I'm doing it."

Lexi's eyes returned to hers and she could have sworn they were a shade darker now. "Why does it feel like no time has passed when I'm talking to you?" Lexi asked.

Charlotte reached her hand out and hovered it by Lexi's hip, almost too afraid to make intentional contact. She was so close she could feel the heat of Lexi's body warm the palm of her hand.

"Charlotte." Lexi's voice wavered and Charlotte froze, her hand halting its progression. "You can't." Lexi glanced over her shoulder and Charlotte heard voices approaching them. "I can't."

Charlotte exhaled as Lexi stepped back. She turned her body back toward the railing, shielding herself from Lexi's rejection. She gripped the cold metal with both of her hands, trying to expel the extra energy that vibrated through her. She'd thought they were on the same page, but Lexi didn't seem so sure. She bit her lip to contain her disappointment and confusion.

Lexi mirrored her position, this time with considerable space between them. A couple wandered by behind them, laughing and canoodling. It was the first time Charlotte was aware of anyone around them. They'd been in this perfect little vacuum, all by themselves for a while. Clearly that time had ended.

"Don't do the lip thing, Char," Lexi said, her voice hushed. "I can't take the lip thing."

Charlotte chanced a glance in her direction and saw a pained look on Lexi's face. She released her lip and soothed it with her tongue. Lexi pouted.

"This is maddening." Lexi sighed and Charlotte wasn't sure if she should be glad that Lexi was affected by her or annoyed that she wasn't acting on it when Charlotte had been convinced they were both interested in the same thing. At least in that moment anyway.

"I'm not sure what to do or say right now." Charlotte frowned, her confusion winning over her frustration in that instance. "Mostly because your eyes were telling me one thing, but your mouth said something completely different, and now I'm a little embarrassed and think maybe I should go lick my wounds elsewhere."

"Wait. Don't go yet," Lexi said as she looked over her shoulder. The lovey-dovey couple were still nearby but appeared to be lost in each other's mouths. "There's a camera right behind us, three actually. All of them are closely monitored by the ship's security to ensure no one falls overboard, since this is a popular area for people to congregate. But that's not the issue, at least not exactly."

"I'm lost," Charlotte replied, unsure of what this had to do with anything.

"You can't touch me, Charlotte," Lexi breathed out. "Because I want you to and if you do, I'll want to kiss you. And if I kiss you, I'm not sure what will happen, because in the short time you've reentered my life, I'm not the Lexi I've been for years. I'm the Lexi I stopped being when you walked out. And I'm scared of that Lexi because she makes heart-driven choices and ignores her head, and she wonders if your lips are still as soft as she remembers."

Lexi ran her hand through her hair and palmed her forehead as she said, "That's it, really—*she remembers*. And if you touch me and I kiss you and it all comes rushing back, then I don't know what will happen."

Charlotte wasn't expecting that response—not that she knew what to expect since she felt like she was flying blind about all this anyway, but she certainly didn't expect that. "That's all? You're worried you'll like touching and kissing me too much?"

Lexi covered her eyes with her hands and nodded. "Yes."

"I gotta be honest with you, that's a pretty high bar you just set. What if you're abysmally disappointed and I don't live up to your expectations? I mean, I could fall completely flat here—I'm having performance anxiety just thinking about it." Charlotte wondered where her filter had run off to.

"I sincerely doubt that." Lexi's hands dropped to her sides and she pursed her lips. "There's one other thing, too."

Charlotte turned to face her fully, eager to hear what this might be. She didn't want to miss any nuances in Lexi's body language, either. "Go on."

Lexi subtly motioned behind her. "The cameras. The cruise company has an iron-clad rule about the crew not fraternizing with guests, as in if you're caught even kissing one of them, they'll drop your ass off at the next port and mail you your last check. It's *that* kind of serious. And you chose the most monitored part of the ship to stand under the moonlight and look gorgeous and say all the right things, and honestly, it's a little rude."

Charlotte laughed. "It is. You're right—I'm sorry."

"You should be," Lexi said, and her heartbeat picked up. "So you can't touch my hip because I'll lose my job and likely my self-control all at once. Which would suck for a lot of reasons, but mainly because I did just maybe get a promotion, and I just found you after you were lost to me—so yeah."

"And it might not even be worth it, since you've probably inflated my kissing skills in your mind as a way to reconcile my awfulness in our teenage breakup," Charlotte added.

"Again, unlikely, but still not the time to test that theory."

"Because of all the cameras." Charlotte wanted to be crystal clear on this, because it seemed like Lexi wanted to kiss her as badly as she wanted to be kissed.

"Yes." Lexi frowned. "And because maybe all those other reasons mean it's just not a good idea in general."

Oof. And just like that, Charlotte was back to square one.

The kissing couple had moved on, but a few more people had sprinkled in around them, so Charlotte took this as her chance to bow out before anything got more complicated or confusing or sexually frustrating.

"You know, it's been kind of a long day. I think I'm going to turn in for the night and just reset a bit." Charlotte stretched and forced a yawn.

"Charlotte, I..." Lexi looked as frustrated as Charlotte felt.

"It's okay. I get it." She didn't but she'd pretend to. "I'd rather have you as a friend or a re-acquaintance than as nothing." She turned to go but paused to ask, "You said if I touched you, you would want to kiss me. That means you didn't already want to kiss me, right?"

Lexi looked down briefly before answering. "I think we both know that that's not the case."

Charlotte felt momentarily victorious. "Yeah, okay, just checking."

She dipped her head to catch Lexi's gaze and said, "I'm teasing you. I won't push you for more than you're willing to give or share. I'm glad we talked tonight. I hope we can have more."

"Thanks. And me, too." Lexi's tone was sincere.

Charlotte walked away and used every ounce of her willpower not to look back. But she hoped the vagueness of her last statement wasn't lost on Lexi. She'd settle for friendship, reunited ex-lovers turned friends, if she had to. But she wanted more, and that surprised her. But just about everything that happened involving Lexi surprised her. And she was all right with that.

# Chapter Nine

*Cruise Day Three: Half Moon Cay*

Lexi had had a fitful night's sleep. Restless didn't begin to describe it. She was hot, she was cold, she couldn't get comfortable, the pillow was too flat. Everything was the worst thing ever and she was cranky, and now the line for eggs was slowing down instead of speeding up and she was going to be late.

"Lexi," Enrique called from the very front of the cafeteria line and waved to her, "come here."

Lexi jumped out of line and jogged to him, ignoring the dozen or so people who groaned as she cut them. She needed this boost today, even if it just meant getting the hard-boiled eggs while they were still hot. It was a win and she felt like she needed a win today.

Enrique held up two eggs and a whole avocado. "Breakfast of champions for my favorite bartender." Lexi looked at him in awe as he placed them on her tray and shuttled her out of line. "Save me a seat? I'll be by in a second."

"Sure thing." She slipped out of line and headed toward the coffee station before thinking better of it. The crew cafeteria coffee was grainy sludge at best. And with a Starbucks in the main atrium of the ship for the guests, there was no real reason to expose yourself to that mud unless it was after-hours or you had a death wish. Neither of those applied to Lexi, but the day was young.

She settled for some watered-down cranberry juice and sat in her favorite seat by one of the few windows. The crew area was mostly below the water, but the gym and part of the cafeteria had a partial view of sea level, which was something she looked forward to seeing before the start of the day. You never really knew what to expect weather-wise unless you checked one of the dozen or so televisions in the main corridors down here. Updates filled those screens—weather forecasts, expected drills, announcements—and there was a constant rolling schedule at the bottom of the screen. It was like a real-time office memo for twenty-two hundred or so people. But Lexi still preferred to *see* the day before reading about it.

Lexi watched as Enrique weaved through the crowd of crew members spilling in for breakfast before their morning shifts began. He lifted his tray high above his head to preserve its contents when a traffic jam at the cereal island formed as one of the sous-chefs dropped off what appeared to be freshly baked pastries. It was a masterful adjustment, Lexi mused.

"Whew," Enrique said as he wiped imaginary sweat from his brow, "I narrowly missed the fresh bagel drop-off."

"You're lucky to be alive," Lexi replied. He was. People took fresh baked pastries very seriously around here since they were a bit of a novelty. The crew had access to the same foods the guests did, but it wasn't always as fresh. "Thank you for the eggs. And the avocado! What black magic did you employ to get that?"

Enrique gave her a broad smile. "I'm covering an extra samba class tonight for Bebe. She's paying me back in avocadoes."

Avocado was a favorite of theirs. It was something they'd bonded on when they first met, hoarding them in their rooms whenever they were available. She was touched he was sacrificing his for her benefit. She had a feeling it had to do with the Zara thing.

They hadn't talked much since Zara's revelation the other day. Lexi needed someone to be mad at, but Enrique wasn't the right target of her anger. She knew that lay squarely on her own shoulders. She also knew they should talk, but she'd been so caught up in Charlotte and Zara and her possible new position, she hadn't had the opportunity to chat with him. At least that was what she was telling herself, even if she knew she had been avoiding him because she felt like she'd overreacted. Because she had.

As if reading her mind, he said, "Look, I feel bad about dinner the other night and how things went with Zara. I'm sorry you felt left out—I know I would have been if I was in your position—but I felt like I had to be there for her. She needed me to be a sounding board, but I get how that sucked for you. And I'm sorry."

Lexi felt bad all over again. "I was wrong to be mad at you. It was

Zara's decision and I need to respect that. I don't have to like it, but I do have to respect it. You're a good friend, to her and me. I'm sure that was a tough secret to keep."

"The worst. Ugh. I feel like I aged a decade over the past month." Enrique looked relieved. "I was hoping I could buy back your love with avocadoes and gossip."

"Done. I'm easily placated." That wasn't true, unless the person meant something to her. Enrique fell into that category, which immediately brought her back to thoughts of Charlotte and how she'd made that observation just the day before. Things seemed to keep circling back to Charlotte. She sighed. "Share this with me. I'd feel terrible eating your bartering fruit alone."

Enrique looked pleased and easily accepted half of the avocado. "I accept your conditions."

Lexi sliced up her half and was sprinkling some salt on it when she realized Enrique had said something else. "Wait, did you say you have gossip for me?"

"Oh yeah," Enrique mumbled between bites of scrambled eggs that were soaked in more ketchup than was socially acceptable. And he was eating them with a spoon. His eating habits were questionable at best. "It's about Charlotte."

Lexi dropped her fork and it bounced off her tray and shot under the table. "Shit."

Enrique didn't miss a beat. He handed her the fork he wasn't using and motioned for her to eat. "You're gonna be late."

"I know, I know." She glanced at the wall clock and started to sweat. They would be docking in Half Moon Cay in a few minutes. She still had to get to Charlotte's room and go over the daily itinerary before the ship opened the doors for passengers to exit in the next hour or so. The ship would only be at the island for about eight hours, so the clock was ticking, and she had to get to Charlotte before she exited the ship. "So, about that gossip?"

Enrique waited for her to resume shoveling food into her mouth before he continued, "I ran into her last night, on the Lido deck. I was coming back from my shift at the dance club and was walking back the long way to avoid the cigarette smoke of the casino, and I found her sitting under one of the deck lights, working on her tablet."

Lexi refrained from asking all the questions that were in her head. Was she upset? Did she mention the almost-kiss? Did she look as beautiful as she did when she was with her earlier? Was her hair up or down? Did she do that nervous habit thing where she put her hand over her heart and looked adorable? Since all of those questions seemed a little too intense, she chose the nonchalant route. "Oh?"

Enrique nodded and used part of his English muffin to soak up his excess ketchup, and Lexi cringed. "She was working on a drawing for a hospital project or something. She said she'd hit some kind of a block that stopped her from creating...something that started with an *M*..."

"Like, she lost her muse?" Lexi asked.

"Yes, that's it." Enrique wiped his mouth but missed a glob of ketchup and Lexi couldn't stop staring at it. "She said she'd been blocked for a while, but she'd had a really interesting and draining day and woke up inspired. She said she couldn't sleep, so she found a quiet place outside to work."

Lexi couldn't take the ketchup anymore and reached across the table with a clean napkin to wipe Enrique's face. He looked surprised but didn't stop her, and she was grateful. "She's got a balcony in her suite, so why not just work there?"

"She said she needed to get out of that room." Enrique shrugged. "I just assumed it had something to do with all the honeymoon stuff that was in there. Maybe it was giving her bad vibes. I offered to remove the rose petals and card when she told me about them."

"What rose petals?" Lexi asked as she checked the time again. She really had to go.

"She said her ex had had someone sprinkle flower petals on the bed. I asked her why she didn't tell you not to leave them, but she said you weren't on last night."

That was true. Lexi's VIP shift had ended earlier than usual yesterday because she'd put in so many hours by the pool. That wasn't unusual on days at sea—there was a strict maritime policy that there were breaks built into their work schedules. A cruise week meant seven days of consecutive work with ten-hour days as the average, but there were only so many hours that could be worked at once, and usually, crew had four to six hours off between shifts. But yesterday, she had front-loaded her work, so her night had ended early, which was why she'd been able to catch Charlotte by the bridge. She'd gone over that interaction all night in her sleepless insomnia. Still, she felt bad all the same. "Jeez, that sucks."

"Totally." Enrique cleared their plates and motioned for Lexi to follow him. "Come on, we can walk and talk."

She had to increase her pace to keep up with his borderline trotting stride. He kept making quick turns and sudden stops which didn't help either. "Was she upset?"

"You know, surprisingly no." He looked down to talk to her, his six-foot-three-inch frame towering over her. "She was really focused, like she'd had a breakthrough or something. She made it seem like it was more like an annoyance. But I thought you should know, all the same."

Lexi nodded. "Thanks." It was then that she realized Enrique was using his frame to clear a path for her to get to Charlotte's end of the ship more easily. They'd nearly reached the crew stairwell on the starboard side by the time she'd realized it. "Wow. Really, thanks."

Enrique gave her shoulder a squeeze, then gave her a bashful smile. "Anytime. Oh, and one more thing."

"Hmm?"

"You think it'd be too forward for me to ask Ahmed out for a drink? Or to play pool?" Enrique asked as he gave her a boyish grin. He scratched the back of his head, looking insecure and it occurred to her that she'd never seen that side of him before. "Or do you think that's a dumb idea? I don't want to make a big deal out of something that's not there, you know?"

Lexi reached out and tapped his overly pumped biceps. "I think you should take a chance and see what he says."

"Really?" Enrique looked hopeful and Lexi's heart melted.

"Really."

"Thanks, Lex. Hey, swing by the samba class later. I could use an extra set of hands, and we both know the only person that's a better samba dancer on this ship than me is you."

"We'll see." Lexi was noncommittal but she figured she might swing by as a show of support anyway—she did eat half of his avocado, after all. "Good luck with Ahmed."

Lexi was convinced he was skipping down the hall, but she knew he'd deny it if she asked.

The overhead speaker crackled with an announcement, and Lexi took off in the direction of Charlotte's room. What little leeway Enrique had carved out for her schedule-wise was long gone by now.

❖

Charlotte rested her head on the tiles of the shower and let the hot water loosen up the tense muscles of her shoulders. She hadn't slept well, and when she did fall asleep, she'd overslept a bit and was slow to get moving. After her talk with Lexi last night, her body felt restless. She didn't want to stay in her room, but she wasn't interested in socializing either. She'd been hung up on a few details that had slowed her Davenport Hospital project progress, but she had a burst of creativity, so she went with it. Of course, her middle-of-the-night attempt at working had done little to help quiet her brain, but she felt renewed and accomplished by the progress she'd made. She was nearly done with the project, and though she wasn't ahead of schedule, she'd surely finish on time. That was a total win, even if sleep had evaded her. Still, last night had been a lot of things, none of which were uncomplicated.

When the water started to lose its heat, she decided it was time to get out. She walked past the wastebasket full of flower petals and tried to ignore the anger that threatened to breach her newly achieved mellow from the shower. Finding those with Veronica's card last night after leaving Lexi on the bridge had done nothing to help her mood or confusion. She'd hoped that the roses would be the only invasion of privacy Veronica had set up, but that didn't seem to be the case. She'd vowed to talk to Lexi today and make sure that any other surprises were stopped. All those petals did was make her mad, not make her want to take Veronica back.

She'd shredded the card the moment she'd read it. It was a seemingly generic note of apology and begging for forgiveness that had almost no depth or sincerity to it. Much like Veronica herself. Charlotte was more and more grateful with every passing day that she'd made the decision to leave her.

She wrapped the towel around her chest and wiped the fog off the bathroom mirror with her hand. She took some of the excess water out of her hair with another towel before she twisted it up onto the top of her head. Beads of moisture ran down her neck, down her back, and between her breasts, as she moved from the sauna-like bathroom toward the bed. She shivered when the cooler air met her skin and her nipples pressed firmly against the tightly wrapped towel encasing her chest. The sensation made her see stars—she'd always been very reactive to any nipple stimulation, but her breasts were especially sore today. Which she knew was largely because she'd masturbated to the thought of Lexi last night. Though she hadn't achieved the ending she'd hoped for.

Charlotte hadn't had an orgasm by herself, or with anybody

else, in nearly a year. The irony of that was that before the wedding, Veronica had made them both take a celibacy vow in hopes of making the wedding night extra special or some other garbage Veronica had fed her that she'd lapped up blindly. Veronica was obviously only being celibate with her, and not with whatever number of women she was cheating on her with. But perhaps stupidly, she had gone along with it.

She hadn't had much interest in sex after the breakup, but when she did start feeling a desire to experience pleasure, she'd found herself frustratingly blocked. At first, she'd hoped it was just about sex with a new partner. After she'd moved out, she'd tried a few one-night stands to reset her libido, but none of those encounters resulted in the orgasm she so desperately yearned for. So she tried a little self love to see if that would work. It didn't. Or rather, it hadn't *yet*. Not exactly, anyway.

Charlotte could come close—she could feel the buildup, and the act felt good and great and hot and wet and then…nothing. She'd just lose it, right before the dam would break, and she'd be left horny and frustrated all at once. But last night was different. Last night she found herself feeling aroused after her conversation with Lexi. She let herself think about Lexi's laugh and her lips as she touched her chest and toyed with the waistband of her panties. She remembered the look in Lexi's eyes when she'd told her to tie that cherry stem, a demand, not a request. And even though their closeness later in the evening didn't result in the kiss she'd found herself hoping for, the desire was there. The chemistry was palpable. And she'd walked away wet, a wetness that stayed with her as she replayed their flirtation from throughout the day.

And as she pulled on her nipples and rubbed them between her fingers, trying to push herself past the precipice while the fingers of her other hand worked her clit, she experienced something she hadn't in a very long time. It wasn't a full-blown orgasm, but it was something. It was the closest she'd come to release in almost a year, and she knew it had everything to do with Lexi.

Just thinking about her now sent a gentle throb to her sex, and her nipples strained harder against the partially wet towel. They ached, and her sex throbbed more, and she wanted to slip her fingers inside and try again. She didn't have to leave the ship for a while longer, since her snorkel excursion on Half Moon Cay wasn't until midday. She had time, right?

❖

Lexi knocked on Charlotte's door for the second time but received no reply.

"Fuck." She dropped her head against the door. She'd missed her. She must have already exited the ship. An unexpected weight of disappointment settled on her chest when she looked up at the door and noticed that Charlotte had slid the *Ready for Service* slider into place.

She looked up and down the hallway to see if any of the housekeeping carts were nearby, but she didn't see any. They must not be on this floor yet. She wondered by just how much time she'd missed her.

She contemplated sliding the papers in her hand under the door, but she hesitated. She'd much rather arrange them on Charlotte's desk, out of the way of housekeeping, with a personal note. She'd felt like she hadn't said enough last night, like she'd left something unsaid. Truthfully, she had. That was one of the things that had kept her up last night.

Her heart wanted to tell Charlotte that she'd missed her, and that since the moment she'd laid eyes on her that first day, she'd been on her mind constantly. Her heart wanted her to lean in and kiss those full pink lips and see if the Charlotte who used to make her toes curl from just kissing alone was still behind those mesmerizing and familiar sparkly green eyes. Her heart wanted her to do and say more than she did last night, and she felt unsettled about it.

"Whatever happened to carpe diem, Lexi?" she scolded herself as she dug in her pockets to find the universal keycard. She gave one final unanswered knock before keying in.

Lexi made it three steps into the room before she realized she wasn't in there alone. From her vantage point in the small corridor that extended from the door of the suite toward the bedroom, she could see Charlotte's reflection in the large glass pane of the open balcony door.

What she saw caused her to stop short, like she was frozen in place and unable to move: Charlotte was on the bed nearly naked, save for a towel that draped part of her lower body. Her head was thrown back and her eyes were closed while one hand toyed with the skin of her chest. And though her knees were bent and obstructing Lexi's view, she was more than positive that Charlotte's other hand was between her legs.

"Oh my God," Lexi heard herself say. Her own voice sounded distant as she honed in on the breathy noises coming from the reflection of Charlotte in the bed.

In that moment, the door to the suite, which Lexi must have forgotten to close behind her, slipped shut with a loud click. Lexi jumped and Charlotte gasped, her eyes springing open and catching Lexi in the glass's reflection.

Charlotte let out a startled cry, and Lexi remembered she was an uninvited witness to Charlotte's private moment.

"I'm so sorry—I thought you were gone." Lexi covered her eyes and stumbled backward as she tried to regain control of her legs.

She could hear Charlotte muttering curses nearby, and she turned away from the rustling noises toward the door to the suite. She ran her hand along the wall to her right to help navigate the short distance, all the while apologizing. "I'm really, really sorry. I'll just—I'll see myself out."

Her hand hit the front door and she opened her eyes and the door at the same time. She slipped into the hallway and jerked the door closed shut behind her, as she fell against it with a heavy thud.

Her heart was pounding in her chest when she looked down and noticed the papers still clutched in her left hand. Fuck. The fucking paperwork. She took in a deep breath and willed her body and mind to slow down. *Just put it under the door and walk away, Lexi.*

A housekeeping cart pulled up beside her, and the crew member said hello, but she couldn't form words or think, so she just shook her head and moved the marker outside of Charlotte's room to the *Privacy Please* setting in an attempt to communicate that he should not fucking go in there right now.

She stepped away from the door and slid the papers underneath it. As she turned to go, she noticed a clipboard with paper on it on the cart next to her.

"Can I borrow this?" she asked the crew member.

"Sure." He handed it to her and disappeared into the room next door with a stack of fresh towels.

Lexi's hand shook as she tried to jot down a quick note for Charlotte. Not that she knew what to say, exactly. Should she try *Sorry I walked in on you masturbating?* Or *Sorry I stood there and watched. I was paralyzed because my legs were suddenly made of stone.* Or maybe the simpler approach of *Can we just forget that happened? Here is my list of recommended restaurants on the island* would suffice. None of those seemed right, but she doubted anything would.

Deciding she would never find the right words, she scribbled down the only thing she could think of and hastily folded it before slipping that under the door as well. She dropped the clipboard on the housekeeping cart and walked down the hall in a fog. That had not just happened, right?

## CHAPTER TEN

Charlotte pushed the poke around her salad plate absentmindedly, her thoughts elsewhere. The weather was perfect on Half Moon Cay, the sun high in the clear blue sky, and a mild breeze helped cut the heat. People all around her were laughing and relaxed in that vacation sort of way. And Charlotte would be too if her morning hadn't gone so terribly wrong.

Finding Lexi in her room this morning would have been a welcome thing, had she not been pleasuring herself to the thought of her and not known she was standing nearby, watching. Charlotte had been too flustered and embarrassed in the moment to be mad. And honestly, she wasn't mad, just sort of mortified. Once she'd covered herself and had a moment to think, she wasn't feeling shameful as much as curious. Just how long had Lexi been standing there?

She replayed the events in her head and had to laugh. Lexi had certainly looked shocked, but Charlotte saw something else there: Lexi also looked a little turned on. Watching Lexi fumble and practically fall out of her room helped to lessen her embarrassment, even if only a little. And she might be laughing about it now, but she wasn't so sure she would be when she had to face Lexi later, which seemed inevitable.

She reached into her beach bag and pulled out the papers Lexi had slid under her door. One was the ship's itinerary for the day. Lexi had starred a samba class on the Lido deck and jotted down in her small print, *this is fun*. At the bottom of the itinerary was information about departing and reboarding the ship. And below that Lexi had circled and starred the bold print that designated the final boarding time for the ship. This was accompanied by a drawing of a winky face.

Charlotte smiled and pushed that aside, reaching for the island map behind it. The map was double-sided; one side depicted the entire island with all sorts of geography markers and longitude and latitude information that was way over her head, but the other side showed the most visited tourist attractions. Just about each one had a note from Lexi, informing her whether it was a waste of time or not. She'd written little tidbits about what type of travel to and from would be required and reasonable pricing for each.

Charlotte circled the area offshore where she was scheduled to have her snorkel adventure and drew a line to the edge of the page. Along the paper's perimeter, Lexi had written out detailed instructions about a secret tiny coral reef at the edge of the island where the beach met the rocks. Lexi told her to ditch the original snorkeling area once she'd had the safety lesson and head there instead. Charlotte was excited to see what Lexi had recommended—she felt special getting what she considered an insider's scoop.

The third paper in the stack was the one Charlotte had seen slide under her door last. She'd read this quickly scrawled note in Lexi's clean but small handwriting over about a dozen times today and it made her laugh every time.

*Enjoy HMC (Half Moon Cay, but shorthand)! The water is clear and beautiful, and the weather should be great. Sorry for walking in on you just now. Maybe next time leave a sock on the door...or use the slider like I told you...or put the dead bolt on. Any or all of the above would have worked. But still, sorry. Have a good time on the island but don't ignore the bold print like you did the privacy marker. ;) PS. I left you a set of snorkel gear at the departure zone of the ship. Just ask Angela to find it for you—the rental equipment on the island sucks. PPS. Sorry again.*

"Ready to snorkel, buddy?" Barb returned to their lunch table with an enthusiastic jig. When Charlotte had mentioned that she wasn't going to cancel the snorkeling excursion Veronica had set up, Barb had offered to join her. She was glad she'd taken her up on it. Cruising alone was one thing, but it was much more fun to have someone to island hop with. Barb was excellent company.

"I am." Charlotte abandoned the remainder of her salad and packed up her beach bag. "Lexi said stay for the safety protocol so we don't drown, but then head to the rocks. I understand there's a bit of a walk—still interested?"

"Are you asking if I'm interested in taking an off-road adventure to an exclusive and unmonitored part of the beach to find coral reef that could possibly result in me seeing or being eaten by a shark?" Barb deadpanned, "Obviously the answer is yes."

"I did not sign up for a shark sighting or biting. Just snorkeling. And maybe some beach walking while I work on my tan. Don't get it twisted, sister." Charlotte bumped Barb's shoulder as Barb paid the lunch check at the restaurant Lexi had recommended with a drooling smiley face.

"Fine, fine. Whatever you say." Barb adjusted the strap holding on her sunglasses and shifted the small gym bag on her shoulder. "But only because your super-hot ex-girlfriend is giving us secret intel. Otherwise, I wouldn't be satisfied with your company alone."

Charlotte slid the sunglasses down from the top of her head and smiled up at the scorching sun overhead. It was hard to feel anything but good in paradise. And even though this morning hadn't gone as she expected, she was still here, under the sun, living a pretty good version—if not the best version—of her life. A life that just six months ago didn't seem possible when she was packing up her belongings and moving out of the apartment she shared with Veronica.

She looked over at Barb and lowered her sunglasses to look at her. "She is super-hot, isn't she?"

"Oh yeah." Barb gave her a high five and all was right in the world.

Charlotte rolled her shoulders and rubbed the back of her neck. Snorkeling had taken a lot out of her. The hike to the rocky part of the beach was no small feat, but what she found there was breathtaking. About fifty yards from the edge of the beach was a small but gorgeous reef. And judging by the fact that there were only five people out there in total, including her and Barb, this really was a hidden gem. As the sun started to shift in the sky and the water got a little cloudier and visibility decreased, they agreed they'd reached their adventure quota for the day, and they made the long but rewarding trek back in plenty of time to board the cruise ship before it left port.

Charlotte had had an excellent day and she had Lexi to thank for it. Now, if only she could face her and tell her that. Not that she knew where to find her, but she was sure she could ask around if she wanted to. The question was whether or not she was ready to see her after this morning...

She'd run into Enrique while boarding, and he'd mentioned that he was hosting the samba class that Lexi had starred on the paperwork. Charlotte had no interest in taking a dance class, but Enrique had practically begged, and Barb was meeting a woman at the casino for Queens and...Studs? Kings? She couldn't quite remember. Regardless, she had no plans, and though she was tired from her day on the beach, this dress was fantastic and needed to go for a walk.

She double-checked her hair and makeup in the mirror and decided she looked great "Don't be a chicken," she said to her reflection as she adjusted the strap of her asymmetrical off-the-shoulder dress. "Take the samba class, embrace cruise life."

She laughed at her own ridiculousness and was happy to see a carefree version of herself in her reflection. *Embrace the adventure.* Her grandfather's words fresh in her mind, she stepped away from the mirror and dug out her cell phone. She turned it on for the first time in a few days.

Although the ship was moving now, they were still close enough to land that she'd likely have a signal. If she did, she'd call Paw Paw and say hello. After a moment, her apps updated: she had several voicemails and about a dozen texts. She ignored the two voicemails and half a dozen texts from Veronica, choosing instead to enjoy Paw Paw's attempt at texting. He was adorable, and technologically challenged. But he tried, which she appreciated. She decided to call and check in.

He answered on the fourth ring, his voice sounding as though he'd been asleep. "Lottie! How are you? Why are you calling? You're supposed to be on vacation."

She could tell by his tone that he was happy to hear from her, even if he chided her a bit. "I missed you, Paw Paw. And I had a free minute. How are you?"

"I'm fine. I'm old and I fall asleep sitting up. That's the exciting stuff happening over here." He cleared his throat. "Tell me about the blue water and the beautiful women."

Charlotte laughed, "The water is gorgeous. It's bathwater warm and it's clear for miles. And there's dolphins. I saw dolphins by moonlight last night."

"That sounds lovely," he said before adding after a brief pause, "but did you meet anyone yet?"

"Paw Paw, this trip wasn't about meeting anyone. It was about getting away and not losing out on an experience that I'd already paid for." Veronica and her family had agreed to pay for the majority of the wedding, but Charlotte was paying for the honeymoon and some odds and ends. And though they both came from fortunate backgrounds, Veronica's family's money made Charlotte's look like chump change. Nonetheless, she'd used her own savings to book the best that money could buy, wanting to treat herself and Veronica without her mother's help, something that now seemed foolish considering she was doing this trip alone. Though she would be the first to admit that this trip had turned out to be exactly what she needed and didn't realize. Most likely—okay, definitely—because she'd run into Lexi here.

"Pish-posh. You're young. You need to sow your wild oats."

"Ew," Charlotte teased him. "I'm not taking relationship advice from my grandfather."

His chuckle was hearty and deep, a sound she loved. "I was successfully married to your grandmother for sixty-one years, so you'd be wise to take my advice."

"You'd have me sleeping with any woman with a pulse."

"If it would help get that rotten Veronica out of your mind, I'd even recommend the women without a pulse." Paw Paw made no secret of his feelings about Veronica's infidelity. Though they got along prior to Charlotte learning of the affairs, Veronica was dead to him now. It was something she was finding easier to embrace every day.

"Has she been around?" Her grandfather had moved in with her and her mother while she was still in high school after her grandmother died. He still lived with Cookie, though he had help to manage the majority of his day-to-day routine. Charlotte knew full well that Veronica and Cookie still spoke. Her mother made no attempt at hiding that. It was one of the things she'd used against Charlotte as leverage to try to get them back together. Little did Cookie know it just drove her farther from them both.

"What do you think?" Paw Paw's distaste was palpable across the line.

Charlotte frowned. "You'd think Mom would take my side, just once. She's a piece of work."

"But still my daughter, so tread lightly." His tone wasn't

challenging but the point was received. He'd never bad-talk her mother. He was old-school like that. Sometimes she loved and hated that part.

"Fine. We'll agree to disagree." Charlotte knew it was a losing battle.

He paused. "I don't disagree. I just know your mother and she's a complicated person. Not unlike her daughter."

Charlotte chose to take that as a compliment. "Complicated isn't bad."

"Exactly," he agreed and she chose to move on.

"By the way, I ran into an old friend here." She pulled her bottom lip between her teeth and worried it a bit. Paw Paw *loved* Lexi. He was more upset than almost anyone that they split. She was grateful to have heard the news about Timothy from him, her closest and most loved family member. He'd even paid for her flight back from Europe to try and find Lexi. And he was the one who had held her when she cried that night, when she was inconsolable at the thought of never seeing Lexi again. He'd helped her mourn the loss of Lexi, and he was the first person she'd thought of when the shock of seeing Lexi again had worn off.

Not that it had fully, but still.

"Someone I know?"

"Lexi Bronson." Saying her name still felt surreal to Charlotte.

"You don't say." She could hear him clap in the background. "Now that's something. How is she?"

"She's good. She seems happy." Charlotte thought about their conversation at the bar the other night. Lexi *was* happy. And she seemed to be in her element here. That made Charlotte happy, too. "She works for the cruise line—she's been doing it a long time."

"Oh, I'm so glad to hear that. Timothy would be happy to know she was seeing the world. He used to talk about traveling a lot." Paw Paw spoke as highly of Lexi's father as he did of her. Their shared love of classic cars often resulted in them droning on and on about their favorite muscle cars from the past, when Charlotte and Lexi were desperately trying to get away from them to do less than innocent things. She'd always had a feeling they both knew and would intentionally drag their conversations on just out of spite.

"I bet he would be. She's good, Paw Paw. She looks great." Charlotte hadn't meant to add that last bit out loud.

"Oh?" Crap, he'd heard. Funny how sometimes his hearing

was better than other times. "And have you been spending any time together?"

She thought about that and frowned. "Yes and no. She's working, so that's challenging. But we've had a chance to talk. And I hope we've mended some broken bits enough to be friends."

"Just friends though." He was goading her.

"We have to start somewhere, I guess." It wasn't lost on Charlotte that their time together was quickly coming to an end. But the reality was this: Lexi lived on a moving ship that had two thousand or so new faces every week. It would be ridiculous to think they would have anything more than the time they spent together this week. Charlotte lived on solid ground and Lexi, well, Lexi lived on the sea with all the opportunities in the world. And a large part of Charlotte was jealous about that. But mostly because after this, her life would go back to boring normal, and she'd know that somewhere Lexi was out there looking incredible and perfect and not being hers.

"Maybe. Or maybe this is the start of something new and exciting. A fresh start, Lottie. Sounds to me like this is exactly what you needed." His confidence made her smile, even if her heart sank a little. She knew it couldn't be, but she didn't want to burst his enthusiastic bubble.

"We'll see, Paw Paw. We'll see."

"We already talked about how wise I am, so just give it a chance to grow wings, Lottie. Don't ground it before it can take flight." The specificity of his word choice was not lost on her. She was the grounded one here, as in literally on solid ground. Lexi, on the other hand, was as free as the blowing wind.

"Okay. I won't." Charlotte chatted with him about her plans for the remaining days of the trip and ended the call feeling both better and worse than before she'd talked to him. On the one hand, she was recharged from talking to her favorite family member, but on the other hand, the reality of the situation between her and Lexi was at the forefront of her mind. It was now or never, because in no time at all, they'd be apart again. Maybe forever. And she wasn't ready to accept that.

"Samba it is." Charlotte discarded her phone and scooped up her room key before slipping it into the hidden pocket of her dress. First, she'd dance, and then she'd find Lexi and make sure she didn't waste any more time.

## CHAPTER ELEVEN

Y ou found me!" Enrique called across the parquet dance floor as Charlotte approached.

She curtsied. "After all the hype you gave this, it seemed foolish to miss out."

Enrique clapped. "No one can resist my Latin charm"—he swiveled his hips and danced toward her as the music changed over to a new song—"or my smooth moves. I get it."

Charlotte let herself get swept into his arms and he moved them across the floor toward the other cruise guests, who appeared to be waiting for direction nearby.

He released her from his grasp and walked toward the speakers at the edge of the dance floor. Once he turned the music down, he addressed the group. "Welcome to Samba 101. For those of you who don't know me, I'm Enrique Martinez, and before you ask, although I look and dance like Ricky Martin, the name is merely a coincidence. Or a curse. I choose to embrace the coincidence side." He shimmied in place and the couples around her laughed.

Charlotte looked over at the other guests and did a quick head count. There were a dozen of them, plus one. Her. An odd number didn't seem like it would work for this lesson. She suddenly felt very alone and second-guessed her decision to come.

"All right, ladies." Enrique stepped toward the group. "Are any of you familiar with this type of dance style?"

There were a few mumbles, some in confirmation, most not. He continued, "Not to worry. I'm here to make you an expert in the foundational footwork moves of the samba. You will leave here with a sway in your hips and a skip in your step, but more importantly, you'll leave here with one very sexy tool in your toolbox to attract the perfect mate." He paused with a grin. "And by sexy tool, I mean you will have samba skills. Not me. I'm sexy, but I'm my own tool, not yours."

More laughter. Enrique was charming. Charlotte felt herself start to relax infinitesimally. He spent a few minutes explaining the African origins of the Brazilian dance style before he started the more formal lesson.

"Let's start with a lesson on how to shift your weight from foot to foot. Please form two parallel lines and mirror what I'm doing." Enrique jogged over to the speakers and turned on the music before resuming his place in the front of the room.

Charlotte fell in line, and the woman on her right appeared to be a singleton like herself. There were four very definite couples here, and the rest of them, she couldn't quite peg. She stayed on the end of the line, nearest the edge of the dance floor, just in case she lost her nerve and decided to bail.

"Start with bringing your right foot behind you, shift your left foot forward a bit, and then slide the right foot forward to meet it." Enrique slowed his movements to a crawl, but he was still too fast for Charlotte.

"You're kidding me." Charlotte nearly tripped on her own feet in an attempt to bring them together. She was usually a pretty decent dancer, but this seemed like a reach for her.

"Can I help?" Lexi appeared at her side with a timid smile.

Charlotte felt her face flush. The plan was to dance first, then find Lexi. That way she'd have time to chicken out. That plan didn't work if dancing *and* finding Lexi happened simultaneously. Particularly if Lexi found her first. "I, uh—that all depends." Charlotte closed her eyes and exhaled. "Do you know how to samba?"

She opened her eyes to find Lexi grinning broadly.

"Ah, my lovely assistant is here to help. Everybody, this is Lexi," Enrique called out over Charlotte's shoulder.

Well, that answered that question.

"Come on over, Lex. Let's meet the ladies." Lexi gave Charlotte's hand a quick squeeze before joining Enrique in the front.

The music continued, but it wasn't loud enough to block out the murmurs of the curious and excited dance novices.

"That's the hot bartender from the pool bar," one woman said to her partner.

"Do you think we get to dance with her?" the brunette in the couple in front of Charlotte asked, and her dance partner swatted her in the arm. "What? It's just a dance."

"Just a dance indeed." Charlotte willed her heart rate to return to normal, but Lexi kept glancing at her, which made that impossible because Charlotte wasn't ready to see her yet. Or ever.

Lexi and Enrique joined hands and did a brief but intense dance together, showcasing their form and skill. Charlotte was shocked at how well Lexi moved—she'd never known her to be a dancer. But she moved her hips with a fluidity that made Charlotte's mouth water, and suddenly other places felt wet, too. And before she realized it, her mind went right back to this morning and how wet just thinking about Lexi had made her, and then Lexi was unexpectedly there and now here and…on second thought, she couldn't do this.

She glanced over her shoulder and saw her out—she was at the edge of the dance floor still, and though a crowd had gathered, she could totally slip out unnoticed and—

"Since we have an odd number, I'm going to pair one of you with Lexi to go through the steps while I teach the rest of the class." Enrique appeared at her side like a ninja and placed a hand on her elbow just as she made her move. "Charlotte, care to volunteer?"

Charlotte gave him her best *hell to the no* face, but he ignored her, tugging her toward the front as he called out orders for the other dancers to get ready.

"I'm not so sure. I think I'll pass." Her objections fell on deaf ears as he handed her off to Lexi and turned back to the group.

Lexi's touch was tentative at her elbow. She nudged Charlotte to look up at her. "You don't have to if you don't want to. But I think we could have fun."

Charlotte knew she could have infinite amounts of fun with Lexi, that wasn't the problem. It was the looking at her in the face part that was the problem.

"One-two-three, one-two-three," Enrique said over his shoulder as he rejoined them at the front. He lowered his voice and said, "Charlotte, it has come to my attention that you and Lexi are already acquainted, yes?"

Intimately, she thought. "This is true."

"Great. Good. Lexi is a fantastic dancer. I'm sure she'll lead you with confidence." Enrique patted her on the shoulder and walked away without waiting for a response.

The look on Lexi's face was a mix of hesitance and amusement. Charlotte would give just about anything to know what was running through her mind.

"Dance with me, Charlotte." Lexi took her hand and turned her so they were facing each other. "I promise it will be painless. And educational."

Charlotte gave Lexi her best dubious expression, and Lexi pointed to the guests in front of them, before adding, "For them, I mean. Educational for them. It's helpful to see a couple dancing when you are trying to replicate the steps."

"A couple?" Charlotte took Lexi's other outstretched hand and resigned herself to the embarrassment that would surely follow. Her mind wandered back to the way she'd felt after her call with her grandfather: her time with Lexi was finite. *Embrace vacation*, she told herself. *Don't waste any time.*

"Yeah, a couple. A couple of attractive ladies that share a past who are dancing together in a friendly way." Lexi's eyes sparkled with mischief.

"Friendly, huh?" Charlotte let Lexi guide her hands into place, one hand in Lexi's grasp, the other on Lexi's upper back, between her shoulders.

"To start, anyway," Lexi said, and Charlotte felt her body heat up again.

"Okay, ladies. Lexi and Charlotte are going to demonstrate a few simple steps, and I want you and your partner to try them. I'll be coming around to help." Enrique walked to the music and turned it up slightly. "One of you has to take the *lead* position, ladies. No arguing—it's just for a dance, not for a lifetime commitment." Charlotte was aware of the laughter around them, but she hadn't broken eye contact with Lexi yet.

He continued, "The lead will push and pull with their hand to help guide the other dancer. It looks like this." Charlotte could see him move in her periphery, but she kept her focus on Lexi.

"Lexi will lead this dance. Ladies who are leads, watch how Lexi initiates the movement and directs Charlotte to follow."

"I didn't agree to being led anywhere," Charlotte said, but it was an empty objection. They both knew damn well that she would let Lexi lead her any which way she'd like.

Lexi initiated the movement Enrique described, and Charlotte rotated easily at Lexi's insistence. "Oh, I don't believe that for a second." Lexi's voice was low and her eyes dark.

"Why do you say that?" Charlotte followed the distant commands of Enrique as Lexi guided her movements with a practiced ease.

"Because you stayed when you could have gone. So you're

willing to try, at least. To be led, I mean." Lexi's hand dropped from her shoulder to her hip and cupped it slightly. "This comes forward with your step, and backward with your rotation."

Charlotte would have argued if she had words or could process anything other than Lexi's hands on her body. "Okay."

"Okay, you're up to being led by me?" Lexi gave her a knowing look and she nodded. "Great. This will be fun."

Charlotte wasn't sure *fun* was the word to use here. Agonizing, sexually frustrating, or masochistic seemed like more appropriate choices right now.

❖

Lexi was not so secretly loving this. She had her hands on Charlotte and was leading her without any resistance, and God, it felt good to touch her. If the look on Charlotte's face was any indication, she was in on the secret and enjoying it herself, as well.

After the unexpected private show this morning, Lexi had been in a daze for what seemed like an eternity. She'd finished her midmorning bar shift and stopped by Enrique's post to propose a plan. She needed to see Charlotte again, and she had a feeling she knew how to make that happen. It took next to no effort to get Enrique to agree to coax Charlotte to come to the class, especially if Lexi agreed to co-teach without dangling any avocados over his head. She owed him and needed him, so it was a mutually beneficial agreement.

She was pleasantly surprised when she walked up and saw Charlotte on the dance floor. The plan hadn't been guaranteed to work, but with some sort of luck, it had.

"You're smiling," Charlotte said. "Why are you smiling?"

Lexi moved them into the next sequence and straightened her shoulders. Charlotte's hand rested between her shoulder blades in a comfortable embrace. It was nice. "I'm having fun. Aren't you?"

"I am." Charlotte followed her foot cues and completed the first four steps of the eight count without difficulty. "But I know that face and there's more to that smile than just fun."

Lexi laughed and Charlotte missed a cue. "Let's start over." She initiated the same sequence again. "And you're right. I was thinking about earlier."

Charlotte missed a step entirely and her foot came down heavily on Lexi's.

"Ouch." Lexi pulled her foot back as Charlotte's hand left her shoulder.

"Wait." She caught Charlotte's wrist with her hand and pulled her back into position. "I was talking about the earlier when I convinced Enrique to persuade you to take this class so I could see you again. And touch you. In public. Without raising any sort of alarms. That's what I meant. *That* earlier."

Charlotte stopped dancing altogether and dropped her hands by her sides. Her mouth was open in surprise. "You did what?"

Lexi gave Charlotte her most flirtatious smile and took Charlotte's hands, swinging them slightly. "I wanted to see you again so I—"

"Manipulated me into an innocent dance class where you had less than innocent intentions," Charlotte replied as she pulled one hand from Lexi's and placed it on her hip. Her pose was threatening. And hot.

Well, when she put it like that... "Yes. And I'm sort of sorry."

"You sound it," Charlotte replied sarcastically.

"But I'm also not that sorry"—Lexi reached forward and ran her fingers along the ones on Charlotte's hip—"because *touching*."

A small smile formed on Charlotte's lips and Lexi rejoiced. "Okay, fine. But I'm only not mad because of touching. And that's all."

Lexi pulled her hand back into position and moved closer as Charlotte scratched between her shoulder blades playfully. "Hi."

"Hi," Charlotte said as she moved with her. They were so close, Lexi could smell her perfume. It was an intoxicating mix of floral and sweet undertones.

She breathed the scent in more deeply. "You look nice."

"You're flirting." Charlotte was picking up the movements better and better with each repetition.

"I am." Lexi stepped even closer and Charlotte gasped. She clawed at Lexi's back again, this time with more force, and Lexi purred.

"All right, dancers," Enrique called out to the group, and Lexi was reminded that they weren't alone. "Let's spice this up a bit, shall we? It's time for you lead ladies to get behind your partners and help them move their hips. Now that you've perfected the step sequence, it's time to speed it up and add some flavor."

Lexi dropped her hands to Charlotte's hips and slowed her sway. She ducked her head to check in with Charlotte and let herself appreciate how that black off-the-shoulder dress made Charlotte's eyes appear to glow green. She was breathtaking tonight.

"You're staring," Charlotte said. "I think we're supposed to be dancing."

Lexi traced Charlotte's face with her eyes. "I'm soaking you in because the next portion of the class puts me behind you, and I don't want to have any trouble remembering that beautiful face."

Charlotte's lips parted and Lexi wanted to taste them. "You'd better get behind me before we both get into trouble."

"Who's leading who, here?" Lexi teased as she followed Charlotte's very astute suggestion.

Charlotte let out a low moan when Lexi slipped behind her. "Are you suggesting I can't lead with you behind me?"

Lexi placed her hand on Charlotte's right hip from behind and gently dug her fingers into the soft flesh. "I'm suggesting you try."

Charlotte pressed her ass against Lexi's pelvis, and it was Lexi's turn to moan. "You were saying?"

"Maybe this wasn't such a great idea," Lexi said as she pulled Charlotte tighter against her front, "the being in the front of the class part."

Charlotte completed the spin Lexi initiated and locked eyes with her, her face flushed, her pupils dark and dilated. "I think it sort of makes this more exciting, don't you?"

Lexi turned Charlotte back toward the other dancers and stepped behind her again, guiding Charlotte to step and sway in place against her hips to the sound of the beat playing around them. "I had no idea you were such an exhibitionist."

"And I had no idea you were such a voyeur," Charlotte said on the next turn, and Lexi almost missed her cue when Charlotte's tongue wet her lips.

"We're talking about the *other* earlier now, right?" Lexi could feel the heat settle between her legs at just the mention.

"Well, I figure we can only dance around the subject for so long." Charlotte was facing the group again, but she ground back against Lexi and Lexi's clit throbbed at the friction.

Charlotte reached behind them and slipped her hand into Lexi's back pocket. The accompanying squeeze made Lexi stutter when she replied. "I-I'm sorry about that. I didn't mean to intrude."

"Go ahead, lead ladies, hold your partner's hip with one hand and rest your other hand on their abdomen if they don't mind. This is the best way to ensure your hips move in sync. And it's great fun, too."

Enrique's voice was like an alarm in Lexi's ear. She should stop this before it got too far.

"And I should have locked the deadbolt." Charlotte's reply was breathy, almost panting. "Mistakes were made all around, but I'm not mad if you aren't."

Fuck. Charlotte wasn't upset about being walked in on, and Lexi would be lying if she said she hadn't enjoyed it. It had been pretty much the only thing she could think about all day—well, that, and how badly she wished she was closer and more involved, that was.

"Not in the least." Lexi barely managed to get out as Charlotte pulled Lexi's other hand to her abdomen and rolled her hips back again. Lexi saw stars. This had officially gone too far, and she was a goner.

"And that concludes our lesson," Enrique called out, and Lexi dropped her hands from Charlotte's body, quickly adding some space between them.

"Thanks so much for coming by. Be sure to check the times for my salsa classes and my Intro to Hip-Hop Dance in your daily itinerary. Let's dance to one last song before we go. Give a big round of applause to your partner and to our guest teacher, Lexi." A smattering of applause and cheers sounded, and Lexi felt like a deer in headlights.

Enrique approached them and Lexi tried desperately to catch her breath.

"That was some demonstration." He looked between them before glancing over his shoulder at the rest of the class which Lexi had entirely forgotten and not helped to teach at all. "I'm good here, Lex, if you need to…get some air."

"Right. Yeah, thanks." Lexi took the out he gave her, and even though everything in her brain told her this was a bad idea, she reached for Charlotte's hand anyway. "Take a walk with me?"

Thinking was overrated.

## CHAPTER TWELVE

I'd love to." Charlotte barely got the words out before Lexi guided her off the dance floor through the crowd of onlookers she hadn't realized had formed. Catcalls and cheers followed them as Lexi maneuvered them out the side door of the Lido deck to the shuffleboard area outside.

Several women were drinking and laughing as they pushed the weighted disks along the painted board on the deck, but Charlotte was too distracted to notice much else. The insistence of Lexi's hand in hers, pulling her along, was all she could focus on.

Lexi slowed her pace and Charlotte bumped into her back. "You still with me?" Lexi asked over her shoulder without looking back.

"You've got me by the hand, Lex." And the clit, she thought, but she kept that to herself.

"Good." Lexi squeezed her fingers and opened a door that Charlotte hadn't noticed. She looked at her with an intensity that made Charlotte shiver. "Just a little farther, I promise."

"Until what?" Charlotte didn't much care where they were going as long as they were going together, and Lexi kept that hungry look on her face the whole time.

Lexi led her into a small stairwell and up two flights before she opened another door that Charlotte barely registered. They stepped out onto a small expanse of deck. It was empty and darker than the other deck spaces she'd been on, largely due to the enormous lifeboats suspended above them.

"Until I can get you alone." Lexi stopped and turned, fully facing Charlotte for the first time since they were dancing. She looked incredible, her eyes bright and intense while her long dirty-blond hair cascaded down her shoulders.

"And what will you do with me then?" Charlotte reached out and delicately fingered the intricate half braid that ran along the crown of Lexi's head, sweeping the shorter front pieces into an elegant part. Her hair looked so beautiful in the mix of moonlight and shadow cast around them, she almost didn't want to touch it. Almost.

Lexi took both of Charlotte's hands in hers and laced their fingers together as she guided her backward. She eased her against the cold wall of the ship, between two jut-outs that provided them with a little privacy, and pressed up against her as she whispered, "Whatever you'll let me do."

Charlotte's breath caught at Lexi's words and the feeling of her body against hers, and her last coherent thought voiced itself. "What about the cameras?"

Lexi pinned their entwined hands above Charlotte's head to the wall behind her, and she leaned in, nuzzling Charlotte's jaw before ghosting her lips across the skin of Charlotte's cheek. "There are no cameras here. Security flaw. Whoops."

Charlotte squeezed Lexi's fingers in hers as Lexi's lips made contact with the skin on her neck. She panted, "A happy accident."

"I'll say." Lexi's lips moved up her neck and closed around her earlobe.

Charlotte's body quaked in response to the feeling of Lexi's tongue and lips sucking the flesh there. "Lex, I—"

"Mmm?" The vibration against the soft skin under her jaw made the steadily increasing pressure between her hips spike.

Charlotte turned her head, catching the blown pupils of Lexi's eyes watching her closely. She tugged one hand out of Lexi's grasp and cupped Lexi's jaw, running her thumb over Lexi's deliciously plump bottom lip.

Lexi shifted against her and released her other hand, guiding it around her neck as she leaned in closer still, lips brushing against Charlotte's. Lexi was driving her crazy.

Charlotte rolled her hips against Lexi's in a desperate attempt to expel some of the sexual energy flooding through her in that moment. Lexi's moan in response was amplified by the sensation of her wetting her lips against Charlotte's, and that was all Charlotte could take. She closed the distance between them, and her body ignited in sparks as Lexi kissed her with a passion she hadn't experienced before. Want and need fought for dominance as Lexi's mouth opened and her tongue teased along Charlotte's lips. She couldn't take Lexi's tongue in fast enough or deep enough, it seemed.

Lexi's hands were in her hair and massaging along her jaw as she did incredible things with her tongue. Charlotte was suffocating and she didn't care because she had never been kissed so fucking thoroughly in her whole life.

Lexi saved her life when she pulled back, breaking the kiss to pant out, "Jesus fucking Christ, Charlotte."

Charlotte sucked in a breath and some of the dizziness diminished. Impatient for more, she pushed forward again, connecting their lips in an unhurried, languorous fashion. Lexi matched her passion and pace, and she lost herself in Lexi's lips and tongue again. She'd missed these lips, and though they were familiar, they were different, too. But still fucking incredible. And soft, had she mentioned soft?

Lexi moved even closer, resting her forearms on the wall behind Charlotte's head. Her proximity made it impossible to ignore the way her chest heaved against Charlotte's. The sensation was titillating. Literally. Charlotte's nipples ached.

Charlotte dropped her head back to breathe, and Lexi kissed along the column of her neck, placing soft, teasing nibbles as she went. Charlotte slid her hand into Lexi's hair and scratched gently at her scalp, the smell of her shampoo mixing with the scent of her skin, a lovely combination of coconut and vanilla. She smelled as delicious as her mouth tasted.

Charlotte rubbed her hands up and down Lexi's back, massaging her shoulders before settling at her waist. She slipped one hand under the bottom hem of the back of Lexi's shirt and danced her fingers there.

Lexi shuddered and her kisses paused as she reacted to Charlotte's touch. Her voice was small, almost shy, when she said, "You remembered."

Charlotte met Lexi's gaze and nodded. "How could I forget your favorite post-make-out massage ritual?"

"Does that mean we're done making out?" Lexi looked disappointed.

"No, not even close." Charlotte reconnected their lips and smiled against Lexi's mouth when Lexi kissed her back. After a moment she pulled back. "Unless you want to be, and then that's okay. Whatever you're comfortable with."

Lexi shook her head. "I feel like I have a lifetime of kissing to catch up for with you."

Charlotte knew what she meant, and the feeling was mutual. She leaned forward and took Lexi's bottom lip between her teeth, tugging it gently. Lexi made the sexiest noise she'd ever heard, so she did it again. "I am all for this plan."

Lexi rolled her hips against her and Charlotte felt that familiar heat from the dance floor return, her heart rate picking up. "I like the way your body feels against mine." Lexi moved again, and Charlotte wished less clothing separated them.

"We do seem to fit together nicely, don't we?" Charlotte grabbed Lexi's jaw and pulled their mouths together again. She needed more kissing, especially if Lexi kept this bump-and-grind thing up.

Lexi stepped back, separating their lips as she dropped her right hand to Charlotte's collarbone. She dragged her fingers in a zigzagging pattern along the asymmetrical neckline of her dress and toyed with the lowest angle, pulling it down a bit. The coolness of the air against her newly uncovered hot skin made Charlotte shiver, and her nipples ached even more. She could feel them tighten and push against the fabric in response to Lexi's teasing. Lexi's gaze dropped to her chest. Clearly, she had noticed as well.

"I wonder," Lexi said as she toyed with her lip between her teeth and Charlotte wanted her lips to be back there, "if you're still as sensitive as you used to be."

Charlotte swallowed thickly, her hips moving against the air slightly, missing Lexi's friction but also anticipating what Lexi might do or say next.

"Are you, Charlotte?" Lexi pulled the top of her dress down farther, almost exposing her nipple. "Do you still like it when your nipples are touched?"

"Fuck." Charlotte felt her sex throb at the mere mention of nipple play.

Lexi gave her a mischievous look and shifted her hips, slipping one leg between Charlotte's and leaning on the arm pressed next to Charlotte's head, keeping her flat against the wall. She leaned in and kissed the skin next to Charlotte's mouth and asked, "Should we find out?"

"You first." Charlotte released the vise grip she had on Lexi's hip to run her hand up Lexi's abdomen and palm her breast through the tight material of her shirt. Lexi closed her eyes and let out a surprised exhale as Charlotte let the weight and fullness fill her hand. It was heavenly. She reconnected their lips and continued to massage Lexi's chest through her shirt until Lexi pressed her thigh against Charlotte's core, causing her to lose her focus a bit.

"My turn." Lexi moved Charlotte's hand to the back of her neck and resumed her teasing, pulling the fabric of the top of Charlotte's dress even lower until her breast was fully exposed. Lexi cupped it and dragged her thumb across Charlotte's erect nipple and Charlotte nearly fainted.

"Oh my God, Lex." Charlotte dropped her head back against the wall and pushed her chest farther into Lexi's hand. She shuddered and squirmed with every deliberate flick and roll of Lexi's fingers around her nipple. That, combined with the pressure from Lexi's thigh against her crotch, was making it harder and harder to form words.

"Some things haven't changed at all," Lexi said, and Charlotte could barely see her smile through her heavy-lidded eyes. Lexi palmed the flesh more aggressively and Charlotte felt a jolt shoot through her like lightning, from her spine to her clit. "Good."

"I need to, we need to—" Charlotte closed her eyes when she felt Lexi's hot mouth descend on the skin just above her breast. She ground her hips against Lexi's thigh and scratched at the back of Lexi's neck when Lexi tweaked and pulled her nipple as she sucked on the skin of her chest. "Lexi, if you keep that up, I'm going to come pressed against this wall, under this lifeboat, and it's going to be loud and incredible and as much as I want that, and you have no fucking idea how badly I want that"—she gasped and hated herself for what she was about to say—"I'd really rather be under you and naked when that happens, so please—"

"Stop." Lexi's mouth and hand stilled at her breast and the pressure against her now wet crotch lessened. "Okay."

Charlotte gasped, afraid to look at Lexi's face but knowing she should. When she opened her eyes, she found Lexi looking at her with patience and understanding, not the disappointment she feared she would find there. "I'm sorry."

"Don't be." Lexi's smile was small but genuine as she adjusted Charlotte's neckline with a tenderness that made other parts of Charlotte ache. She moved her thigh from between Charlotte's legs but leaned into her, shielding her as Charlotte's body continued to thrum with a mix of sensations and emotions. It was overwhelming, all of it.

Charlotte felt herself start to fall apart. This was too much to handle.

"Why are you crying, baby?" Lexi's thumb brushed her cheek while her hand cradled her face. "It's fine. We don't have to."

Charlotte let the tears fall mainly because she knew she couldn't stop them. This had been an emotionally challenging week—year, really. And she felt safe here, pressed against the wall by Lexi's warm body and kind heart and soft hands. Lexi's tender kisses and thoughtful affections were exactly what she knew her body needed to give her the release she had been searching for. She knew she could come from Lexi's touch in the cloak of darkness against the ship with the sounds of the water crashing behind them, and she knew it would be glorious and fierce and earth-shattering. But she didn't want it to be like this, and when she relived this decision in her mind later, she might never forgive herself, but she wanted what she knew she'd had in the past: Lexi, all of her, over and under her, bringing her to life like she had when they were younger. Lexi had been the best lover she'd ever had, and she had a feeling that reopening that door would devastate her, but she wanted it opened. She wanted that door blown right off the fucking hinges. Consequences be damned.

She laughed and pulled Lexi's lips to hers for a passionate kiss before resting their foreheads together. "I'm not crying because I stopped you from giving me a life-changing orgasm."

"Well, shit, if it was going to be life-changing, maybe you should have let me," Lexi teased her and pecked her lips.

Charlotte accepted Lexi's nuzzle and exhaled, knowing she'd made the right decision. "I'm crying because this feels so natural and so right. And I really, really, really want to do this with you again, but I want there to be less clothes. And I want some hair pulling and more of that I'm-going-to-suffocate-if-she-keeps-kissing-me-like-this feeling."

Lexi hummed and leaned back. She brushed an errant hair from Charlotte's forehead and tucked it behind her ear. "Well, then the crying is totally acceptable. Because I want those things, too."

Charlotte wiped away the last lingering tears and looped her arms behind Lexi's neck as she admitted, "There's one other thing, too."

"Oh?" Lexi's free hand found her hip and her thumb traced along the fabric of Charlotte's dress in a lazy circular motion. "What's that?"

"I haven't had a successful orgasm in almost a year. And that was going to be *very* successful, but not how I wanted it to be forever immortalized."

Lexi's expression was almost comical. "A year?"

"A year." Charlotte nodded. "It's been a long year."

"Jesus, fuck." Lexi gave her a pained look. "Not that I want to talk about that woman, ever, but you were going to marry that chick and she wasn't giving you orgasms?"

Charlotte laughed and felt her body start to unwind a bit, the tension leaving her ounce by ounce. "She had the brilliant idea that we should be celibate before the wedding."

"And you were." Lexi's expression darkened, but not with lust like before. This looked like anger. "But she wasn't."

"Well, she was with me." Charlotte didn't feel any sting when she said that this time. Veronica seemed to have less and less impact on her.

Lexi straightened for a moment before she leaned more onto the arm that remained next to Charlotte's head. She ran her other hand through Charlotte's hair as she spoke. "I sort of really hate that bitch, Charlotte. Like, full stop."

"I'm realizing more and more that we weren't right for each other for about a hundred reasons. But, yeah, I've felt that way recently, too." The realization was refreshing, but not entirely painless. She'd given three years of her life to Veronica. That was time she'd never get back.

"I could have told you that before I even knew the story," Lexi said, still standing close.

"Oh?" Charlotte replied, letting herself relax into her closeness. Lexi was so warm.

"She sent you red roses. Red is your least favorite rose color." Lexi shrugged. "Seems like a dumb mistake to make if she was really trying to win you back. If you're going to do something clichéd, at least get the color right, you know?"

Charlotte couldn't stop the hearty laugh that bubbled from her lips. "You know, you're right. I hadn't even thought of that."

"I'm here to remind you of the important things," Lexi said with a smile.

"That you are. And you're doing a bang-up job of it." She placed one last lingering kiss to Lexi's lips before she turned and directed her attention to the strong arm by her head. Lexi's shirt sleeve had ridden up and Charlotte could see even more tattoos than before. She kissed the soft skin on the inside of Lexi's arm and Lexi looped an arm about her waist, cuddling her close.

"How far up do these go?" Charlotte pushed the remaining fabric up higher in an attempt to get the full picture.

Lexi laughed but continued to hold her tightly. "Just beyond my shoulder—so far, that's where I've stopped."

"Do you plan to go farther?" Charlotte was talking about the tattoos but also about them.

Lexi seemed to consider this. "Maybe. I've always gotten tattoos as a way to remember something important that happened in my life. So I guess the answer is yes. Though I haven't gotten one in a while."

Charlotte examined the images. They all seemed to follow a similar theme: water. Lexi had a mermaid on the inside of her forearm, a dark-haired beauty holding a triton. Her tail curled and ended just short of Lexi's wrist, deep blues and teals surrounded her like waves of the ocean. Charlotte pushed Lexi back to get a better look at her arm, extending it and turning it in her hands to see the rest of the scenes. A sea turtle floated near her biceps and schools of fish wove between seaweed and a colorful coral reef that wrapped around her triceps. A sleek, beautiful shark was partially obstructed by crashing waves on the back of her forearm, and an anchor rested in sand just below her elbow. Cursive black script lined the sand there, so delicate and small you'd miss it if you weren't looking closely. It read *Timothy Alan Bronson*.

"He was my anchor in the storm of life." Lexi's voice was soft.

Charlotte looked up to find Lexi watching her. Lexi didn't pull her arm back or resist Charlotte's curiosity—she just let her explore. Even if that exploration hurt her. That was so very much a Lexi trait, Charlotte thought. "He was a great man, Lex. And he raised a great woman."

"I know." She nodded. "And thank you."

Charlotte paused her inspection but made a mental note to continue in better light and with less clothing, like they'd discussed. She slid her hand down Lexi's arm and held her hand, lacing their fingers together as she pulled Lexi against her again. "Let's do some more of that kissing, but keep it PG-13 for a bit, okay?"

Lexi's flashed her a toothy grin as she leaned in to connect their lips. "This sounds like an exciting challenge. I'm in."

"Good." As Charlotte opened her mouth to Lexi's tongue, she hoped she could stick with her suggestion of keeping it hot and heavy, but not too hot. That was possible, right?

# CHAPTER THIRTEEN

You're out late." Zara flicked on the lamp by her bed and propped herself up on her elbow.

Lexi blinked and shielded her eyes from the unexpected interrogation light. "Were you waiting up, Mom?"

"Someone has to." Zara pushed her pillows against the wall and leaned against them as she sat up.

"Oh? And why is that? I'm a grown-up." Lexi kicked off her shoes and sat heavily onto her bed, tired and fatigued from the day, but also feeling very much alive. She had been right about Charlotte's proposition being a challenge. It had taken all of her willpower to keep things from getting X-rated, something Charlotte did little to avoid with all those sexy sounds and shudders when Lexi touched her skin. But, God, how good it felt to touch her again. It felt like coming home in a way. Lexi was addicted already. And that was bad, very bad.

"That all depends. Did you sleep with her?" Zara gave her a knowing expression and Lexi felt herself blush.

"Who told you?"

Zara crossed her arms over her chest and clucked. "Enrique. He squealed like a little piggy. He said you two nearly had sex right on the dance floor in front of a few dozen people. Subtlety never was your specialty, huh, Lex?"

Lexi dropped her head and sighed. "Fuck."

"You didn't answer that question yet," Zara pointed out. "Did you two...?"

"No," Lexi said. Not yet. But she had every intention to.

Zara nodded and scooted forward, shifting to sit at the edge of her bed with her feet on the floor. "But you want to."

Lexi looked her right in the eye when she replied. "Yes."

Zara got up and stood in the small space between their beds. Lexi looked up at her and noticed the packed boxes that were illuminated by the bedside lamp. She hadn't noticed them in the dark, but they were impossible to miss now.

"You're packing." She had to say it out loud for her heart to accept it. "Because you're leaving me."

Zara sat next to her on her bunk and placed a hand on her leg. "I'm not leaving *you*, I'm leaving the ship. And my job. For a new adventure."

Zara tapped the compass tattoo on Lexi's arm and smiled. Lexi knew that had always been Zara's favorite—it was gold and seemed to sparkle and glimmer. Lexi had gotten it when they'd met. She told Zara it was meant to glitter like the gold nose ring she had worn in her nose since she'd joined the cruise life. That had been true, but she'd also gotten it because finding Zara felt like finding lost family. Zara had helped Lexi find direction in her life. A life without seeing her every day felt like too much to handle.

"I know," Lexi said as she looked up at her best friend and fought the sadness to accept the inevitable. "I'm being melodramatic."

Zara pulled her into a bear hug and patted the back of her head. "And you're so very good at it."

Lexi let herself be held and savored the moment. "I still have feelings for her."

Zara ran her fingers through Lexi's hair and rocked her a bit. "I know."

Lexi leaned back to ask, "How?"

"How do you still have feelings for her or how do I know?" Zara settled against the wall behind Lexi's bed and brought her knees up to her chin.

Lexi scrambled up next to her and copied her position. "Both." She looked at Zara and sighed. "She apologized to me today. She told me she was trying to limit my pain, and hers, by ending things before she went off to school. She said that she was overwhelmed by her feelings for me and the path she had laid out for her future, and that she fucked up. She said she was imperfect and broke things off with me in a shitty way."

"Wow." Zara's eyes widened momentarily.

"I didn't disagree with her on that last part," Lexi added.

"And why should you?" Zara replied. "Look, the way I see it, you never got closure the first time. And though she broke things off with you, she didn't leave you for someone or do it in an intentionally malicious way, right? She said so herself today. It sounds like you meant to her as much as you've always told me she meant to you. So that's something, I guess. Do you believe her?"

"I do." A part of Lexi had always thought that, but it had been easier to vilify Charlotte than deal with feeling lost and abandoned. She had let herself believe that she was left behind because she wasn't interesting enough. She felt foolish about that now. She tried to lighten the heaviness of the conversation with humor. "But she still dumped me."

Zara nudged her foot. "Because she was trying not to hurt you, and probably to help lessen the hurt to herself, too."

"I suppose."

Zara shook her head. "You're pretty thick sometimes, Lex."

Zara turned to face her, sitting in that lotus yoga position Lexi could never quite achieve. "Put yourself in her shoes—she loved you, and she had goals, two separate things that maybe at one point overlapped. But she was going to college and had a plan long before she met you, right? That's what you told me. You told me she was studious and hardworking and had a lot of plans."

"Which was ridiculous because I was sort of a slacker and lived in the moment," Lexi replied. That was true. She and Charlotte were opposites when they met. She wondered if that was still true today.

"Except that's not true because we both know you're a low-key planner—*cough cough*, beachfront bar dreams—even if you like to play it cool and act all uninterested for the ladies. And we also both know you're a number savant in there," Zara said as she tapped Lexi's temple, "and that you and Charlotte got together because she needed a tutor to help with her SATs and you were matched to her needs."

"Which turned into tutoring a lot more than math," Lexi recalled. Charlotte had had a lot of needs that she'd met. And that was mutual. She smiled in recollection.

"And see? That stupid grin on your face answers your initial question. You have good memories with her, obviously." Zara paused, seeming to consider something. "Did you ever think that maybe there was no villain in this story? Maybe there were just a couple of hard decisions and two coming-of-age teenage kids with a bunch of hormones trying to sort everything out and not doing the best job of it?"

Lexi hadn't considered that angle before. She thought back to the last night she'd seen Charlotte. They'd talked for hours, cried for even more hours, but that night had been bittersweet and wonderful at the same time. They'd shared a really powerful and intimate night of lovemaking in the back of Charlotte's grandfather's beloved '57 Chevy. Charlotte had borrowed it as a nod to their first hookup. Before she left, Charlotte had drawn a heart on the inside of her left wrist and kissed it. Lexi put her hand there now, as if she could still feel those lips on her skin. Lips that were on hers just a few moments ago. That still felt surreal to her.

"I'll take your silence and that faraway look in your eyes as understanding of my very legit and spot-on point," Zara said, but there was no boasting in her tone. "And to answer the other part of your first question, the how I *know* you still have feelings for her part…"

"Yeah?" Lexi was dying to know.

"Because I see it all over your face. I see it in the way you smile when you catch her looking at you, and I see it in the extra shake you give her cocktails when you pour them, as if you are trying to make them extra special. Or perfect, just for her." Zara eyes were bright as she added, "And I hear it in the way you hum that song your dad used to sing you at night. Which you've been doing all the time—while you're folding laundry or annoyingly tapping your fingers on the desk while I'm trying to nap between day shifts. You're humming because you're happy. Charlotte makes you happy. Or at least, seeing her again has made you happy."

"Well, damn." Lexi was feeling a little exposed at all the truth bombs being dropped.

"Yeah, the Disney princess humming thing was cute for, like, a minute, but now it's annoying. So chill with that, okay?" Zara teased.

"What am I going to do without you, Zee? Who's going to set me straight?" She leaned into her best friend and wrapped her in a tight hug.

"Hopefully, no one. You being gay is your most interesting quality."

Lexi tickled Zara's side. "Rude."

"You don't need a sounding board, Lex. You've always been the keeper of your destiny." Zara pulled back and motioned around the room. "And you don't need me or my stuff around for you to find your way. It's just stuff. And I'm still just a phone call away. You know, in case you fuck something up and need a pep talk."

"My she-ro."

Zara laughed as Lexi hit her with a pillow. "And don't you forget it."

Lexi considered the boxes for a moment. "Why are you already packed? You've got a few days, still."

Zara crawled off her bed and stretched. "I'm shipping the majority of my stuff back home. I'm swinging by North Carolina to see my little sister at her college dorm before I head home, and my plan is to leave with only a small backpack and a suitcase. Ahmed arranged for the baggage crew to put my stuff in the storage area and have it shipped Priority up to Connecticut. That will give us some more space and me one less thing to worry about as I finish tying up loose ends."

The boxes made this all very official. Lexi couldn't even imagine what this space would look like without Zara and her belongings in it. "Better to be tying up loose ends than having a screw loose, I suppose."

Zara rolled her eyes and flopped onto her own bed. She crawled under the covers and said, "I really hope for your sake Charlotte isn't turned off by your lame dad jokes."

"She used to love my lame dad jokes," Lexi recalled. "Or at least she pretended to."

"Mm-hmm." Zara yawned and clicked off her bedside lamp, casting them both in darkness. "That woman must be a damned saint then."

Lexi lay back on her bed and mulled over their discussion. She could confidently say that Charlotte's breathy noises and needy kisses and groping probably knocked her out of the saint category, but she was angelic, nonetheless. Lexi felt a flutter of butterflies in her abdomen as she remembered how hard it had been to walk Charlotte to the door of her suite and not follow her in. The look on Charlotte's face had told her that she was very much on the same page. Now all Lexi had to do was find a way for the two of them to be intimate, and check all of Charlotte's and her boxes, without losing her job in the process.

Charlotte was the forbidden fruit that she absolutely could not stop thinking about, and tonight's make-out session had done nothing to dull that fact.

## CHAPTER FOURTEEN

*Cruise Day Four: Grand Turk*

Charlotte had paced back and forth in her suite for the past five minutes. She'd been anxiously awaiting Lexi's arrival since she'd woken up. Not that she'd slept well for the second night in a row, but last night had been different. She'd been too riled up and excited to sleep. And not just sexually excited, which she'd certainly been, and chose not to act on, but *really* excited, like the kind of excited a kid was on Christmas morning. Because making out with Lexi had felt like Christmas goddamn morning and she was dying to open her presents. And by presents she meant her legs, to let Lexi in. Which was all she'd been thinking about since she woke up. She needed to find a way to have sex with Lexi. Because she wanted to, and she needed to. And because Lexi made her feel like a little kid again, excited and happy and reborn.

A knock at the door halted her nineteenth lap. She had to stop herself from running to the door and yanking it open.

Lexi greeted her with a broad smile and an extravagant plate of cut fruit and berries. "Good morning."

"Indeed." Charlotte stepped back, and Lexi stepped in.

Lexi closed the door behind herself while she balanced the fruit platter in one hand. She walked into the suite and deposited the platter on the desk next to Charlotte's bed.

Charlotte fidgeted with her fingers, hovering nearby but unsure of where they stood or what she was allowed to do. Because what she wanted to do involved being naked and that king-sized bed over there, but she had a feeling now wasn't the time.

Lexi gave her a knowing smile and walked over to her. "Come here."

Charlotte slipped into her arms as easily as she breathed and accepted Lexi's kiss just as seamlessly. "Now *that* is a good morning."

"Wait until I wake you up with my tongue"—Lexi licked across her lips, clearly not talking about kissing her mouth—"because *that* will be a good morning."

Charlotte was significantly more turned on than she'd been a minute ago. "Well, fuck."

Lexi laughed and kissed her again. "Mmm. I hope so."

Charlotte stepped back and the back of her knee hit the bed. She pulled Lexi with her as she lowered herself down to the mattress. Lexi crawled over her as she scooted up the bed and she savored the feeling of Lexi's full weight draped across her body. "Why should we wait until some yet-to-be-determined morning?"

Lexi moaned in her ear as Charlotte palmed at her clothed breast and tugged at her uniform pants. She really needed Lexi out of these clothes to do all the things with her that she wanted. Charlotte managed to unbutton the top of Lexi's slacks before Lexi's hand grasped her wrist and stopped her. "Wait, Charlotte."

Charlotte whined as Lexi pinned her wrist above her head, reminiscent of last night, which did nothing to slow down her libido.

Lexi's hot mouth was on hers as she dominated her tongue, slowing Charlotte's kissing down while Lexi moved against her body in an easy but unhurried rock. Charlotte's unpinned hand scratched at Lexi's lower back but didn't wander like she wanted it to. Lexi had to set the pace here since Charlotte clearly couldn't control herself around her.

Lexi rewarded her restraint with a harder, teasing body roll, and Charlotte was deliciously uncomfortable again. "That's a good girl."

"I'm not feeling very good at the moment. And I'm not thinking very pure thoughts, either." Charlotte closed her eyes and wrestled her hand free from Lexi's grasp to intertwine their fingers. Lexi pulled back from her lips and propped herself over her on her elbows.

"I know, me neither." Lexi's blue eyes shone with the want Charlotte felt in her core.

"Remind me why we're waiting again?" Charlotte slipped her hand out of Lexi's to run both of her hands along Lexi's face and trace that gorgeous jawline to those pouty lips.

Lexi turned her head and kissed Charlotte's fingertips before she replied, "Because I came in this room to drop off your daily itinerary and the hallway cameras might notice if I don't emerge for hours and hours. That's why."

"You don't think we can make it quick?" Charlotte was desperate.

Lexi raised an eyebrow in her direction. "Do you want it to be quick?"

"No." Charlotte's answer was automatic. She most certainly did not want it to be quick.

"Neither do I." Lexi kissed her, and she felt momentarily less frantic about the whole situation.

"Fine." Charlotte settled against the bed and rested her hands at Lexi's lower back. "Do you have a plan as to how we'll work around this obstacle?"

Lexi's smile was blinding. "I do, actually."

Charlotte sat up so fast that Lexi fell off to the side with a thud. "Sorry."

Lexi shifted on the bed next to her and stretched. "It's okay. You're excited. I am, too. I get it."

"Do you, though?" Charlotte climbed over Lexi and straddled her hips. "Because I'm *really* excited."

Lexi's hand rested on Charlotte's hip, holding her in place as Lexi looked down at the crotch of Charlotte's capris. "I can feel that. Yes."

Charlotte rocked forward, pressing her chest against Lexi's as she spoke. "Then you know how anxiously impatient I am to hear your solution."

"Fuck this job." Lexi grunted as she gripped Charlotte's hips and rolled them against hers. "I'll get a new one."

Charlotte let the little diversion go on until she felt that familiar pressure begin to build between her hips. She broke their kiss and leaned back, pulling Lexi's hands to cup her breasts over her shirt while she slowly rocked against her, winding herself back down while still prolonging the play. "I doubt that was the original plan. Tell me your suggestion."

Lexi licked her lips and massaged Charlotte's chest as she panted. "I'll get fired from my job when the cleaning staff catches us having really loud sex, and then we run off to an island somewhere and have lots of sex for the rest of our lives."

Charlotte's insides tightened when Lexi's fingers found her nipples again. "That sounds and feels incredible. Don't stop."

Lexi did though. She stopped.

Charlotte looked down with a frustrated sigh. "Stopping was not in your proposition. I was paying very close attention, I assure you."

Lexi's hands left Charlotte's chest and she whimpered at their loss. Lexi guided Charlotte off her hips and positioned her on her side, facing her. "I know. And I got carried away because you are so fucking sexy I want to do terrible things to you, but you were doing that thing you do when you're about to come, and I didn't want to ruin your plan even though I really wanted to ruin your plan."

Charlotte willed her heartbeat to slow, but Lexi was in her bed, just a few inches away, and she was still buzzing with a sexual energy that did not seem to diminish, even though they weren't touching anymore. "What thing was I doing?"

"That breathy little pant you used to do when you were getting close. When your cheeks flush and you close your eyes like you need to concentrate. That thing." Lexi gave her a one-shoulder shrug.

"I don't do that." Charlotte was lying, she totally did.

"You used to and apparently you still do." Lexi's expression was playful. "Which I'm more than fine with and glad that I still have that effect on you. But I'm not going to let you dry hump me to get the first orgasm you've had in a year."

"It's certainly not dry, and it wasn't just humping. There was groping, too," Charlotte replied.

"We mustn't forget the groping." Lexi placed her hand on Charlotte's hip momentarily before grabbing her hand. "Reach into my back pocket, Charlotte."

"That seems like a good idea to you?" Charlotte asked as she did what Lexi said. She found an envelope and some folded paper there. "What's this?"

"Pull it out," Lexi said, and she did, but not before squeezing Lexi's ass first, because she could.

Charlotte rolled onto her back and held the papers above her to examine them. Lexi scooted closer to walk her through them.

"We are going to be docked in Grand Turks today until just after dinner. This is a map of the island with some of my suggestions for things to do and see." She pointed to the paper with the map on it. "This"—she pointed to the other paper—"is information about the excursion you booked, the trail for the horseback riding on the beach, and the to and from transportation details."

"I think leaving the ship is a terrible idea. I'm suddenly not so excited about horses." Charlotte turned to face Lexi and Lexi kissed her on the lips, but it was much too brief for Charlotte's liking.

"Leave the ship. Enjoy your vacation," Lexi said. "I'm working at one of the pool bars for the entire afternoon, so I won't be able to sneak away—"

"And make out with me under the life rafts," Charlotte concluded.

"Exactly." Lexi nodded toward the envelope Charlotte still held in her hand. "Open that."

Charlotte did as she was told and pulled out an ornate card embossed with gold script and a nautical design. It was an invitation to the Officers' Lounge for a VIP dinner with the captain. "Why are we excited about dinner with the captain?"

Lexi laughed. "Because it's a cool thing to experience and there's bottomless champagne. Plus, Captain Correia is an incredible lady. You'll have the finest dining experience of the whole ship in an intimate setting with the most gorgeous view of the sunset you can get anywhere on the ship. And champagne. There will be lots of champagne. Did I mention that?"

"Well you had me at the first champagne mention, to be honest," Charlotte said, suddenly thirsty. "But still, what's with the invite?"

"All VIPs are invited to dine with the captain—it's part of the package. I just rearranged some things to make sure it's tonight and not the last night of the cruise," Lexi said.

"Well, that's good since I won't be here on the last night of the cruise." Charlotte hadn't given that much thought until now. "Oh my God, I won't be here on the last night of the cruise."

Lexi sat up, looking bewildered. "What do you mean you won't be here? Where will you be?"

"In Aruba." Charlotte had completely forgotten her original plans since reconnecting with Lexi. She lost all sense of time around her. "When I called off the wedding, I reorganized the honeymoon as best as I could, to maximize the things I wanted to do since I no longer had to negotiate with someone else."

"What does that mean, exactly?" Lexi asked, her expression unreadable.

"I'm getting off the ship when we dock in Aruba. I extended my stay at the Hotel Mooremont and moved the dates up. Originally, we were going to get back to land and take a flight back there, but when I realized things had changed, I moved the booking up. So I wouldn't have to spend extra days cruising alone." Although initially she had thought this was making the best of a bad situation, she was sorely regretting that decision now. "But that means less time with you." She looked up at Lexi's disappointed face and swallowed. "Lexi, I had no idea I'd find you here. I never would have—"

"Booked the cruise?" Lexi's tone was flat.

Charlotte shook her head, "No, I never would have shortened the trip."

Lexi sighed, seeming to consider this new information. "The Hotel Mooremont is a swanky place. The nicest and most luxurious on the entire island. You have great taste."

"Well, it *was* supposed to be for my honeymoon," Charlotte replied, but she regretted that immediately. "That's not the point, I mean, that doesn't matter. What matters is..." *You.* Charlotte stopped herself from saying what she wanted to, afraid she might scare Lexi off.

Lexi was quiet, her expression unreadable.

Charlotte was at a loss for words, unsure of what to say. She tried to regain some footing, "I interrupted you—what were you saying about rearranging the captain's dinner?"

"Hmm?" Lexi seemed distracted.

"The dinner?" Charlotte tried again. She took Lexi's hand in hers, but Lexi's grip was loose, almost noncommittal.

"Oh yeah. I moved it to tonight because I'm working in the Officers' Lounge tonight. That way I could be there with you while you have dinner without, you know, being there *with* you." Lexi was looking out onto the balcony as she spoke, anywhere but at Charlotte's face, it seemed.

Charlotte reached out and touched her chin, turning her head back to face her. "I'd like that. But I'd rather be there with you, *with* you."

"But you can't be." Lexi tried to turn her head, but Charlotte held her in place.

"But I want to." Charlotte held her gaze and made a decision: She would be brave. She would take a chance. She wouldn't let fear stop her from being honest with herself, or Lexi, about what she wanted. "I'll change my plans, Lexi. I'll stay on the ship until the end—the rest of it doesn't matter." She motioned between them. "This matters. I don't want to miss out on any of this."

Lexi's face softened and Charlotte took the opportunity to press a reassuring kiss to her lips. "I mean that. Truly."

Lexi rested her forehead against Charlotte's and let out a shaky breath. "Are you ready to hear my grandiose plan of how to get you someplace where we can be together uninterrupted now?"

"Absolutely, one thousand percent yes." Charlotte meant every hyperbole of that.

Lexi pulled back and smiled at her. "Tomorrow is a day at sea, but the last stop before Aruba"—she swallowed thickly and Charlotte's heart broke a little—"is Curaçao. I'm working an extra shift this afternoon on the ship, and I changed up your dinner with the captain to cover for someone else, so that I can have the entire afternoon off while we're docked in Curaçao."

"This keeps getting better. Go on." Charlotte could feel the excitement starting to return after the somber realization she might lose time with Lexi. "What's the plan?"

Lexi laughed. "I was going to suggest we tweak your Curaçao excursion plans a bit so we could rent one of those private cabanas on the beach for a little longer than originally planned."

"You mean to reserve it all day from the moment the ship docks until it reboards." The wheels were already turning in Charlotte's head.

"Exactly. Or we could get a room with a view not far from there, to get the best of both worlds, beach access for you and some privacy should we need it. What do you think?" Lexi's expression was hopeful.

"I think Curaçao can't get here fast enough," Charlotte said, but she knew that meant her time would be coming to an end as well.

"I'll get the information together and see what I can set up." Lexi stood from the bed and ran her hand through her hair.

Charlotte joined her and pulled her into an embrace. "Thank you for reworking things and moving things around."

"Sure," Lexi said but a sadness tinged her reply. Charlotte knew why. She felt it, too. "I should head out before anyone gets too suspicious about my time in here. The breakfast is on me today—enjoy the fruit. And have a nice time on the island."

"Lexi…" Charlotte wasn't ready for her to go.

"It's better if I just head out—trust me." Lexi's smile didn't reach her eyes. "Dinner with the captain is a formal affair. You'll want to wear something fancy. The directions of how to get there are on the back of the card. I'll see you tonight."

Charlotte accepted the kiss Lexi gave her before she left, but it was missing the heat from the ones before Charlotte's disclosure about

Aruba. She touched her lips, trying to regain the excited feeling she'd had just a few minutes before, but part of her felt like it had left with Lexi just now. Damn it.

❖

Lexi's throat felt tight when she left Charlotte's cabin. It was amazing how one simple conversation could change everything.

Her legs moved on autopilot to the crew quarters. She poked her head into her room, hoping to find Zara there to talk about Charlotte potentially leaving early and how that made her feel sick to her stomach, but Zara was nowhere to be found. She headed to the only other person she knew who would hear her out and be exactly where she expected him to be.

Ahmed's door was closed, but she knew his shift had started fifteen minutes ago, and she had to talk to someone, or she was going to combust. So she knocked and walked in without waiting for an answer.

"I know why she didn't book any excursions in Aruba, Ahmed. It's because she's—whoa!" Lexi walked in to find Ahmed and Enrique in a passionate kiss. The sound of her voice broke them apart and she covered her eyes. "Why do I keep walking in on people at the most inopportune times?"

Ahmed cleared his throat. "Probably because most people wait for a reply when they knock."

"It was an emergency," Lexi squeaked out and tried to retreat through the door.

"Is everything all right?" Enrique sounded concerned and Lexi felt doubly bad for ruining their moment *and* sort of exaggerating the emergency part.

"It's not a real emergency, just a gossip one. Sorry." Lexi was almost out in the hallway when Ahmed called her back in.

"The moment is ruined. You might as well tell us your gossip as an apology." His exasperated sigh was not lost on her.

"I'll come back." Lexi shook her head and started for the I-95 again.

"Stop being noble—you've already screwed that up." Ahmed straightened his shirt and pointed to her usual chair. "Close the door. Sit. Spill."

Lexi did as she was told because, truthfully, she was a little dazed. "So, are you guys, like, a couple now?"

Enrique looked at Ahmed who was suddenly looking a little sheepish.

"Yes," Enrique replied with a smile as he squeezed Ahmed's shoulder.

"Nice! I told you it'd all work out." Lexi cheered but stifled her excitement when Ahmed stopped blushing and shot her a death look.

"Told who what?" Enrique looked between them and Ahmed cleared his throat again.

"Nothing." Lexi changed the subject because Ahmed was boring holes into her skull, and it was starting to hurt. "Charlotte didn't book any excursions in Aruba because she's leaving the ship early."

"She's what?" Ahmed's jaw dropped. "Who leaves a cruise early?"

"That's what I said silently in my head, while I also screamed and had a tantrum." Lexi sighed and dropped her shoulders. "But you'll be pleased to know I kept it together until I got into the stairwell."

"Then what happened?" Enrique asked.

"There was probably definitely ugly crying. It's all a blur, to be honest." Lexi hated feeling so vulnerable. Charlotte just got under her skin in so many wonderful and awful ways.

"So I take it things are going well between you two?" Ahmed tried to connect the dots, but Lexi didn't have time for a formal retelling of the whole ordeal.

"Yes, we kissed and made out and maybe started rounding a few bases, but then she stopped it, and I'm glad she did because I really want to be in a cabana by the beach with her when the moment is right, but she's leaving the ship early, and I just got her back, and she's already almost gone." Lexi was out of breath by the time she'd rambled that out.

"Whoa." Enrique leaned against the bookcase behind Ahmed's desk and whistled. "That's a lot."

"Right?" Lexi felt seen.

"I thought you two had totally had sex after the dance. Talk about hot and heavy." Enrique fanned himself.

"Was it that obvious?" Lexi cringed.

"If it were possible, I'd expect Charlotte to have gotten pregnant," he replied.

"I miss all the good shit down here." Ahmed pouted and Enrique left the bookcase to give him a quick hug. It was adorable.

"So what do I do?" Lexi looked at them expectantly.

"About what?" Ahmed looked at Enrique like he'd missed something.

"About Charlotte—God, follow along," Lexi whined and talked directly to Don Julio. "He's too head over heels to feel my pain, Donnie. It's just you and me now."

"His nickname is DJ, not Donnie," Ahmed corrected. "And I heard you, I just don't see what the problem is."

"She's leaving the ship—that's the problem." Lexi felt like she had to spell it out for him.

"But she was always going to leave the ship," Enrique supplied. "She was only here for a finite amount of time and then she was going to be gone. The only thing that's changed is she's leaving two days earlier than was expected. But she was always leaving."

"Oof." Lexi felt dizzy. She was always leaving. That wasn't even up for debate. Lexi had blocked that realization out. "She's leaving, again."

"You okay?" Ahmed asked, but she didn't feel okay.

"I might faint." It was a strong possibility.

Enrique was next to her in the next blink, his hands out to catch her. "Maybe you should lie down."

Ahmed stood from his seat on the other side of the desk and knelt in front of her. He placed his hands on her knees and locked eyes with her. "You're going to be fine. You can handle this. Let's talk through the important parts."

"Okay." Lexi did not feel like she was going to be fine.

"She's here until Aruba, right?" Ahmed recounted the facts.

"Yes." Lexi could handle one thing at a time. This was thing number one.

"So that gives you some time to figure out what you want. And I'm thinking what you want is to keep the reconnection alive, beyond the end of the cruise. Am I right?"

"I guess so, yes." Lexi hadn't given it much thought, but she supposed he was right. If she'd been okay with this just ending, then she'd probably feel less like she was dying right now, right?

"So it's simple. Enjoy the time you have with her and have a frank conversation with her when it's over. If she's on the same page, then you'll find a way to make it work," he said matter-of-factly.

"And if she's not?" Lexi didn't want to think about that option.

"Then you have to let her go. And be prepared for what that

means." Ahmed's expression was hopeful. "But let's not jump to conclusions. Try talking to her first. Feel it out a bit."

Enrique's soft brown eyes regarded her with affection and pity. She accepted both. "He's smart *and* cute, huh?"

"He is. You're totally right." Lexi was glad she'd talked to them but still felt unsettled about all the change that was happening around them. "I'm glad you two figured out that you were perfect for each other."

Ahmed adjusted his glasses and coughed, clearly uncomfortable with all the feelings talk when it had to do with him, but Enrique looked touched. He was such a softie.

"I'll leave you to your, uh, good-morning tonsil hockey." Lexi stood on shaky legs for a moment until she felt strong enough to go. "Leave a sock on the doorknob next time. God, I sound like a broken record around here. The sock thing totally works."

"Or just wait for a reply before you come in like a cannonball," Ahmed quipped.

"Bye, boys." She waved and saw herself out, happy for her friends but feeling like her world was unraveling a little more with every crashing ocean wave.

## CHAPTER FIFTEEN

Charlotte agonized over her dress choice for tonight's dinner. It was vacation, after all, and though she'd packed a few nice outfits, most of her clothing was bathing suits or cover-ups. Sure, she had some casual touristy looks and outfits that could become evening wear with a few accessories, but she really didn't have anything formal. Except her green dress which she loved, but it was a little revealing. Too revealing?

She toweled off from the shower and began to get ready, taking extra time on her eye makeup and lip gloss choice. She wanted to look nice tonight—she wanted to look good for Lexi. Lexi. Who she'd thought of all day while on the island. Who she thought of ceaselessly while she was zoning out on the horseback ride along the beach, which was a bad idea since she nearly got bucked off at one point, but still, even then her mind was on Lexi, not on hitting the rough sand below.

She'd spent the better part of today daydreaming about those endless blue eyes and soft lips. And the look of disappointment on those lips when she'd said she was leaving early. It was the same disappointment Charlotte felt in her own stomach. Her gut ached and her heart broke. She'd had so much heartbreak this year, and she wasn't sure how much more she could take.

She thought about that now. This tryst with Lexi was leading her straight to Heartbreak City, with a population of one. She knew in her heart of hearts that she'd broken things off with Lexi in their youth to save Lexi from the pain she knew Lexi'd suffer while she was gone, but she'd been shocked at how visceral her own pain had been. She realized she'd never quite healed, because having Lexi back in her life these days made her feel whole in a way she hadn't since she'd left her. Which was exactly what she was about to do again—she would be leaving, again. And that thought killed her.

She slipped on her dress and worked the side zipper until it was entirely closed. She smoothed down the fabric over her hips and breasts and slipped on her heels. She dug through her closet for a clutch, because this dress did not have pockets. It was so tight it didn't even allow for panty lines, something that gave her more pause than usual considering Lexi would be in the room. Did she really want to be without panties around Lexi? Yes. But also, maybe not.

She stepped in front of the mirror and bounced the light curl she'd worked into the ends of her hair. She took in a deep breath and watched the dress strain to contain her chest. The heart-shaped neckline was deeper than she'd usually go with, but the real showstopper of this dress was the thigh-high slit on the left. Charlotte was grateful she'd inherited her mother's natural athleticism. Her leg looked toned from her minimal exercise routine, and tanned from her time in the sun this week. This dress was to die for, but she'd only worn it once before.

Veronica had bought this for her for their anniversary. She'd worn it to dinner and that was about as long as it had lasted. She'd packed it for exactly that reason—she was angry that Veronica had tainted another beautiful thing in her life. She wanted to take back what was stolen from her. She felt beautiful in this dress, and she wanted to do the dress justice. She wanted to wear this dress for herself and she wanted to wear it for Lexi.

"I hope you know what you're doing, Charlotte," she said to her reflection before she grabbed her clutch and headed for the door. The truth was, she had no idea what she was doing. None.

Lexi was at a crossroads. She both wanted and didn't want to work in the Officers' Lounge tonight. On the one hand, it was always a really fun event with lots of great conversation and amazing views of the ocean, something she never grew tired of. But she'd also be seeing Charlotte tonight, and after the day she'd had, she wasn't sure she'd be very good company.

She'd spent the majority of the day working the pool bar, but with the ship at port, the guest volume was down significantly. So she'd had a lot of time to herself, which was not a good idea because all she did was think about Charlotte and what she wanted to do and say to Charlotte. The *do* part seemed to be the most vivid daydream, which did nothing to help the mixed emotions she was having. She was all over the place, it seemed.

She'd felt marginally better after the talk with the boys, but not much. And she'd stalked the spa area during her lunch break to catch Zara up on the goings-on between guest appointments, but Zee didn't have much to add except to reiterate what Ahmed said: *Enjoy the time you have and stop putting an expiration date on it, unless you want to put an expiration date on it.* That was what bothered Lexi the most. Did she or didn't she?

The truth was she wasn't confident one way or the other. Maybe this was just what it was supposed to be—a week of reconnection, maybe kissing and sex, but a chance for closure. But maybe it was supposed to be a door opening and a new chapter beginning. That was what she couldn't decide. Was this some kind of luck? Or fate's cruel game? She wasn't sure she'd ever know for sure.

She got to the lounge early to prep the bar and make sure everything was just right. At least, that was what she told herself even if she knew she really went there to keep her idle hands busy. Her feet wanted to find Charlotte or jump into the ocean, either or. But her brain told her to get to work. So she tried.

"You can do this." Lexi double-checked her formal uniform attire in the reflection of the refrigerator door in the room behind the bar. She rolled her shoulders and shook out her hands, getting ready to mix drinks for the next few hours. "Just go in there and be normal and talk to Charlotte when you can."

And that was the perfect plan, until Charlotte walked in and took her breath away. Up to that point, Lexi had been successfully schmoozing the other guests, shaking drinks and making easy conversation. Until Charlotte stepped through the door, that was. Then everything went to hell.

Lexi tried not to stare, but that would have been impossible because Charlotte came in as radiant as a goddamned emerald sun. And Lexi wasn't the only one that noticed. Just about every head near her turned to Charlotte, including the captain's, which caused Lexi to bristle a bit.

Captain Correia was in midconversation near the door when Charlotte entered, and Lexi watched as the captain interrupted the guest she was speaking with to turn and address Charlotte. Lexi couldn't hear what they were saying from her station behind the bar, but there was laughing. It occurred to her that she'd never seen Correia laugh so openly with anyone before, herself included.

"Something wrong?" Angela, who was serving as backup bartender tonight, asked next to her.

"What? No." Lexi forced herself to look away from the interaction. She must be imagining things. She counted the red and white wine bottle selection for the fiftieth time to keep busy. "Why would you say that?"

"Oh, I don't know." Angela bumped her hip. "It's just that you were shooting eye daggers at the captain. I assumed maybe it had something to do with that woman in the green dress."

"Hmm?" Lexi didn't look up, for fear that her face would confirm Angela's accusation.

"You used to date her, right? The green dress girl?" Angela didn't let up.

Lexi looked up at her. "What makes you say that?"

"That woman she hangs with, Barb, I think her name is, told me you two had some history. And when it comes to beautiful women, I've never seen you scowl at, well, anyone before. You know, since you're kind of the resident bar hottie, especially during this theme week. But there was definite scowling just now." Angela was looking in the direction of the captain when she was speaking. "Plus, I was getting coffee at the Starbucks on the Lido deck when you two commandeered Enrique's samba lesson."

Did anyone *not* see that lesson? Lexi wasn't sure if she should feel complimented by the bar hottie comment or annoyed that there was gossip going around about her and Charlotte, but she didn't have time to process those feelings because Charlotte's laugh drew her attention toward where Angela had been looking.

Correia had her hand on Charlotte's forearm, and Charlotte was laughing that full-bodied carefree laugh that Lexi loved. She did not, however, love Correia touching her. Since when did she touch anyone?

"The captain seems to like her." Angela added fuel to the fire. "Does she know her, too?"

Correia motioned for the tray of pre-poured champagne flutes to be brought over.

"I'll take it." Angela moved to take the tray, but Lexi stopped her.

"You need to pour another glass." Lexi reached for a clean flute and went for the chilling champagne bottle.

"Why?" Angela was already on the other side of the bar, tray in hand.

Lexi poured the glass and handed it to Angela. "Because you put a strawberry on the rim of every glass."

"So what? It looks better." Angela shrugged.

"Charlotte's allergic to strawberries." Lexi nodded toward the captain but couldn't bring herself to look at her. She wasn't used to feeling jealousy, but she certainly felt it right now. She didn't trust herself with this feeling. Just one more feeling Charlotte seemed to evoke in her, it seemed.

Angela paused. "You know what, on second thought, maybe you should bring the tray by."

"What? No, that's fine." Lexi didn't like this idea. Not one bit.

Angela put the tray on the counter and slipped back under the bar. "No, I insist. I'll help prep the passed hors d'oeuvres. You should go—the captain is waiting." Angela gave her a smirk and Lexi hated her in that moment.

"Fine." Lexi slipped under the bar and grabbed the tray, starting as far away from the captain as possible, hoping to work off a little frustration before she got there.

By the time she got to Charlotte and Correia, she had only two flutes left on the tray, one with and one without a strawberry.

"Bronson," Correia said as she gave her a bright smile that Lexi wanted to wipe off her face immediately, "what took you so long?"

"Lots of thirsty guests, Captain. Sorry." Lexi had tried to avoid looking directly at Charlotte this entire time, but she couldn't any longer. She chanced a glance and found Charlotte watching her, a small smile on her lips. Lips that were wet and delicious looking, she might add. Crap.

Correia reached for the strawberry flute to hand to Charlotte, but Lexi stopped her. "That's for you, Captain."

Correia shook her head and gave Lexi a questioning expression. "We always serve the guests first, Bronson. You know that. Ms. Southwick here should get the fancier glass."

Correia addressed Charlotte next. "We seem to have run out of fruit. I can have Lexi fix that for next round."

Charlotte held up her hand, gently pushing the glass back to

Correia. "Thank you, Captain. But I think Lexi was trying to tell you that this glass," she said as she pointed to the one remaining on the tray, "is for me. I'm allergic to strawberries."

Lexi handed the glass to Charlotte, even though she'd been intentionally extending the tray in Charlotte's direction. Clearly, Charlotte wanted her to hand it to her directly.

"Thanks," Charlotte replied as she ran her fingers along Lexi's before taking it. Her touch was electric.

Lexi had to stifle a shudder. "Of course." She turned to go but Correia stopped her.

"Lexi's the best bartender on the ship. Good catch, Bronson." That was probably a normal exchange, but Lexi felt like it was mocking. She had to get out of there. She wasn't in her right mind.

"Sure thing." Lexi strode away before anything else could stop her, and she ducked under the bar entrance, safely positioning herself near all the glass bottles and sharp knives. She muttered to herself, "Get it together, Lexi."

"Hors d'oeuvres are up," Angela said as she reemerged by her side with two trays of food.

"Of course, they are." Lexi took a tray and waited until Angela was on the other side to pass it to her.

"I'll go this way." Angela motioned away from the captain, and Lexi wondered if she could get away with murdering her on the spot.

"Sounds like a plan." She gave Angela her best fake smile and headed toward ground zero.

Lexi was relieved to find that Charlotte was no longer standing next to Correia. In fact, she didn't see her at all. Where had she gone?

She finished circling her side of the room and returned to the bar with the empty tray. She'd had two orders for sangria while she was walking around, so she started muddling some fruit.

"I thought you liked her." Charlotte's voice sounded from across the bar.

Lexi looked up and was mesmerized by the green in Charlotte's eyes. The dress made her eyes sparkle more than usual. She looked stunning tonight. "I do."

"You might usually, but you don't tonight," Charlotte replied, a knowing smile on her lips.

"I'm not sure what you're talking about." She wasn't fooling anyone, and she knew it.

"I think that fruit is plenty pulverized by now," Charlotte said.

Lexi redirected her attention to the fruit she had muddled to death. "So it is."

She mixed the rest of the drink parts and poured the contents of the shaker into the two glasses on the counter. She motioned toward Charlotte's near-empty flute. "Would you like another?"

Charlotte hesitated. "Not yet. I should pace myself."

"Worried about overindulging?" Lexi teased as she put the sangria glasses on the empty serving tray next to her.

"Only when it comes to you." That got her attention.

Angela walked up to the bar with an empty food tray, and Lexi pushed the drinks toward her. "Can you bring those to the ladies by the window?"

"Bring them yourself." Then Angela noticed Charlotte and seemed to reconsider. "Sure thing, boss."

Once Angela was out of earshot, Lexi redirected her attention to Charlotte. "Do you think you can have too much of me? Is that what you're saying?"

Charlotte leaned her elbows on the bar, and Lexi was aware of just how low her neckline dipped. "I'm willing to find out."

Any concern Lexi might have had about the captain went out the window. "I was a little jealous before, I'll admit."

"I know"—Charlotte reached across the bar and took a cherry from the fruit tray near Lexi's hip—"but you shouldn't be. Because the only thing I've been thinking about all day is how wonderful it's going to be to not see an inch of Curaçao."

Lexi bit her lip to stifle a moan. She slid a cocktail napkin toward Charlotte to give her hands something to do. "You sure you don't want to see the beaches? The sand is famously beautiful—white and powdery."

Charlotte popped the cherry into her mouth and produced a tied stem for Lexi, her timing markedly improved from last time. "So, you're saying it's soft enough not to bother my knees when I'm kneeling in front of you? Because that's pretty much the only thing I care about."

"Fuck, Charlotte." Lexi was gripping the bar so hard her hands hurt.

"That's the plan." Charlotte handed over the stem, pressing her fingers into Lexi's shaky palm as she did.

The dinner bell rang behind Charlotte, and Lexi jumped about a mile.

"I guess it's time to take my seat." Charlotte stepped back from the bar and patted her lips with the bar napkin Lexi had slid toward her. "Thanks for the champagne before, and the cherry now."

Lexi watched Charlotte glide away, the dress seemingly painted on her body. The seat Charlotte chose was off to Lexi's right, and as she sat, the slit in her dress exposed the near entirety of her left leg, directly in Lexi's view. The small wave Charlotte gave her once she was seated told Lexi her seat choice was no accident. Lexi exhaled. "She's going to be the death of me."

❖

The meal had been exquisite. It was everything Lexi had promised her and more. As the fifth and final course came out, Charlotte was starting to reconsider just how much give this dress would allow. Thankfully, this course was dessert, which she always seemed to have room for.

"Have you enjoyed your dinner tonight, Charlotte?" Captain Correia had dropped the use of her surname at her request, but it had taken a reminder or two.

"I have. Thank you again for the invitation." Charlotte had been impressed by the captain's charm. She'd been surprised when she'd taken the seat to her left. She'd expected her to sit at the head of the table near the front of the ship, not at her end. She was more than aware that the seat choice had caught Lexi's attention, as well. Lexi had been the designated wine pourer for their end of the large formal table for most of the evening, and though she'd tamped down some of her scowl from before, Charlotte could still see it reappear every now and then. It was honestly making her a little hot.

"Well, dinner with the captain and her officers is part of your VIP package, but I'd be a fool if I didn't tell you the pleasure is all mine," Correia replied, this time reaching out and touching Charlotte's arm as she spoke. "There will be after-dinner cocktails while the sun sets after dessert, and I hope you'll stay for them."

Up to this point, the captain's flirtation, although present since the moment she'd walked in, had been rather subtle. There was nothing subtle about the look Correia was giving her now, though.

"I've been promised a beautiful sunset," Charlotte replied, "and while I wouldn't miss that for anything, I think I'll be turning in a bit early tonight. I'm feeling a little fatigued."

"Oh." The captain looked disappointed. "Are you not sleeping well? If there is anything I can do to make your accommodations more comfortable, please let me know."

*Ooh, she's real smooth.* "The accommodations are fine, thank you. Just a long day of being a tourist catching up with me a bit."

Correia seemed to survey her curiously but only nodded in acquiescence of what she said.

The dessert came to the table in that moment and Charlotte was grateful for the distraction. She had no intention of leading the captain on, but she didn't want to offend her either. Pissing off Lexi's boss seemed like a bad idea.

Petite individual warm chocolate cakes were placed in front of all the guests. They were delicately adorned with strawberries and whipped cream with some sort of red glaze, and they looked delicious. But the plate placed in front of Charlotte was entirely different: a key lime tart, something that she had no doubt was Lexi's doing. Key lime was her favorite.

She looked up to find Lexi watching intently from the bar. She gave her a brief nod and a smile in gratitude. She thought she'd been discreet, but Correia must have noticed.

The captain commented, "Her attention to detail seems more keen than usual." Her tone was unreadable.

Charlotte made sure to make direct eye contact when she replied, "I'm sure it has something to do with the fruit glaze on the plate. Strawberries find their way into everything."

"Hmm. Perhaps." Correia looked back at Lexi, who did a rather impressive job of looking busy, even though Charlotte had seen her staring while Correia was talking.

Charlotte finished her dish and excused herself from the table, taking the moment to walk toward the floor-to-ceiling windows in front of her. Lexi had been right about the view; the Officers' Lounge was located midship and had an unobstructed view of the sunset. It was beautiful. The colors were unreal, a mix of glowing orange and pink. The horizon appeared to be on fire, and it was a fire that she could see stretched for miles.

"My favorite part is the way the sunset reflects on the water's surface." Correia's voice at her shoulder caused her to sidestep a bit.

She wanted to share this with Lexi, not Correia. She looked toward the bar but didn't see Lexi, though in her periphery she did notice the captain's hand hovering near her hip. The slit leg hip at that. She sidestepped farther, this time making it more obvious.

"You have a beautiful ship, Captain. Thank you for a lovely evening." Charlotte bowed her head in appreciation and turned to leave.

Correia's fingers hit her wrist, slowing her progress, but Lexi's appearance at that moment resulted in the contact ceasing.

"Can I get you anything, Captain?" Lexi's voice was terse.

"I'm fine, Bronson," Correia replied before she turned her attention toward Charlotte. "Anything for you, Charlotte?"

"On my way out, but thanks anyway." Charlotte flashed Lexi her best apology smile and made it two steps away when she heard Correia speak again.

"I heard you two had quite the dance class the other day. Seems like something I should have seen for myself. Will it be happening again, I wonder?"

Charlotte froze. Lexi's warnings of cameras being everywhere were fresh in her mind. She was more than confident that the dancing could be explained away, but what happened afterward…that would be more difficult.

Lexi replied, "Enrique is the best dancer on the ship—I was merely assisting. But I think my samba days are behind me."

"Is that so?" Correia's voice had ice in it. Charlotte wanted out of there and fast.

"Well, ladies, thanks for the lovely evening, I'll be on my way." Charlotte left as quickly and inconspicuously as possible, but she had a feeling that wasn't the end of that discussion.

## CHAPTER SIXTEEN

Lexi wanted nothing more than to check in with Charlotte, but Correia had dragged on this dinner for an hour longer than was necessary, two hours if you asked Lexi, and she was feeling bitter. Lexi had stopped serving her alcohol over dinner when she'd felt she was getting a little too friendly with Charlotte, but Angela had missed the cue and switched the captain to something harder than house wine. This was the first time Lexi had seen the captain lose her composure.

When she stumbled while attempting to get out of her chair, Lexi stepped in.

"All right, Captain"—Lexi gripped her elbow to steady her—"I think it's time we call it a night."

Correia attempted to shrug off her hand but succeeded only in falling forward, nearly knocking over the dark amber liquid in the glass on the table. "I'm fine," she slurred, clearly not fine.

"Be that as it may, my shift is over." Lexi tugged her arm again, and when the captain resisted a second time, Lexi tried a little tough love. She leaned closer and lowered her voice as she said, "And aside from the overtime I don't want to be working, you're also making a scene. So get up."

Correia blinked and her eyes seemed to focus as she nodded. Lexi used her strength to help yank the captain out of her chair and did her damnedest to take the majority of her weight so she wouldn't sway.

Most of the room had cleared, but a few senior male officers remained. And though they seemed to be engrossed in some sort of conversation, she'd bet they'd noticed Correia start to unravel. She had to get the captain out of there immediately.

Lexi looked over at Angela and Angela pointed to the bar checklist and gave her a thumbs-up, indicating that she would close the bar on her own. Lexi was grateful she'd stepped up toward the end when it had become apparent that something had to be done with Correia. She felt confident that Angela would be discreet as well, but that was Correia's problem, not hers.

Correia was silent during the short walk down the hall toward her private quarters. Lexi was grateful the lounge was on the same floor, because Correia was taller than her by at least three inches, and though Correia was fit, she was deadweight right now, and Lexi was sweating trying to keep her up.

When they approached Correia's door, the captain spoke for the first time. "Sally's mad at me."

"Sally? As in Staff Captain Sally?" Lexi grunted in exertion as Correia reached for the door and lurched to the side. "Chill, Cap. Let me do it."

Correia said nothing, her eyes glazed as Lexi rested her against the wall.

"Where's your key, Captain?"

Correia reached into her pants pocket and held it out to no one, since her aim was about five inches from where Lexi's hand was.

Lexi grabbed the card and unlocked the room, heaving Correia in with her as she went.

The room was dark, save for the light of the moon shining through the open balcony door. Lexi fumbled for a light switch, stepping on what sounded like paper as she went. She found a light near the bathroom door and flicked it on, using the wall to help her get Correia to the waiting unmade bed.

Correia dropped like a sack on the edge of the bed and flopped backward, making no attempt to safely maneuver herself into any position. Lexi pulled off her shoes and helped get her legs on the bed before she pulled the covers over her. She went into the bathroom and ran some water from the tap in a glass she found on the bar, then put the water and a bottle of ibuprofen next to the bed.

"She's mad. And I think she's going to leave me," Correia mumbled from beside her.

"Who's mad, Cap?" Lexi nudged the papers strewn about the room by the open door and marched over to close it, in an attempt to limit the hurricane of printer paper.

"Sally. She's the most important person in my life." Correia's voice cracked. "She's mad and she's going to leave me. And it's all my fault."

Lexi wasn't sure if she meant that in a romantic *She's going to leave me* way or like in a Zara was moving on and maybe Sally was, too kind of way. But when Correia started to openly sob, she decided maybe this was romantic after all. She couldn't believe Ahmed was actually right.

"Hey, hey." Lexi walked back toward the bed and patted the captain on her shoulder. "It's late, and you've had a lot to drink. Have some water, take some meds, and sleep it off. I'm sure that whatever is happening between the two of you can be figured out with a steady head and a new day."

Correia accepted the glass and pills Lexi gave her and hiccupped them down before rolling to her side and murmuring to herself, "Okay, sleep now."

Lexi waited for a moment for the captain to start snoring before she shut off the light and walked to the door. She closed the door behind her and walked right into a red-eyed and tired looking Sally.

"Uh, Sally…Captain. Hi." Lexi stopped so short she skidded in her shoes. "It's not what it looks like. I was just dropping her off." The last thing she wanted to do was encourage the ire of the ship's primary staff disciplinarian.

Sally nodded but said nothing. She just stood there looking drained, and Lexi took that as her cue to go.

"Okay, well. I guess I'll see you around." Lexi stepped around her and walked as fast as she could without breaking into a jog. As she turned the corner, she saw Sally key into the captain's room and close the door.

What the fuck was that? Lexi poked her head back into the lounge to make sure Angela had locked up before she set out to find Charlotte and apologize. For what, she didn't know, but she felt like she should apologize for something.

❖

Charlotte sat by the piano in the bar at the edge of the Club Lounge and ran her finger along the rim of her soda water. She had been too frazzled leaving the dinner earlier to go back to her room, but she was dressed a little too fancy to just wander around on the decks of the ship without a purpose. She heard the music from a few floors above and followed the sounds to this area. The people watching was fantastic, and the piano was lovely. So she settled in and sipped her drink, enjoying the moment.

It occurred to her that she really hadn't explored the ship much. She'd stopped by the casino during her wandering tonight to say hello to Barb, who had made herself a fixture there, but aside from that, she really hadn't left the top decks or her room. In fact, if Lexi wasn't guaranteed to be in an area, she didn't bother going there. Part of her thought she should be annoyed by that fact, but she wasn't. She wanted to be where Lexi was, if at all possible. And so far, that had been very possible. Though she wasn't able to *be* with her the way that she wanted to, she knew that time would come. Or at least, she hoped it would.

"Charlotte, right?" A pretty blond server gave her a warm smile.

"Yes?"

The server looked relieved. "Okay, good. They said you were in a green dress, and I have to say, that is some dress—you look great."

"Thank you?" Charlotte sat up a little straighter as she asked, "Who's *they*?"

"Oh, right." The server palmed her forehead. "Housekeeping was looking for you. They said they dropped off something perishable at your room."

Housekeeping knew she was in a green dress? She doubted that. "Okay, thanks for the update. I'll get right back there."

"Great, I'll let them know." She left without another word, and Charlotte tried to make it look like a nonchalant exit, even though she wanted to run, not walk, back to her room.

The distance felt like an eternity in those heels. But when she turned the corner to her hallway, she was pleased to see a familiar face waiting by a housekeeping cart outside of her suite.

"You're working for housekeeping now, huh?" Charlotte keyed into her room and Lexi followed closely behind her with a stack of towels and fresh linens so tall they nearly obscured her face.

"I'm a Jill of all trades, what can I say?" Lexi closed the door and deposited the linens on the table nearby.

"Are you trying to tell me I should freshen up my linens, or are those towels perishable?" Charlotte pointed to the stack as she spoke.

"Oh, well, these are for later when we make a mess of the sheets already on your bed. And the towels are for after I have my way with you in the shower, once we mess up the bed." Lexi's expression was dead serious.

"Oh?" This was news to Charlotte—excellent news, but news all the same. Charlotte stepped closer to Lexi as she asked, "And how is all that going to happen?"

"You worry too much." Lexi reached for Charlotte's hand and pulled her close. "Are you stressed? Because I can probably help with that."

"Do I seem stressed to you, Lex?" Charlotte wrapped her arms around Lexi's neck and closed her eyes when Lexi's lips connected with the skin under her jaw.

"You seem delicious. And this dress changed my life tonight, so I'll be taking it off you with my teeth." Lexi nipped at her pulse point and Charlotte felt her body flush.

"Again, I ask, how do you intend for that to happen?" Charlotte dipped her head to connect their lips and moaned when Lexi's tongue danced against hers.

"All will be revealed in due time. Oh, and besides fresh linens, you ordered room service, too." Lexi pulled back from the kiss and flashed her a mischievous smile. "Stay in the dress—I meant what I said about taking it off you. But let Enrique in when he gets here. It should be about fifteen minutes or so, okay?"

Charlotte was excited and nervous all at once. "Okay."

"Good girl." Lexi pressed one final kiss to her lips before she slipped out the door and disappeared.

Charlotte's knees felt shaky as excitement and energy surged through her. She went to the bathroom to freshen up and take a sip of water. It was hot in here, right?

Fifteen minutes later, a knock at her door signaled that her room service had arrived. She opened the door and was greeted by Enrique.

"Charlotte," he said with a broad grin as he entered her suite and closed the door behind him. He pointed to the contents on the top of the cart as he said, "I come bearing champagne, fruits and cheese, and Lexi."

"And Lexi?" Charlotte had barely gotten the question out when her confusion was resolved. Lexi slipped out from beneath the cart, crawling out from under the white cloak of the tablecloth.

She stood up with a stretch and dusted off her shoulders with a groan. "That was fucking way tighter than I thought."

"Anyone want to fill me in on what's happening here, or should I just fill in the blanks?" Charlotte would be lying if she wasn't thrilled to have Lexi in the room, but she wasn't sure she was ready for an audience, considering all the things she'd been daydreaming about since they'd last spoke.

"I called in a favor—" Lexi started.

"All your favors. All of them. Plus five that you didn't even have in your favor cache." Enrique unloaded the tray and shot her a quick thumbs-up before he dropped the tablecloth back over the cart and maneuvered it toward the door of her suite.

"That, too." Lexi gave him a grateful expression. "Anyway, I'm your nightly entertainment. And these are your snacks."

Charlotte just wanted one last bit of clarification. "So Enrique is merely the mule to get you to the room, right?"

"Did you want him to stay?" Lexi looked mortified.

"That's my cue." Enrique gave her a quick wave. "Have a nice night, ladies."

Lexi closed the door and leaned against it, wiping her brow and breathing out a sigh of relief. "I thought he'd never leave."

"You don't even deserve him," Charlotte said as Lexi looped her arms around her waist.

"I don't. But I'll never have a fresh avocado again for the rest of my life while I cruise with Enrique, and I have a few other friends willing to take the next few pickup and drop-off shifts, so we're good." Lexi jested but Charlotte knew Lexi was playing a dangerous game, one that now included her friends. She tried not to think about it. Especially since Lexi's hand at her rib cage took priority attention now.

"I'm glad you're here." Charlotte leaned into Lexi's touch and let herself get enveloped by Lexi's arms.

"I was hoping you'd say that." Lexi pressed a soft but brief kiss to her lips. "Because I sort of inserted myself into your evening plans. And I never asked if that was okay. Is it?"

"*So* okay." Charlotte brought their lips back together and held the kiss while she appreciated Lexi's word choice. "Is that the only thing you plan on inserting yourself into tonight?"

Lexi pulled back and shook her head. "You mean besides the riveting conversation I planned on inserting into this moment?"

"Besides that." Charlotte tugged at Lexi's shirt, untucking it from her pants. She pressed her palm to the hot skin of Lexi's abdomen and relished in the feeling.

"I have a few things in mind." Lexi repositioned Charlotte's hand to her hip and Charlotte gripped it in frustration. "We need to get you out of that dress, Charlotte, before you get all grabby-hands on me, and I fuck you while you're still clothed. Deal?"

"Damn." Charlotte let go of Lexi's hip and waited for Lexi to make the next move. She didn't want to delay this any longer. She couldn't take the teasing anymore.

"Good." Lexi kissed her deeply and intertwined their hands. She pulled back and brought Charlotte's fingers to her lips, where she kissed each one slowly, teasing her tongue along each tip. "I intend to take my time with you tonight."

Charlotte shivered at the promise of a night filled with Lexi doing all sorts of things to her, starting with the way she was sucking on her forefinger. "And if I don't last?"

Lexi's tongue left her finger and slid into her mouth with another searing kiss. "Then we'll do it all over again until you can't anymore."

Charlotte's hip bucked in response to Lexi's words and mouth. "Get me out of this dress, Lex. Now."

Lexi smiled against her lips and pulled back, running her lips across Charlotte's, teasing her. She released her grip on one of Charlotte's hands to trace along Charlotte's left hip. "This slit, well"—her fingers found the edge of the dress and dipped lower—"a slit this high should be a crime."

Charlotte's leg quaked as Lexi's fingers moved from her hip toward the inside of her thigh, following the fabric with great attention. "I'm glad you like it."

"Very much so." Lexi moved the fabric inward, exposing the entirety of her left leg to the cool air in the room. "Tell me, a dress this tight makes it hard to wear panties, right?"

"Mm-hmm." Charlotte was squeezing their still joined hands so hard she was afraid she might break them.

Lexi pulled the fabric farther and Charlotte felt the coldness of the room air settle across her hot, swollen sex. Lexi dipped her head to make direct eye contact with Charlotte when she asked, "So the question remains, did you even bother wearing any?"

Charlotte's mouth hung open, but she had no words. Lexi's eyes were dark, but they never left hers while she spoke, all the while touching the soft, tender skin on the inside of Charlotte's leg—so close, yet not close enough.

Lexi's lips parted as she traced up infinitesimally, skimming Charlotte's naked wet lips. "Oh. This is very naughty of you."

Charlotte let out a shaky breath as Lexi added more pressure to her exploration, touching and teasing, winding Charlotte up more and more. "Lexi."

Lexi smiled and pressed against her a little harder. Charlotte felt her clit twitch in anticipation. She wanted this so very badly. Lexi's voice was a low purr when she said, "I want to see you naked. Let's get rid of this gorgeous dress, shall we?"

Charlotte nodded, unable to speak as Lexi's hand left her crotch and danced up her side. Charlotte missed her touch along her most intimate of areas, but the way Lexi slowly lowered the zipper at her side was giving her something else to focus on, specifically the torture of it all. This was blissfully agonizing. She wanted it to stop *and* never end. It was a delicious dance of want and need. She was hungry for it.

Lexi's mouth was on hers as she got to the bottom of the zipper. Her lips were unhurried against Charlotte's as the dress slacked beneath her touch. She was taking her time, it seemed.

"I've been thinking about doing this since the moment I saw you again." Lexi breathed across her lips as her palm traced up Charlotte's now naked rib cage and cupped the side of her breast. "The idea of holding you in my palm, all of you, has quite literally kept me up at night."

Charlotte could now add the feeling of being sticky to being hot, damn. She pulled back from Lexi to look into her eyes. She wanted to see her face when she did this.

"And tell me"—Charlotte took the hand at her side and eased it under the fabric of the top of her dress, putting the weight of her naked breast into Lexi's palm—"does this live up to your expectations?"

Lexi licked her lips and glanced down at her hand, squeezing it slightly and making Charlotte moan in response. She liked being in Lexi's hand again. Lexi looked back up at her as she replied, "More than you can ever know."

Charlotte leaned into her touch as she released Lexi's other hand to free her own. She tugged at the bottom of her dress and savored the feeling of it slipping down her body, the silky departure one more delightful sensation overwhelming her senses. She took back Lexi's hand as she stepped out of the dress and guided it between her legs, pressing Lexi's fingers to her as she leaned more fully into the hand cupping her breast. "And here? What about touching me here, Lex?"

Lexi's eyes traced down her naked front and paused at the space between her hips. Her fingers massaged at her chest, and she teased

Charlotte's erect nipple as her other hand slid along Charlotte's sex, palming it firmly.

"My imagination failed me, because there isn't a thing about this that doesn't blow those daydreams out of the water." Lexi separated Charlotte's lips with her fingers, gathering wetness as she spoke. "You are even more beautiful than I remember. And you feel ready for me—are you?"

Charlotte felt light-headed from all the touching and teasing. And talking. God, when did Lexi get so good at dirty talk? She wanted Lexi in her, deep, right now. Her body was buzzing with energy and anticipation. She had to slow herself down from *over*feeling it all. "So ready."

"Good. Because I don't think I can wait any longer." Lexi's lips pressed against her mouth and her fingers left her sex as she wrapped Charlotte up in her arms and walked her backward toward the bed.

Charlotte had never been so glad to be horizontal in her life, a feeling that exponentially increased as Lexi settled on top of her, her lips and hands hungrily taking all that Charlotte had to give. The feeling was incredible. And the knowledge that it didn't have to stop before it got interesting made the feeling that much more exciting. Charlotte was turned on and excited and fucking horny as fuck, and Lexi was giving her life.

Lexi kissed her neck as her hand traced along the outside of Charlotte's thigh, bending her knee and gliding along her calf to her foot. She eased off one of Charlotte's heels, then the other, before she settled back on top of her. "I'd be lying if I said I wanted those shoes off of you, because they do incredible things to your legs, but I have a lot of plans and those are much too sharp and pointy for what I have in mind."

"Which is what, exactly?" Charlotte shifted her hips toward the hand Lexi had bracing her thigh. She wanted to feel her touch again.

"Oh, you know, your knees on my shoulders while we get reacquainted. It'd be hard to lose myself between your legs if your heels are branding my back." Lexi took the hint and returned her palm to Charlotte's middle, stroking and teasing again.

The visual of Lexi between her legs made her clit pulse with need, and her body quaked when one of Lexi's teasing swipes got a little closer than she was expecting. "Fuck."

"All night." Lexi licked at her earlobe and Charlotte shivered.

"Get out of these clothes and let me see you." Charlotte tugged at Lexi's shirt and spread her legs wider, inviting Lexi in.

Lexi leaned back and knelt over her, straddling her hips as she pulled off her shirt and tossed it aside. Charlotte reached up and ran her hands along Lexi's toned and tanned stomach. Her fingers traced the natural grooves of her abs and slipped beneath the fabric of her bra. Lexi closed her eyes at the touch unhooking her bra, and Charlotte's hands enveloped her breasts without resistance now. They were full and round and fucking perfect.

"It feels good, touching you," Charlotte said as she caressed the skin of Lexi's chest. She sat up to get closer to her, dragging her thumb across one of Lexi's nipples before closing her lips around it and licking.

Lexi's hand threaded into her hair and held her close, and Charlotte sucked on the skin between her lips, teasing it with her teeth and tongue as Lexi scratched at her scalp. She moved her other hand from Lexi's breast to pull at the button on her pants, fumbling until Lexi's hand closed over hers.

"All in good time." Lexi placed a firm but gentle hand along her clavicle and pressed her onto her back. She looked incredible kneeling over her, all long blond hair and perfect everything. Charlotte wanted this image burned into her brain for later. And always.

Lexi rose up enough to ease her pants off her hips but left her panties on to Charlotte's great disapproval, before she lowered herself back down. But Charlotte forgot to complain because Lexi's skin was hot against her own and she needed more, so much more.

Lexi slid off to the side a bit and eased Charlotte's legs apart, gliding along the inside of her thigh and making Charlotte tremble with want. "I want to feel you. All of you. But if you touch me, I'll get distracted by how good *that* feels and then I can't give you what you need," Lexi said as she wound Charlotte back up with her teasing touches.

"Which is what?" Charlotte lifted her head to connect their lips because there was so much talking and not enough fucking, and Lexi's mouth was life changing but not as life changing as whatever she was doing with her fingers in this moment.

"Every. Little. Thing," Lexi breathed out against her lips as she slipped inside her, one tentative finger at first before she added a second, and Charlotte's entire existence was rattled to the core.

"Oh my God." Charlotte had never been so turned on in her life.

Ever. Never. And as Lexi slipped in deeper, filling her, she realized that this was everything she'd needed and more. She rolled her hips to meet Lexi's slowly building thrusts and scratched at Lexi's back, trying to slow herself down and ride Lexi's fingers harder at the same time.

"You feel so good." Lexi kissed her hard and she struggled to remember to breathe as their pace quickened.

"Lexi, I need—" Charlotte felt herself climbing at a feverish rate, but a part of her worried she'd fail again, stuck at the precipice and unable to climax.

"More." Lexi sucked her bottom lip between her teeth and tugged her mouth open, kissing her deeply as Charlotte felt her curl the fingers of her hand to rub against Charlotte's insides, sending shock wave after shock wave through her center and bringing her that much closer. But when Lexi's free hand found her naked breast and her fingers closed around her nipple, pulling and pinching while she thrust deeper and deeper, Charlotte felt that fear fade away, the block a distant memory as she felt herself start to let go.

"Don't stop, Lexi. Don't stop," she panted against Lexi's mouth, unwilling to separate long enough to breathe because she didn't dare lose this feeling or dim the lightning that was running through her with every roll of her hips and stroke of Lexi's fingers inside her.

"Never." Lexi brushed against her lips and with a firm twist of Charlotte's nipple, she sent her tumbling over the precipice into ecstasy, one continuous tremor after the next.

Charlotte cried out but Lexi didn't stop, instead meeting her roll for roll, slowing but not stopping to drag out what Charlotte would describe was easily the best and longest orgasm of her fucking life. And she could die right here, right now, because nothing could top this moment, ever.

After what seemed like an eternity, the aftershocks began to fade. Charlotte was only barely aware of Lexi slipping out of her, but that was mainly because she was overwhelmed by the feeling of Lexi scooping her up into her arms and rolling her to rest on Lexi's chest.

Charlotte closed her eyes and breathed in Lexi's scent. Her flushed cheek rested against the warm skin of Lexi's clavicle, and she'd never been more comfortable.

"Hey, Lex." She kissed the skin in front of her before settling into the crook of Lexi's arm and snuggling closer, catching her breath and letting her body come down.

"Yes?" Lexi kissed the top of her head and her heart melted.

"You just gave me the orgasm of a lifetime."

Lexi laughed and the sound vibrated against her cheek. "Curse broken, huh?"

"Obliterated." Charlotte looked up at the bright eyes regarding her with affection. Her heart swelled another size or two.

"That's good, right?" Lexi's smile told her she was very aware of what she had just done.

"Very good. The best even." Charlotte leaned forward until her lips were nearly on Lexi's before she added, "Just one thing, though?"

"What's that?" Lexi leaned forward to kiss her, but Charlotte pulled back.

"I'm not done yet."

Lexi's smile broadened. "Ready for more?"

"So ready." Charlotte nodded. She shifted so she was on top this time, and she traced her fingers along Lexi's naked torso as she spoke. "But first, I have a really important question."

Lexi's eyes fluttered closed at her touch. "Hmm?"

Charlotte took a moment to appreciate the beauty beneath her, the way Lexi's lips parted when Charlotte touched her hip and the way she bit her bottom lip when Charlotte tugged at the offending fabric covering what she was so desperate to feel and see. It was a glorious visual. One that she had no intention of forgetting anytime soon. "Do you taste as good as I remember?"

Lexi's eyes opened and the lust on her face told Charlotte everything she needed to know.

"Let's find out, shall we?" Charlotte licked her lips and directed her attention lower. Because tonight was just getting started, and she was definitely all right with that.

## CHAPTER SEVENTEEN

L exi was fine being in control and taking the lead because Charlotte had been so vulnerable and honest with her before. But also because she knew she had a goal and a focus, and she knew she couldn't let herself get caught up in Charlotte because this woman was even hotter than she remembered and her touch felt like fire on her skin. She wanted to be engulfed by her.

So it should have come as no surprise to anyone, least of all to herself, that the mere notion that Charlotte might go down on her right now was sending her into a blind panic. A sexy super-turned-on panic, but a panic, nonetheless.

Because she could be brave and lead and give Charlotte what she needed, but could she do this? Could she feel that tongue inside her and still be okay afterward? Because this was uncharted territory and what the fuck was Charlotte doing because that was really distracting and—

Charlotte's tongue dragged across the crotch of her panties and she forgot how to think. "Fuck."

"Get these out of the way and I'll do just that." Charlotte pulled at the band of her underwear with her teeth, and Lexi wasn't sure she'd ever be the same.

She lifted her hips and Charlotte discarded them off to the side, pausing only for a moment before lowering herself between Lexi's legs. "You're gorgeous." Her lips closed over Lexi's clit, and Lexi reached out to stroke her hair, half because she needed to feel grounded, and the other half to make sure this wasn't a dream.

Charlotte looked up at her and lapped at her sex, her eyes never leaving Lexi's. It was easily the hottest thing she'd ever seen.

"Yes, like that." Lexi lifted her hips and rocked against Charlotte's mouth, her body clenching and releasing in anticipation of Charlotte's tongue entering her. She wanted that, to feel her inside. "Deeper, Charlotte."

Charlotte nodded and smiled against her sex before she slid inside, and the slow, controlled thrusts of her tongue drove Lexi crazy. She gripped at her hair and rolled against her face again.

"There's the hair pulling I've been waiting for." Charlotte slipped out long enough to egg her on before sliding her tongue in deeper.

Lexi pulled on Charlotte's hair and was rewarded with Charlotte's fingers on her clit while her tongue continued to lavish attention to Lexi's core. She was so turned on that she wouldn't last long. The anticipation of tonight had been coursing through her long before she found herself alone with Charlotte. And so far, she'd been more than pleased with the outcome.

Lexi's leg started to shake next to Charlotte's cheek, and Charlotte paused long enough to ask, "Can I touch myself while you come in my mouth? It's kinda been something I'm dying to do."

"Jesus fuck, Charlotte." Lexi barely strung those words together as she watched Charlotte's free hand slip between her legs, her hips bobbing while she licked and sucked on Lexi's clit. The sensations would have gotten her there regardless, but the image of Charlotte fucking herself with her face in Lexi's pussy was more than she could take, and she came hard and fast against Charlotte's mouth.

Charlotte cried out against her lips, and Lexi came again, the vibrations and noises of Charlotte against her bringing her right back to the edge and back again.

She cupped Charlotte's face and eased her away from her sex because it was too much and not enough and she needed to breathe. And kiss that incredible mouth.

"Come here." She guided Charlotte by the jaw up to her mouth, savoring the wetness along her lips and cheeks as she kissed her slow and deep. "You are something else, Charlotte Southwick."

Charlotte purred against her mouth and cuddled up beside her. "That's a good thing, right?"

"A very good thing. The best, even." Lexi parroted Charlotte's phrase from earlier and dropped her head back against the pillow with a laugh. "Damn, girl. Just, damn."

Charlotte shifted next to her and maneuvered the covers out from under them as she moved to Lexi's side again, pulling the comforter over them both. "My thoughts exactly."

Lexi closed her eyes as her heartbeat began to slow. She soaked up the feeling of Charlotte's weight against her. It was intoxicating.

"And just so you know"—Charlotte kissed her jaw and she turned to meet her lips—"you taste better than I remember."

Lexi moaned and Charlotte kissed her deeper. "Charlotte," she warned.

"What? Do you have somewhere else to be?" Charlotte straddled her hips, and the comforter pooled at her waist, her green eyes sparkling in challenge.

"No." Lexi couldn't think of anyplace she'd rather be. "I'm all yours."

"All night," Charlotte said as she bounced on her lap a bit.

Lexi felt the warmth from Charlotte's center glide over her abdomen and she nodded. "All night."

"Then let's not waste it." Charlotte rolled her hips again and Lexi couldn't think of a better way to spend the evening.

"Let's not."

Lexi stretched and her muscles groaned. She looked to her left and took in the glorious sight of Charlotte still sleeping, naked, on her side, facing away from her. Her dark hair fanned over the white pillow case and the comforter slipped off her shoulder in such a way that it almost looked intentional. She was quietly sleeping, and Lexi was glad to have tired her out, a feat that had taken most of the night, not that Lexi was complaining. It was as if Charlotte had had some sexual rebirth, like she couldn't be satiated. And if she was being honest, Lexi fucking loved it. She loved getting reacquainted with Charlotte's body. It was both familiar and different, but still fantastic.

Kissing Charlotte, feeling her over her and under her, felt like coming home. And a part of her felt reawakened, too. She'd never been a lover who cherished closeness or cuddling. She'd always been one to tango and slip away, but this was different. It hadn't even occurred to her to slip out and head back to her quarters. That wasn't even an option. She'd spent the few hours they weren't fooling around, wrapped up in Charlotte's limbs, kissing her while she slept, or being tickled awake by Charlotte nuzzling her neck. It was scary how quickly she'd slipped into bed and into old habits with Charlotte.

But she wasn't scared. Not exactly, anyway. She wanted last night to last forever, but there was something magical about this quiet, serene morning that tugged at her heartstrings. The breeze from the private balcony cooled the Caribbean air just enough to warrant a blanket on their naked skin, but not enough to stir the beauty sleeping beside her.

The ocean was a hypnotizing blue from her vantage point on the bed. She wanted to bask in it for a few minutes, the quiet and the beauty. She didn't often have the chance to appreciate this view. She wanted to savor it.

She slipped out of the bed and grabbed one of the honeymoon robes that lay draped across the chaise at the bottom of the bed. She was pleasantly surprised how easily she and Charlotte reconnected in the bedroom. They'd had no trouble sparking that flame. Chemistry had never been something they'd lacked, and clearly that hadn't changed. She pulled on the plush robe and grabbed a few mints from the abandoned dessert tray before she stepped through the slider. She lowered herself onto one of the waiting lounge chairs and let the coolness of the mint on her tongue wake her up a little more.

In the serenity of the vastness before her, she let her mind wander. First, to last night, but then, to the next few days. Her time with Charlotte was winding down, and though she'd successfully been able to ignore that while they were together last night, the new day brought one less with Charlotte. It was a bittersweet realization.

"I could really use a pep talk, Dad." She looked up at the only cloud in the sky, giving it a wave. "I think I'm getting in over my head."

She thought about her father and how she'd often asked his advice over the years. She'd felt that he'd answered her in some way or another, like he'd sent her luck or some small signs to know he cared. That he'd heard her struggling. She hoped for a sign like that now, now that her heart ached in a way it hadn't in a long time. The way seeing Charlotte again opened old wounds but also gave her peace. The way time was ticking away, and she wasn't sure she could slow it like she wanted to.

"I don't want to lose her again, Dad. I just found her. I feel like I found a part of myself along the way, too. Like I'd lost some." She looked up at that cloud and shook her head. Her emotions were all over the place. Charlotte's reappearance in her life reminded her of the time that had passed and the anniversary that was fast approaching. "It'll be ten years this year, Dad. Ten years since you're gone. That's a lifetime."

Charlotte stepped onto the balcony wearing a robe similar to Lexi's and sat at the edge of the lounge chair, facing her. "I wasn't sure if you'd still be here."

Lexi reached out and intertwined their fingers. "Is that why you were so averse to sleep last night? Were you afraid the morning would bring an empty bed?"

Charlotte laughed and took one of the mints Lexi had placed beside her, popping it into her mouth and closing her eyes as she sucked it. "No. Not consciously, anyway." She looked up at her. "Mostly I just couldn't get enough of you."

Lexi scooted over and pulled Charlotte into the space next to her. She leaned forward and kissed Charlotte's lips, laughing when Charlotte slipped the mint into her mouth with her tongue. "Thank you."

"For the mint? Or the sex?" Charlotte looped her arms around Lexi's neck and nuzzled her nose.

"Both." Lexi let herself enjoy the moment. "You're very generous."

"And you have incredible stamina." Charlotte pressed a brief kiss to her lips before she cuddled into her side.

"I work out." Lexi wrapped her arm around Charlotte and looked out at the water. The day was already underway and she'd have to leave soon.

Charlotte's hand slipped between the lapels of her robe and stroked her stomach. "I noticed that."

Lexi closed her eyes and let herself enjoy the tender swirls Charlotte made against her abdomen. "What else did you notice?"

"I noticed that you hold your breath before you come, like you're saving energy."

Lexi laughed. "Do I?"

"Mm-hmm," Charlotte continued, "and I noticed that you stayed close to me all night, never letting me get too far away. You had a hand or an arm around me the whole time. I liked that."

"You're very touchable." Lexi deflected a bit. She was feeling a little exposed.

"I noticed that you snore a little—"

"I do not." Lexi scoffed but Charlotte kissed away her frown.

"You do. It's adorable."

"Agree to disagree." Lexi closed her eyes again as the pattern of Charlotte's touch changed.

Charlotte's swirls broadened until her palm rested flat against Lexi's stomach. It was warm and felt lovely. "I noticed that you look almost hungry when you kiss me. And that look intensifies by about a million when you touch me. And I noticed that it feels unbelievable to be looked at in that way. Like I'm the most beautiful person you've ever seen. Which can't be true because you work in literal paradise, yet it feels true."

"You are." Lexi looked at her and was surprised by how vulnerable Charlotte appeared in that moment. "It is true. You are the most beautiful person I've ever seen. You just…you *do* something to me. I can't explain it. I know you and yet I'm rediscovering you, too. And that is beautiful in itself."

Charlotte cocked her head and smiled.

"What?"

"You're very much the romantic." She tugged Lexi's hand up to her chest and pressed their joined hands to the skin there. "That's something new. You were always sweet and thoughtful and romantic, but now, now you're like this incredibly deep, introspective, amazing human being. It's wonderful. You're wonderful."

Lexi opened her palm and rested her hand over Charlotte's heart. She felt such a palpable love between them still, more than sex and lust and familiarity, deeper than that. She felt it now, when her heart spoke before her brain could slow it down. Charlotte made her feel things she wasn't ready to feel. She made her feel things she'd tried to ignore and forget.

"I also noticed something else." Charlotte pressed her hand to Lexi's. "I also noticed you talk to the clouds."

Lexi smiled. "I was talking to my dad."

"What about?" Charlotte's voice was soft.

"You. And what to do with you," Lexi replied candidly.

"Do you often ask him for sex tips?" Charlotte teased.

Lexi slid her hand up to cup Charlotte's cheek. She trailed her eyes over her face, soaking her in. "No, I don't think I need any guidance in that department. We seemed to pick up where we left off rather easily, don't you think?"

"Oh, I think we've gotten much better at that stuff," Charlotte replied. "But I'm willing to test that theory lots more. If you're up for it."

Lexi kissed her and rested their foreheads together. "I feel confident that I couldn't have enough sex with you in a lifetime. Ever."

"This information pleases me," Charlotte replied and Lexi warmed at her dorkiness. "What did your dad say about me?"

Lexi paused. "He doesn't say much of anything, really. Mostly it's just me babbling into the abyss and trying to sort out my shit that way."

"And this time? What shit is there this time? With me?" Charlotte asked, her expression patient but attentive.

"This is different with you." Lexi motioned between them as she leaned back, regarding Charlotte closely as she spoke. "This feels almost too easy. That worries me."

Charlotte nodded. "I know what you mean."

"Like it's too far, too fast. You know?" Lexi didn't want to give voice to that concern, but she couldn't stop herself either. She owed it to both of them to be honest.

"What do we do? Just...stop?" Charlotte looked like she hated that idea. Lexi did, too.

"I don't think I can." Lexi felt pulled to Charlotte in so many ways. "I don't want to."

"Me, neither," Charlotte replied, before she asked, "So what do we do?"

Lexi shrugged. "I go to work, and you vacation, and we overlap when we can."

"You make that sound so easy." Charlotte frowned.

"It is." Lexi rested her head against the back of the lounge chair and turned to face Charlotte. "It has to be."

"Because you can't fuck the guests," Charlotte replied with a small smile.

"Exactly."

"But you already did," Charlotte pointed out.

"And I plan to again," Lexi said. She did. As much as she could.

Charlotte reached out and slipped her hand beneath the fabric of Lexi's robe again, this time palming at Lexi's naked breast as she spoke. "Then it's decided. Work, vacation, sex. The order of which can be shuffled as necessary."

Lexi nodded. The feeling of Charlotte touching her chest took all of her attention. Words could wait.

"When do you have to leave?" Charlotte's mouth descended on her neck and Lexi felt herself heat up.

"Soon." Lexi turned her head to connect their lips and moaned when Charlotte's playful palming intensified to something much more intentional.

"Then let's make this one quick. Until later. When we can take our time with each other. Sound good?" Charlotte rolled Lexi's nipple between her fingers, and she had to will herself to answer.

"So good."

# CHAPTER EIGHTEEN

*Cruise Day Five: Day at Sea*

Charlotte yawned and shifted lower in her lounge chair, adjusting her linen shirt and undoing a button by her chest. She was wearing her bathing suit, but she hadn't been able to drag herself out of this chair yet today, probably because the view of Lexi from here was spectacular.

"You seem more tired than usual. Late night?" Barb asked from behind a travel magazine.

Charlotte yawned again and shook her head. "Not a ton of sleep. I'll make it up later." She hoped that was a lie.

"Dreaming about little miss hottie bartender all night?" Barb pushed her sunglasses into her hair, and Charlotte noticed the very apparent sunglass tan Barb had honed over the past few days. It suited her—she looked athletic and happy.

"Something like that." Charlotte looked back to the bar and watched Lexi shake what was probably the hundredth cocktail in the past hour. She admired the strong, muscular arms that never seemed to tire, especially last night when she did so much more than daydream about Lexi.

Barb gave her a broad smile and patted her on the shoulder. "I think you should go for it."

Charlotte laughed because she had, multiple times, including this morning on the balcony. "I'll take that under advisement." She changed the topic, this time to Barb's love life. "So, how's Marlene?"

Marlene was the name of the woman Barb had been spending all her free time with. They shared a love for gambling, and Barb had sheepishly mentioned that she thought Marlene was pretty.

Barb looked shy and examined her cuticles. "She's good. We have dinner plans before the dance tonight."

"That sounds fun." Charlotte paused. "What dance tonight?"

Barb gave her a hearty laugh. "The White Party. I hear it's a tradition on these cruises. All the ladies get dressed up in their best white attire and head to the dance club. There's prizes and free drinks and live music. I'm looking forward to it."

Charlotte had totally forgotten about the dance. It had been one of the highlighted events in her cruise information. "Shit."

"You're going, right?" Barb asked as she sat at the edge of the lounger. "I wanted to introduce you to Marlene."

"I, uh, I'm not sure." Charlotte didn't want to commit until she'd talked to Lexi to see if she was off later, but more importantly, she was second-guessing the white outfit she'd packed, out of spite.

Barb frowned but seemed to get over it quickly. "Well, let me know. I'm going to take a quick dip to cool off. I'll be back."

She pulled off her tank top and headed down to the pool, diving in headfirst with sunglasses on and all. Barb was the best.

"She's got a serious stroke of luck this week." Lexi's voice sounded to her right.

"Oh?" Charlotte turned, happy to hear her.

Lexi took a seat on Barb's lounger and continued, "Rumor has it she's been cleaning house at the tables in the casino. She won a pretty snazzy excursion in Curaçao the other night—I think they just want her off the ship, to be honest. So she stops taking all their money."

Charlotte took off her sunglasses and folded them, placed them by her side, and reached out to discreetly run her fingers along the outside of Lexi's thigh. "Curaçao, huh?"

"Tomorrow's stop." Lexi pushed her thigh into Charlotte's touch before shifting away. "Still want to explore the island together?"

Charlotte laughed. "You know how I feel about Curaçao. I'm positively thrilled to see none of it."

"It's a beautiful island—you should see *some* of it," Lexi replied. "I can show you some of the most popular sights."

"As long as at least one of them includes you naked, then I'm good," Charlotte said.

Lexi gave her a once-over. "I'm sure we can work something out."

"Good." Charlotte noticed for the first time that Lexi had a tray with her. "What's that?"

"Ah, sustenance. And hydration." Lexi pulled the tray onto her lap and pointed to its contents. "A Miami Vice for your friend and a mango daiquiri for you, because vacation. Water for you both to stay hydrated in the hot sun. And chicken fingers and french fries for you because you've been watching me at the bar all day and haven't eaten anything."

Charlotte accepted the bounty and replied, "That sounded judgy. And you'd only know that if you were also watching *me* all day."

"Point taken." Lexi produced three ketchup packets from her pocket. "And it's not judgy—I just want to ensure you have enough energy for later."

Charlotte let out a grateful squeal at the appearance of her favorite condiment and popped a fry into her mouth. "These are delicious." She paused. "What's happening later?"

Lexi took a fry and shook her head. "Did you listen to anything we discussed this morning on the balcony?"

"You mean before or after you started moaning and writhing? Because anything that wasn't that part was boring, and maybe I zoned out." Charlotte shrugged.

Lexi took a sip of her water and stretched. "Okay, well, I mentioned that I'd misplaced my schedule for the eightieth time and wasn't positive, but since I've located it, I'm now positive that I'm working the party tonight."

"Boo." Charlotte frowned. "That does not sound like something conducive to us getting room service in my room. Together. Emphasis on the *service* part."

Lexi smiled and Charlotte forgot why she felt sad. "That means I'm going to be working the bar at the White Party tonight. So you should come down and dance and be near me, so I can flirt with you all night until I'm off—"

"And can get off with me afterward, right?" Charlotte was skipping some steps, but she didn't care.

"Exactly." Lexi leaned in and lowered her voice to say, "You know, I've had a long-standing tradition of packing at this party. Usually I do it for tips and because it's fun, but tonight, maybe tonight I'm doing it because I want you to know I'm doing it."

Charlotte stopped midchew because…was Lexi saying what she

thought she was saying? "Seriously?"

Lexi shrugged. "I guess you'll have to go to the party to find out."

Well, that changed things. "I'll be there."

"I was hoping you'd say that." Lexi glanced over her shoulder at the bar. "I should head back—people look thirsty."

"We're on the ocean. There's water everywhere. They'll survive." Charlotte didn't want Lexi to go.

Lexi gave her a knowing look. "You and I both know that there is only so long we can keep this conversation PG out here. Especially if you keep unbuttoning that shirt."

Charlotte looked down. "My tits do look fantastic right now, don't they?"

"Yes, they do. Which is why I have to go over there, away from you, because they're very distracting." Lexi stood up and took the now empty tray between her hands. "One more thing…"

"Yes?" Charlotte intentionally leaned forward.

Lexi's eyes followed the movement. "That text app I put on your cell last night only works if you check your phone."

"Oh, right." Properly chastised, Charlotte leaned back and pulled her cell out of her bag. The screen showed four missed messages from Lexi asking her if she was hungry or needed a drink. "Sorry."

"It's okay. I was looking for a reason to come over here anyway." Lexi gave her a small wave and started walking toward the bar. "See you later."

Charlotte watched her walk away, because she could.

"Is it safe to come back now?" Barb's presence beside her made her jump.

"What?"

Barb sat back on the lounge chair, water dripping from her swim trunks as she motioned toward the bar. "I saw your friend here, so I stayed in the water a bit longer. What'd I miss?"

"Not much." Charlotte played coy. "Except for maybe I *am* going to the White Party tonight."

"Awesome." Barb stole a fry and gave Charlotte a high-five as she accepted her drink. "It's gonna be epic."

Charlotte raised her glass in cheers and hoped Barb was right.

❖

Lexi exhaled as she closed the door to her room. She was tired, happy but tired.

"Fancy seeing you here." Zara's playful tone greeted her. "I assume the morning food cart pickup by Enrique went well?"

"Like a well-oiled machine," she said with a smile.

"What's next on the agenda?" Zara asked.

"Gotta freshen up before the dance tonight." Lexi already had her shirt half over her head when Zara spoke. She had enough time to squeeze in a quick nap and a shower before the second part of her shift started, if she didn't dillydally, that was.

"Nice hickey," Zara said.

Lexi froze, the bottom of her shirt still covering part of her head. "What hickey?"

"The one on your chest. Just a bit north of your nipple, I'd say." Zara sounded amused.

Lexi struggled to get the rest of her shirt off and looked down at her sports bra clad chest. "Damn."

"I'll say," Zara replied, "That one's gonna be there for a bit."

Lexi admired Charlotte's work. "A memento."

"Have you given that any thought? The afterward stuff?" Zara's tone was gentle, but her questions pierced Lexi all the same.

"Yes. Off and on. It's hard to ignore." Lexi plopped down on her bunk, arms stretched over her head. She played back this morning's introspection before Charlotte joined her on the balcony. "It's going to gut me, I think."

"Then don't let it." Zara sat up and Lexi looked at her.

"How?"

"Don't let her go." Zara shrugged.

"What, like, kidnap her?" Lexi wasn't sure what she meant.

"That sounds like a crime. But also, kind of kinky." Zara seemed to consider this. "Not what I was getting at, though."

"You mean, like, just get off the ship? And leave my life behind?" Lexi sat up and looked at her.

"No one said that, Pessimistic Patty." Zara rolled her eyes. "I'm just saying, maybe this doesn't have to end after the cruise docks. Maybe you two can carry on a long-distance relationship."

"A long-distance international relationship, you mean. One where I don't have a mailing address that's not a PO box and where I'm in a different country almost daily." Lexi sighed.

"You'll find a way to make it work, if you want it to." Zara's gaze didn't falter. She was giving Lexi her serious face. Lexi was very familiar with this face. This face meant she should pay attention and heed Zara's advice. "Do you want to?"

"Of course," Lexi answered before she'd thought about the words. But she did. She didn't want to give Charlotte up. "But how?"

"Well, that's the hard part, right?" Zara yawned. "You have to find out if you're compatible outside of vacation mode."

"Vacation mode?"

"Yeah, Charlotte's free and clear right now. She's in paradise. Real life is a distant memory, until it's not," Zara replied. "You, on the other hand, are in real life. This is your life—a week here, a week there. You live a mobile existence. Thousands of new faces cross your path on a weekly basis. It's different."

"It sounds so, I don't know, *empty* when you say it like that." She might be projecting here, just a bit, and she acknowledged that.

"Well, is it?" Zara turned the question back to her again. That was an annoying habit she'd had of late.

"It didn't seem that way." Lexi flopped back onto her side. "But it probably will now that I know Charlotte is out there, existing and being perfect without me."

Zara yawned again. "Right. So maybe consider having the talk about continuing the relationship after the cruise. Maybe it's more possible than you think."

Lexi yawned, because it was clearly infectious, and squinted at Zara. "I know why I'm tired. But why are you tired? And why are you spreading those yawns like a contagion?"

"I was up late on the phone last night." Zara covered her mouth to stifle another yawn. "You remember my ex, Johann?"

"The track star from community college?" Lexi had heard about him a few times, but only during moments of nostalgia from Zara.

"Well, I got to thinking that I should look him up." She crawled under the covers and settled against her pillow. "Since I'm going to be back home and all. And…" She looked a little sheepish as she said, "I've seen what reconnecting with Charlotte has been like for you. Maybe I'll find the same luck with Johann. Lord knows I could use a good lay."

Lexi crawled under her own covers and mulled that over. "If it could be anything like the night I had last night, then you'd better skip visiting your sister and head back home posthaste."

"Stop bragging." Zara rolled over. "We have only so much time to nap. And I think we both could use it."

"You won't hear any arguments from me." Lexi closed her eyes and let the wonderful fatigue from last night wash over her. She didn't regret a minute of it. Not now, anyway.

## CHAPTER NINETEEN

Charlotte sat at the edge of her bed and tried to quiet the panic that was brewing. "You can do this. You have to do this. You don't have any other choice because you packed like a spiteful asshole and this is what you've got to work with."

She looked at the second suitcase she'd packed but had yet to open. This had been a last-minute decision. She'd packed this after a particularly heated argument with Veronica, but she was regretting that now. Not the argument—Veronica was being a total bitch—but maybe the whole let's-bring-this-along-it-won't-be-weird thing. She'd done this in a fury, and with a clear head, her decision seemed rash.

"Well, at least it's white." She unzipped the suitcase and pulled out the wedding dress she'd never had a chance to wear. "And you paid for it to sit in your fucking closet like an overpriced eyesore, so you might as well wear it."

She pulled out the gown and draped it across the bed. The bed she'd shared with Lexi last night. A bed that remained unmade because she didn't want housekeeping to come in and notice anything out of the ordinary, just in case there was some evidence of Lexi in the room. Which she knew there was lots of, since she and Lexi had *really* utilized all the spaces in here. She was just being cautious. The last thing she wanted was to bring any trouble to Lexi.

Lexi. Who had been on her mind since the moment she'd been wheeled out the door this morning and, especially, since she'd talked with her earlier by the pool. Charlotte felt that familiar tightening in her abdomen. Just the prospect of what Lexi had proposed turned her on. She was in deep and she knew it.

She looked at the dress, her gorgeous custom-made dress, and sighed. The hand-sewn details and beading made it one of a kind.

She'd picked every piece of fabric and tulle—this was her dream dress, through and through. And right now, she was extra happy she'd splurged and made sure it was a convertible one: poufy and over the top for her walk down the aisle that never happened, but sleek and sexy for the reception that had gone to waste. She disconnected the formal and elegant frilly top skirt and put it back in the suitcase. The cocktail length gown that remained was still magnificent, but much less pomp and circumstance-y. She could totally wear this to a fancy White Party tonight, and yeah, it was a wedding dress, but it was way less of a wedding dress without the flowing skirt and train attached.

She faced the mirror and held the sweetheart neckline against her chest. "Oh, Charlotte," she said to her reflection, "how did we end up here?"

She swayed side to side and let the dress flow back and forth, the expensive fabric glistening under the less than flattering overhead lights of the suite. This was a really beautiful dress, even under less than beautiful circumstances.

She gave herself one last appraisal in the mirror and placed the dress on a nearby hanger, allowing it to settle and relax into its full perfect shape. She dug in the side pocket of the suitcase and pulled out the gold leaf and pearl hair clips she'd bought, to complement the dress. She'd planned out her hairstyle so many times, she was sure she could do it on the fly now. And though she didn't have a professional stylist or makeup artist with her like she would have had on her big day, she knew she would do a fine job with what she had. She would be absolutely stunning tonight because she deserved to be. And to feel. Because Veronica shouldn't be able to ruin something beautiful, and reconnecting with Lexi reminded her of just that.

After more time than was anticipated, Charlotte hustled down the corridor, headed toward the elevators. Prepping had taken longer than she'd expected, but she figured showing up late to the party was fashionable, right? Not that she had to rush there to meet anyone; she'd had a nice dinner with Barb and her new boo, Marlene, before they'd separated to get changed. They had plans to have drinks together at the party, but nothing set in stone. Except that she would be seeing Lexi. That was guaranteed, and the thought made her walk a little faster.

She was excited to see her, even though a bit of her still felt self-conscious about the whole dress thing. She pressed the button to the elevator at midship and boarded it, lost in her thoughts, eager to get to her destination.

"Ms. Southwick," Captain Correia said to her left. "It's nice to see you again."

"Oh." Charlotte hadn't realized there was anyone in the elevator car with her. She tensed. "Hello again, Captain."

"You look nice. Are you headed to the dance?" Correia's expression was friendly, but not overly friendly like last night. Charlotte relaxed a bit.

"I am." She regarded the captain, who was wearing a more formal version of the white uniform she had seen the other night. "Are you as well?"

Correia looked embarrassed. "I am, but just to drop by. I have dinner plans with my colleague here." She motioned to another person in the car that Charlotte had been completely oblivious to, a smaller bookish and serious looking red-haired woman who appeared to be about the captain's age. "This is Staff Captain Sally Dashel. Sally"— she addressed the captain—"this is Charlotte Southwick, one of our VIPs this week."

Sally pushed her glasses up her nose and nodded. "It's nice to meet you."

"You as well." Charlotte shook her hand and crossed her arms, trying to distract from the whole wedding dress outfit and all. "Where are you headed to dinner afterward?"

"Oh, the Officers' Lounge," Correia replied.

"Fun." Charlotte breathed a sigh of relief when the elevator door opened and saved her from making any more awkward small talk. "Well, I guess I'll see you inside. Have a good night."

"You, too." Correia gave her a small wave and Charlotte ducked out the door, turning toward the sound of the music coming from down the hall.

She caught sight of the officers leaving the elevator behind her in the large mirror on the wall and swore she saw them hold hands briefly before exiting the doors. But she was probably imagining that because she was eager to see Lexi and hold her hand, and other things, like immediately. Lexi had her feeling some sort of way, it seemed.

"You made it." Barb's voice called out from the entrance to the club. "Wowee. That's some dress."

Charlotte curtsied and pulled her friend into a hug. "Where's Marlene?"

Barb blushed and Charlotte thought it was adorable. "She went to the bathroom, I'm just waiting for her."

"You are such a gentlewoman," Charlotte teased. "I'm going to head in and get a drink. Meet you there?"

"Yeah." Barb opened the door for her, and Charlotte was immediately met with loud, thumping beats from the dance floor inside. Barb raised her voice to add, "We have a little table with some of the casino crew off to the right by the stage. Stop by and say hi."

"Will do." Charlotte slipped through the doors and stepped into the darkened room. Strobe lights flashed on the periphery and a smoke machine was working somewhere nearby, pumping a subtle but seemingly constant fog along the floor. The colorful lights by the stage illuminated the fog, casting a pretty rainbow glow on everything.

Charlotte weaved between the tables and couches of the club, headed toward the main bar in search of Lexi, when Enrique's voice on speakers overhead caught her attention.

"Okay, ladies!" He cheered, and Charlotte moved to get a better view of him on the mainstage, in his go-go dancing booty shorts glory. "It's time to play a few games. We'll be giving out prizes for the best dancer. First up is a good old-fashioned Macarena. Who's with me?"

Charlotte was surprised by how many people cheered around her. But she was even more surprised by the number of people that moved toward the dance floor.

"Let's go, Charlotte." Barb appeared at her side and grabbed her arm, pulling her toward the center of the room.

"The Macarena?" Charlotte shook her head. "I'll pass, thanks."

"C'mon," Barb said, as she flashed her best puppy-dog eyes. "Don't make me look like a fool out there. I'm trying to woo a pretty lady."

As if on cue, Marlene waved from a nearby table, filled with people Charlotte assumed were the casino crew members Barb mentioned before. The woman in the white dress shirt with the diamond and heart embroidery on the chest pocket was sort of a dead giveaway. Charlotte had no idea there were such hard-core gamblers on this ship. Barb seemed to have hit the jackpot, in every sense of the word. She was glad her friend was having such a good time this week.

"Fine." Charlotte relented and allowed herself to be pulled toward the dance floor. "But only because Marlene is so sweet, and I think you two are cute together."

Barb gave her a broad smile. "I think so, too."

"All right ladies, get in position—here we go!" Enrique called out and that familiar, annoyingly catchy song started up. As the women around her started to flap their arms and sway side to side, Charlotte started to second-guess this decision.

"Oh no." Barb reached for her hand and pulled her back in line. "You're not leaving me yet. Live a little. It's vacation."

Charlotte laughed and stepped back in line because Barb was right and she was already in a wedding dress at a White Party, so what did it matter if she couldn't get the moves right or if she sort of hated this song. It was all about having a good time. And as she got up on tiptoe for a better view of the main bar and hopefully a Lexi sighting, she anticipated just how good a time could be waiting for her.

❖

The party had been well underway for over two hours now, but Lexi still hadn't seen Charlotte. She checked and rechecked her phone for any messages, but she found none. She was starting to think that maybe, just maybe, she'd been stood up.

She adjusted the belt of her pants and shifted self-consciously. She might have chosen a smaller piece if she'd realized that was a possibility. Though she was holding out hope that it wasn't, and maybe Charlotte was just late.

"This is a thirsty group," Angela grumbled as she reemerged from the walk-in refrigerator behind the bar. "This is my second refill on cocktail fruits since the party started. It's like everyone is trying to avoid scurvy."

Lexi nodded in agreement. They had been busier than usual today. "I'm just glad I came in early to prep the fruit."

"We might need more." Angela frowned as she refilled the bar top fruit caches. "Or everyone is getting cherries and orange slices only."

"They'll survive." Lexi had made sure to grab an extra jar of cherries from the kitchen when she was on her way here. Charlotte was fresh in her mind when she'd made that decision.

She'd experienced a mix of emotions since her chat with Zara earlier. Though she'd napped hard, waking up had been difficult. And getting notice that her promotion had been approved shortly after waking up had been hard, too. She'd be spending a lot less time behind the bar in the future, a future that didn't include Zara, and one that would surely take her out of her comfort zone. And Charlotte? Would it include Charlotte? She wasn't so sure. Where was Charlotte, anyway?

"Whoa." Angela stopped muddling the drink in her hands and nodded toward the dance floor. "You can stop brooding, because your girl is here."

Lexi looked up and felt her jaw drop. Charlotte was dancing in the center of the floor, under the bright lights overhead, moving to the music in a glittering, glowing gown. She looked like a disco ball out there, all shiny and gorgeous. "Holy shit," Lexi muttered. She dropped her hand reflexively to the front of her pants in a gentle caress that sent a surge through her.

"I'll say." Angela reached past her for some fresh mint leaves, and Lexi pulled her hand away from herself. "That girl knows how to make a statement."

Lexi watched Charlotte move until she felt Angela elbow her in the ribs. "Lex, there's a line forming. And you're drooling. Mix, mix, shake, shake, okay?"

"Yeah, sorry." Lexi shook her head and tried to focus on the thirsty patrons in front of her. It appeared that Charlotte had gotten quite a few people's attention, since half the line in front of her was looking back toward the dance floor and not at the bar. She could relate.

"I'll have a mojito," the short-haired brunette across from her called out, "extra lime juice."

"You got it." Lexi grabbed a nearby shaker and tossed in some mint leaves, forcing herself to keep her eyes on her work for fear of losing focus again, something that seemed inevitable.

Somewhere in the time it took to fill the dozen or so drink orders, she'd lost sight of Charlotte in the mass of people who had filtered onto the dance floor, but as she went to go out in search of her, Captain Correia sidled up to the bar.

"Captain." Lexi gave her a calculated smile. She hadn't seen her since last night, and she wasn't exactly sure where they stood or what the captain remembered about how the evening had ended. Then a smaller yet no less significant fear occurred to her: Would the captain's height advantage and sight line make the bulge she was sporting just below bar height more perceptible? Because that would be embarrassing. And awkward.

She decided to pretend like everything was normal. "What can I get you?"

Correia shook her head and held her hand up in a friendly decline. "Nothing, thanks. I just wanted to stop by to see how the evening was going."

Lexi leaned in to hear her as the sounds from the stage amplified. Enrique was chanting something and wiggling his butt around and everyone seemed to love it, which explained the sudden volume increase.

Lexi called out, "Things are good. Busy. Lots of happy, thirsty guests."

"Good." Correia matched her volume and looked back at the crowd behind her. "Everyone loves a White Party."

"That they do." Lexi opened the dishwasher to her right and a puff of steam came out. This was the fourth wash she'd done this hour alone. The White Party was a notoriously busy event for the ship. It meant all hands on deck, too. She had two floating bars on either side of the room set up to help offset some of the long lines that formed at the main bar. Which reminded her, she should check on their supplies…

"I meant to tell you, thank you for last night." Correia leaned across the bar, her volume more discreet this time.

Lexi nodded, unsure of what to say. "Sure thing. I hope you're feeling better."

"I am." Correia gave her a small smile and motioned over to the end of the bar, where Lexi could just make out the profile of the staff captain. "Things are good. Thanks. I mean that."

Lexi figured the captain was talking about a few things in that moment, and she exhaled a sigh of relief. "Good. I'm glad."

Sally made eye contact with her and Lexi held up an empty glass in her direction, raising her hand in question. "You think she wants a drink?"

Correia was looking at Sally and made no attempt to look at Lexi when she replied, "No, this isn't really her scene. We have a dinner in the Officers' Lounge in a few."

Lexi wondered if it was a private dinner or not, but she had the decency to keep that question to herself. She didn't want to poke the bear or anything. Or spend any more time talking to the freakishly tall captain. Was she taller than usual? Or was Lexi just paranoid?

"Oh, and congrats on the promotion." Correia looked back at her and added, "When do you start the new role?"

"When I get back from vacation," Lexi replied, already feeling anxious about her decision.

"Sounds like the perfect time to start something new, then." Correia gave her a wave as she stepped back from the bar. "Have a good night. Thanks again."

Lexi watched as Correia joined Sally and they both disappeared into the darkened part of the room, in the direction of the club entrance.

"Can I get a mango margarita?" someone asked behind her.

"Sure thing." Lexi looked up and paused, delighted to see who was asking. Charlotte was leaning against the bar, looking incredible, and giving her the once-over. She smiled as she asked, "Is that all you want, miss?"

Charlotte's eyes lingered down by Lexi's crotch before meeting her gaze. "Not by a long shot, but I'll settle for a drink to start."

Lexi grabbed the ingredients and went to work, fully aware that she had a captivated audience just a foot or two away. She made a show of working the shaker and was careful to position Charlotte's glass on the crotch level surface of the beer cooler while she slowly drained the shaker's contents into the cup. She was pleased when Charlotte's attention never faltered.

She popped two cherries on the top and handed the glass across the bar, shivering when Charlotte rubbed their fingers together as she took the drink.

"Thank you very much." Charlotte's lips closed over the straw and Lexi's mind went somewhere dirty.

She watched her with rapt attention and leaned forward, the bulge in her pants bumping the beer cooler and sending a shock wave through her center. She slapped her hands to the bar's surface to steady herself.

"Something distracting you?" Charlotte glanced down at her pants while she licked her lips, and Lexi wondered if she could casually vault the bar's surface to get closer to her. Though she wasn't feeling anything casual about the look Charlotte was giving her.

"You, mostly." Lexi dropped her hand to her pants and gripped the bulge for Charlotte's benefit, though she'd be lying if she said she hadn't enjoyed the brief friction for herself, as well. "But this is a little distracting, too. I guess."

Charlotte's lips parted and she raised an eyebrow as she said, "That doesn't look all that *little* from here."

Lexi grabbed the toy through her pants and pulled on it with more force, rocking her hips forward and savoring the sensation against her clit as she replied, "I think you'll be more than satisfied, if that's a concern of yours."

Charlotte sucked on the straw of her drink for a moment before she replied, "No concerns here."

"Good." Lexi shifted and returned her hand to the bar's surface, mirroring the position of the other one. "You look amazing tonight."

Charlotte placed the near-empty glass on the bar and pushed it toward her. "And you look positively fuckable tonight. But thank you for the compliment."

Lexi groaned when Charlotte took a tied cherry stem out of her mouth and dropped it into the abandoned glass. The mouth on that woman was something else entirely.

"How much longer are you behind that bar?" Charlotte asked, her intentions as loud as an air siren.

"I have to go check the inventory on the bars in the back in a few, so just as long as it takes me to work through that line, I'd say." Lexi pointed toward the now seven-person-deep line that had formed behind Charlotte.

"Hurry up, Lex," Charlotte said as she stepped aside for the next person to place a drink order. "Nobody likes to wait."

Lexi watched Charlotte walk away and deliberately leaned against the beer cooler while she did it. She had every intention of sharing the amazingness of the friction she felt right now with Charlotte later, a later that couldn't come soon enough.

## CHAPTER TWENTY

Charlotte wasn't sure how much longer she could wait. When Lexi had told her that she'd be slipping out from behind the bar what seemed like an eternity ago, all she could think about was Lexi slipping into *her*. Something that was impossible if every single woman in this room kept going up to the bar. For fuck's sake, didn't they have any other bartenders on this ship?

Needless to say, the last twenty minutes had felt like a lifetime, and she was anxious to see and feel Lexi again. Now would be a good time.

She left her spot on the couch near Barb and her casino crew because she needed to move. Or scream. Or rub one out. Neither of the last two seemed socially appropriate, so she decided to check out one of the smaller bars and wait for Lexi there.

As she headed toward the bar closest to the club entrance, she finally caught sight of her favorite bartender. Lexi was holding a tray and delivering drinks to one of the VIP tables at the edge of the dance floor.

Charlotte made sure to position herself right in Lexi's way as she turned to leave.

"There you are." Lexi looked relieved before her expression changed to turned on, which Charlotte appreciated.

"Been looking for me?" Charlotte wanted nothing more than to be pinned to the wall to their right, but she knew that wasn't possible. She settled for flirting and driving up that tension eight more notches, because she loved it and she knew that Lexi did, too.

"Always," Lexi said in that sexy tone that made Charlotte weak.

Charlotte wanted to reach out and take Lexi's free hand, and something told her if she did, Lexi wouldn't resist the contact, but it wasn't worth it. Right?

Lexi took a step forward and Charlotte's heartbeat picked up. "Walk with me."

She matched Lexi's cadence and followed her as Lexi led them to the nearby bar. Lexi stood at the corner, halfway between the front of the bar and the entrance area to where the bartenders were working, and she guided Charlotte to her immediate right, facing her forward, with her abdomen pressed to the bar's edge.

"Two shots of tequila, Derrick," Lexi called out, and the handsome brunet behind the bar nodded.

"Who are those for?" Charlotte asked.

"Us." Lexi placed the empty serving tray on the bar top in front of Charlotte.

Charlotte felt Lexi's hand under the bar caress her leg and play with the hem of her dress. She dropped her hand instinctively to reach for Lexi's, but she gasped when Lexi guided her hand to the bulge in her pants. "Oh."

"Lime and some salt?" Derrick placed the two shots on the tray Lexi had placed in front of her and waited for their reply.

"Absolutely. Extra lime, just enough salt." Lexi didn't let on that she was encouraging Charlotte to grope her under the bar top. Charlotte would have complimented her on her ability to maintain her cool if she wasn't otherwise engaged.

Derrick left the requested ingredients and headed to the other end of the much quieter bar to take a few drink orders. Charlotte was glad they were alone again.

Lexi bit her lip as she made eye contact with Charlotte again. "You have no idea how good that feels."

Charlotte pulled a little harder. "Oh, I'm sure it'll feel even better when we're alone. Which is when, exactly? Because this teasing is getting me awfully riled up."

Lexi's hand found Charlotte's hip after Charlotte intentionally rubbed aggressively against her crotch. "Soon."

"How soon?" Charlotte moved her hand up to toy with the button at Lexi's waist. She reveled in the way Lexi canted her hips forward in response.

"Fuck, Charlotte. You aren't making this easy." Lexi's complaint contained no bark, but Charlotte pulled her hand back just the same. It was getting hard to behave.

"Sorry, not sorry." She brought her hand up to the bar, a safe distance from where she'd like it to be. "You know, if you asked, I'd get up on this bar right now and let you have your way with me in front of all these unsuspecting guests. Just FYI."

Lexi let out a shaky breath and shook her head. "You're going to be the death of me."

"You're the one who told me you were packing and put my hand there." Charlotte shrugged. "The way I see it, I'm just showing my appreciation to your sexually adventurous side by consenting to you fucking me in public."

Lexi looked stunned. "I need a drink."

"Lucky for you there appear to be two already waiting." Charlotte smiled, pleased to see the effect she was having on Lexi. If only Lexi knew the effect she was having on her.

"Give me your hand." Lexi held out her hand and waited for Charlotte to comply.

"Didn't we just discuss this? That's a dangerous request," Charlotte teased but complied all the same.

Lexi took her hand and brought it to her lips, licking a strip along the back of Charlotte's hand from the knuckle of her forefinger to the base of her thumb, and Charlotte thought she might faint. Lexi pulled back and dashed some salt over the area before handing Charlotte a lime and sliding a shot toward her. "Lick, sip, suck."

Charlotte raised the shot glass in cheers as she waited for Lexi to get her shot ready as well. Lexi made a show of licking her own hand, and Charlotte got the feeling that the tables had turned between them. She liked it.

"Ready?" Lexi asked.

"More and more by the second. Especially if you keep licking me like that," Charlotte replied honestly.

"Good," Lexi said as they took their shots together.

Charlotte squeezed her eyes shut as the tequila burned its way down her throat and the salt and lime dulled the taste on her tongue, pulling the tartness of the fruit to the forefront of her palate. She wasn't a typical shot taker, but she'd do that again with Lexi anytime.

"Just so you know"—Lexi's lips were by her ear—"I intend to lick you like that again later, right before I fill you."

"Lex." Charlotte opened her eyes and Lexi pulled back, a wicked grin on her face.

"Soon." She squeezed her hand before waving Derrick back over and rattling off a drink order.

Charlotte felt exposed in that moment, like anyone watching could see how fast her heart was beating in her chest, or how hard it was to catch her breath. Lexi had a way of bringing her from zero to a hundred with seemingly no effort at all. She thought she was turned on before, but she was wrong.

"I have to finish up here—the party is going to start to wind down." Lexi glanced toward the dance floor and motioned to the seated guests on the couches around the stage area. "It'll be drink heavy for a bit before the lights come on and the water starts pouring, so I'll be tied up awhile more. But..." Lexi paused, looking back at her. "I'd like to see you after, maybe finish what we started here."

Charlotte's eyes fell involuntarily to Lexi's pants. She blinked them shut with a laugh. "Sounds great."

"Look at me—I want to tell you something," Lexi implored.

Charlotte opened her eyes and found herself blown away by the affection in Lexi's. She was closer now, her voice softer, almost inaudible with the loud singing and music behind them. "You look incredible tonight, beyond incredible, really. The only thing getting me through tonight is knowing that I'll get to end it wrapped up in you. Buried deep inside you. Kissing those perfect lips until you tell me to stop. So it'll be soon. Okay? Because I don't think I can wait much longer."

Charlotte had no words. Lots of feelings, but no words. She placed her hand over her heart to will it to slow long enough for her to string words together.

Lexi gave her a knowing smile. "I love that you still do that."

Charlotte frowned as she found her voice. "I hate that I can't kiss you right now."

"Kiss me later. Kiss me all night." Lexi took the drinks from Derrick and loaded her tray, spacing them out in a way that Charlotte supposed would help her balance them. "I'll message you when I'm headed your way."

"Okay." Charlotte watched Lexi walk back toward the tables, thinking how much she'd like to kiss her forever.

"Can I get you anything else?" Derrick's voice broke her from her reverie.

"No, thanks." She couldn't have what she wanted, anyway. At least, not for more time than she was willing to be patient for, annoyingly. As much as she enjoyed the naughtiness of sneaking around, a part of her wanted to luxuriate unabashedly in Lexi's affections. She wanted to hold her hand and sit on her lap. She wanted to feel like Lexi was hers, for keeps and not just temporarily. But that didn't seem possible. Right? Or could it be? She vowed to talk to Lexi tomorrow when they could be together in Curaçao. Not just behind closed doors, stealing kisses and touches in fleeting moments. It surprised her how much she was looking forward to tomorrow, especially with the promise of what was to come tonight.

She let herself get lost in her thoughts as she made her way back to Barb and company. If Lexi was going to message her, she'd better be by her phone. And since this dress didn't have pockets, that phone was in her room. She'd rather not waste time here and risk missing any communication from Lexi.

She bid her friends good-bye and took the long way back to her room, walking outside along the ship's balcony, soaking in the smell of the sea and the gentle breeze from the ship's steady movement in the water. The world continued to spin, and the ship continued to move, even though her heart beat so hard it felt like it would break. She was in too deep with Lexi now to not end up getting hurt. Lying about that to anyone, especially herself, was an exercise in futility. And she knew it.

# Chapter Twenty-One

The night ended in a blur for Lexi. After seeing Charlotte slip out the back door of the club, she didn't bother paying attention to much else. She knew that Charlotte would be waiting for her, and she wanted to get to her as fast as possible. So she put her head down, mixed more drinks than she could count, and managed to have the bar cleaned up and closed before all the house lights had come on. She had places to be, and waiting around here was not one of them.

She swiped her ID to update her time card and jogged down the I-95 toward her room. It was late, the corridor was mostly empty, but she could hear crew members talking and cheering from the crew bar down the hall. On any other night, she would be there with her friends, recounting the day's activities and playing darts until fatigue forced them back to their rooms. But not tonight. Tonight she had much grander plans.

She keyed into her room and texted Zara when she noticed she wasn't there. She'd need her help tonight to get back to Charlotte's undetected.

She changed into a sexier bra and put on a fresh uniform shirt, knowing full well that she would stay with Charlotte until the last moment possible before work tomorrow. And being dressed for work when that happened would allow for her to extend every moment to its fullest. She slipped a fresh pair of panties into the cargo pocket on her work pants and brushed her teeth, eager for the night ahead of her.

She braced a hand against the sink while she brushed, and her fingers shook. She was positively vibrating with excitement at the prospect of seeing Charlotte again. Tonight had been a lot for her, a challenge to maintain any sort of professionalism. And in truth, she found herself ambivalent about getting caught. Which was dangerous.

But Charlotte had a way of making her not care about anything in the world outside of the time they spent together. She hadn't felt that way in a long time, not since her, anyway. It was funny how just a few days with someone could make a decade's worth of time seem like it never happened. She'd had so much life away from Charlotte, and yet she felt like she was truly *living* now that she was in her presence again. That only further complicated her feelings about the trouble that was Charlotte.

"You beckoned, m'lady? Is it time for us to depart?" Zara asked as she closed the door to their room behind her.

Lexi laughed and spit into the sink. "Does that mean you're my trusty steed?"

"You did not just call me a horse." Zara gave her a look.

"Lady-in-waiting?" Lexi tried again.

"You are no queen and I am not your personal assistant." Zara laughed as she perched at the edge of her bed. "I will accept Duchess of Deviance or Countess of Collusion."

"Ooh, if we go the countess route, can I call you CC for short?" Lexi sprayed on some perfume and double-checked herself in the mirror.

"Sure thing, Casanova." Zara swung her legs as she spoke. "Shall I get your chariot?"

Lexi laughed and rolled her eyes. "Do I look okay?"

"You look great." Zara stood and took Lexi's hands in hers. "You look happy. Like, really happy. It suits you."

"Thanks, Zee." Lexi leaned forward and rested her forehead against her best friend's. "I really appreciate your help."

Zara gave her a kiss on her cheek and pulled her into a hug before jumping backward. "Alexandria. You did not just let me hug you without telling me you were packing heat, girl. That's just rude."

Lexi covered her face with her hands and apologized. "I'm sorry. I kind of forgot."

"Forgot?" Zara's voice was comically high. "That's some *thing* to forget, Lex."

Lexi was laughing so hard her eyes were watering. "Stop, you're going to fuck up my eyeliner."

"You're lucky I don't fuck up your face," Zara joked as she shook her head. "Whatever. That's gonna be uncomfortable as eff when you have to pretzel into that food cart in, oh, say, five minutes."

Lexi stopped laughed and braced herself against the nearby wall. "Oh, fuck."

"Mm-hmm." Zara shook her head again. "The things you do for love, girl. Damn." Zara opened the door to their room and stepped into the hall before she said, "Meet me by the kitchen in two."

Lexi didn't have a chance to reply before Zara closed the door, leaving her to her thoughts. Something Zara said was ringing in her ears. Love. Was she in love with Charlotte? She couldn't be. They'd only just reunited. It wasn't enough time, was it?

As she gathered up the rest of her belongings and sped down the I-95 in the direction of the kitchen, she contemplated just that.

Lexi swore on her life that Zara took the long way to Charlotte's room. And hit every bump along the way. She didn't remember this cart being as tight the last time. Finally, as claustrophobia was setting in, the cart stopped, and she heard Zara knock on a door.

"Room s*ervice.*" Zara dragged out the second word with an exaggerated pronunciation. Lexi stifled a laugh.

She heard the door open and Charlotte greeted Zara before ushering her into the room.

"Charlotte. It's so nice to finally meet you. I'm Zara." This was their first-time meeting, and Lexi was a little nervous. But it sounded like it was going well, which was good.

Another large bump, which Lexi assumed was a threshold, caused her to nearly tumble out from under the tablecloth cover. She didn't dare speak until she was sure the coast was clear, but it seemed as though Zara and Charlotte were having a freaking epically long discussion about God knew what, and Lexi couldn't be contained any longer.

She cleared her throat. "Any chance I can come out now?"

"Oh," Zara said as she lifted the cloth, a smirk on her face. "I forgot about you."

Lexi tried, and failed, to exit the bottom of the cart gracefully. As she toppled onto the floor, Zara's hearty laugh echoed in her ears.

"That's what you get for calling me a horse," Zara teased.

Lexi stood up and brushed herself off, careful to give Zara her best side-eye once she was upright.

"You called her a horse?" Charlotte was leaning her hip against the table in the small kitchenette area of her suite. She was wearing that beautiful gown from earlier. Lexi smiled. She was glad to see it still on her.

"Not exactly." Lexi swept an errant hair behind her ear.

"Yes, exactly," Zara said as she covered the cart again. She handed the items from the top of the tray to Lexi and wiped her hands on the towel by her waist. "Your food, Duchess."

Lexi curtsied. "I'm indebted to you, Countess."

"Thank you, Zara," Charlotte said, walking toward her and taking her hand. "I really appreciate it. Especially since Lexi seems to lack the common decency to express gratitude without insulting you."

"You're probably too good for her." Zara gave Charlotte a nod. "You two lovebirds have a good night. Message me in the morning when you're ready for your pickup."

"Love you! Mean it!" Lexi called out and Zara waved her off.

"Yeah, yeah." Zara blew her a kiss and disappeared into the hall, closing the door behind her.

"Duchess?" Charlotte asked, staying put.

"It's a long story." Lexi placed the tray on the nearby desk and stepped toward Charlotte. "We can talk later, or never. Because I am dying to get my hands on you in that dress."

"Oh? This old thing?" Charlotte said as she ran her hand along her bodice.

Lexi stepped closer, so that Charlotte was only an arm's length away now. "That's twice in the last few days that you've stopped me dead in my tracks with a beautiful dress."

Charlotte reached for her hand as she replied, "And here I thought you were only interested in seeing me out of my clothes. You surprise me, Lexi."

Lexi pulled Charlotte to her, releasing her hand to grasp both her hips and draw Charlotte against her front. "I'm full of surprises."

"I can feel that." Charlotte's hands settled on Lexi's jaw and she connected their lips in a sweet kiss. "I'm excited to be filled by these surprises you speak of."

Lexi closed her eyes and the discomfort from the food cart melted away as a new sensation, a much hotter one, took priority. She ran her hands up Charlotte's sides, gently fingering the beadwork and lace as she went. She pulled back and looked at Charlotte's gown. It was stunning.

"This looks amazing on you. Like it was—"

"Custom-made?" Charlotte's hands clasped behind Lexi's neck in a casual embrace.

"Yes." Lexi drifted one hand over Charlotte's ribs and up over the cup of her breast, dancing along the delicate stitching of the heart-shaped neckline.

Charlotte's eyes were on Lexi's curious fingers when she replied, "Well, that's good, because it is."

"Oh?" Lexi dragged her thumb to the lowest dip of the neckline and caressed the skin there. "Something for this trip?"

"Not exactly." Charlotte kissed her again, slowing her train of thought. "More like for my wedding. But it seems to be bringing me luck on this trip, so I'm good with it."

Lexi pulled back from Charlotte and gave her a once-over, paying more attention to the dress in front of her. "Oh my God, this is a wedding dress."

"Was," Charlotte corrected. "That was its intended purpose, but it's been repurposed as a White Party dress. Which I'm surprisingly okay with."

Lexi stepped back, taking Charlotte's hands in hers. "I need to see this more clearly. You know, give it the appreciation it deserves."

Charlotte gave her a curious look. "I thought you gave it plenty of appreciation," she said as she tried to step closer to Lexi, but Lexi resisted.

"No, no way. This changes things. I want the whole experience." She paused. "Unless you don't want to talk about it, or want me to breeze over it. Which I can totally do, but I'd rather not."

Charlotte looked shy. "What should I do? Like, twirl or something?"

Lexi laughed. "You should totally twirl. Here"—she sat at the edge of Charlotte's bed and waited—"it's custom-made, right? Tell me about all the stuff you love about this dress."

"Seriously?' Charlotte gave her an incredulous look. "There was kissing and most likely definitely sex and now you want to talk about dresses?"

"There will be more kissing and an entire evening of mind-blowing sex," Lexi assured her. "And it's not *some* dress, it's your non-wedding dress. And it's exceptional. Much like you. So I'd like to know more about it. Please and thank you."

Charlotte seemed to consider this. "Okay, but only because you promised sex."

"So much sex," Lexi replied.

"Fine." Charlotte placed her hand on her hip and motioned to the fabric. "I picked out the fabric myself from a series of spools the designer had on hand."

"And the beadwork?" Lexi asked, loving how Charlotte seemed to glow at her very genuine interest.

"Hand-sewn. I chose a mix of flat and rounded beads to ensure maximum glitteration occurred," Charlotte said.

"I'm not sure that's a word, but I like it," Lexi replied.

"But if we're doing this, I should be honest with you about something." Charlotte looked shy again.

"Anything. Lay it on me."

"This is only a part of the look. There's more." Lexi followed Charlotte's eyes to her closet.

"You have something in the closet to complete this look?" Lexi was intrigued. Was it a veil? Shoes? What?

Charlotte exhaled, "Okay, close your eyes."

Lexi followed orders very well. This was easy. "Done."

She heard the closet door open and close. The sound of a zipper was shortly followed by some wrestling of fabric. "I'm ready."

Lexi kept her eyes closed. "I feel like I should hum the 'Wedding March' here."

"That seems excessive." Charlotte laughed.

"No, no. I want this to be authentic." Lexi started humming, pausing only to ask, "Can I look now?"

"You can." Charlotte sounded timid.

Lexi opened her eyes and gasped. Charlotte stood before her in the most incredible dress she had ever seen. She'd thought the gown before the addition of the skirt thing was gorgeous, but this, this was a whole different thing entirely. "Charlotte. My God. You look…"

Charlotte dipped her head and looked down.

Lexi stood and walked to her, taking her hand and bending to meet Charlotte's gaze. Her heart broke at the emotion she saw there. Sadness. A heaviness that felt out of place in the beauty of this dress and the beauty of this woman. "I'm glad you showed me."

Charlotte nodded but cast her eyes down again. Her grip on Lexi's hand was so tight it almost hurt.

Lexi tried again. "You are so, so beautiful, Charlotte. This dress, it's just an extension of the beauty you already possess. I am grateful you shared this with me. I'm so—" Lexi lifted Charlotte's chin and held her gaze as she spoke from her heart. "I'm so lucky to have found you again."

Charlotte smiled and the falling tears seemed less heavy, though Lexi knew they were plenty significant. This must be hard for Charlotte. All jokes and innuendo aside, she realized that this was a substantial moment. She wanted to honor that emotion. "I would definitely marry you in this dress."

"Oh?" Charlotte laughed and let herself be pulled into Lexi's arms.

"Most definitely." Lexi danced them in place as she spoke. "I'd probably marry you even if I didn't know you. That's how amazing this dress is."

Charlotte rested her head on Lexi's shoulder and swayed with her. "Married at first sight, huh?"

"I would've married you across a courtyard," Lexi said, as she nuzzled her nose against Charlotte's. "That's how magical you look."

"That would be a tricky distance to finagle a first kiss," Charlotte noted.

"Well, I'd clearly have to run across the courtyard to you. I'd vault shit. Full on parkour." Lexi added, "No obstacle would be too great. You would have to be mine."

Charlotte looked up at her and the glow from before had returned, the sadness seeming to have retreated. "Any obstacle?"

"Even the ocean wouldn't stop me. Vastness be damned." Lexi leaned in but stopped, wanting Charlotte to make the first move.

"I'm going to hold you to that." Charlotte brushed her lips against Lexi as she spoke. "Not to change the subject or anything…"

Lexi shuddered as Charlotte's hand left the spot on her waist where she was hugging her and traveled across her abdomen, pressing against her shirt as it explored. "I'm open to subject changes," she replied.

"Good"—Charlotte flicked open the button of her pants and tugged the zipper down—"because I've been waiting for this surprise of yours all day and I'm getting impatient. Especially since you keep telling me I'm magnificent and marriage-worthy."

"So much both." Lexi moaned as Charlotte's mouth met hers. "And fuckable. That, too."

Charlotte kissed her deeply before pulling back to add, "In this dress."

"In and out of this dress." Lexi reclaimed her lips as she let her hands explore Charlotte's chest. "But let's leave it on to start."

"Fuck." Charlotte exhaled and Lexi walked her backward toward the metal-framed kitchenette table near Charlotte's bar.

"So much that, too." Lexi gripped Charlotte's ribs and helped hoist her up on the table. The massive skirt put an inconvenient barrier to where Lexi needed to be. "The skirt might have to be retired, though."

"Screw formality." Charlotte reached behind her back and wiggled out of the skirt, perching at the edge of the table in the less formal version of the gown. "Now, screw me."

Lexi laughed and stepped closer, easing the hem of the dress up and over Charlotte's hips and stepping between her legs. "I can do that."

Charlotte wrapped her legs about Lexi's waist and pulled her closer still, and this time nothing stopped the bulge in Lexi's pants from reaching Charlotte, a fact made evident by Charlotte's deep moan and rolling hips. She purred. "Mmm."

Lexi kissed her as she massaged her breast before she snaked a hand down the front of her body and between her legs. She toyed with the damp fabric over Charlotte's cunt, teasing and rubbing until Charlotte moved against her fingers in a steady rhythm.

"Take those off," Charlotte mumbled between kisses, lifting her ass off the table to help Lexi free her of her panties. She tugged at Lexi's shirt. "This, too. And those pants."

"Bossy." Lexi did as she was told, and Charlotte rewarded her by guiding her hand to Charlotte's wet center. "Oh, my."

"I've been waiting for you." Charlotte threw her head back when Lexi eased a finger into her. She gripped at her shoulder when Lexi added a second. "Yes."

Lexi thrust in slowly, savoring the way Charlotte tightened around her. Charlotte's lips and tongue were on her mouth, moving in tandem with Lexi's fingers. Charlotte's hands massaged her upper back before freeing her of her bra. She cupped Lexi's chest as Lexi spread her fingers slightly, helping stretch Charlotte for what was next.

"Lex," Charlotte gasped out as her grip on Lexi's chest became more forceful. "Please."

"Please what?" Lexi added a third finger and thrust in faster, curling her fingers as she pulled out. Charlotte was plenty wet now. She was ready.

One of Charlotte's hands left her chest to reach for the phallus between them. She gripped the head of the dildo and pulled, jerking back and forth as she continued to roll her hips against Lexi's hand. She deepened her kissing as she tugged and rocked, pausing only to beg, "Please. This. Lexi, please."

"Put this on," Lexi said as she slowed the kiss. She used her free hand to reach into the pocket of the pants she had discarded nearby to hand Charlotte the condom she'd brought.

Charlotte opened the wrapper with her teeth, before her hands expertly dressed the dildo between them. All the while Lexi continued to move her fingers in and out of her, making sure to keep Charlotte primed.

When Charlotte was finished and her lips found Lexi's again, Lexi slipped out of her to coat the head of the dildo with her wetness. She guided it to press against Charlotte's center, and gripped Charlotte's hip with her free hand to slow her movements. She eased forward, careful to listen and feel for Charlotte's reaction.

"More, Lex," Charlotte panted against her mouth as she shifted forward to the edge of the table. "I'm ready."

Lexi pressed forward, breaking their kiss to look between them. She watched as Charlotte accepted the head and rolled against it. Lexi pulled back a bit before sliding back in, deeper this time. She loved the position the table afforded her. She could stand to her full height and still pleasure Charlotte—it was exhilarating.

Charlotte moaned, and she reached back to brace herself as Lexi closed the distance between, burying the dildo completely. Lexi started a slow rhythm, thrusting in and out until Charlotte hooked her legs behind Lexi's waist and rocked with her, keeping Lexi buried inside her while she moved.

Lexi leaned forward, bracing herself against Charlotte, pressing her naked chest against Charlotte, who was still wearing the dress, as Charlotte placed hungry, sloppy kisses along her face and mouth.

Charlotte panted in response and breathy little sounds of pleasure spilled from her lips as Lexi's pace quickened. Lexi felt her clit twitch and ache with each thrust, the delicious friction winding her up as she sank into Charlotte over and over again, but the angle wasn't enough to give her relief. Not that she really gave a damn with Charlotte grinding against her and looking so fucking perfect. She'd do this forever without complaint.

Charlotte's hands found her face and she was pulled into a kiss so startling and intense that she momentarily lost her rhythm.

"Get me out of this dress and take me to bed." Charlotte

continued to roll her hips, keeping Lexi inside her, but her pace slowed considerably.

Lexi felt out of breath. That kiss, those sounds, this back and forth, it was overwhelming and erotic and romantic and *everything*. And the way Charlotte was looking at her right now, with adoration and affection, with such trust, made Lexi feel like she'd never breathe again.

She wrapped her arms around Charlotte and lifted her from the table, holding her close as she turned and lowered her to the bed. She watched in awe as Charlotte eased the toy out of herself and stripped, first of her dress, then of the lacy strapless bra she wore underneath.

"Come back to me," Charlotte said as she reached for Lexi, pulling her between her spread legs, but stopping her before their hips could meet. She reached down to play with her clit while Lexi watched, teasing Lexi until she felt like she might explode from the sight alone.

"You are so fucking sexy." Lexi wanted to taste her. All of her. She missed her lips and the feeling of her skin moving against her. The light sheen of sweat on Charlotte's chest made that glow from earlier glisten, renewed, and as much as she was enjoying the show, she wanted to be over Charlotte, feeling her writhe beneath. Because of her.

Charlotte slipped a finger into herself with a contented sigh before running that finger across Lexi's bottom lip. She flexed forward and kissed Lexi, breathing out a command, "Fill me," that Lexi knew she'd fantasize about forever and ever.

Guided by Charlotte's hand, Lexi slid back into her and quickly resumed the pace they'd had before they hit the bed. Charlotte arched underneath her, clutching at her back and shoulders, one leg wrapping around her waist and while the other anchored her against the bed.

Lexi could feel Charlotte's strength as she braced herself against the bed's surface and pushed back into Lexi's thrusts. She was meeting her passion with every movement, and Lexi couldn't remember another lover who'd felt this compatible. Or this right. Or this fucking good.

And as Charlotte cried out, her body shuddering and quaking beneath her, Lexi followed her across the precipice, giving in to the orgasm that had been building since their position change. Her heart raced and her pulse throbbed as she tried to catch her breath, all the while struggling to maintain her rhythm as she came undone, not wanting to cut Charlotte's pleasure short. But Charlotte rescued her. She flipped her on her back and straddled her hips, rocking against her slowly, dragging out Lexi's pleasure with every intentional grind.

Charlotte lowered herself against her, circling her hips, the thrusting from before gone now. And as she kissed along the column of Lexi's neck, Lexi basked in the feeling of the intimacy, the contact she shared with Charlotte. She'd missed this kind of closeness, she realized. The kind of closeness that comes from giving a part of yourself away and having the other person share themselves in return. Charlotte was vulnerable to her in so many ways tonight. And seemingly without hesitation, at that. Lexi's gut told her to be honest with her, to tell her she was afraid of all the things Charlotte made her feel, but that she didn't think she could live without those feelings either.

"You feel so good." Charlotte sucked on her earlobe, her hips circling even slower now.

Lexi vibrated with the aftershocks of her orgasm, renewed sparks jolting her with Charlotte's lazy pelvic teasing. "And you are still making me see stars." She turned her head to connect their lips.

"Are you complaining?" Charlotte asked, her continual motion unchanged.

"Never." Lexi rolled them to their sides and held Charlotte close, lazily kissing her as her tremors started to fade. It was unhurried and wonderful.

After a few minutes, Charlotte pulled back, easing the toy out of her and helping Lexi strip down to nothing. Lexi let her lead, appreciating the gentle touches and caresses Charlotte made against her skin, cradling her hip, massaging her low back, the touch of a familiar lover. Of a reunited first love. And as Charlotte curled into her chest, her head nestled against her collarbone, Lexi let herself daydream of what a life full of Charlotte might be like, if it was even a possibility, and what, if anything, she'd have to give up to have that.

# CHAPTER TWENTY-TWO

*Cruise Day Six: Curaçao*

Charlotte had been staring at Lexi's empty pillow for the past fifteen or so minutes, trying to wake up but also trying to hold on to the memories of last night. Not that that was going to be hard, since she was delightfully sore from their play. But last night had felt like a dream, and a part of her didn't quite believe it had happened at all.

She rolled to her back and pulled the covers up to her chin. The sheets smelled like Lexi's perfume and shampoo. And sex. Since there had been a fair share of that last night as well. And a little this morning, though she might have been dreaming that bit. Lexi had slipped out that morning when it was still dark out, but she'd made sure to kiss Charlotte good-bye and hold her close. That's where it got a little hazy, because Charlotte's memory told her they'd shared more than a quick hug, and her body buzzed when she thought about it. But could she really still have been horny after last night? Yes. Yes, she could be. Because Lexi had flicked a switch in her that seemed to make her insatiable. In regard to Lexi, at least.

A soft breeze from the open porch door caused something to flutter near the bed. She looked over toward it and smiled—it was the skirt of her dress. Through the open closet door, Charlotte could see that Lexi had hung up her non-wedding dress, with the fancy and elegant skirt, on a hanger. Even from her vantage point on the bed, she could see that Lexi had zipped it and used the garment straps to ensure it would stay in place. She'd taken care to handle it with a gentleness that seemed unnecessary. Previously, the dress represented a failure and loss in Charlotte's life, but after last night, it held a new meaning. Last night, when Charlotte succumbed to the power of her emotions and trembled with shame and sadness over the extravagant material reminder of her failed relationship, Lexi looked at her and told her she was beautiful. She told her she was worthy of love and respect and kindness, and Charlotte believed every word because she could see the sincerity on Lexi's face. She could feel it in the loving way she touched her. And in her kiss.

And just like that, something that had brought her great pain was transformed into something that brought her great joy. And love. A feeling of true, unconditional love and affection. That was what she'd felt last night, between the sensual touches and soul-shattering climaxes. She'd felt loved. And it was the first time she'd felt that in well over a year. Longer, if she was honest with herself. It was the first time she'd felt that whole and complete since, well, Lexi.

"I'm going to fall head over heels for you all over again, Lexi," she said to no one. But she knew that wasn't true—she was *already* there. It had happened somewhere over the last few days, like an accelerated courtship that also turned back the clock a decade or so. Her heart raced now when she saw her like it had when they were sneaking kisses in the back of her grandfather's classic car. All the time and no time had passed all at once.

She climbed out of bed and retrieved her phone from the desk. Her battery was nearly dead—it had been long forgotten once Lexi entered the room last night. Before she had entered *her.* The memory made Charlotte tingly all over again. *Oh, no, don't start that.* She shrugged off the feeling, deciding if she fell down that rabbit hole, she'd never get off this ship. Which didn't seem like all that bad an idea since Lexi was here, but still.

She plugged in her phone. She had a few messages on the texting app from Lexi. There was a sweet good morning text and some updates about her schedule. To accommodate for their planned rendezvous in Curaçao today, Lexi was working the very early and late shifts on the boat. Charlotte was going to depart from the boat midmorning and meet up with Lexi at one of her favorite local restaurants before they started their day together. Or resumed their day, together. Whatever. All she knew was that she was going to be seeing Lexi again and what day or time or universe didn't matter as long as it was soon.

She checked the clock and cursed. She was going to be late if she didn't hustle. Evidently, she'd slept longer than she'd anticipated. Not that she could blame her body for trying to store up some sleep—she hadn't exactly been generous in that department lately. She tossed her beach bag on the delightfully unmade bed and threw in all the necessary items for a day of sex at the beach. Or just the beach. Whatever Lexi had in mind, she was game for. She didn't really care what it entailed as long as Lexi was there. And she was just fine with that.

❖

Curaçao was gorgeous. And the weather was perfect, which made the island that much more gorgeous and perfect, and damn, Charlotte was on cloud nine from last night and she probably wouldn't have minded a storm right now, but still. She was glad she left the ship. Lexi was right—she would have been sad to miss this.

She checked the paper map Lexi must have slid under her door while she was in the shower. Though she would have rather Lexi joined her in the shower, finding the cute little notes she'd scribbled along the ship's itinerary for the day was an unexpected surprise.

She followed the instructions and made her way toward the island bar Lexi recommended. She took her time, weaving between the shops along the way, embracing the island culture and friendliness she found endlessly. She was eager to meet up with Lexi, but also in no rush to miss what Curaçao had to offer. What life had to offer.

She ran her hand along a colorful watercolor-like rainbow fabric at one of the pop-up shops along the main road and appreciated the contrast against her newly tanned complexion. This beach wrap needed to come home with her, she decided. It was the only token she'd gotten for herself this whole trip, and she was excited about it. As she carried the garment to the register, she thought about how different this week had gone than she had anticipated.

These last few days on the ship had been eye-opening for her in a lot of ways. She realized she'd lost a lot of herself in her relationship with Veronica. She'd let her own friendships lapse in favor of spending more time with Veronica's friends, something that was painfully evident when they separated and her support system went with her ex. And she worked too much. Or, at least, she wasn't using her time efficiently. She often worked on weeknights and weekends, particularly since she and Veronica had split. There was nothing exciting about living at home with your mother as you neared thirty, and she'd holed herself up in her room more than she wanted to admit.

But the world existed outside those four walls. She could see that so clearly now. She'd let herself wallow for long enough, and it was time for a change. It was time to work less and travel more. It was time to be the Charlotte she had dreamed of becoming all those years ago, when the possibilities seemed endless and the world was new and exciting. It wasn't lost on her that those times, the easier ones when she loved herself more and worried less, those times involved Lexi. And though she also realized that those times were in her youth, when she had less world experience and less responsibility, she also realized that even though she had grown up in a lot of ways from that young teenage girl, in some ways she hadn't. She still wanted to believe in endless possibilities. She wanted to believe in love, true love. And now that Lexi was back in her life, whatever that meant, those things seemed more achievable. She didn't want that to end. Everything felt simpler. And she knew some of that might be because she was on vacation and all, but she didn't care. The way she felt right now was fantastic. And she didn't want that to change.

She paid for the wrap and placed the neatly folded cloth in her beach bag. She decided she'd wear it later on the beach, or as a cover-up for activities that didn't involve clothes. Activities with Lexi. And though she wanted nothing more than to spend the day lost in Lexi's eyes, she realized she would, at some point, have to address the elephant in the room. Or on the ship, as it were.

She'd decided to extend her time on the cruise ship and not depart tomorrow when they docked in Aruba like was previously planned. She hadn't changed her reservations at the hotel yet, but she knew that wouldn't be an issue, since she was shortening her stay, not extending it. She had money set aside to pay for the flight back down to Aruba, that wasn't an issue. What was an issue was the Lexi situation. She wanted to make sure Lexi knew that she was serious about continuing this reconnection, whatever that panned out to be, and she was hopeful and open-minded. And she wanted Lexi to be as well. They needed to talk about life after the cruise, and that should happen sooner rather than later.

She turned onto the street Lexi had marked on the map she'd left her and spotted the colorful signage of the bar just a short distance away. Her anticipation grew as she approached, but so did her trepidation. She didn't want to acknowledge real life, but she knew she had to, regardless.

She was a little nervous, though, nervous that she might be more invested than Lexi. Not that Lexi had given her any indication that that was the case, but they'd successfully avoided talking about it, and she knew that was intentional on her part. She'd wanted to live in the moment with Lexi and not plan her life out to a failure like she had before. She needed to *live* more, and she couldn't do that if she was planning all the time.

Before she knew it, she found herself at the beach bar. The hostess greeted her with a warm smile, and the soft sound of island music played in the background, mingling with the laughter of tourists and locals, scattered throughout the open air dining room patio just beyond the restaurant's entrance. Charlotte smiled reflexively. Everyone seemed happy in paradise, so why wouldn't they be? It was contagious.

She made her way toward the bar facing the beach at the back of the restaurant, the butterflies in her stomach doing cartwheels with every successive step closer to her destination. Lexi had told her to snag two seats for them to have a quick bite. She scanned the bar and frowned when she only saw one empty seat available. She was a little late, but she hadn't expected that to be a big deal. Clearly, she was wrong.

She made her way toward the empty seat when someone caught her wrist.

"Looking for someone?" Lexi asked as she massaged the skin on the inside of Charlotte's wrist.

"Seems like I found her." Charlotte smiled as Lexi pulled her in for a lingering kiss.

Lexi pulled her up onto her lap and kissed along her jaw, nibbling the skin along her neck. "I missed you."

"Maybe we should skip lunch and get to that hotel room." Charlotte reconnected their lips and relished the passion she felt there. Lexi held nothing back when kissing her. It was a welcomed feeling of affection.

"All in good time," Lexi said after a few more kisses. She nodded toward the empty seat next to her. "That's for you."

Charlotte felt herself blush. "I was supposed to get here first."

"I was eager, and I left work a little early"—she poked Charlotte in the ribs—"but you are a touch late."

Charlotte leaned away from Lexi's tickling and grabbed her hand, holding it to save her ribs from the assault. "I slept in late. I'm going to blame it on all the *touching* from you that kept me up all night."

Charlotte slid off her lap and pulled the empty seat closer.

Lexi intertwined their fingers once she was settled and asked, "Do you regret that?"

"Not even a little." Charlotte played with Lexi's fingers as she looked at her. "Part of me hoped the night would never end."

Lexi stroked the back of her hand as she replied. "I know what you mean."

Charlotte rested her head on Lexi's shoulder, savoring the moment. The bartender came by and Lexi ordered them both drinks and food. Charlotte told her to choose whatever she liked from the menu—she wasn't picky.

"We're going to have a really fun day," Lexi said as she kissed the top of Charlotte's head.

"I don't doubt that for one moment." And she didn't. Every moment she spent with Lexi had been a fun one. "What's on our agenda today?"

"Well," Lexi said as she stretched, "I was thinking I'd take you for a quick tour of this side of the island, and then maybe we could hit up the beach. I put in a call to my favorite local beach guy and he reserved us a cabana toward the far end of the beach. You know, to, uh, afford us a little privacy." Lexi looked shy as she added, "I can still book a room for the afternoon like we'd discussed, but I thought you might like the beach. This is a nice one, quiet, not too crowded. It's a little bit of a walk, but it's my favorite one on the island. We'll see the best waves and have the softest sand without any real interruption. It's one of the best parts of Curaçao. I'd hate to rush your time here."

"That sounds perfect," Charlotte replied, because it did. "I told you before—I don't care what we do, as long as I'm with you while we're doing it."

"Good." Lexi looked touched. Charlotte hoped Lexi knew she meant what she said.

"Listen, before I lose my nerve and find every other way possible to occupy my mouth today other than using it to tell you how I feel," Charlotte began, her palms sweating as she spoke, "I wanted you to know that I decided to stay on the ship until the end of the trip. I'm not getting off in Aruba like I thought I was. I—I can't. Not when I've been so looking forward to today"—she motioned between them—"and this. I didn't want this to be the bookend of our time together. Not that I think it won't be fantastic or swoon-worthy, but I'm not ready to leave you yet. I'm not ready, Lex."

Lexi blinked, seemingly caught off guard by her honesty. Charlotte second-guessed her rambling but couldn't seem to stop herself either. "I know we haven't talked about life after this cruise and I hope I'm not getting ahead of myself here, but I—"

Lexi's lips against hers silenced her words but spoke volumes at the same time. She exhaled against the warmth of Lexi's mouth and leaned into the gentle caress of Lexi's fingers along her cheek.

Lexi pulled back from the kiss and pressed their foreheads together, her fingertips still soothing along Charlotte's jaw as she spoke. "I'm not ready for you to leave, either. You're not getting ahead of yourself. And even if you are, I'm right there with you. Okay?"

"Okay." The last of Charlotte's trepidations and insecurities drifted away with the warm breeze off the water behind them.

They broke apart as the bartender dropped off their drinks and they sat in a comfortable silence, save for the outrageously loud and excited beating of Charlotte's heart that she was sure the entire restaurant could hear.

"I'm glad we're doing this," Charlotte said, unable to help herself.

"Me, too." Lexi's smile told her the feeling was mutual.

❖

Today had been a perfect day. Like, really perfect. So perfect that Lexi practically floated through security and back to her room. She knew she'd walked because she'd held hands with Charlotte the whole time, laughing and joking, and kissing, often, until they got close to the boat, but she still swore she'd floated all the way from the beach. Everything else was a blur. She only had eyes for Charlotte, and she was okay with that.

She keyed into the room and found Ahmed pacing back and forth in the narrow space between her and Zara's bed.

"Hey, Ah—"

"Where have you been?" Ahmed looked frantic.

"On the island," Lexi said as she dropped her bag on the bed. She had to side-step to keep from getting run over as Ahmed made a sharp turn and continued his pacing. "What's up?"

The toilet flushed and Zara emerged from the bathroom. "Don't you check your phone anymore?"

Lexi patted her pocket but didn't find the phone in its normal spot.

She'd put it in her bag when she and Charlotte had settled into their cabana space. She hadn't needed her phone at the time, and honestly, Charlotte didn't give her a lot of time to get out of her pants before she tried to get into them. They swam for the majority of the afternoon, slipping in and out of the cabana until it was time to head back to the cruise ship, and she'd completely forgotten about the rest of the world, let alone about her phone.

"It's in my bag." She pulled it out of the front pocket, powering it on. "I went to the beach."

Ahmed groaned. "There's a signal at the beach, Lexi. It's a tourist island. You know you're supposed to keep your phone handy when you're on shift."

"I'm not on shift." Lexi had never seen him so freaked out. "I don't have another shift until later. I was off midday—you helped me reorganize my schedule." She looked back at Zara for some help. "Wanna fill me in as to why the hamster fell off the wheel here?"

Zara sighed as she sank into her desk chair. "Ahmed. Take a breath. Tell her what you told me."

Ahmed stopped pacing and stomped his foot. His eyes filled with tears as he looked at her. "Sally came by the office today. She asked for your employee file. I thought it was about your promotion, but she had the head of security with her."

A pit formed in Lexi's stomach. "What did she want?"

"Everything. She wanted all the details of your whereabouts for the week: your schedule, your time cards, all of it." His eyes were red as he added, "She asked for all your VIP appointments, too. She wanted to know if you were placed with anyone other than Charlotte this week. I told her you weren't. I didn't know what to do, so I gave her what she asked for. But I don't know, Lex. Something seemed wrong. She seemed mad."

Before Lexi could reply, there was a knock at her door. She looked between her friends, unsure of what to do, but she knew that knock was for her.

"Ahmed, go hide in the bathroom," Lexi whispered as she walked toward the closed door. "The last thing we need is you looking like a snitch."

Ahmed covered his mouth and nodded, following her orders. Zara gave her a sad frown as she cut her off at the door. "I'll do it."

She looked through the peephole and paused, then looked back at

Lexi with a face that told her she should be worried. "We'll figure it out, Lex. Whatever happens, we'll figure it out."

When Zara opened the door to reveal Staff Captain Sally Dashel standing there with her clipboard and the chip on her shoulder, Lexi knew it before she had to be told. She was fired.

## CHAPTER TWENTY-THREE

Charlotte took another lap around the top deck, stretching her legs and hoping to clear her mind. She and Lexi had had an incredible day, but she'd been unable to reach her since they'd boarded separately. At first, she'd assumed Lexi might have started her evening shift early, but when she stopped by the restaurant bar she was supposed to be covering that night, she was told Lexi's shift had been picked up by someone else.

She figured she must have gotten the dates switched, but when she checked the text Lexi had sent this morning, she realized she wasn't wrong. Lexi wasn't working there that night like she was supposed to be, and she wasn't returning any of her messages, either.

Charlotte increased her pace, hoping the briskness of her walk would give her clarity. They'd had a good day, right? She couldn't remember a more fun day at the beach with anyone, ever. And they'd kept it mostly light, playful touches and kisses, aside from that not so PG interaction in the cabana, but it had been great. Granted, it was their first time together without having to sneak around or work around Lexi's schedule, but she'd thought it had been a good day.

Her anxiety set in as she wondered if maybe she'd chased Lexi off. Maybe she'd come on too strong. Charlotte had initiated that conversation about continuing to talk with Lexi after the trip, and Lexi seemed to be agreeable to it, but maybe she'd rushed it a bit? They still had a few days left…God, did she fuck this up? She totally did, didn't she?

Her phone vibrated in her pocket and she nearly dropped it overboard in her clumsy rush to see if Lexi was messaging her.

She frowned when she realized it wasn't a message from Lexi, but one from Veronica. It just said, *Call me. Please.* Not a chance, she thought as she slipped the phone back into her pocket. She stopped walking and leaned against the railing, looking out at the receding view of Curaçao as the ship moved on to its next destination. They were too far to hear the music from the port, but Charlotte could still see the dancing lights of the restaurants and bars along the beaches. The weather had been mild today, warm but not windy. But as the lanterns and lights swayed and the breeze picked up around her, she realized the tide had turned, and with it, the weather had changed as well. She hoped that wasn't true for what was happening between her and Lexi.

She'd run into Barb and Marlene on the walk here earlier but had declined their invitation to dinner. She cited fatigue, but the truth was, she didn't want to be out of her room or tied to an engagement she couldn't back out of the moment Lexi messaged her. But after waiting in her room without any word, she got restless. So she decided to walk. And she wasn't sure how much time had gone by, but she'd have guessed a considerable amount.

But the more she thought about it, she was tired, so maybe it would be better to just head back to her room and wait it out there. She'd see Lexi in the morning regardless, right? She'd get her answers then.

She pushed off the railing and made the long walk back to her room, keeping an eye out for her favorite bartender but not being surprised when she didn't see her. She keyed into her room and flicked on the cabin lights, moving slowly with a fatigue and anxiety that she hadn't had before. Something felt off about this. Why hadn't Lexi contacted her?

She stepped into her space and noticed something was different. The room had been cleaned. The sheets were changed and the bed made and some sort of towel animal sat at the end. The roses Veronica had sent were starting to wilt. She'd neglected them in a way she wouldn't have if she'd been home, or if they were from someone else. They sagged in a way that she felt very familiar, since her elation from earlier seemed to dwindle by the moment.

She sat at the edge of her bed, looking out to the dark balcony, and sighed. Reaching for her phone to double-check her messages again, she bumped into the towel animal and something caught her eye.

It was an elephant, and at the tip of its trunk was a single yellow rose. When she reached for the flower, she noticed the small scrap of paper folded in its mouth. Her hand hovered over it, almost afraid to read its contents.

"Get a grip, Charlotte." She exhaled and picked up the paper. It was from Lexi, but it was brief. *Meet me by the life boats.* The note included a crude little map and a meeting time. Charlotte checked her phone for the time. A lump formed in her throat as she realized that was over twenty minutes ago. Had she missed her?

She shoved the map into her pocket and grabbed her room key, swapping out her sandals for sneakers. If she planned to get there anytime soon, she'd have to run for it. She exited her room and jogged down the hall, maneuvering between guests in the small corridor as she went. She got to midship and pulled out the map. There was no way she knew how to get there without this, since she'd blindly let Lexi lead her before, in a haze of lust and neediness. Now, as she looked over the many doors and stairwells Lexi drew for her, she wished she'd paid a little more attention the first time.

She ducked into one of the unmarked doors Lexi identified on the map, and she climbed the two flights of the service staircase two steps at a time until she hit a familiar looking door. She looked left and right, as instructed by the notes, and waited until the faint voices in the stairwell above faded before she wrenched the little used door open with great effort.

The wind nearly pulled the door from her hand, but she stopped it just before it clanged against the metal wall of the ship. She threw her body weight against the door to get the creaky hinges to comply, and the door swung shut with a loud thud.

"Well, that's one hell of a way to make an entrance." She heard Lexi's voice before she saw her. Lexi was seated against the wall, in the alcove they'd made out in, wearing dark clothes and holding a cell phone for light.

"Lexi." Charlotte still hadn't caught her breath from the sprint to get here, or all those damn stairs, but she was relieved she hadn't missed her. "Sorry I'm late."

Lexi stood, but she remained in the dark, unmoving. "It's okay. I figured it was a long shot you'd even get my note."

Charlotte headed toward her. "Well, I wasn't expecting the carrier elephant, but I was glad to hear from you."

"Yeah, sorry. I can't—" Lexi's voice was soft. "Messaging seemed like a bad idea."

"Why? Is something wrong?" Charlotte barely got the question out by the time she'd reached Lexi and saw the tear-streaked expression on her face. "What happened, Lex?"

Lexi reached for her and Charlotte took her hand, pulling Lexi against her chest. She held her while Lexi sobbed, her distress quiet but strong as she shuddered against Charlotte. Charlotte ran her hands through Lexi's hair, soothing her shoulders and upper back while Lexi slowly composed herself. "Tell me what happened."

Lexi looked up at her, her eyes wet and deep, deep blue in the dimly lit space beneath the life rafts. Charlotte caressed her cheek, waiting for her to say something.

"We've been caught." Lexi gave her a half smile as she shook her head. "I was foolish to think we wouldn't. I mean, it's not like we didn't push the envelope."

Charlotte pulled her hand back, bringing it to her chest as she felt her heart rate pick up. "What do you mean? What does that mean?"

"It means"—Lexi sighed—"I can't sneak into your room anymore or grind against you in plain sight on a dance floor. Or kiss you the way I want to in broad daylight because the cat's out of the bag."

Charlotte instinctively looked over her shoulder for cameras.

"We're still safe here, for now," Lexi said.

A realization settled over Charlotte and she felt sick. "Did you get…fired?"

New tears filled Lexi's eyes as she shook her head. "Not exactly, no."

"But sort of?" Charlotte knew what this meant for Lexi. She was so close to her severance package opportunity. She'd planned her whole future around it.

"I'm on suspension. I've been relieved of my position as your VIP attendant, and my schedule for the last few days of the trip has basically been relegated to lower deck work. But I haven't been formally fired, no." Lexi wiped a tear from her face, but a new one replaced it immediately.

"Oh, thank God." Charlotte pulled Lexi into a hug before she leaned back and asked, "Why are we still crying? That's good news, right?"

"It is," Lexi said, "and it isn't. The only reason I wasn't fired is because they didn't catch us hooking up on the ship. Someone saw us kissing at the bar in town today. They snapped a picture and reported it to the staff captain. So they went back over the tapes here, and though they could see us interacting, closely, they didn't see anything overtly obvious."

"Boy, am I glad I didn't kiss you at the White Party like I wanted to," Charlotte replied, knowing that Lexi had dodged a bullet, because Charlotte had *really* wanted to kiss her after that tequila shot.

Lexi gave her a half smile as she continued, "So, my privileges to leave the ship have also been suspended until the end of this tour. And I have to take a bunch of HR courses about interacting with guests and what's allowed and not allowed…"

"And your promotion?" Charlotte was dying here.

"I still have it. But I'm on probation and will have to jump through some hoops to get out of that, but it's fine because I won't lose my severance eligibility," Lexi said but her expression still looked grave.

Charlotte tightened her hold around Lexi's waist. "This is a lot. And I imagine it's incredibly stressful and scary for you, and I know it's my fault, and I'm sorry. I had nothing to lose in this, but you had everything to lose and I was selfish, and I pushed you more than I probably should."

Lexi's face broke and the tears from before returned. "Charlotte, I'm not upset because I almost got fired." She wiped her cheek in vain. "Okay, maybe I am a little upset about that. But I'm more upset about what this means for us. And you saying perfect things like that isn't making this any easier."

"You lost me," Charlotte said.

"I can't see you anymore." Lexi sniffled. "My every move is going to be monitored over the rest of this trip. I'm taking a risk even being here right now, but I didn't want to go dark on you. Not after last night and today, and—"

"Finding you again." Charlotte's heart broke as she understood what was happening. Lexi was breaking things off with her.

"Exactly." Lexi sighed. "How can I go from making love to you in your wedding dress to pretending that you and I aren't on the same ship in paradise? I can't. I can't unfeel what I've felt this last week, and I can't pretend that you aren't here, and that you don't have a piece of my heart. Because you are and you do and I'm the *most* upset about that."

"You're upset that you have feelings for me?" Charlotte asked, a tightening in her chest making her throat hurt.

"Yes. No. I don't know." Lexi looked down, and Charlotte released her hold on her. "Because I *do* have everything to lose. And this is just vacation for you, right? You go back to your normal life after this, and I am barely holding on to my career. And that's my fault, because I knew the risk when we started this. But it's like I can't not kiss you or touch you. It's like my heart only beats for you, and I forgot how paralyzing that felt until you showed up on this ship and everything from the past rushed back to the surface. I can't lose everything again. I just can't."

Charlotte didn't want to hear any more, she couldn't. "So that's it then, huh? You're feeling too much, too fast, and I somehow represent something temporary to you, so you'd rather end things before they get more involved, right? And that talk we had earlier about trying to maintain some sort of relationship, even a friendship after this trip? Is that off the table now?"

Lexi wouldn't look at her. "I don't know. I need some time to think."

"I can't believe after all I've shared with you, after how honest I've been through this whole thing, you actually believe that this was just a temporary weeklong fling for me."

"I don't think that." Lexi looked up at her, eyes still wet with tears. "I just don't know what to think."

"You need some time," Charlotte replied. The feeling of rejection and hurt almost stung as much as Lexi's indecisiveness.

"Charlotte." Lexi reached for her, but she stepped back, out of reach.

"I'm sorry I screwed up your life. It wasn't exactly in my plans, but I acknowledge my part in it. And I'm sorry for that, but not for anything else. I'm not sorry for seeing you again and I'm not sorry for feeling things with you again." Charlotte felt herself start to unravel. She had to leave before she couldn't hold back the tears anymore.

"Wait." Lexi reached for her again and this time she paused. "Wait. I just…I'm sorry. I need a little time. This was a lot, it's—I'm sorry."

Charlotte saw the pain and conflict on Lexi's face, and she felt for her, but her own sadness bubbled at the surface, and she knew she couldn't keep the disappointment at bay much longer. She stepped forward and cupped Lexi's jaw, leaning in to place a soft kiss to her lips.

She spoke against those lips, keeping her eyes closed to help find the strength to say what she had to. "I love you. I have always loved you and I never stopped loving you, even when I left all those years ago. And you can take all the time you need. I'm not sorry for finding you again, and I'm not sorry for realizing I still loved you. But I'm sorry if that hurt you." She kissed her once more and pulled back. This time she couldn't look Lexi in the face, knowing it would hurt too much. "Find me when you're ready to, Lex. I'll be there."

She turned and ran for the door, pulling it open with more force than was required, and she ducked into the dark service stairwell as what little composure she had fell apart. She managed to keep her tears mostly silent until she was in the privacy of her own room, but then her walls crumbled, and her heart ached like it had so many years before. She knew Lexi was gone from her life, and she wasn't sure she could live with that. Again.

# CHAPTER TWENTY-FOUR

*Cruise Day Seven: Aruba*

Lexi's eyes stung and her ribs hurt from crying. She'd slept collectively two hours last night. She couldn't sleep because every time she closed her eyes, she saw Charlotte running from her, crying and not looking her in the face. Charlotte had told her she loved her, she still loved her. She'd never stopped loving her. And Lexi hated herself for feeling so weak in that moment that she said nothing. She just let her go.

She sighed as the numbers on the clock inched on. She hated that someone else was going to Charlotte's room today to give her the itinerary. She hated that she couldn't just knock on her door and apologize for panicking last night. She hated how a beautiful day ended so horribly.

But she'd panicked. She knew that the only reason she wasn't full-on fired yesterday was because she'd helped Captain Correia from making a bad decision—ironically with her actions toward Charlotte—and got her back to her room safely. Sally had confirmed that once they were alone in the room together. Lexi was being cut leniency as a one-time favor. She was grateful, but she knew she was on borrowed time. And she also knew that she'd likely be moved to another ship, but that was a worry for another day. Right now, all she could worry about was talking to Charlotte and trying to make things right again.

Zara slipped through their closed door with breakfast in hand. "C'mon. You gotta get up and eat. Your shift starts soon, and I can tell by the sheet marks on your face that you haven't even moved since I left."

Lex waved her off and closed her eyes. She was exhausted. And sad. She was glad to be pushing papers around down here and not having to be sunny and optimistic topside.

"Lex," Zara said as she combed a piece of her hair off her forehead. "You can't be late. You don't want to give them a reason to second-guess their decision."

She turned to face Zara, annoyed at the pity on her face, but realizing that she should try to show some grace right now, even if she felt none. "I know."

"I brought you some hard-boiled eggs and a muffin. The coffee looked like tar, so I left it behind. Scarf this down quick and shower. I'll swing by your post on my lunch break. Sound good?"

Lexi took the food and nodded. She was grateful Zara was handling her with kid gloves right now. She'd been a damned saint last night. These were her last few nights on the ship, with her friends, and Zara should be out partying, not consoling her heartbroken bestie. Lexi felt guilty about that.

"I'll see you later." Zara kissed her forehead and disappeared into the bustle of the corridor.

The silence of the room felt deafening. Lexi sat up and shook her head. She could do this. She could do her early shift and find a way to get in touch with Charlotte that wouldn't result in her getting fired. Maybe she could swing by the casino and see her friend Barb...That might work. There was a chance, anyway.

She stood up, feeling a little better about herself. *Eat, shower, go to work. Find Charlotte.* She could do that—she could do one small thing at a time. She had to.

❖

The day had been busier than she'd expected. She'd spent the majority of the morning working with the suppliers, doing inventory for the bars, and reviewing some of the less than glamorous parts of her usual job that she used to put off for the last day of the cruise when the bar service was limited.

Zara stopped by during her lunch break to cheer her up and spend some time with her, and that was nice, but not enough of a distraction.

The ship had docked in Aruba and it was mostly empty now. But Lexi wasn't able to leave the ship, even though she had a break midday, as part of her suspension. That felt doubly frustrating since she'd bet Charlotte was on the island, enjoying herself. She replayed Charlotte's words from last night. She'd told her she'd wait for her, that she'd be there when she was ready. That gave her a little comfort. She wasn't sure she had a plan just yet, but she didn't want Charlotte thinking Charlotte was more invested in their relationship than she was. That wasn't true. Charlotte had taken the words right out of her mouth last night, but she hadn't been able to say that. She hadn't been able to move. There was a lot to unpack about the things she felt about Charlotte, but she was willing to put in the time, once she knew Charlotte knew her feelings on the matter as well.

She headed toward the top deck to take a walk. No one said she couldn't *be* up there—they just said she couldn't work up there. Maybe she'd catch a glimpse of Barb or swing by the casino like she'd planned. There wasn't any harm in taking a stroll, right?

The pool bars and loungers were mostly empty, and she didn't notice Charlotte's friend anywhere, so she headed inside toward the casino. She was nearly through the doors when she heard Enrique call out to her.

"Lexi, hold up," he said as he jogged up to her.

"Hey." She didn't feel like talking, but she was glad to see a friendly face all the same. Zara had called an emergency meeting last night in their room. Lexi had barely survived telling Zara what had happened, so it should have come as no surprise that she'd cried through most of Zara's retelling of the story to the boys. Ahmed cried right along with her. He was emotional like that. She was glad to not be the only one sobbing, honestly.

"I have something for you." Enrique looked left and right before pulling Lexi through the doors to one of the outdoor deck areas.

"Okay," she said.

It was quiet there, save for one older woman reading her e-reader at the other end of the deck. She was smiling. Whatever she was reading must be funny.

"Charlotte wanted me to give you this," Enrique said as he handed her a folded piece of paper.

Her chest warmed and she felt the pit in her stomach lessen a bit. Her mind started to race—she had questions. "How did she look? Was she okay? When did she give it to you?"

"You want the truth?" Enrique looked hesitant.

"Yes." The paper shook in her hand. She was anxious to see what Charlotte had to say.

"Tired. She looked tired, and a little sad." Enrique frowned and she mirrored it.

"Oh." Though she wasn't sure it was possible, she felt even guiltier about their exchange last night.

He sighed and placed his hand on her shoulder. "She gave it to me as she was leaving the boat. I'm sorry—I tried to find you as soon as I could. I wanted you to hear it from me."

"Hear what from you?" Lexi looked down at the slanting script on the page. "Did she mention when she'd reboard tonight?"

"She's not," Enrique replied. "She's gone, Lexi."

"What?" Lexi was only half listening as she skimmed the start of the letter, but her eyes locked on the underlined *I'm sorry* in Charlotte's script. Suddenly Enrique's words held more weight. "Wait, what?"

"She had her luggage removed and she departed the ship. She's not coming back," he replied, his expression sympathetic.

"No." Lexi didn't believe him. Charlotte wouldn't just leave, would she?

He squeezed her shoulder but said nothing.

Shit. This really happened, didn't it. She left, again.

"I have to get back to the boarding zone, but I'll swing by your room later with Ahmed." He motioned toward the letter. "She told me to make sure you read it in private. I'll leave you to it."

Lexi dropped onto the nearby lounge chair once he was gone. Her hands were sweating as she held the paper. Part of her didn't want to read it. But she knew she couldn't live without knowing what Charlotte had to say.

She let out a shaky breath and looked down at the paper.

*Lexi,*

*I'm sorry. I'm sorry for leaving you all those years ago and I'm sorry for complicating things for you now. I'm sorry.*

*Now listen, before you say anything (yes, I realize this is a note, just go with it), I want you to know this was wholly my decision and I'm sure I'm going to regret it later, but I decided to leave the ship rather than put you at risk of making a mistake you couldn't take back. But I'm done with sorrys now. I'm not sorry for how you made me feel. Or how being with you made me remember how alive I once was. And I'm not sorry for any moment I spent with you. I'm not*

*sorry for any of it. And I hope you aren't either. I meant what
I said last night—take as much time as you need. All I've
done is take away the temptation, for us both.*

*I love you. Find me when you're ready.*

*Charlotte*

Lexi reread the letter three more times before she folded it and
tucked it in her pocket. Charlotte was gone. Again. And even though
the letter reiterated what she'd said last night, a part of Lexi couldn't
get past the fact that Charlotte had left. Though her heart ached at
Charlotte's promise to wait, a piece of her recoiled from the familiar
loss. From fear. From abandonment. From being alone, again.

As they pulled up to the airport, Lexi drummed her fingers on
her lap. Enrique and Ahmed had stayed on the ship, prepping for the
next week's cruise, so she was accompanying Zara to the airport alone.
Which she was more than fine with, except for the whole Zara was
leaving part. That sucked. But doing it alone was fine. She'd rather
have the quiet moments with Zara without distraction. It gave her
time to process and mourn. Two things that had been hard to do since
Charlotte left.

She'd immersed herself in work and in celebrating Zara's last few
days. She'd successfully avoided spending any time in her own head,
except for at night. Nighttime still haunted her, and sleep evaded her.
She felt restless constantly. But the daytime was filled with distractions,
and she let herself fade into the background, not thinking, just moving.
Just working. Just surviving. It had been the longest few days of her
life. Well, since her father had died, she supposed.

The driver pulled up to Zara's terminal and they both got out. She
tipped him via the app on her phone and unloaded their bags from the
trunk. They both were traveling light: Zara had only a small suitcase
and her backpack, since Ahmed had shipped most of her belongings
for her. And Lexi had only a small carry-on and a backpack. Where she
was going required little in the way of clothing or accessories.

"Stop crying. You're making me cry." Zara wiped her cheek and
shook her head.

"You started it." Lexi sniffled and searched for a tissue or a napkin
or a safety blanket, since hers was leaving.

Zara hugged her again and held her tight. "I'll be seeing you soon—it's fine. I'm going to Connecticut, not the moon."

"It feels like the moon." Lexi was pouting, she didn't care.

Zara stepped back and appraised her for a moment. "So, what did you decide?"

Lexi sighed. "I haven't."

"What are you waiting for?" Zara asked. "The way I see it, Lexi, you're at a crossroads right now. You can either go to Key West like you planned and spend your weeklong vacation with a bunch of nameless, faceless beautiful women. Or you can go to Aruba and fight for Charlotte."

"It's not that simple." She scuffed her shoe on the thickly lacquered floor of the airport.

"It is," Zara replied. "You're making it harder than it needs to be."

Lexi had mixed emotions about Zara's statement. Was she really? Because it didn't feel like that. To her, it felt like she was protecting what little unbroken heart she had left. Even if she went to Aruba, and Charlotte welcomed her arrival. How would she know what would happen then? How would she know that Charlotte was alone?

She'd gone back and forth about this for the past few days. Ahmed told her that on the final cruise day, Charlotte's ex had requested her room be filled with flowers, all kinds, every surface covered. It appeared as though Veronica hadn't gotten word that Charlotte had left the ship. Ahmed quote-unquote *lost* the VIP paperwork and didn't charge Veronica for the request but also didn't call her to let her know. But what was to say that she wouldn't try some grand gesture and just show up somewhere? Not that Charlotte had given her any indication that she should be worried about Veronica as a possibility of anything, but the truth was, Lexi wasn't sure what kind of future she and Charlotte could actually *have* together. If she did go to Aruba and take a chance, wouldn't she just be prolonging the inevitable heartbreak of them separating again? Could she handle that? She didn't think so.

An announcement overhead interrupted her reflection. They were calling Zara's flight to the gate.

"I have to go," Zara said.

"I know." Lexi gave her a smile, even though it killed her a little.

"I'll call you later on." Zara adjusted the bag on her shoulder and grabbed the handle of her rolling suitcase. "Love you. Make good decisions."

"Always," Lexi replied. "Love you, too."

"I put something in your backpack when you were showering this morning. Just a little going away present. Check it out." Zara blew her a kiss and waved. "See you later, Lex."

"Bye, Zee."

Lexi watched her friend leave, and though she was sad, she wasn't as devastated as she'd thought she'd be. Maybe because they'd talked about the million ways they could maintain their friendship. Or maybe because she understood why Zara was leaving. Change wasn't a bad thing. It was just something Lexi had to get used to, because it was inevitable, it seemed. Life moved on, even if she wasn't ready for it to.

She turned toward the flight screen a few yards away and maneuvered herself closer to see which terminal her flight left from. It was a bit of a distance from Zara's, but she didn't mind the walk. It was worth it to have spent more time with Zee, to savor all the moments, even if they were fleeting.

She walked toward the terminal and stopped by the small local coffee kiosk to grab a bottle of water for the flight. She was emotionally and physically dragging, but she felt like caffeine would only make her feel more dried out and sluggish than renewed. Water felt like a safe bet. As she reached into her bag to grab her wallet to pay, she saw the small package Zara had mentioned. She pulled it out, paid the cashier for her water, and walked the rest of the way to her gate, holding it gingerly in her hand.

Once she confirmed everything was on time, she dropped into an empty seat and placed the parcel on her lap. A piece of twine tied the middle of one of Zara's hair wraps that Lexi had always admired. It was a running joke between them that Lexi would steal it someday, not to wear, but to have as a good luck charm. Clearly, Zara had remembered those conversations. She unwrapped the cloth and found an envelope with a folded pink Post-it on it.

She opened the Post-it. In Zara's bubbly print was a note: *You don't need luck in this life. You just need to follow your heart. Don't live in the past forever, or you'll miss your future. Xo, Z*

"That was deep," Lexi said as she opened the envelope. What awaited her made her heart skip a beat. Inside was a one-way ticket with her name on it to Aruba, dated for today, in less than an hour.

She got out of her seat to check the nearby flight board. The terminal for this flight was about halfway across the airport from here. If she hurried, she could get there in time. But that didn't give her a lot of time to think. Or overthink, as it were.

She ran to the nearest window and looked out at the clouds overhead. She found the biggest one and asked, "What do you think, Dad? Play it safe and try to forget her? Or take the risk and see where it takes me?"

She didn't have to wait for his answer. It was right in front of her all along.

## CHAPTER TWENTY-FIVE

The pictures online did nothing to showcase the beauty of this suite, Charlotte thought as she settled against the California king bed and stretched out. The bed was in the center of the room and three of the walls that surrounded her were panoramic folding glass doors that led to two separate private patios, one for dining and one for bathing in a luxurious steel bathtub or under an outdoor rain showerhead. And the doors at the foot of the bed led to a private and exclusive portion of beach just for her. The Hotel Mooremont did not disappoint in its luxuriousness.

This was the most expensive room in the entire hotel, and she had saved for months to get it. And while the weather had been perfect and the accommodations unmatched by anything she had experienced in her life, she wasn't quite *happy* here. It wasn't the staff—it was her. Once she'd told them she wasn't on her honeymoon and that they could lay off with all the daily reminders of that fact, it had been easier to stomach being alone. But still, she had a lot of space to herself and she wasn't sure how she felt about that. Mainly because she didn't want to be here alone. She wanted to be here with Lexi.

She couldn't really be disappointed, though, could she? She was the one that left the ship, after all, and Lexi had a job. It wasn't like Lexi could just up and leave with her for a week in paradise. Charlotte wasn't even sure that was something Lexi wanted. Their last conversation left her feeling insecure and heartbroken. She knew a good part of that was on her, but knowing that didn't make it hurt any less.

Leaving the ship had been devastating for her, especially because she knew Lexi would find out after the fact. Even though it had been an impossible decision to make, it was the right one, and she knew that. She'd done her best to communicate her feelings to Lexi the night before she departed, and again in that letter she'd entrusted to Enrique. She hoped he'd delivered it to Lexi, and she hoped her message had been received. But she'd heard nothing from her in the time she'd been here. It had been four long days of silence. She didn't dare message her after she'd asked for space, but she was dying a little bit every day, wondering if she was thinking about her. Especially since it seemed Lexi was the only thing she could think about at all.

The quiet *had* helped her settle her mind a bit, though. She was grateful for the reflection time. She'd finished her work project and met her deadline. She'd caught up on emails and spoken to her grandfather a few times, but mostly she'd had a chance to think about what she wanted in this life. And what she didn't want. She felt a clarity she hadn't felt in a very long time. It was empowering and sobering. Her life would never be the same after that cruise, after this trip. And she was fine with that. Things had to change, and that change had to start with her.

She looked up at the large banana leaf–inspired fan blades that were moving slowly above her, circulating the warm but comfortable Caribbean air. The bed was her favorite part of this suite because she could see everything from it. She could see and hear the ocean from the short walk to her private section of beach just beyond the foot of her bed. Or she could look to her right and admire the beautiful steel bathtub outdoors, made for two, beneath the cover of a few trees and some moveable privacy walls. She'd taken a soak in that tub last night, after she'd opened up the ornate hinged door that led to the beach. She'd luxuriated in the warm bathwater while she looked out at the ocean, the sounds of the island birds and crickets lulling her into a peacefulness she didn't think she'd achieve. But she did. And from this place on the bed, beneath this fan, she felt the stress melt away from her bones again like last night. Her shoulders relaxed and her breathing slowed, and she felt herself falling asleep. She didn't fight it—it was vacation, after all.

She was awoken by a gentle caress on her cheek. She blinked awake to find Lexi there, looking at her lovingly. The initial shock of her being there faded into joy. This was how she always wanted to wake up.

"You came," Charlotte said and Lexi nuzzled her cheek.

"I couldn't stay away if I tried," Lexi said, her voice soft and reverent.

Charlotte reached for her, to pull her close, but when her arms closed around her shoulders, Lexi disappeared.

Charlotte opened her eyes. It was only a dream. Lexi wasn't here, and as much as she wanted her to be, that wasn't her decision to make. She sighed and let the disappointment wash over her. She closed her eyes and tried to chase the dream. She tried to find Lexi, to make it feel real, to will it to be real.

A knock at the door woke her sometime later. She wasn't sure how much time had passed, because the sun still shone brightly outside. Her nap must have been brief. The knock sounded again, this time louder.

"Just a minute," she called as she tried to get her bearings. She must have been out cold, because she was having a hard time waking up, though she had no trouble remembering the vividness of Dream Lexi next to her in the bed. That seemed like a cruel twist of fate.

She moved to the edge of the bed and sat up, steadying herself with her hands before she stood and walked toward the door. She gave herself a quick appraisal in the mirror along the corridor to the door and was relieved she didn't look as sleepy or out of sorts as she felt. That was good.

"Be right there." She opened the door without looking through the peephole, more because she was rushing to answer it than out of intentional neglect. She still felt a little foggy.

"Hi," Dream Lexi said from the doorway of her suite.

"You're not real." Charlotte frowned, angry at her subconscious. This was torture.

"Wait." Dream Lexi reached out and stopped the door from closing. "I assure you, I am."

Charlotte shook her head. "You aren't. This is another dream and when I reach for you, you'll vanish. Because in my dreams you are perfect and you love me and I can feel your touch, but in real life, I'm here in paradise alone. So you aren't real. And that's okay, I guess, because at least I can see you from time to time, even if only in my dreams."

Dream Lexi blinked, not saying anything, and Charlotte sighed. She'd clearly reached the end of her dream sequence again.

She turned away from the open door, because what was the point of closing an imaginary door? But as she stepped into the room, she felt a very real hand on her wrist.

"I do love you," Lexi said, pulling Charlotte back to her. "I do love you and I'm not perfect, but I am here."

Charlotte scanned her face. The affection from her dream was there. The look of love Dream Lexi had given her was there, too. Charlotte raised her hand to touch Lexi's face, but she hesitated for fear Lexi would disappear again.

"I'm here, Charlotte." Lexi pressed Charlotte's hand to her face and she didn't disappear.

Charlotte gasped as Lexi turned her head to kiss her palm. "I'm going to be real with you—if this is a dream, I don't want to wake up."

Lexi laughed and pulled Charlotte to her, her arms wrapping around Charlotte's back, holding her close. "This is just the start. I promise."

Charlotte closed her eyes and breathed in Lexi's scent. Her skin was warm, so warm it made her want to melt into her body. She rested her head on Lexi's collarbone and felt Lexi's lips on her forehead. "I wasn't sure you'd come."

"I'm sorry I'm late." Lexi squeezed her shoulders and ran a hand up and down Charlotte's back.

Charlotte nodded, unsure of what to say. Her emotions were a mess right now. She was relieved to see and feel Lexi, but part of her still didn't trust it. Had Lexi told her she loved her?

"You have excellent taste in vacation accommodations." Lexi's voice vibrated against her cheek.

Charlotte laughed. "The best money can buy." She looked up at Lexi and leaned in to kiss her, just to see if she could.

Lexi kissed her back, soft and slow, and Charlotte felt her chest warm at the sensation. She was here, really here. "You're not a dream."

Lexi shook her head. "I hope that means I'm not a nightmare."

"I've never felt that way about you," Charlotte replied simply. That was a fact.

"Good." Lexi stepped back and stretched. "Care to give me a tour?"

"Might as well, you've been in my doorway long enough, I suppose." Charlotte tugged Lexi into the room and closed the door behind her.

As Lexi pulled in her suitcase and dropped her bag, Charlotte went about orienting her to the space. She pointed to the private section of beach just outside the open accordion style glass doors at the end of the bed. "That's the beach." She motioned toward the outdoor bathtub and shower. "That's the outdoor shower area." She turned toward the center of the room. "And that's the—"

"Bed." Lexi stepped into her space, her hands cupping Charlotte's jaw. Her deep blue eyes had that endless hungry look she'd seen so many times on the cruise ship. Like she couldn't be quenched. Like she was looking for a piece of her soul. "I meant what I said before." Lexi leaned in and kissed her. This kiss was deeper than before—this kiss was wanting. "I love you, Charlotte. And I don't want to be without you."

Charlotte shivered and her knees felt like they might buckle when Lexi's tongue dragged against hers. "I might have to lie down for this."

"I think that can be arranged." Lexi kissed her once more and lifted her up, carrying her to the bed.

Charlotte reached for Lexi, pulling her down on top of her as she moved up the bed to the pillows. "If you keep kissing me like that, I'll love you forever."

"Good." Lexi propped herself up on her elbow, looking down at Charlotte with a small smile as she said, "I love you."

"I love you, too," Charlotte replied, placing her hand over Lexi's heart, just to feel the beat beneath her fingertips.

"I'm sorry I'm late." Lexi leaned close, grazing her lips against Charlotte's as she spoke.

"You did say that." Charlotte arched her back when Lexi's free hand found her chest.

Lexi kissed along her jaw to her ear. She sucked her earlobe between her lips and bit down gently as she whispered, "Let me show you how sorry I am. Let me show you how much I love you. Let me love you, on this bed, in paradise, all day long. Let me love you forever."

Charlotte let out a shaky breath. She felt her emotions bubble over at Lexi's promise, but she wanted to be sure. She turned to look at Lexi, shifting Lexi's lips from her skin. She ran her hand through Lexi's hair and caressed her cheek as she said, "Don't say it if you don't mean it, Lex. If you aren't ready—"

"I'm ready." Lexi slid off to her side. She pressed Charlotte's hand more firmly against her skin, and Charlotte felt Lexi's heartbeat rebound beneath the pressure.

"Then show me." Charlotte smiled and Lexi kissed the tears off her cheeks.

Lexi kissed her with that same passion she'd had on the ship, on the beach at Curaçao, behind closed doors, and in the dark under lifeboats. Lexi kissed her like she was the only person on this earth, and she succumbed to the adoration like she had time and time before, because there was nothing quite like the way Lexi kissed. There was nothing quite like the way Lexi loved. And Charlotte wanted a lifetime of those sensations.

She pulled at Lexi's shirt and pushed at Lexi's pants, trying to free her of the clothing that separated them, and as Lexi stripped, Charlotte watched, enjoying each and every inch of skin exposed. The colorful tattoos, the faint tan lines, the small scars of a life well lived—Lexi was a beautiful creature, inside and out, and she wanted nothing more than to be enveloped by her. All of her.

And as Lexi undressed her, with care and affection, kissing her skin and massaging her back, Charlotte knew that Lexi felt the same way about her. She felt loved. She felt appreciated. She felt adored. She felt home.

❖

Charlotte smiled at the sound of Lexi filling the outdoor bathtub. It had been a sort of ritual that they began their nights that way.

"Nightly soak time, huh?" she asked as she stepped onto the private deck. The sun had retreated, and the breeze brought a comfortable coolness with it. It was the perfect weather to soak outside in.

Lexi gave her a shy smile. "Well, it is our last night here. I'd hate to break tradition."

"Mmm." This was a tradition Charlotte was going to miss, much like everything else that didn't include paradise and Lexi never more than an arm's length away. But the nightly soak had become a favorite of theirs because of the simple, uncomplicated intimacy it provided. They shared their deepest conversations in that tub, and those fears and revelations inevitably led to comfort seeking, which seemed to morph into foreplay. It was like they cleansed their days to dirty their nights and start all over again. Charlotte loved it, and she knew Lexi did, too.

She leaned against the decorative wooden pillar to her right and admired the way the black lace panties Lexi wore framed her ass in an alluring heart shape as she bent over the edge of the tub. "I'm going to miss this view," she said.

"Just the view?" Lexi looked back at her and gave her a sly smile. She turned around and crossed her arms over her chest, and the loose-fitting, barely buttoned light blue linen shirt puckered in the most enticing way, exposing the swell of Lexi's breasts. The color of her shirt brought out the deep blue of Lexi's eyes, but Charlotte was only vaguely aware of that when there were so many other parts of Lexi on display at the moment.

"Not just the view, no." She stepped forward and ran her fingers along the lightweight fabric, playing with the rolled cuff along Lexi's forearm. She liked seeing Lexi in clothes—not as much as she liked her out of them, but she liked getting to know her style. It was a sort of beach-chic. Lexi had lots of smart warm-weather-appropriate yet flattering clothes. And some really, really fucking sexy underwear, Charlotte noted. Not that she'd had much time to appreciate any of it. Since Lexi's arrival, they'd pretty much only left the room for an occasional meal here or there, preferring instead to order room service. The majority of their time had been spent cuddling together in the bed or sunbathing naked on the private section of beach outside her suite before showering under the midday sun, in the outdoor stone shower. Each day followed a similar agenda, something she hadn't minded at all. She never tired of Lexi's touch, or her taste. And she couldn't remember another time in her life when she had been this happy or this free. She never wanted that feeling to end.

"That's good to know." Lexi's voice was soft. "Still, I'm glad that even though this is our last night here, it's not our last night on the island."

"Me, too." Charlotte abandoned the cuff to trace along the colorful art on Lexi's forearm. Lexi had convinced her to stay an extra few days after her reservation here ended. Lexi had some more time off before she was due back to the ship. Since Charlotte had finished up the Davenport project and had nothing else urgently waiting, it had been an easy decision to make.

"I think you'll like the next place." Lexi uncrossed her arms and turned her hand over for Charlotte to continue her playful inspection, something she did often. She was trying to memorize Lexi's art, and learn all of the things she'd missed in their time apart. Lexi was patient with her. As she'd always been.

"As long as it has a bed and you in it, I'm fine." Charlotte caressed the chest of the mermaid on Lexi's inner forearm. She found herself drawn back to this dark-haired beauty time and time again. There was just something about her—she was mesmerizing.

"You're easy to please, then." Lexi dipped her head and caught Charlotte's gaze.

"Did you just call me easy?" Charlotte accepted the kiss Lexi placed against her lips.

Lexi smiled against her mouth. She slipped her arms around Charlotte's waist and untied the sash of the robe she was wearing. She leaned back and eased the robe off Charlotte's shoulders as she replied, "That's my favorite thing about you. Well, that and the fact that you're naked under this robe right now."

Charlotte shivered as Lexi dragged her fingertips down her arms, moving the cloth away from her skin and claiming it as her own. Lexi seemed to undress her a little differently each time and Charlotte *lived* for it.

"But do you really need a bed? Because there are lots of other places we can have fun." Lexi tossed Charlotte's robe off to the side and pulled her close as she walked them both toward the now filled tub.

"Oh? Did you have someplace specific in mind?" It was warm, but Charlotte's nakedness chilled her a bit now that the sun had set. Lexi's body heat was comforting, but that bathtub was looking better and better.

Lexi pressed her up against the edge of the tub and reached past her, dipping her fingers in the water before she danced them along Charlotte's collarbone, torturing her. "The tub seems welcoming enough. Cozy, warm"—Lexi leaned forward and spoke into the shell of Charlotte's ear—"wet."

Charlotte swallowed thickly and turned her head to connect their lips. Lexi kissed her slowly as she grasped her hips and lifted her up onto the teak bench that was level with the top of the tub. Charlotte exhaled as Lexi pushed apart her legs and stepped between them, sliding her hands up Charlotte's back and pulling her flush to Lexi's front.

"Sounds perfect," Charlotte breathed out as Lexi moved her lips to the skin of her neck, sucking and nibbling as she went. It was driving Charlotte crazy. "But you're overdressed."

She reached out and unbuttoned Lexi's shirt, helping her out of it as she took in Lexi's tan-line-free chest and abs. "Now those." As she reached out to toy with one of Lexi's nipples, she pointed to Lexi's panties. "Those should come off before they get soaked."

"Too late." Lexi's voice was full of want and Charlotte was right there with her.

"Then we shouldn't wait any longer, should we?" Charlotte gave Lexi's chest one more squeeze before she moved out of her grasp and eased into the hot water behind her. "Oh, Lex, this is heaven."

Lexi finished undressing and joined her, causing the water level to crest the tub's edge, the sounds of splashing water a distant memory as Lexi wrapped Charlotte up in her arms, turning her to kiss her deeply.

Charlotte wrapped her legs around Lexi's waist and settled against her chest as Lexi leaned against the curve of the tub, easing them both into a recline that afforded Charlotte all kinds of friction and grinding potential. She capitalized on all of it.

Lexi's hands were in her hair, pulling her head back to lick along her neck as Charlotte rolled her sex against Lexi's stomach. The water around them swelled and sloshed with each more aggressive movement Charlotte made, but she didn't care because now Lexi's hands were at her chest and teasing along her clit, and thinking was getting hard.

"Lexi," she panted after a particularly deft swipe of Lexi's thumb caused her hips to buck in response.

Lexi kissed her as her fingers left Charlotte's body and Charlotte whined in frustration.

"I want to try something." Lexi's tongue dragged against her bottom lip before she nipped it playfully. "Indulge me."

Charlotte traced her tongue along Lexi's before sighing. "I *was* indulging you."

Lexi pulled back and laughed, caressing Charlotte's cheek with her hand. "You were. And you were doing a very, very good job of it, too." Lexi's hands found her hips and she gripped them. "Spin around for me. Sit on my lap, Charlotte."

Charlotte complied without complaint and she leaned her back against Lexi's front, as Lexi's fingers gently clawed up and down her thighs, making her legs quake with want. "That feels amazing." She closed her eyes and dropped her head back against Lexi's shoulder as she squeezed the outside of Lexi's thigh. "Don't stop."

"We haven't even gotten started yet." Lexi nuzzled along Charlotte's cheek.

Charlotte opened her eyes at the feeling of Lexi's hand leaving her skin and the sound of the water splashing again. She watched as Lexi reached over to the teak bench next to them. Lexi reached between the small stack of rolled towels she'd arranged there and pulled out a medium-sized purple silicone toy.

Charlotte reached for it and Lexi placed it into her hand. She ran her thumb along the ribbed shaft and squeezed the bulbous tip between her fingers, feeling the silicone's pliability under her pressure. "What's this?"

"This is the new waterproof toy I got for vacation and haven't had the opportunity to use yet," Lexi replied as she kissed Charlotte's jaw. "I was thinking we might give it a try."

Charlotte leaned into Lexi's affections as she examined the toy more closely. There were two raised buttons toward the base. She pressed the one marked with a plus sign and the toy began to vibrate, causing her to nearly drop it from surprise.

"It's got four speeds," Lexi said, her lips still close to Charlotte's ear. "Hold down the plus sign to speed it up, the minus sign to slow it down. Simple. Easy. Effective."

Charlotte pressed the plus sign again and marveled at the change in speed. "Well, damn."

Lexi's hands found her thighs underwater again, and she eased Charlotte's knees apart as she sucked on the skin of Charlotte's neck.

Charlotte closed her eyes at the sensation, and her clit throbbed with want when Lexi's hands stroked and massaged along her inner thighs.

"Are you ready?" Lexi asked as she took the toy from Charlotte, submerging it and dragging the vibrating phallus along the inner thigh her hand had just been teasing.

Charlotte moaned at the feeling, her legs spreading instinctively as Lexi brought it closer to her pussy. "Yes."

Lexi's free hand left her thigh to finger her clit before replacing her fingers with the vibrating tip of the toy.

Charlotte flexed forward at the contact, the jolt causing her clit to twitch and spasm. She was plenty wound up from all the kissing and caressing already, and the speed of this would make her come quickly. "That feels...incredible." She slowed her breathing to draw out her words, to draw out her pleasure.

"Good." Lexi held her tight as she continued to drag the toy over Charlotte's clit, pressing it against her before pulling it back each time Charlotte dug her fingers into Lexi's thighs in warning that she was getting too close, too fast. Lexi seemed to want to draw this out. Charlotte wasn't so sure she had it in her.

"Lexi," Charlotte cried out when Lexi adjusted the speed of the toy, the vibration making her jump. "Fuck."

Lexi pulled the toy back and removed one of Charlotte's hands from her thigh, wrapping it around the toy and closing her hand over it. "Slip this in, Charlotte. Help me guide this into you."

Charlotte whimpered at the command and tried to spread her legs farther as she and Lexi brought the toy between her thighs, pressing the tip against her lips before easing it inside.

"Oh my God." Charlotte moaned at the feeling of the ribbed silicone gliding inside her. The vibrations were less shocking along her inner walls than they were to her clit, but they still managed to overwhelm her a bit. "Lexi, I can't, I'm going to…"

"Don't stop, Charlotte. Move it in and out," Lexi coached as she pressed the button once more, increasing the pulsing to its top speed. "C'mon, love. Don't stop yet."

Charlotte clutched at Lexi's thigh to ground herself as her sex clenched around the dildo with each thrust in and out, her G-spot trembling against the pulse of the toy. She lasted only a few more thrusts when Lexi's hand left the toy to rub against her clit, and she came hard and fast in the water, shaking and crying out as she came undone again and again.

After the third series of spasms, she pulled out, shifting away from Lexi's touch to catch her breath and let her body wind down. She tried to blink the stars out of her vision, but they only seemed to recede when she squeezed her eyes shut and took deep breaths.

Lexi gave her a slow, gentle kiss and smiled against her lips. "I love feeling and hearing you climax. It might be my favorite thing."

Charlotte laughed and turned off the toy, dropping it into the base of the tub in favor of snuggling into the embrace Lexi wrapped her up in. "You give the best hugs."

Lexi squeezed her tighter. "And orgasms? Where do I rank in that department?"

"At the top," Charlotte teased. "A-plus effort there. Gold stars abound."

Lexi cheered before adding quietly, "I'm glad you weren't turned off by the toy thing."

"Why would I be?" Charlotte turned in Lexi's arms and was pleased when Lexi scooted forward to accommodate. She wrapped her legs around Lexi's waist and sighed at the pleasurable ache this new position afforded her.

"I don't know." Lexi shrugged. "It was something different. Sometimes that freaks people out."

"More than strap-on sex while wearing a wedding dress?" Charlotte asked with a smile.

"Fair point." Lexi laughed. After a pause she said, "I'm so glad you vacationed on my ship. I'm so glad I found you again."

"Me, too." Charlotte was glad to be facing Lexi in this moment. She marveled at the emotion she saw on Lexi's face, emotion she knew was for her to see and feel, and she did. Lexi was so vulnerable with her that it was amazing. It was humbling.

She rested her head on Lexi's collarbone and savored the closeness. The warmth was leaving the water, but she didn't much care. She could stay like this until the end of time.

Lexi placed a kiss on the top of her head, and Charlotte looked down at the strong tattooed arm holding her close. "What was your first tattoo?"

"Hmm?"

She leaned back to find Lexi's eyes closed with a peaceful expression on her face. She reached out to cup her jaw. She kissed her because her lips looked so plump and inviting.

Lexi blinked her eyes open when she ended the kiss. "What's that now?"

"Your first tattoo, what was it?" Charlotte leaned back to examine Lexi's arm as she continued, "Can I find it? Or did you cover it up? Like, was it a regret tattoo? Is that why you have a whole sleeve? Was it that bad?"

"Whoa. Slow down." Lexi scrunched her nose and smiled. "What makes you think I covered it up?"

"I don't know." Charlotte shrugged. "I've never gotten a tattoo because a part of me was afraid I'd regret it later—like, I'd change my mind but there would be something permanent on me reminding me I made a silly mistake or had questionable judgment. No one wants to be reminded about questionable judgment. It's questionable for a reason."

Lexi laughed. "I love the way your brain works."

Charlotte delighted at the compliment. "I'm right, aren't I? It's something you covered up."

"Yes and no." Lexi looked amused.

Charlotte frowned. "That's vague."

Lexi reached behind herself and pulled the plug out of the drain as she asked, "Do you remember the last night we spent together, before we broke up and you went off to school?"

"I do." Charlotte remembered it vividly. It had been the last time she'd seen Lexi, after all. She'd relived that night often in the days and months following their breakup. The water level dipped below her shoulder and she shivered, sad their tub time was ending.

Lexi replaced the plug and turned the hot water on, much to Charlotte's delight. Tub time was *not* over. Excellent.

"Well, that night you told me you loved me, and you kissed me once before leaving. But you did something else—do you remember that?" Lexi rubbed her arms over Charlotte's shoulders, warming her.

Charlotte thought about the question Lexi posed. She remembered the lovemaking, and the kissing, and the seemingly endless tears and the— "I drew a heart on your wrist with that pen I found in my grandfather's car. I have no idea why, but I just felt the need to—"

"Mark me. Brand me as your own." Lexi shut off the faucet and reclined, draping her arms along the edge of the tub.

Charlotte cocked her head to the side. "I suppose I did. It wasn't wholly conscious, though. We did that kind of thing a lot throughout our relationship, doodle here and there. It just seemed to fit the moment."

Lexi nodded. She looked beautiful in the moonlight; her casual recline in the tub was effortlessly sexy. "That was my first tattoo. Your heart on my wrist."

Charlotte immediately reached for Lexi's hand, searching for the heart, but she didn't see it. Her shoulders slumped. "You covered it up. You did regret it." The realization wounded her.

Lexi reached for her and pulled her back onto her lap, touching her chin softly to guide her gaze to meet hers. "I didn't. And I don't."

Charlotte shook her head, feeling suddenly very emotional. "I don't understand."

Lexi sighed, but her face showed no signs of frustration. Charlotte saw only love there. "I love you, Charlotte. I loved you then and I still love you now. And though we've lived many moons apart, my love for you has never wavered. Not really, anyway." She continued, "When you left that day, I wasn't ready to let you go. And though I changed, and I grew up, I don't regret that tattoo. But instead of leaving it as the outline of an empty heart, I had it shaded in and added to the story of my life." Lexi turned her arm so it was palm up, and she pointed to the tail of the mermaid. "It's still there, Charlotte. Your heart became the start of my story."

Charlotte raised Lexi's arm to look at it more closely. She could see it now: in the center of the first row of scales, just above the fin of the mermaid, her heart acted as a sort of keystone, as if holding the scales around it in place. The outline around it was darker than the scales, but if you weren't looking closely, you could easily miss it.

She leaned forward and kissed the heart, as she had when she first drew it. She closed her eyes, breathing in the smell of Lexi's skin, and savored the feeling of Lexi's pulse beating rapidly under her lips. Lexi was so full of life and love, and Charlotte wanted to soak all of it up and hold on to it forever.

"I love you, Lex." She spoke into the soft skin of Lexi's wrist before reaching for Lexi and connecting their lips. "I've always loved you."

Lexi kissed her back, brushing the tears off her cheeks as she replied, "I hope you always will."

"I will." Charlotte nuzzled her nose, overcome by the emotions and revelations of the moment. Her shoulders shook and her hands trembled, but not from the cold. She was buzzing with joy and her body danced as Lexi embraced her, pulling her even closer. Kissing her. Charlotte wanted tonight to never end, and in some ways, she knew it never would.

# CHAPTER TWENTY-SIX

L exi held Charlotte's hand as she took her toward the beach bar near their new hotel. She'd been glad they'd been able to book her usual room when she stayed over at the island. Marco, the hotel manager and a friend of hers from her years of cruising, had pulled some strings for her, and she knew she owed him one. Still, the room wasn't nearly as luxurious as Charlotte's place, but it had a view of the beach, a king-sized bed, and shower big enough for two. And Charlotte seemed more than happy with that arrangement.

"Is this the place you were talking about?" Charlotte asked as they walked along the shoreline toward the restaurant.

"Yeah," Lexi replied, "this was on the list Omario gave me. I've been here once or twice, but not in a while. I'm curious to see how it's changed, if at all."

Lexi had told Charlotte about the real-estate listings and research she'd been doing, one night during their bathtub confessionals. She had no reservation telling Charlotte anything, but verbalizing this made it feel very real. She'd been touched when Charlotte told her she wanted to know more about it. When she had encouraged her to show her, she'd made the phone call to the bar owner, Miss Camille, the next morning, to set up a meeting over lunch today.

"It's cute," Charlotte said, her tone sincere. "The beach access is incredible."

Lexi walked with her around the perimeter, pointing out the pluses and minuses she'd noticed along the way. There was a good-sized parking lot, but the broken shells that formed the parking surface needed to be redone. The exterior had significant wear, but it appeared to be mostly cosmetic wind and weather damage. But the carved wooden doors and original Dutch-inspired wood storm shutters were in good shape and had great character.

The inside was well lit, with a U-shaped bar and three open walls showcasing the beach and the views of the island. Tables dotted the floor off the bar, leading up to an elevated platform where a set of drums and some other musical instruments sat, waiting to be played. On the beach side, just below the elevated stage, a dozen or so other small two- and four-person tables sat, worn and weathered from years of use, in a roped-off patio area with a few faded and aging umbrellas overhead. But the bar was busy—not full, but nearly. And the aged tables and chairs were populated by happy tourists and singing locals. The bar moved out colorful, fruity cocktails at a blistering pace by island life standards, and though the place needed work and some upgrades, it was great. It had promise. It had potential.

"You must be Lexi," a deep, gravelly voice called out from the bar, and an older woman waved her over. She appeared to be in her late sixties, though her eyes and smile shone with a youthfulness that didn't fit the gnarled hands that reached to shake Lexi's. "Welcome to Sebastian's, I'm Miss Camille. But you can call me Cami."

"Thank you for meeting with me," Lexi said. "This is Charlotte."

"You're a looker, Miss Charlotte," she said in her thick Caribbean accent. "Those eyes must make emeralds jealous."

"You keep that up and I'll leave this one behind." Charlotte winked at Lexi and Cami laughed.

"You're too young for me, girl." She smiled and a gold tooth winked in their direction. "I swore off pretty young girls and hard liquor long ago. Too much trouble for an old lady like me."

"That must make tending bar on an island hard, no?" Lexi asked as she and Charlotte sat across from Cami at the bar.

"Not really. I'm only here behind the bar on the slow days. I'm mostly doing the business behind the scenes now. It's too much work and too much for these old bones to manage. I'm riddled with arthritis and I've got a bad back." She handed them each a plastic cup of water and leaned against the bar. "My hard-partying days are over. But I'll still partake in an island fruit sangria from time to time. Much to my doctor's horror, I'm sure."

Lexi laughed and accepted the water. It was nice and cold.

"What can I get you ladies?" Cami asked as she handed them a tattered laminated double-sided meal and drink menu.

"What's the best thing on the menu?" Charlotte asked and Lexi rubbed her knee under the bar top just because she was close enough, and because she could.

"The battered fish and plantains are a local favorite, and the fish tacos are popular with the cruisers," she replied, her voice full of charm.

Lexi looked at Charlotte, who nodded, and she replied, "We'll take one of each."

"What can I get you to drink?" Cami asked as she pulled out a shaker. "The popular island drink is the Aruba Ariba—it's sweet and like a planter's punch. Or the locally brewed Balashi is good, too. You can't go wrong with either."

They both chose the Ariba, and Lexi watched as Cami moved behind the bar with ease, her complaints of arthritis and back pain seemingly unfounded as she glided behind the bar. But Lexi didn't miss her wince when she bent over the icebox, bracing herself on the bar surface as she filled one cup at a time. Cami caught her watching.

"I move faster than I look—I know that." Cami mixed their drinks and placed them down on the bar. "But don't be fooled. I'm ready to give up the hustle and bustle. I'll miss this place, but I'd rather be a patron than a boss these days. Have someone make me meals and feed me grapes, you know?" Cami laughed. "Omario told me you wanted to talk. Make me an offer so I can retire."

Lexi laughed and shook her head. "You don't mess around, do you?"

Someone called from the open kitchen area, and she waddled back and forth, bringing them their lunch. "I'm just letting you know I'm open to a conversation. Omario said you're good people, that you're around here a lot. I don't want to talk to any more developers. They want to turn Sebastian's into a hotel and erase my husband's legacy. I'm not interested in that."

"Sebastian was your husband?" Charlotte coughed out, midsip. "What happened to all that talk about pretty ladies?"

Cami handed her a napkin. "He was open-minded. And I wasn't about to be told no. We were childhood sweethearts, and we made a good match in life and in business. But we had our fun outside of the marriage, too." She shrugged. "It worked for us. He was a good man, and I'm not about to let them build a Marriott over the bar top he hand carved. You know?"

Lexi nodded. She'd heard this story before. The island was changing, as bigger ships came in every day and with them great economic opportunity, but some of the charm of the island was lost along the way. Sebastian's had charm and Cami oozed it. "Let's talk."

"Atta girl." Cami patted Lexi's hand before she limped over to a young couple sitting nearby, taking their order and engaging them in conversation.

"You're serious about this, huh?" Charlotte asked, but there was no judgment in her voice.

"I'm just gathering information." Lexi looked at Charlotte and leaned in to kiss her. She closed her eyes at the sensation of Charlotte's lips against hers and she nodded. "What can a conversation hurt?"

"Nothing, nothing at all." Charlotte pecked her lips before sipping her drink. "You need to learn how to make these—this is awesome."

Lexi laughed. "That it is." She stirred her drink and looked out at the white sand beach and gorgeous teal-blue water lapping at the shore before she looked back at Charlotte. "I'm serious about you, too."

Charlotte looked at her and she fell in love with her all over again. Those eyes captivated her. They always had. "Good, because I'm serious about you."

"I want to try and make this work after you leave. After we both leave paradise." Lexi took her hand and squeezed it. "I want to see what the future holds for us. It'll be challenging, I know, but I want to try."

Charlotte cuddled against her chest. "That sounds like an adventure I'm more than willing to undertake."

Lexi raised her glass in toast. "To rediscovering lost loves and starting new adventures."

Charlotte clinked her glass and added, "To second chances and new beginnings."

Lexi couldn't think of a better way to agree with Charlotte than kissing her in that moment. And for all moments, she hoped.

# CHAPTER TWENTY-SEVEN

Charlotte looked at her phone and checked her texts again. Nothing. Still nothing.

These past eight months had been a challenge. Not in keeping up the relationship, but in missing the feel of someone next to her. She felt emotionally fulfilled by Lexi, but she missed her physically. That was a testament to the way Lexi made her feel when they were together—she knew that. But it didn't make the distance any easier.

"Paw Paw, three minutes till lunch!" she called out as she stood up and stirred the contents in the pot, not because they needed stirring, she'd just done that two minutes ago, but because she was restless. And it made her feel like she was doing something useful.

She walked to the sink to rinse off a few spoons and then stared out the kitchen window into the midday sky, thinking about how much had changed since the cruise. She'd made some bold steps in her career, quitting her full-time job to pursue commissioned work and establish a business of her own. She was finally using those two years of business school she'd taken before she switched over to design work. It was about damn time she applied some of that knowledge. She'd been inspired by Lexi's encouragement for her to live her life more and to acknowledge the worth of her time as that, *her* time. And though these days and months had been long in some regards, time was still her most precious commodity. She knew that now more than ever.

She looked around her mother's kitchen and sighed. *Her mother's kitchen.* Because she'd uprooted her career, she was begrudgingly still living in her mother's guest house. Which meant that, after her initial return home, avoiding Veronica was impossible. But after an honest and frank discussion with the minimal amount of rage and anger possible, Veronica stopped calling and stopping by uninvited. The truth was,

Charlotte didn't feel rage anymore. She felt like that part of her had healed some. She wasn't afraid to be honest with herself or Veronica, like she had been before. And though in the past she hadn't wanted to accept the failure of their relationship or how she had become complacent long before she caught Veronica in bed with someone else, that time was over. The cruise had been eye-opening for her. She felt like herself for the first time in a long time. She forgave Veronica, but she told her she had no interest in seeing her again, even as a friend. And though Veronica looked devastated by that last bit, Charlotte felt no remorse about speaking her truth.

Her grandfather's good-natured laughter in the next room broke her from her trance. She set the table for two, since her mother was out of town. Her relationship with Cookie was about the same. Cookie had been less than pleased that she'd sworn off getting back together with Veronica, but after a few months, she stopped bringing it up. Once she'd found out Charlotte had reconnected with Lexi, that opened up another can of judgment worms, but it was seemingly short-lived. Her mother had met someone new and was around less than usual, which was just fine with Charlotte.

She checked her phone again and thought about Lexi. Oh, how she missed her. It had been almost two months since she'd kissed Lexi. Two months since she'd felt Lexi's touch and her tongue. And it had been two long months since she'd come the way she wanted to. And though they talked frequently and had phone sex often, it wasn't the same. She missed her touch and she wanted to see her again. Now.

"She'll call, Lottie," Paw Paw said as he wheeled his walker into the kitchen. "Stop staring at the phone."

Charlotte put her cell phone down and stood to pull out a chair for him. She helped him lower himself into it and pushed it closer to the table for him to eat.

"Thank you." He lifted his chin while she tucked the linen napkin into his dress shirt. "I don't need the bib, Lottie. I know your heart is in the right place, but just because I'm old doesn't mean I can't keep my shirt nice."

She laughed and squeezed his shoulder. "We're having chowder for lunch, and you're wearing the bib."

He gave her an excited smile, his eyebrows comically high as she placed the bowl in front of him. "Is this Timothy's recipe?"

"I think I finally perfected it." Charlotte had been practicing Lexi's father's signature chowder recipe for weeks in preparation for the next time she'd see her, whenever that was. She wanted to surprise her, but in truth, she wanted something to look forward to. The last few times she'd brought up when they'd see each other again, Lexi had skimmed over it and changed the subject. And the last few conversations, Lexi seemed distracted. It had been over a week since she'd heard anything from her at all. Charlotte tried not to dwell on it.

Paw Paw squealed with delight and slurped a too full spoonful, dribbling some of it to the napkin bib below. "It's wonderful. Well done."

Charlotte used the bottom of the napkin to wipe his chin before she pointed to the mess. "Thank you for the bib, Lottie," she teased.

"Mm-hmm. That." He took another spoonful and closed his eyes with a happy hum. "This is great."

"Do you have enough for one more?"

Charlotte nearly dropped her spoon at the sound of Lexi's voice.

"Lexi." She looked up to find her girlfriend smiling at her broadly from the doorway of her mother's kitchen, a sight so reminiscent of their past life together that nostalgia almost won out over excitement. Almost.

"I heard it was time for lunch." Lexi walked in, dancing her fingers along Cookie's marble countertop, looking sexy and confident in her vintage leather jacket and tight jeans. "You know how I hate missing lunch."

Charlotte stood, walking toward her but stopping just short of her. "If I recall, it's your favorite meal of the day."

Lexi dipped her head and lowered her voice as she replied, "Favorite? Well, I don't know about that." She stepped into Charlotte's space and cupped her cheek as she leaned in to add, "I think we both know *you* are my favorite meal. I can never get enough, and you always leave me wanting more. It's just a thing you do, Charlotte. I hope it never stops."

"I need you to flirt less and kiss more because this has been a damn long two mon—"

Lexi's lips descended on hers and words were an afterthought to the electricity she felt from Lexi's touch. Lexi pulled her into a hug, and she felt home again.

"Ahem." Paw Paw cleared his throat and Charlotte broke apart from Lexi's kiss, mildly embarrassed. "Finally. Lexi, I thought you'd never get here. You look great. How are things? How's the life of a pirate?" Paw Paw's face lit up as he talked to Lexi, and Charlotte didn't think she could handle the adorableness of it all.

"Well, I have my fair share of scallywags to keep in line, but the bounty is mighty fine." Lexi gave Charlotte a look and Paw Paw laughed.

He motioned to the bowl in front of him. "She's been feeding this to me weekly. I've been the resident food tester, which is probably not great since I can hardly smell or taste anything, but this is by far her best batch. I think. Who can really know?"

"Best batch of what?" Lexi asked as she slid her hands along Charlotte's arms, clasping their hands together.

"Charlotte made your father's chowder." He motioned for her to take the empty seat next to him and waved Charlotte back to the table to join them. "She's hungry, Charlotte. She's wasting away—look at her."

Charlotte stepped out of Lexi's embrace and looked between her and her grandfather. "Wait, you knew Lexi was coming all along?" She turned to Paw Paw as the realization set in that she was totally set up. "Is that why you asked me to prepare the chowder today for lunch and asked me to free my schedule?"

"You caught me red-handed." Paw Paw swelled with pride, not showing the least bit of remorse for his deception. "Good thing today was the day you perfected the recipe, huh?"

Charlotte shook her head before directing her attention to Lexi. "And you? You were in on all of this?"

Lexi raised her hands in a show of innocence. "No way. Don't blame me. He's the brains here. The total mastermind. I just told him I'd be in town and that I was hoping to see him when I got here. I knew nothing of the chowder."

"Old coot's still got it." Paw Paw snickered by her side as he used his bib to wipe his face. "Now, if you'll excuse me, ladies, I have a canasta tournament to get to." He turned to Lexi. "Will you be around for dinner?"

"That's up to Charlotte, but I'd love to if that's all right." Lexi gave Charlotte her best puppy dog eyes, though they were clearly unnecessary since of course, obviously, always. Duh.

"Dinner's at six sharp, Paw Paw. No dillydallying at the club." Charlotte went to help him out of his seat, but Lexi beat her to it.

"You got it, Lottie." Paw Paw stage-whispered to Lexi, "She's a tough one. Be sure you mind your p's and q's."

"I'll even cross my t's and dot my i's, sir." Lexi saluted him and Paw Paw giggled all the way out of the room with his aide and out of sight.

"You two are trouble," Charlotte said, but she was beyond excited to have her two favorite people together again. It didn't seem real.

"I'm in good company, then." Lexi sat in the chair Paw Paw had recently vacated and reached for Charlotte's hand. Lexi looked at her, a look of surprise on her face. "So, my father's chowder, huh? Is that why you asked for the recipe a few months ago?"

Charlotte squeezed her hand briefly before heading toward the range. She took a bowl to the stovetop and filled it, suddenly feeling a little insecure about all her recipe progress. She was thrilled that Lexi was here and all, but she would have liked to have a little heads-up before it was time to get Lexi's stamp of approval. Or disapproval.

As she set the bowl down in front of Lexi, Lexi took her hand, stopping her from returning to her original seat.

"I wanted to surprise you. I was hoping to get the portions right—you were a little vague, so…" Charlotte felt sheepish.

"He was a little vague in that he cooked off the cuff with most things. That's why I could never get it right. He didn't exactly leave me a detailed recipe," Lexi replied. "I can't believe you did this."

Lexi held Charlotte in place while she tried her first spoonful. She said nothing but tried a second and then a third. After the fourth spoonful without any comments, Charlotte started to panic.

"I'm going to need a little something, Lex. Anything. I'd even take a Gordon Ramsay–like insult at this point. I'm dying here." Charlotte wanted to pace but Lexi held her hand tight. It was maddening.

"It's perfect." Lexi looked up at her with tears in her eyes. "It tastes exactly like I remember it tasting. You did it."

"Oh thank God." Charlotte let out a shaky breath and a nervous laugh. "You really had me going there for a minute. I thought I really fucked that up."

"You most certainly did not." Lexi squeezed her hand once more before releasing it. "Sit with me—eat with me while it's hot."

Charlotte rubbed Lexi's shoulders before she took the seat next to her. Lexi finished her bowl in record time and Charlotte served her a second helping, touched at the way Lexi rested her hand on Charlotte's knee while she ate.

"Paw Paw looks great," Lexi said as she wiped her mouth with a happy sigh. "He hasn't aged a bit."

"He loves you," Charlotte said as she began clearing the plates from the table.

Lexi joined her at the sink, carrying the still partially full pot. "What's not to love?"

Charlotte shook her head and spooned the extra chowder into a container for Paw Paw for later. She turned to Lexi, resting her hip on the counter of the sink as she replied, "I haven't found anything just yet. You seem perfect to me."

"Ah." Lexi leaned in and kissed her. "Then my plan is working. You're in too deep now, girl. You're all mine."

"I can live with that." Charlotte looped her arms around Lexi's neck and let herself be pulled to Lexi's front. "I missed you."

Lexi rested her forehead against Charlotte's. "No, I missed you. And I missed Paw Paw. And I missed this." She motioned between them. "I missed family. And no matter how many months or years have passed, this is still where I feel most at home. And most loved. When I'm with you. And making fun of you with Paw Paw. Like old times."

"See, you had me there. You were saying all the perfect things and then—"

Lexi kissed her. "I love you."

"Better." Charlotte smiled.

"I'm a fast learner," Lexi replied.

Charlotte could stay wrapped up in Lexi's arms forever and stare into those gorgeous baby blues for just as long, but she needed a little more first. "How long are you here?"

"Well, that sort of depends." Lexi released Charlotte from her embrace and stepped back, leaning against the kitchen island behind her. "I have some errands I need to run and some loose ends I need to tie up while I'm in town. But I'm pretty open. I just have to swing by the hotel to check in at some point, but I came here first because I wanted to see you."

"A hotel?" Charlotte was offended. "Why are you staying at a hotel?"

Lexi looked a little embarrassed. "I wasn't just going to expect it was okay to crash Biscuit's guest house without asking you first. Plus, I know we haven't talked much recently. I didn't want to assume you'd be thrilled to see me, either."

"First of all, Cookie is out of town. So screw her. Secondly, you are staying in my bed, with me, no debate on that front. And thirdly, I'll always be thrilled to see you, but what was with the radio silence this past week? You really know how to make a girl panic." Charlotte promised to always be honest with Lexi. This was as honest as it got.

"I know. Work's been…tough. I have to catch you up on some things." Lexi reached for Charlotte's hand. "But since I'm no longer checking in to a hotel and I haven't seen your mother's guest house in a long time, care to give me a tour? I could use a shower and a nap. It was a long flight and I'd like to get out of these clothes."

"This is a reasonable request." Charlotte loved the idea of getting Lexi undressed, but she had no intention of letting her sleep. Not now anyway. Not when there was catching up and reacquainting to do. And if the look Lexi was giving her now was any indication, she didn't think she'd get any resistance on the matter. "Right this way, my love."

Dinner had been a blast. Lexi and Paw Paw got along so well, it was as if no time had passed between them. And when Paw Paw headed to bed, Lexi dried the dishes after Charlotte washed them, and the domesticity of it all felt like a warm blanket. All of today had felt that way, actually. The afternoon—the afternoon had been like a dream come true. Her mother's guest house got the best light of all the rooms on the property, and basking in that midafternoon sun with Lexi, naked in her bed, writhing under her touch, well, that was poetry in and of itself. And to Charlotte's great surprise, napping had occurred. For both of them. After they'd played, of course. But she felt refreshed and energized still. Lexi had a way of doing that to her.

"I was hoping we could go for a drive," Lexi said as she took the final dish from Charlotte and ran the towel over it.

"Sure." Charlotte would go anywhere with Lexi. That was an easy yes.

"Great," Lexi replied. "I'm going to pull the car around. I'll meet you out front."

"Kiss first," Charlotte said, and Lexi obliged. She wasn't sure she'd hit her kiss quota for the day. Or if there even was one. She doubted it.

"See you in a few," Lexi said as she left the kitchen.

Charlotte unloaded the strainer and put the dishes back, one by one. She liked to keep the kitchen tidy, and she liked the methodical nature of unpacking things and putting them in their place. It made her feel calm.

The sound of her grandfather's walker behind her caught her attention.

"Everything all right, Paw Paw?" she asked as she turned to face him.

"Just came down for some milk and cookies, Lottie." He gave her an impish grin. "And to tell you to say *yes*."

"Say *yes*?" Charlotte laughed. "Say yes to what?"

He wheeled over to the counter and pulled out two oatmeal raisin cookies. Charlotte poured him a glass of milk and slid it to him. He cheered like a little kid and dipped his cookie into the milk as he replied, "To adventure."

"I did." Charlotte leaned against the countertop watching him. "I went on the cruise and embraced adventure. And I found Lexi along the way. It was a total win-win. Your advice was sound."

"Adventure happens over and over. I just wanted you to remember that." He started in on his second cookie. "I'm glad Lexi's back in your life. She's good for you. You're good for her. It's a good match."

Charlotte handed him a napkin to subtly alert him to the fact that milk was dribbling down his chin. "Thank you."

He gave her a look before taking the napkin and passive-aggressively wiping his chin. "I knew it was there. I just wasn't done making a mess yet." He wrinkled his nose at her and adjusted his glasses. "Anyway, it's bedtime for me and now my sugars are probably too high, but I wanted you to know I want you to take a chance and say yes to adventure. All adventures. Unless they seem dangerous—then, use your judgment. It's the spirit of the statement, not the literal meaning, but you probably get that, so I'm going to bed. Night, Lottie."

"Night, Paw Paw." Charlotte watched him shuffle out of the room, completely mystified about what he was talking about. She looked up at the clock and jumped. She was supposed to meet Lexi out front, and she'd better get a move on it.

The night was warm, but not warm enough to be out without a jacket. She chose a medium-weight one, noticing Lexi had taken her leather jacket off the hook in the guest house. As she made her way around her mother's house to the front drive, she heard a familiar purr.

"I thought you were going to stand me up," Lexi said as she leaned against her grandfather's '57 Chevy.

Charlotte hadn't seen that car in ages. His long-distance walking had declined so much in recent years that they only brought it out for special occasions because he was worried that taking the wheelchair in and out of the trunk and back seat would ruin the aesthetic of it. Charlotte assumed he didn't want to look his age in the car, since it was something he associated with his young and wild days. She never pushed him. She just made sure that someone came out every few months to run it and get it tuned for him. In fact, he'd asked her to prep it last week. She'd done so blindly since his birthday was approaching.

"In a car like this?" Charlotte said as she dragged her fingers along the still shiny coat of paint. "That would be foolish."

"Agreed," Lexi replied. "Ready?" Lexi walked to the passenger door and held it open for her.

Charlotte slipped inside and ran her hands along the soft, smooth leather of the front seat. Her grandfather had made sure to keep it in its original condition, resisting any upgrades besides a reupholstering her grandmother had surprised him with fifteen or so years ago. Otherwise, it was untouched, which Charlotte knew, from interviewing mechanics over these last few years to keep it that way, was a feat in and of itself.

Lexi closed the door to the driver's side and put the car in gear, easing out of the driveway with care. She reached across the seat for Charlotte's hand and held it as they drove.

"I thought you only talked to Paw Paw about visiting," Charlotte said, knowing full well they were both dirty rotten liars.

Lexi cast her a mischievous glance. "Maybe that was a fib."

"Mm-hmm," Charlotte replied as she looked out the window. The night was clear, there weren't many clouds in the sky, and thankfully, it had been a dry day today. The last few had been rainy and gray, which had done little to improve her mood given the way she missed Lexi and that beautiful ocean paradise they'd shared together. But the sun had come out today and brought Lexi with it. And she was grateful.

After driving awhile, Lexi took them toward the private beach access for locals, a path Charlotte hadn't taken in years. "Are we going to the beach?"

"We are." Lexi pulled the car into the farthest spot in the parking lot, next to one of the large sand dunes. The tall sea grass waved next to them, almost eclipsing the height of the car. The parking lot was mostly empty, save for one car near the entrance, under the streetlamp, but Lexi had chosen a more secluded, darker area to park in. Charlotte didn't miss that fact.

"And are we actually going to the beach? Or are we making out like teenagers in my grandfather's car?" Charlotte hoped it was the latter, but Lexi had been surprising her all day.

"Maybe a little of column A and a little of column B." Lexi rolled down her window a bit as she shut off the car. "I was hoping to talk a bit, too."

"Okay," Charlotte replied. "Everything all right?"

"So all right," Lexi said, her tone sincere. She turned to face her. "I'm sorry about last week. I want to tell you about it."

Charlotte unbuckled her seat belt and faced Lexi, leaning against the car door. "I'd like that."

Lexi ran her hand through her hair and sighed. "You know how I told you I wasn't loving the new job or the new ship? That I missed my friends and was having a harder time than I expected?"

Charlotte nodded. Lexi hadn't complained much, but she could tell she wasn't happy.

"Well, it wasn't just that. It was that I missed you," Lexi said. "I hated being in paradise every day without you. Because it didn't feel right. It doesn't feel right. And the hardest part of all of it is that before I saw you again, I thought I was happy. But I wasn't. I was just going through the motions, not realizing what I was missing. But I was missing you." Lexi continued, "My father's anniversary came and went, Charlotte. And I was at sea, schmoozing people I'd never see again and looking up at the sky, trying to find some direction. But my internal compass always pointed me back toward you. Do you remember when I told you my dad was my anchor in this world?"

That was the first night they'd finally kissed, when Lexi had let Charlotte examine her tattoos. "Yes."

Lexi reached across the seat and took her hand. "What I didn't mention was that he might have been my anchor, but I realized, you are my sun and my moon and my wind. He grounded me, but you *move* me. And I don't want to be in paradise without you. I can't. Because nothing has been the same, not since you. And now that you're in my life again, I want you there always, every day."

"What are you saying?" Charlotte was touched by Lexi's words. She vibrated with excitement to hear what she had to say next.

"I quit cruise life, Charlotte. I filed my paperwork for my retirement and I resigned." Lexi moved closer to her. "I don't want to be away from you any longer. I want to be in paradise with you. Always."

Charlotte didn't know what to say. The prospect of seeing Lexi every day, all day, and spending every night in her arms was literally everything she'd hoped for these past eight months. Those weekends when they could reconnect, as sparse as they were, had fueled her and kept her warm when she'd felt alone. She'd lived for those moments. And now? Now there was the chance for that to be her actual life. "Are you serious? Because I want you to be serious, Lex. Don't play with my emotions."

"I'm serious." Lexi put her hand on Charlotte's knee. "Move with me to paradise. Wake up there every day with me. Start a new life with me. Take that adventure."

Lexi's use of Paw Paw's words made it all crystal clear. "You told him, didn't you?" Charlotte wiped the happy tears from her eyes.

"I *asked* him." Lexi's expression was full of emotion as she spoke. "I asked him if I could take you with me, if he'd approve. He said he would, as long as you came back to visit and told him all about your adventures."

"I can't leave you two alone for a moment, can I?" Charlotte shook her head, grateful to have two people in her life who loved her so much, they would conspire behind her back.

Lexi ran her hand along Charlotte's hairline, tucking her hair behind her ear. She leaned close as she said, "Come with me, Charlotte. Say yes."

"Yes." Charlotte's only hesitation would have been her grandfather, but since Lexi had clearly been conspiring with him and had gotten his blessing, there was nothing left keeping her here. Her heart was with Lexi, and her home, too.

Lexi beamed. "I love you," she said as she leaned in and kissed Charlotte, and Charlotte felt her words in that kiss and in the way she touched her face. The way she pulled her close, the way she moved against her, gentle and affectionate and so sure.

Charlotte kissed her through the happy tears on her face and opened her mouth to let Lexi deepen their connection. She pushed at Lexi's jacket to slip her arm around Lexi's waist, but Lexi leaned back, breaking their kiss.

"I think this is cause for celebration," Lexi panted out as she motioned toward the back seat. "What do you say we move this back there, for old time's sake."

"I like the way you think." Charlotte was already out of the car and into the back seat before Lexi got her jacket off.

Lexi crawled over her and Charlotte lay across the bench seat, pulling Lexi on top of her as Lexi's hands danced over her abdomen and chest. Charlotte tugged at Lexi's shirt and lifted her hips as Lexi undid the button to her jeans, easing them off.

Lexi kissed across her mouth as she slipped beneath Charlotte's panties and teased her lips. Charlotte could feel herself already wet and ready for Lexi. She spread her legs as best she could in the small space, and Lexi rewarded her with two confident fingers sliding inside.

"Yes," Charlotte breathed out, her body still primed from their play earlier, as Lexi moved in and out of her, kissing her mouth and massaging her clit with every thrust.

Charlotte reached under Lexi's shirt and underneath her bra to cup her breast, pulling and pinching at Lexi's nipple as Lexi's hips canted against her thigh. The close quarters afforded them the perfect amount of friction, and Charlotte felt herself climbing quickly.

"Let me feel you," she said as she clawed at Lexi's pants, struggling with her button and zipper until Lexi pulled back enough for her to gain the access she so desired. "Oh, Lex," she purred, thrilled at how Lexi's body reacted to her touch.

On Lexi's next thrust, Charlotte dipped inside her, hooking her fingers against Lexi's tight walls and rubbing the ridged tissue there. Lexi ground against her hand, her kisses getting sloppy along Charlotte's lips and jaw as she responded to Charlotte's fingers in her sex.

"Come with me," Lexi pleaded, and Charlotte felt herself out of breath, moved by the double meaning there. She'd been holding out as long as she could but feeling Lexi tightening around her fingers was too much for her to handle.

"Yes," Charlotte cried out as she spread her legs farther apart, straining against the confines of the back seat and the jeans that pooled around her knees as Lexi bottomed out inside her, the heel of her hand pressed firmly against Charlotte's clit, sending her into ecstasy. She shook and shuddered as Lexi clenched around her fingers, filling her hand with wetness as she came above her with a quiet curse in her ear, her breathing fast and desperate.

Charlotte slowed her thrusts but continued to rub along Lexi's inner walls, prolonging Lexi's pleasure as hers continued to roll through her, slow and steady, winding her down from her orgasm into the delightful bliss and afterglow that sex with Lexi always seemed to produce.

"I swear, you get better at that every time." Lexi laughed as she kissed Charlotte's mouth, sucking on her lips playfully. "It's uncanny."

Charlotte eased out of Lexi and shuddered as Lexi slipped out of her but pressed firmly against her clit, teasing her briefly. "Same, girl. Same." She laughed as she pushed Lexi's hand away from her, feeling too sensitive to continue their play.

"You know," Lexi said as she kissed her sweetly, "it's been a long time since I had sex in the back of a classic car. Or any car, really."

"Oh?" Charlotte nuzzled her nose, luxuriating in the weight of Lexi draped across her. "How long has it been?"

"Not since you, baby," Lexi said, her eyes sparkling. "Not since you."

Charlotte smiled, grateful to be in this moment, with this woman, in this life. And though she hadn't expected her life to take her in this direction, she was ready to start over, in paradise, with Lexi. In fact, she couldn't wait to get started.

## Epilogue

*One Year Later: Aruba*

Lexi felt a soft kiss between her naked shoulder blades, and she smiled. She reached back and intertwined her fingers with the ones gently massaging at her hip. "Good morning."

"Morning." Charlotte spooned behind her and kissed her cheek. "Today's the day."

"It is." Lexi blinked her eyes open, suddenly feeling very awake. Today was the day.

Charlotte slipped her hand out of Lexi's and squeezed her hip, underscoring each word as she said, "Today. Is. The. Day."

Lexi turned to face the love of her life and laughed at the tousled hair and enthusiastic expression that awaited her. "You did say that."

Charlotte frowned. "You're not excited. Why aren't you excited? I'm excited enough for the both of us, but still, why aren't you excited?"

"I am excited." Lexi pressed a brief kiss to her lips. "I'm just also really, really nervous."

"Oh." Charlotte's frown lessened. "That's fair. I'd be nervous if I'd planned to own a beach restaurant and bar and saved for over a decade to achieve that goal and then suddenly it was opening day. I get that. I mean, it *could* totally flop. Then having a bar named Some Kind of Luck would be really unlucky."

Lexi felt her eyes bulge. "Not helping, Charlotte."

Charlotte laughed and kissed her, pushing her flat on her back as she climbed over her. "I'm kidding. You survived three soft openings with no problems, you've gotten great press, and thanks to yours truly, your website and marketing have been off the hook."

"Have I told you how glad I am that you're using your new business platform and graphic design savvy to help the bar?" Lexi was so proud of Charlotte's success since branching out on her own, but she was even more proud of the beautiful art and designs Charlotte produced. She blew her away, constantly. She was magical, in so many ways.

"And without any fee outside of the physical attention you so freely lavish on me. I'd say it's a win-win all around." Charlotte gave her a mischievous grin. "But back to my first point, you're going to do great tonight. Your dad is going to throw a hell of a party up there celebrating Some Kind of Luck's raging success, and we have our best friends as reinforcements tonight to make sure everything goes off without a hitch. It's going to be perfect. Trust me."

"How can you be so sure?" Lexi asked, as she rested her hands on Charlotte's thighs.

"I just have a good feeling is all." Charlotte repositioned Lexi's hands over her naked breasts and gave them an encouraging squeeze. "Like this, right? I have a good feeling about this, too."

Lexi palmed the warm flesh and teased her thumb along Charlotte's nipple. "Well, this is a feeling I like very much."

"Right? So good." Charlotte closed her eyes and rocked her hips against Lexi's lower abdomen.

Lexi glanced down, taking a moment to appreciate the fact that Charlotte was completely void of all clothing. She dropped one hand to Charlotte's hip and traced in, eliciting a purr from Charlotte. "I bet I know something that will feel even better."

Charlotte stopped her just before she reached her goal. "And if you start that, you'll be late getting Zara and Johann from the airport, and I'll be late getting the boys from their ship."

Lexi groaned because Charlotte was right and she hated that, not because she was right, but because she was naked and perfect and all hers. She made a playful attempt to bypass Charlotte's hand. "You sure?" she asked.

Charlotte laughed and brought Lexi hand's to her lips, sucking on her first two fingers before she replied, "Yes. But only because I want to think about how bad I want you while I watch you absolutely kill your opening tonight." Charlotte lay down on top of her and kissed her lips as she said, "And I'm sort of kind of counting on you fucking me on that bar after closing, to celebrate your grand opening with my grand opening. That okay with you?"

Lexi moaned against Charlotte's lips and nodded. "Well, then. It sounds like I'm going to get lucky no matter how tonight goes."

"I'd count on it." Charlotte gave her a quick peck before she climbed off her and headed toward the shower. "Now hurry up. You know how Zara hates to wait."

"Love you," Lexi called out, feeling more excited about tonight than she had a few moments before. Tonight *was* going to be a big night after all. She could feel it.

❖

"And that's a wrap!" Ahmed called out with a clap as he closed the front door of Some Kind of Luck after the last patron exited. "Let's clean up this joint and get our tequila on."

Enrique hooted next to Lexi behind the bar and pulled Zara into an exaggerated tango toward one of the three dishwashers. They returned with six sparkling clean shot glasses.

"Just a sec," Lexi said as she ran a fresh cloth across the bar, wiping the section of the bar top she'd kept from the old Sebastian's, a nod to Miss Camille and her late husband. She was glad to see Cami here tonight. And she was touched when Cami noticed the piece of her husband's hand-carved bar, immortalized in Lexi's upgraded bar space. Cami wiped her eyes with a grateful nod and Lexi knew she'd made the right decision to keep it. "Okay, now we're ready."

Zara's boyfriend Johann held up two fresh limes, and Lexi watched as Zara gave him a sweet kiss. She was glad her best friend was happy. Johann seemed like a great guy. Lexi was looking forward to seeing them more this week while they vacationed here. Having Zara here for this moment in her life made it feel like everything had come full circle.

Charlotte dimmed the house lights now that everyone had been ushered out and sat across from Lexi with a broad smile on her face. "Can I say it now?"

Lexi gave her a look, but Enrique elbowed her in the ribs.

"C'mon, Lex," Enrique chided her. "I think it's safe enough."

Charlotte squirmed as she waited for Lexi's nod of approval. Lexi made her wait longer than was necessary because she knew she'd pay for it later. She was looking forward to it.

"Fine," Lexi said, acting as underwhelmed as possible, though her entire being buzzed with excitement of her first real success as a small business owner.

Charlotte cheered and motioned to the room around them. "Tonight was nothing less than amazing. It had nothing to do with luck and everything to do with hard work, but it was a success all the same."

"Nothing to do with luck, you say?" Lexi asked as she leaned across the bar, looking at her favorite human with adoration and affection.

"Well, maybe some kind of luck." Charlotte blew her a kiss and their friends cheered.

"I love the idea that we are paying tribute to your dad at the end of every night, by saying that phrase." Ahmed sat next to Charlotte and rested his chin on his hands. "It's so damn romantic."

"Isn't he the cutest?" Enrique asked, giving Ahmed moon eyes as he clutched three saltshakers to his chest like a set of priceless pearls.

Lexi laughed but she didn't tease them too much. She got it. She was madly in love, too. And Ahmed and Enrique were as adorable as ever, still going strong, still cruising together, the picture of love and affection. It was touching.

"Is it time to drink yet?" Charlotte asked and Zara cackled to Lexi's left.

"She's got a point, Lex." Zara lined up the six shot glasses and motioned toward them. "Care to do the honors?"

Lexi nodded and grabbed the tequila bottle she'd tucked away for this very moment. She filled each glass, and Johann placed a lime slice in front of each of her friends, while Enrique deposited the saltshakers between each couple.

Lexi raised her glass in a toast and looked around at the people that had become her family. "To those that I love most in this world... and Johann"—she gave him a playful wink and her friends laughed—"I couldn't have done this without you. Thank you for all of your support and aggressive real estate listing stalking, because without you I don't think I'd be here, right now, about to drink this super-expensive tequila behind my *own* bar."

"Hear, hear!" her friends cheered and Lexi held Charlotte's gaze as she downed her shot, the comfortable confidence of knowing Charlotte was by her side during this endeavor warming her almost as much as the tequila did. The look Charlotte gave her told her they were on the same page, in this together. A new adventure, a second chance, with a first love.

"Well, we're going to turn in," Enrique said from his new position across the bar. He wrapped his arm around Ahmed's waist as he asked, "We'll see you in the morning?"

"Not too early," Zara added as Johann helped her into her denim jacket.

"Agreed." Ahmed pushed his black-rimmed glasses up his nose after a heated kiss from Enrique. "In fact, maybe we should see you in the afternoon."

Lexi rolled her eyes. "Just send out a message on the text thread when you lazy bags of bones get your crap together."

"Harsh." Zara gave her a quick hug as she turned toward the door. "You sure you don't want us to stay and lock up?"

Lexi chanced a look at Charlotte who raised an eyebrow in her direction. "No, I think we're good. Thanks anyway."

There were a few seconds of comfortable silence after her friends had left before Charlotte said, "I'm so proud of you, Lexi." Her eyes were bright with tears. "Look at this place. Look at all you've accomplished."

Lexi looked around at the space and nodded. She'd spent months perfecting the details, pouring hours of sweat equity into this place, and it had paid off. She'd kept the general layout of Sebastian's but overhauled it to be a welcoming, beach-chic dining experience with a bar that had literally come from her wildest dreams. She'd spared no expense to make sure it was equipped with everything a successful restaurant and bar would need. And so far, she'd hit a home run. It was making her emotional just thinking about it.

"Now"—Charlotte's voice was lower as she pulled Lexi's attention back to her—"I do believe we have some celebrating to do."

Lexi cleared the bar and slipped underneath the serving door, joining Charlotte on the other side. "There is no one else I'd rather celebrate with."

"Good." Charlotte placed her hands on the bar and helped Lexi lift her up to the bar's surface. "Then let's not waste any time."

And as Lexi stepped between Charlotte's open legs, her lips pressing against Charlotte's as Charlotte began to unbutton her shirt, she couldn't agree more. "Let's not."

# About the Author

Fiona Riley was born and raised in New England, where she is a medical professional and part-time professor when she isn't bonding with her laptop over words. She went to college in Boston and never left, starting a small business that takes up all of her free time, much to the dismay of her ever patient and lovely wife. When she pulls herself away from her work, she likes to catch up on the contents of her ever-growing DVR or spend time by the ocean with her favorite people.

Fiona's love for writing started at a young age and blossomed after she was published in a poetry competition at the ripe old age of twelve. She wrote lots of short stories and poetry for many years until it was time for college and a "real job." Fiona found herself with a bachelor's, a doctorate, and a day job but felt like she had stopped nurturing the one relationship that had always made her feel the most complete: artist, dreamer, writer.

A series of bizarre events afforded her with some unexpected extra time and she found herself reaching for her favorite blue notebook to write, never looking back.

Contact Fiona and check for updates on all her new adventures at:

Twitter: @fionarileyfic
Facebook: "Fiona Riley Fiction"
Website: http://www.fionarileyfiction.com/
Email: fionarileyfiction@gmail.com

# Books Available From Bold Strokes Books

**A Moment in Time** by Lisa Moreau. A longstanding family feud separates two women who unexpectedly fall in love at an antique clock shop in a small Louisiana town. (978-1-63555-419-9)

**Aspen in Moonlight** by Kelly Wacker. When art historian Melissa Warren meets Sula Johansen, director of a local bear conservancy, she discovers that love can come in unexpected and unusual forms. (978-1-63555-470-0)

**Back to September** by Melissa Brayden. Small bookshop owner Hannah Shepard and famous romance novelist Parker Bristow maneuver the landscape of their two very different worlds to find out if love can win out in the end. (978-1-63555-576-9)

**Changing Course** by Brey Willows. When the woman of her dreams falls from the sky, intergalactic space captain Jessa Arbelle had better be ready to catch her. (978-1-63555-335-2)

**Cost of Honor** by Radclyffe. First Daughter Blair Powell and Homeland Security Director Cameron Roberts face adversity when their enemies stop at nothing to prevent President Andrew Powell's reelection. Book 11 in the Honor series. (978-1-63555-582-0)

**Fearless** by Tina Michele. Determined to overcome her debilitating fear through exposure therapy, Laura Carter all but fails before she's even begun until dolphin trainer Jillian Marshall dedicates herself to helping Laura defeat the nightmares of her past. (978-1-63555-495-3)

**Not Dead Enough** by J.M. Redmann. In the tenth book of the Mickey Knight mystery series, a woman who may or may not be dead drags Micky into a messy con game. (978-1-63555-543-1)

**Not Since You** by Fiona Riley. When Charlotte boards her honeymoon cruise single and comes face-to-face with Lexi, the high school love she left behind, she questions every decision she has ever made. (978-1-63555-474-8)

**Not Your Average Love Spell** by Barbara Ann Wright. In this romantic fantasy, four women struggle with who to love and who to hate while fighting to rid a kingdom of an evil invading force. (978-1-63555-327-7)

**Tennessee Whiskey** by Donna K. Ford. After losing her job, Dane Foster starts spiraling out of control. She wants to put her life on pause and ask for a redo, a chance for something that matters. Emma Reynolds is that chance. (978-1-63555-556-1)

**30 Dates in 30 Days** by Elle Spencer. In this sophisticated contemporary romance, Veronica Welch is a busy lawyer who tries to find love the fast way—thirty dates in thirty days. (978-1-63555-498-4)

**Finding Sky** by Cass Sellars. Skylar Addison's search for a career intersects with her new boss's search for butterflies, but Skylar can't forgive Jess's intrusion into her life. Romance is the last thing they expect. (978-1-63555-521-9)

**Hammers, Strings, and Beautiful Things** by Morgan Lee Miller. While on tour with the biggest pop star in the world, rising musician Blair Bennett falls in love for the first time while coping with loss and depression. (978-1-63555-538-7)

**Heart of a Killer** by Yolanda Wallace. Contract killer Santana Masters's only interest is her next assignment—until a chance meeting with a beautiful stranger tempts her to change her ways. (978-1-63555-547-9)

**Leading the Witness** by Carsen Taite. When defense attorney Catherine Landauer reluctantly becomes the key witness in prosecutor Starr Rio's latest criminal trial, their hearts, careers, and lives may be at risk. (978-1-63555-512-7)

**No Experience Required** by Kimberly Cooper Griffin. Izzy Treadway has resigned herself to a life without romance because of her bipolar illness but wonders what she's gotten herself into when she agrees to write a book about love. (978-1-63555-561-5)

**One Walk in Winter** by Georgia Beers. Olivia Santini and Hayley Boyd Markham might be rivals at work, but they discover that lonely hearts often find company in the most unexpected of places. (978-1-63555-541-7)

**The Inn at Netherfield Green** by Aurora Rey. Advertising executive Lauren Montgomery and gin distiller Camden Crawley don't agree on anything except saving the Rose & Crown, the old English pub that's brought them together. (978-1-63555-445-8)

**Top of Her Game** by M. Ullrich. When it comes to life on the field and matters of the heart, losing isn't an option for pro athletes Kenzie Shaw and Sutton Flores. (978-1-63555-500-4)

**Vanished** by Eden Darry. First came the storm, and then the blinding white light that made everyone in town disappear. Another storm is coming, and Ellery and Loveday must find the chosen one or they won't survive. (978-1-63555-437-3)

**All She Wants** by Larkin Rose. Marci Jones and Tessa Dalton get more than they bargained for when their plans for a one-night stand turn into an opportunity for love. (978-1-63555-476-2)

**Beautiful Accidents** by Erin Zak. Stevie Adams doesn't believe in fate, not after losing her parents in a car crash. But she's about to discover that sometimes the best things in life happen purely by accident. (978-1-63555-497-7)

**Before Now** by Joy Argento. The instant Delaney Peyton and Jade Taylor meet, they sense a connection neither can explain. Can they overcome a betrayal that spans the centuries to reignite a love that can't be broken? (978-1-63555-525-7)

**Breathe** by Cari Hunter. Paramedic Jemima Pardon's chronic bad luck seems to be improving when she meets police officer Rosie Jones. But they face a battle to survive before they can find love. (978-1-63555-523-3)

**Double-Crossed** by Ali Vali. Hired thief and killer Reed Gable finds something in her scope that will change her life forever when she gets a contract to end casino accountant Brinley Myers's life. (978-1-63555-302-4)

Printed in the USA
CPSIA information can be obtained
at www.ICGtesting.com
JSHW082023220524
63639JS00001B/71